THE DEPTH OF THEIR REGRETS

Book Two in The Depth Series

E. Lynn

CONTENTS

Dedication	VII
Prologue	1
1. Harmon	11
2. Skylar	17
3. Harmon	27
4. Skylar	37
5. Harmon	42
6. Skylar	49
7. Harmon	54
8. Skylar	63
9. Harmon	82
10. Skylar	88
11. Harmon	93
12. Skylar	98
13. Harmon	104

14.	Skylar	107
15.	Harmon	112
16.	Skylar	117
17.	Harmon	128
18.	Skylar	134
19.	Harmon	144
20.	Skylar	151
21.	Harmon	157
22.	Skylar	162
23.	Harmon	170
24.	Skylar	175
25.	Harmon	187
26.	Skylar	193
27.	Harmon	201
28.	Skylar	209
29.	Harmon	218
30.	Skylar	225
31.	Harmon	233
32.	Skylar	240
33.	Harmon	245
34.	Harmon	254
35.	Skylar	258

36.	Harmon	264
37.	Skylar	269
38.	Harmon	275
39.	Skylar	282
40.	Harmon	287
41.	Skylar	291
42.	Harmon	296
43.	Skylar	302
44.	Harmon	310
45.	Skylar	319
46.	Harmon	323
47.	Skylar	327
48.	Harmon	332
49.	Skylar	337
50.	Harmon	344
51.	Skylar	349
52.	Harmon	352
53.	Skylar	356
54.	Harmon	361
55.	Harmon	369
56.	Skylar	373
57.	Harmon	379

Epilogue - Six Months Later   384

About the author   387

Acknowledgements   388

Also by   389

DEDICATION

To all who wonder,

It is never too late for a fresh start, take that leap.

PROLOGUE

SKYLAR

The stench of cigarettes in the alley behind Club Ten was nauseating on its own. Couple that with the dumpster, which looked as if it hadn't been emptied in three weeks, and dry heaving seemed an inevitability. Skylar wished the city had a rule about being farther from buildings before lighting up. *Preferably a mile—or two.*

"Skylar!" Zelda shouted.

The urge to walk away from her made Skylar's legs itch to run down the dark, dingy alley toward the passing cars on the fluorescent street ahead. Instead, she attempted a sad smile and turned back to Zelda.

"I hate clubs, and you know it," Skylar whined.

"I know, I know, but you did say you wanted to find a guy." Zelda's eyebrows wiggled up into the electric-blue bangs that hung over her face.

Skylar couldn't deny it. "We've been here nearly two hours, and the only guys who have approached me seem like they wouldn't be able to find their way out of a paper bag with a gaping hole in the side."

"You said you wanted a lay, not an engineer..."

Skylar fought not to roll her eyes. "Can't these men at least manage a conversation about more than their favorite beer?"

Zelda took the time to contemplate Skylar's question. "In my experience," she hedged, "one-night stands don't usually require much talking."

Skylar groaned. That was exactly her issue. She wasn't interested in sex without a connection. She needed to feel that the person was a good partner—which was why she hadn't been with anyone since her last relationship ended nearly two years ago.

It was turning out to be a shit night.

"Give me another," Zelda consulted her phone as she tipped her head from side to side, "thirty minutes. If we have no prospects by then, we'll leave." The way she said it made it all seem so simple.

Skylar opened her mouth to object, her denial teetering on the tip of her tongue, but it was drowned out by the slam of the door they'd just exited. When she turned to see who had interrupted their solitude, Skylar's mouth dropped when she saw the man standing at the threshold. Tattoos—that was the first thing she noticed. She'd never been with a man with tattoos. Maybe it was the way they contoured his sculpted arms. Either way, they were enticing. Then she took in the broad chest, the stubbled chin, and finally the ice-blue eyes staring back at her as if to devour her. Perhaps that was wishful thinking.

"Ladies." He gave an easy smile and nod.

Skylar couldn't find words. Finally, a man had caught her interest, and she couldn't speak. *Fantastic.* It was as if his gaze had turned her to stone.

"Hey there," Zelda crooned, nudging Skylar in the back to step forward.

Is my interest that obvious?

Mr. Tattoo's eye raked over Skylar's body, and she was, for the first time that evening, glad Zelda had all but forced her into the jumpsuit she reserved for special occasions. It accentuated her curves in a way that made the material appear like an extension of her skin. When his eyes made their way back to hers, he gave her a small, appreciative smirk.

I can make this work.

A warm blush filled her cheeks as she tried to remember how to walk. This was ridiculous. The last time she'd been so nervous about a man—well, it had been a boy at the time—was when she'd gone on her first date in high school. Butterflies had run amuck in her belly all night, and she got the feeling that tonight would go the same way, especially since she no longer had the urge to go home. When she stepped up beside him, she inhaled his woodsy scent, but the rotting stench around them dampened the effect. With a small smile in greeting, she tried to focus on her next move.

She stepped closer to the metal door, its black paint peeling at the edges, all of which would likely flake off with a strong gust of wind. The detail hadn't seemed important to her until that moment, but now, she needed to focus on it to pull herself together. Before she could get her own greeting out, another man filled the entire doorway, his features serious and borderline terrifying. His size made her falter.

He nodded to Mr. Tattoo. "Boss."

"Nick, I said I'd be back in a minute, fuck."

Nick, the giant, stepped outside, leaving just enough room for Skylar and Zelda to slip past.

"We were just heading back in," Zelda said as she questioningly raised her brows at Skylar.

Skylar's brain ran about three minutes behind. Whether that was from the haze of cigarette smoke, the poisonous stench from the dumpster, or from the allure of Mr. Tattoo, she wasn't sure. But forming coherent words, let alone full sentences, seemed out of the question. So, she turned to Zelda, gave an awkward nod that felt as if her head was too heavy for her neck, and followed her friend inside.

Mr. Tattoo extended a hand, grazing Skylar's forearm. "Let me get you a drink?"

Again, she nodded. *Fuck. I'm turning into a bobblehead.*

"We'll be at the bar." Zelda came to her rescue again, leaning around Skylar to look back at Mr. Tattoo.

As they weaved past the lines at the bathroom and down the hall to the dance floor, Skylar groaned. "What am I doing?"

"Honestly, I'm not sure, you spaz." Zelda cackled. "But if you finally want to get that cheating shit out of your mind, you need to loosen up."

"I know." Skylar rolled her shoulders as if that was the best way to loosen her tongue and speak to Mr. Tattoo in a somewhat-educated manner—or at all would suffice, at that point.

The bar was packed. Zelda, while on the toes of her black heels, managed to spot one open stool and pointed it out to Skylar. It stood between a couple that looked to be in the throes of a rather heated debate and a woman wearing less clothes than should be socially acceptable. Skylar wasn't one to shame anyone about their personal choices, but she did think undergarments should remain just that—*under* other clothes.

The woman's white thong was pulled up over her hips and glowed in the black lights.

"One moment, loves," the bartender called from a couple of stools down.

In Skylar's minimal experience, most of the time when they arrived at the club, at least two bartenders, sometimes even three, manned the space. Tonight, the poor lady was on her own. She poured drinks, swiped cards, and took orders all at once. The way she never seemed to miss a beat amazed Skylar.

"Take your time," Skylar called over the bump of the overhead speakers. She had taken the seat between the couple and the woman at her left, who seemed to be having a full-on conversation either with herself or her drink. Perhaps she'd had too much.

Skylar wished she'd gotten the man's name before they'd walked away, or asked him where she should meet him. The bar was packed and stretched almost the entire width of the building. Zelda had said this was where they would be, but there were dozens of seats. It was the best place to meet someone—Skylar was overthinking it.

The dance floor was packed and difficult to distinguish one person from the next. "What if he can't find us?" Skylar voiced her worries.

Zelda scoffed. "Girl, if he can't find us with my bright-blue hair, then he's dumber than the Guinness guy who only wanted to talk about his black and tan."

The bartender made her way to Skylar and Zelda. "Sorry about the wait, loves. My other half called in sick tonight, so I'm a lone ranger. Anyway, enough about me. What can I make you ladies?" As she asked, she poured a beer from the tap for a man three seats down.

"Vodka soda," they said in unison.

"Do you already have a tab going?"

"Actually, they can go on my tab, Liza."

Something warm tickled the back of Skylar's neck as Mr. Tattoo and Nick slid into their little bubble. The warmth spread from Skylar's neck around to her face, and she was thankful for the black lights that would make it difficult for someone to see her blush. The woman next to her vacated the chair, and he took the seat as the bartender nodded.

"I'll have another scotch." He held up his glass with the remnants of ice and some amber liquid. "I'm Cannon, but most people call me CJ."

He extended a hand, brushing a blond lock off Skylar's shoulder to expose the front of her square-neck jumpsuit. It showed off her curves, and the wide pant legs made it harder to see what she thought of as extra weight around her middle and thighs. His gaze dropped appreciatively to her bust. It wasn't one of those sleazy looks that made her want to run and hide. It made her feel sexy. But perhaps that was because she wanted a one-night stand and *he* was sexy. If he rolled his sleeves any higher on his forearms to expose more of those tattoos, she would be ogling too.

"Your drinks." Liza slid the drinks to them. Her smile, which had seemed nice and kind earlier, looked stiff and forced now.

Liza removed the empty glasses and turned before Skylar could get a good look at the woman. She wondered where the change in her demeanor came from. Then again, she was working a busy bar on her own. Taking a glass in each hand, Skylar handed Zelda one, not missing the wink Zelda sent her way. CJ leaned into Skylar. "So, do I get to know your name?"

The music was so loud, they nearly needed to shout as a song Skylar didn't recognize blared through the speakers.

"Skylar," she said with what she hoped was a sweet smile. Drink in hand, it seemed less difficult to speak. Or perhaps it was the easy way he smiled that calmed her nerves.

The three of them chatted for several minutes while Nick stayed off to the side, neither joining in the conversation nor moving more than a step or two away. They kept the topics light, covering their basic likes, dislikes, and some of their favorite stories. CJ exuded confidence.

The underdressed woman from the stool earlier bumped into the back of Skylar's chair then knocked into Zelda, who stumbled in her heels. Nick caught her before she hit the floor. Zelda was a wild card, and from the snarl on her lips, she was displeased with the large man's hands on her and the woman who'd nearly bowled her over. Nick helped her back to her feet without a word.

Zelda straightened her high-waisted shorts and crop top. Where Skylar was curvy, Zelda was rail-thin. It didn't matter what the woman ate, drank, or did. She didn't gain weight, and she usually drank more caffeine in a day than what Skylar drank in a week just to keep herself upright. Skylar had encouraged her to see a physician because something must be going on.

"Zelda, are you all right?"

Zelda shook herself off as she stood to her full height. "I'm good." The glare she leveled at the other woman would make most people cower. She was the epitome of small but mighty. Not only was she extremely intelligent, but she also had a sharp tongue, and she'd proven her physical capabilities in a few instances as well. Her stubborn and independent streak meant she would have preferred to hit the floor than have a stranger touch her. But Nick wasn't someone Zelda would be able to take down.

CJ stood from his stool. "Nick," he said as he nodded at the tipsy woman who was still struggling to find her bearings.

Nick took her under the arm and led her to the front door. The club was packed to near capacity, but something about Nick made the crowd part as he approached. The fact that he towered over most of the people there probably played a large role.

"I have a private box upstairs." CJ pointed to a long row of what Skylar had assumed were mirrors to help reflect the lights back around the club. "You ladies want to join me?"

Skylar looked to Zelda. She wanted to go upstairs with him, but her doubts started to creep in. Zelda widened her eyes, tilted her head ever so slightly, then tipped her chin in a way that said, Skylar should agree.

"You good?" Zelda asked just loud enough for Skylar to hear.

Skylar met CJ's ice-blue gaze then nodded.

"Get it, girl," Zelda whispered in Skylar's ear then stepped back. "That woman jacked up my ankle. I'm going to head home after I finish this." She rotated toward the bar top, then turned back to point a finger in CJ's face. "Treat her right, or my older brother, who is a *cop*, will be around to help with any issues." Then she smiled sweetly and winked at Skylar. "I'll wait up for you."

CJ smirked at Zelda's sass. He either found her amusing or thought she was too small to consider a threat. However, her brother was the exact opposite of Zelda, and he took his older-brother duties extremely seriously, which seemed to extend to all of Zelda's and her sister's friends.

"I will make sure she returns home with her glass slippers intact." CJ extended his hand to help Skylar down from her stool.

Her heels hit the ground, and she felt a little unsteady on her feet. CJ adjusted his hand to link his fingers with hers. The small gesture made her stomach swoop, even if it was only to prevent them getting separated as they made their way through the crowd. Or so she thought that was the purpose for it. But as they did with Nick, the crowd parted for CJ and her at his side. People must have sensed the air of authority about him. Skylar vowed that when they got to some quiet place, she would ask him why Nick had called him boss and why he'd so easily been able to escort that woman out the front door.

Two men, all in black, guarded a small door off to the side. One man inclined his head and opened the door for them to enter. "Mr. Adams."

That was something to work with. Now she had his last name too. If only she could be sure to remember it. She glanced over her shoulder once more and caught Zelda's eye as Zelda saluted her with what was left of her vodka soda.

Skylar stumbled as she entered the dark stairwell. Just as she thought she would tumble back down the stairs, CJ tugged on her hand, keeping her upright.

"Thanks."

"I made a promise. I can't let you lose your slippers on the stairs."

Skylar laughed at the reference to one of her favorite childhood movies. When they reached the top of the stairs, CJ led her past three other doors before stopping at the last door off the hall.

Stepping inside the room, she peered through what had looked like mirrors from below but were actually windows. The view was almost dizzying. She had to be at least thirty feet above the people below. "I had no idea these were windows."

The room was nearly the size of her apartment. Along the back wall, a sectional couch faced the windows, a coffee table centered before it. A recliner sat just to the right of the couch, also looking down at the floor of the club. On the opposite side of the room stood a mini bar and pool table. The room could comfortably hold twenty people.

"Makes having some private time easier." CJ lounged on the black leather sectional as he studied Skylar over the rim of his glass.

Chills spread over her body. She had never felt more like prey than now. It was as though she was about to be devoured, and she had no idea how to feel about it as her heart hammered in her chest.

Zelda's words from earlier rang in her mind. *The best way to get over one man is to get under another.* Skylar was convinced Zelda had gotten the line from a movie but couldn't remember which one.

When she stepped closer to the glass, she was almost afraid to touch it. It sloped outward, tilting over the dance floor. It was enough to make her stomach queasy. The people below looked to be having such a great time, their bodies packed onto the dance floor like tree trunks on the logging trucks she used to hate driving behind. They'd been common while living in New Hampshire. Now that she thought about it, she hadn't seen any since moving to Arizona. She shook her head to stop that random train of thought.

Just as she brought herself back to the moment, tattooed arms wrapped around her waist. That deeply masculine scent enveloped her, and she allowed herself to be swallowed by the heat of the man behind her.

CHAPTER ONE

HARMON

FOUR WEEKS LATER

"I'LL BE BACK AT the office on Thursday. If there is any way you can have that woman out of there before I return, I would prefer it." Harmon's patience was running thin. His *new* assistant —well she probably couldn't be considered new anymore —had booked him on a flight to the *wrong* Portland. He was supposed to be heading to Portland, Oregon. He had a ticket to Portland, Maine. Though, he figured the area would be beautiful this time of year, the flight would take him in the completely wrong direction.

It was not the first of her screwups.

"She's trying her best," his boss's assistant, Naudia, tried to reason with him.

Harmon wedged the phone between his shoulder and his ear as he balanced his coffee and took the handle of his carry-on bag in the other. "That might be the problem." When Naudia remained silent, he continued, "If this is the best she can do..." He didn't need to finish.

Shuffling followed on Naudia's side of the phone, and Harmon wondered if she was moving somewhere more private for their chat. "Has she retained anything she's been taught?"

"Not that I've seen. Naudia, she still can't use the damn coffee machine."

She scoffed. "That thing is finicky. It gives me a hard time every morning."

Harmon ran a hand down his face, the stubble scratching his palm. "She has cost the company more money in her eighteen months of employment than I've made in wages this year."

That was an exaggeration, but sending him to the wrong state for a business trip was one of her more expensive blunders. Harmon had overlooked the others, though he likely shouldn't have. Last year, she'd wanted to help coordinate the office holiday party. She'd been tasked with buying the party favors. She'd ordered a pallet of jingling bell bracelets; their company had less than fifty employees, and she'd ordered fifty *cases*. Nearly four thousand of those stupid rattling bracelets arrived at their office.

Then she was supposed to order him a new high-quality printer. She ordered a damn printing press to the tune of just under six thousand dollars. He wasn't entirely sure how she'd pulled that one off, but to see a printer that cost almost as much as a used vehicle had nearly fried his brain. Both orders had been easily returned. She was no longer allowed to purchase anything over a thousand dollars without his approval—which was what led him to stare at his boarding pass to Portland. She'd tried to send him to Maine, during one of the busiest weeks of his life.

"I know." Naudia still sounded hesitant.

Harmon rolled his shoulders as he waited in the horrendously long line of people at the airport service desk. He only hoped the woman behind the counter would be able to work some kind of magic that would result in him getting to the correct Portland in time for his meeting the next day. Mr. Wilton did not like to work from Thanksgiving to New Year's, and his investments always experienced some emergency requiring personal attention, so before they got too close to the imminent deadline, Harmon chose to set up a meeting. Flights around Thanksgiving would have been far worse. Plus, phone calls and video chats were out of the question for dear old Mr. Wilton. The man might be wealthy, but he was also paranoid to the extreme. He worried that if he had a video call, people would gain access to his entire portfolio.

Harmon wondered if letting his assistant go the week before a holiday was cruel. He shrugged; it was only Halloween. The line shifted ahead as a woman wrangling three children looked more than a little flustered as they all rolled their suitcases.

"I'll take care of Mandy myself on Monday." He hung up, not wanting to hear Naudia fight for the woman to stay. Perhaps it was the women with children, or the reminder of the holidays, but he couldn't ask Naudia to do the dirty work. It would ruin both her and Mandy's coming days—possibly even the rest of their year.

As he scrolled through his phone, he was surprised to see Porter and Verity, his best friend and his wife, had shared a post about a house down the street from them that was for sale. They lived in a nice cul-de-sac a few towns away, one that was quiet and a great place to live. He saved the post as the line moved forward another inch.

Four more people stood between him and some damn sanity. As he mindlessly scrolled through more social media posts, he was startled to see none other than Mandy had sent him a follow request.

"Not fucking likely," he mumbled as he denied the request.

The older woman directly ahead of him in line turned to glare at his use of profanity. Not in the mood for other people's judgement, he raised a brow at her—in a way, inviting her opinion. She huffed and spun back around. A couple finished, and the line shifted again. He'd been in line over twenty minutes.

How long does it take to figure things out?

Doing his best to immerse himself in the life of anyone other than himself, he nearly choked on his next breath when he stopped on a photo of Verity and Jackie, *his* Jackie—well, who used to be *his* Jackie. She wore a formfitting beaded mermaid wedding dress. He knew she'd been seeing someone, the first person he'd heard of her dating since their split. Something foul churned in his stomach. *How can I be jealous? We split over ten years ago?* But as he scrolled through the comments telling Jackie how beautiful she was and how Verity made a lovely bridesmaid, his coffee prepared to make a reappearance. Unable to implement any form of self-preservation, he scrolled the remainder of the way through the comments. Each congratulation felt like another dagger to his already-damaged heart. Some of the comments were a few weeks old. Scanning the post more closely, he noted the date they'd been uploaded, nearly a month ago. His social media scrolling was reserved for moments of severe boredom, so it had been easy for him not to see the photos. But neither Verity nor Porter had mentioned a single thing over the last several months about the wedding, planning it, or even that it took place after the event. Something toxic swirled in his gut. It felt more like betrayal than he wanted to admit.

"Umm, sir?"

Shaking himself out of his strange stupor, Harmon nearly tripped over himself to reach the counter. "Sorry about that. I need some help."

***

Settled into a coach seat that felt far more like it belonged in a kindergarten classroom, Harmon once again cursed Mandy. Had the woman been able to do much of anything properly, he would have been stunned. He'd spent almost his entire day at the airport waiting. The only upside was that he had a window seat; however, being seated next to two women who didn't seem capable of shutting their mouths was becoming a new form of torture. Their flight would be touching down at five in the morning, and he had hoped he could take the time to nap on the flight. Apparently, with the gossip queens next to him, that was not an option. The women were wound tighter than the spring in the pen one of them clicked incessantly. If the windows could open, Harmon would have sent it sailing down through the Arizona sky before takeoff.

For hours, he had to sit there and listen to the two women, whom he discovered were sisters named Harmony and Melody. It would have been funny had he not been so annoyed. Their brother's name was likely Saxophone. The similarity between Harmon's name and the one woman's was strange enough on its own. But finding out how closely tied the two women's names were had seemed ridiculous—until he'd realized they were sisters and their parents clearly had a vast love for music.

More annoyingly was when Harmon disembarked the flight, he couldn't help but walk with a limp after being crammed into the too-small seat for hours. He'd waited for all other passengers to leave, not wanting to be stuck in the way of other people getting their overhead bags. With his eyes closed, he tried to take a few calming breaths as Harmony's and Melody's voices finally faded. If he never saw those two women again, he could die happy.

It was just after six in the morning as he got into the driver's seat of his rental car. How Mandy had gotten a rental at the correct place but a flight to the wrong one, he would never understand.

First things first, if he wanted to behave like any sort of human for his meeting in less than two hours, then he needed caffeine—or to find a place to pull over and nap where he wouldn't look like a psycho. As he passed a hospital, he wondered if they could set him up with an IV strong enough to keep him awake for the next several hours.

Because Mr. Wilton took everything he did just so, they would inevitably spend no less than half an hour discussing their personal lives—to catch up. Then they would look at each and every one of Mr. Wilton's investments, spending ten to fifteen minutes on each one—never more, never less, even when there wasn't much of an update. Usually, Harmon didn't mind. The man was structured. But with how the previous day had gone, Harmon worried his already-thin patience would be tested to the point of pushing him over the edge.

CHAPTER TWO

SKYLAR

"Zelda, what the hell do you mean?" It had been a month since her hookup with CJ, and Skylar felt certain she was hearing things incorrectly.

Zelda flinched. "Don't make me repeat it."

"I'm going to need you to spell that out for me one more time, nice and clear." Gingerly sitting down on the edge of the couch, Skylar braced herself.

"Fuck me. Your pal CJ was in court today for an arraignment on a drunk driving charge." Zelda sighed, eyeing her as if to ask if she was sure she wanted Zelda to continue.

Skylar nodded.

"Fine. While he was talking with the judge, a woman stormed into the courtroom. She accused the man of cheating on her. She ranted and raved about the fact that, legally, they were still married and that she hadn't been able to find him in weeks. Kept saying she only knew where to find him because of his embarrassing mug shot in the newspaper..."

"He's married?"

"It would appear so." Zelda shook her blue locks out of her eyes and groaned when the timer went off for the chicken cordon bleu Skylar had prepared.

Skylar didn't move.

Zelda hopped off their threadbare secondhand sofa to free their dinner from the squawking oven. They had been living together for the last three years. Knowing someone else was in the apartment made Skylar feel safer, and it helped them save funds.

Skylar watched Zelda weave around the full baskets of laundry—clean laundry—some of which was haphazardly piled on end tables, and the fake Christmas tree they'd bought to put up the weekend after Thanksgiving but that still sat in its neat white box pushed against the wall. From the couch, Skylar had a clear view into the kitchen. The apartment had an island and was barely big enough to accommodate their dining table. As it was, it sat pressed against the wall with only three chairs surrounding it. Her mind swam with the glaringly obvious reasons CJ hadn't called her. Arrested. Married. The drunk-driving charge made her sick to her stomach. It was stupid to put not only his life on the line but those around him. Plus, to be married, not tell her, then screw her against those windows looking down over the rest of the club—all together, it churned her stomach.

The breading on the chicken no longer smelled delicious. It smelled tainted with broken vows—ones she'd unwittingly helped break.

"Does that make me a home-wrecker?"

"Hell no!" Zelda tried to examine the chicken under the kitchen's bright LED lights. "Does this look pink at all?"

In a slight haze, Skylar picked her way into their kitchen. The living room might look like a bomb had gone off, but their kitchen was spotless other than the few dishes Skylar had used to make their meal. Leaning around Zelda, Skylar, too, examined the now-mutilated dinner she'd worked so hard on.

"No, that's fully cooked. And that one is yours."

Zelda shrugged, got the ranch out of the fridge, and settled onto the couch to watch her favorite crime show. One would think that being a court reporter would make her want an escape from the crimes people committed. But nope.

"Have you decided what you're going to do when the diner closes?" Zelda asked during a commercial break. She would only talk during commercials and would often stop in the middle of a conversation, sometimes in the middle of a sentence, when the show returned. Then she would pick it back up as soon as the ads started again.

Skylar rolled her head around her shoulders. "Not really. I'll check the help-wanted ads this weekend." She cut into her chicken and took a small bite. The news of CJ being married stung, another line in her ever-growing list of why she had trust issues.

Zelda wrinkled her nose, added more ranch to her plate, and went back to her show.

Skylar's life just seemed to develop more and more drama. Between the diner closing, CJ, and her family troubles, she didn't know what was more stressful. The CJ problem wasn't really stressful, more a situation that made her feel dirty. Though she hadn't known about the wife, she couldn't suppress her feeling of being tainted.

"I'll grab a paper on my way home from my sister's on Saturday."

"Thanks." Groaning, she fell back against the couch. *Time to spruce up my resume.* "How is Lara?" If she didn't have to work, she would be tagging along with Zelda for the visit.

"She's good. She'll be moving to pediatric nursing in a few weeks. You know how she likes the little beasts."

Skylar nodded. Lara had a way with children. It didn't matter how old, they gravitated to her. That was one area where she and her sister couldn't differ further. It wasn't that Zelda disliked kids. It was more that she was at a loss for what to do with them, and that, in turn, made her nervous.

During the show, she updated her resume during commercials, and Zelda helped with ideas about what she could do. No college degree—she'd hardly graduated from high school after what her mother had gone through. And she had spent most of her adult life waiting tables. The prospects would be slim. She and Zelda had met during one of her closing shifts at Retro, the diner she'd worked at. Zelda and her sister, Lara, had stopped in, and Skylar was the girls' waitress. The three had gotten along well. Amazingly, they had found they liked the same music and were planning to go to the same festival that weekend, so they met up. One thing had led to another until Zelda and Skylar were renting their apartment together.

"All right, I think that should be good enough."

"Want me to read through it? Add some fluff?"

"Fluff? This isn't a damn sandwich, Z. I need a job. I can't fill my resume with crap."

"Not *crap*. Fluff." Zelda drew out the vowel sound in the word. She put out her hands and made grabby fingers at the laptop.

Rolling her eyes, Skylar passed it over.

Zelda squinted at the screen then pulled a pair of massive glasses out of the tote bag Skylar hadn't even realized was tucked under the end table. "Okay. 'Good worker'? Really, Sky?"

"What? I am."

With a crack of her fingers, Zelda dropped her hands to the keys. "Works well in high-stress situations, proficient at multitasking. Hmm." Her eyes zipped back and forth as she hemmed and hawed over the content. "Has learned to use multiple types of computer systems and is comfortable with technology." Zelda raised a brow as if to ask if Skylar disagreed with anything she'd said.

"How can you come up with all that shit, and I can't think of anything?"

Zelda shrugged. "Easy, you're too hard on yourself." She thrust the computer back at Skylar, then zoned into her television show just in time to watch the house quickly become surrounded by men and women in bulletproof vests and black helmets.

"Thanks," Skylar mumbled. She had a closing shift that next night and didn't want to stay up too late. "I'm going to head to bed."

"'Kay. I might stay up and game."

Skylar smiled and shook her head. "When was the last time you didn't before bed?"

"Good point, I'm not sure."

After tossing the dishes into the dishwasher, Skylar swore to herself she would fold the baskets of clean clothes before she left for work in the morning. They would not live out of the baskets anymore.

As she lay in bed, that feeling of being a shit person filled her again. Pulling her phone from her nightstand, she decided to do some amateur recon on the man who'd lied to her. Well, he hadn't lied. She'd never asked if he was single. So, her assumption could be her own fault in a way. And it sounded as if they were separated. She hoped. *That would make it less bad, right?*

It had taken all her willpower not to look him up sooner. When she'd left Club Ten, she had given him her number and assumed he would call. Zelda had given her hell when she'd found out, telling her that it went against the first rule of one-night stands. Skylar needed that manual. Without too much difficulty, she found CJ Adams and spent far too long scrolling through the photos of him and a gorgeous redhead. Perhaps Skylar was being judgmental and stereotyping, but if that was his wife, it didn't really surprise her that the woman had lost her patience and caused an issue in the middle of her husband's arraignment.

It was unbelievable. His entire account was public. The comments proved to be entertaining. Under a few of his photos, he'd received some interesting offers from women. Their obvious flirting with a married man grated on her nerves.

With a frustrated sigh, she shut down the app and plugged in her phone. *Tomorrow will be a good day.* She would go to work, make plenty of tips, then get everything she, Zelda, and Lara would need for their Halloween night. She hated shopping on weekends and didn't want to risk getting too close to the holiday. They planned to hand out candy and have a small dinner. Skylar did most of the cooking since Zelda had, on more than one occasion, burnt toast to the point where the building's smoke alarm went off and the fire department showed up. The neighbors thought it was funny the first time it happened at two in the morning. The second time, they were less entertained—and even less so on the third and fourth times. The landlord had told them if Zelda couldn't get her cooking under control, they would need to leave. Since Skylar liked the apartment and living with Zelda, she did whatever she could to make sure they didn't burn the building down.

As she slept, her dreams were filled with giant raw, headless, naked turkeys chasing her. It was equal parts terrifying and hilarious. Probably her subconscious stressing about Thanksgiving. Not only was it a busy holiday for her to cook, but it was also only three days before the diner closed for good.

***

The diner was insanely slow the next day. It was as if the world was letting her know that she soon would no longer have an income, and to drive that point home, she had to work a shift making nearly nothing in tips. Worse still, one of the people who had come into the restaurant had been a snobby bitch who'd done everything she could to degrade Skylar. Unlucky for Miss Bitch Pants, Skylar didn't care. Not entirely, anyway.

When Skylar got to the grocery store, she took a cart from the lot to use. One nice thing about working closing shifts—when she decided to go grocery shopping afterward, the store was nearly dead. Nothing was worse than fighting with some senile old man for the last jar of pickles. Because that had happened. She now tried to shop when the store was less likely to be crawling with other shoppers. Even on the Tuesday before Halloween, it was slow.

By the store's front door, she found a newspaper. It wouldn't hurt to get more serious about job searching, something she should have done two months ago, when she'd been told about the diner closing. But something inside her had thought they would change their minds. Each day they got closer to closing, the more she doubted that would be the case.

With her dream about Thanksgiving and slimy, raw turkeys chasing her, she figured she might as well start picking up what she needed. As she rounded the corner to find the damn jar of cranberry sauce Zelda loved, Skylar's power walking ended with her cart slamming into the side of someone else's. *Shit.*

"Oh, goodness, I am so sorry," she rushed to say as her eyes trailed from where their carts had collided up to the pair of deep-chocolate eyes staring back at her. If tall, dark, and handsome needed a cover model, she'd found him. Well, average, tan, and handsome. Her petite height made most people seem like giants.

The man gave her the same scrutiny, and she became ultra-aware that she was still wearing her dirty waitressing garb. To go along with the diner's fifties vibe, she wore a dress that was reminiscent of Snow White. Hers was far less tattered but no less dated. Everyone at the diner had to wear fifties-esque clothing. The color or pattern didn't matter so long as it gave off the right "mood," according to her boss. Skylar loved the style, so she never complained. But she looked like a housewife stuck in the wrong decade.

"Don't worry about it." He continued to look her over, almost as if worried he was hallucinating.

"I don't wear this all the time." She cringed. "Well, I mean, I do when I'm working. This is my uniform. For work…" she added lamely. She would soon be diving into the endcap of prepackaged stuffing if this got any more awkward.

"It's cute." He gave her a small smile.

As she took a closer look at him, he seemed exhausted. Dark circles rimmed his eyes, his button-down and slacks were beyond wrinkled, and his shoes were scuffed. He glanced down at himself. "I don't always look like this, but I suppose that's what two flights, one insanely stressful meeting, and less than four hours of sleep over two days will do to a person."

Her eyes widened. "Less than four hours of sleep? I'd be a bear."

"I'm not far off," he said with a small chuckle. "So, where do you work that you have to dress like a fairy-tale princess?"

Ah, so he got the Snow White vibes too. "Have you ever been to the diner just outside of town called Retro?"

He drew his brows together, then the confusion vanished after a moment. "Do you have to wear roller skates?"

"Oof, thank god, no. I would have killed either myself or someone else by now if that were the case."

He burst out laughing, and his dark eyes wrinkled at the corners.

Pretending she didn't take note of the way her stomach swooped at the sound, she adjusted her grip on her cart.

"So, do you have a name? I would like to say that when I'm less tired, I'm… smoother? More smooth? I don't know which it is, but I haven't… I don't know." He ran a hand over the back of his neck.

"Skylar, and you're fine." Though her stressors were stacking to precarious heights, she was surprisingly at ease and happy talking to this stranger at the stuffing capital of Arizona.

"Skylar," he said in a way that made her stomach float, like he just wanted a taste of it.

Wow, I'm either too tired to function properly, or I have officially lost my mind.

"I'm Harmon." He offered her his hand.

She took it, fully expecting to feel the smooth hands flagging him as a stranger to manual labor, based on what she assumed was his normal life of starched shirts after his mention of flights and meetings. But his hands were coarse with the evidence of hard work. She almost felt bad for the assumption. Too many times, she'd been bamboozled by men.

"Well, maybe I'll see you around." He gave a parting smile. "I need something quick to eat and a nice long sleep."

"I hope so—to seeing you around, that is." As she spun her cart, she cringed. *I hope so. What the hell, Skylar?*

"Me too," he called to her retreating back.

Chapter Three

HARMON

AFTER STUFFING HIS FACE with the microwave rice bowl, he dropped onto the couch, far too lazy to make his way down the hall to his bedroom. With his face pressed into the leather cushions, he replayed his meeting with Skylar in his mind. He was already kicking himself for not asking for her number.

I know where she works, so running into her again shouldn't be too hard.

It took several minutes of a mental berating for Harmon to convince himself that falling asleep on his couch would only hurt him more the next day. Grumbling about Mandy's ineptitude, the ladies on the plane who couldn't stop talking, and his aching legs, he shuffled to his bedroom.

The motion of shucking off his pants exhausted Harmon even more. By the time he fell between the sheets, his eyes were already shut.

***

"Fuck me." He sat up in bed and ran a hand over his face. It was five minutes before his alarm was set to go off. Why he woke up every morning
before he had to, he wasn't sure, but what he did know for certain was
that it was damn frustrating. Five minutes wasn't shit for sleep, but it
was better to sleep than stare at his phone as the time changed. Leaning
over, he turned on his nightstand lamp. The bedroom was furnished
with the bare minimum—bed, dresser, nightstand, and light. The gray
walls were empty as well, a reflection of his life. "Way to be depressing,
asshole. Goddamn, I've been living alone too long."

While Harmon got dressed, he wondered if it was really worth putting
up with Mandy to let her work the last two days that week. He had come
to the conclusion that they would be her last few days, but he worried he
might not be able to keep his annoyance and temper under control that
long.

He spent the drive to work giving himself a pep talk about how he
planned to take care of the issue and made it to his office just on time.
Despite waking early by only a few minutes, he was still exhausted and
moving slower than he wanted to.

"Good morning!" Mandy called from her desk before he had fully
opened the door.

Chipper as always... "Morning." He made his way to his desk, still so
frustrated with her that he could barely look at her. He couldn't continue
to overlook her mistakes.

"How was...?" Her brows pulled together, and she tipped her head to
the side.

"Portland, it was fine." With that, he opened and closed his office door with a resounding snap. "I won't survive these next two days," he mumbled.

His phone rang with an inter-office call almost the minute his ass touched the seat, and he picked it up on the second trill. "This is Harmon."

"You haven't fired that poor girl yet, have you?"

"Naudia, what the hell?"

"I just wonder if you should wait until after the new year?"

"That doesn't teach her anything, nor does it do me any good."

Naudia paused, no doubt sharpening her verbal pencil. "I know, but she needs the money."

"And I need someone with attention to detail," he snapped.

Unfazed, as usual, Naudia continued. "I talked with her yesterday while you were traveling..."

Harmon knew he wasn't going to like where this was going even before Naudia finished what she wanted to say. He sighed. "And?"

The resignation in his voice must have tap-danced through the phone because Naudia seemed emboldened.

"She's behind on her rent as it is. When I told her what had happened with the flight, she looked as if she would drop to the floor. So, please, if you're going to let her go, give her some notice. Let her know it's not working out, and... I don't know, tell her she can stay for another couple of months."

Harmon's brows furrowed. "You want me to give someone a two months' notice that I'm going to fire her?" He had to ask for clarification because that seemed to be too much. "What will stop her from completely giving up and being a *worse* assistant?"

"Tell her that if she has another screwup, she's out, but that you will give her a few weeks to line up something else."

"I'll think about it. Any other wise words for today?"

Naudia was a plethora of information and could often talk some sense into Harmon when he was on the brink of jumping off a ledge. She was the mother of the office, and each one of them knew they would be lost without her.

"Nope, but Sebastian wants to talk with you about Portland."

Harmon nodded then remembered she couldn't see him. "Okay, I'll be down in a minute." When he hung up, he hung his head as he thought about Naudia's proposal. The last thing he wanted to do was turn someone homeless, but he also didn't want to create extra stress and work for himself because of Mandy's lack of meticulousness. Pushing himself away from his desk, he exited his office, avoiding Mandy's eyes—if he didn't see her, he didn't have to speak to her—and made his way down the hall to Sebastian's office. They had an array of advisors, accountants, and other administrative employees. Harmon and a few others were focused on the investment side of the business, while the accountants on staff assisted with keeping the books for other businesses, and each person had an assistant. He passed several employees' offices on his way to Sebastian. Harmon had moved to the area just a few years prior, when he'd no longer wanted to be close to Jackie, and his parents, who had been a bit suffocating since the loss of Cecelia. So, moving nearer to Porter and Verity was the next best option. When the position at SOS Accounting and Investing had opened up, Harmon had applied, and within a month, he was house shopping then giving his notice to his previous employer. The names of the founders were Sebastian, Otis, and Scott. The correlation between that and the distress signal, they claimed, was incidental.

"Morning, Harmon," Naudia called from her desk as he passed. She was always cheerful and talking in a singsong voice.

"Morning again, Naudia."

"Go right on in. He's expecting you." Naudia waved him to Sebastian's closed office door. The building was set up so the assistants all sat in what doubled as a waiting room, while their bosses' offices were located off that area.

Harmon nodded. It wasn't every day that his boss wanted to talk with him directly. Sebastian liked to give all his financial advisors free rein, and Harmon appreciated that. Nothing was more annoying than bosses who thought they needed to check in every couple of hours, harping on what needed to be done. It made him feel claustrophobic.

He knocked on the doorframe before pushing the door open.

"Harmon, glad you're back. How was Portland? And I do hope you actually made it to the right city." Sebastian motioned with his weathered hand for Harmon to take a seat.

Sebastian's office was set up in a similar fashion to Harmon's, but instead of a small love seat at the back, Sebastian's office was large enough to accommodate an entire coffee bar, two armchairs, and a small sofa. The smell of fresh-ground coffee assaulted Harmon's senses. He liked coffee but didn't want his entire office to smell of it at all times throughout the day.

Harmon rolled his eyes as he sat because, of course, Naudia had told Sebastian about the Flight Fiasco, as Porter had aptly named the comedy show of an experience. "I did make it. All went well. To no one's surprise, Mr. Wilton made no changes to his portfolio. His daughter is now moving to Paris to teach English as a second language. His wife just joined a Thrills and Chills Book Club in their area, and Mr. Wilton joined a knitting class. He says it should help him regain the last of the mobility he lost after his stroke in the spring."

Sebastian nodded as if absorbing all Harmon had said. While Mr. Wilton was a creature of habit, he was also a kind man. He liked to make sure all was well, and he and Sebastian had been friends for a long time. When the firm had expanded and Sebastian needed to reduce his load of clients, he'd entrusted that friend to Harmon. It had been a moment of immense satisfaction for Harmon to be trusted with such an account.

"Strokes." Sebastian shook his head. "They just sneak up on a person."

Harmon nodded; he wasn't sure what else, if anything, he could add to that statement.

"I am glad his daughter is back to traveling the world. That husband of hers was no good."

Again, Harmon nodded. He didn't know the exact details, but he'd heard enough gossip to understand the man had been cheating on her for several years. The ex-husband was another of their clients. And it had been a bit awkward when they'd all found out about the divorce, infidelity, and some of his other transgressions.

"I hope the change is good for her. She always seemed like a nice person." Indeed, she was one of the nicest people Harmon could recall meeting on his travels.

"Anyway, the other thing I wanted to talk to you about is Mandy."
Harmon almost groaned.

"She has been making things more difficult than easier for you for some time now... How do you see this going in the future?"

It was never good when Sebastian noticed someone's assistant lacking. That meant they were fucking up on an impeccable level. Each person was tasked with disciplining, hiring, and firing their assistants. So, Sebastian would only get involved in extreme cases. Not what Harmon wanted his boss to notice.

"I was just talking with Naudia about that. I think I am going to let her know she has until the end of the year to find employment elsewhere. Give her time to find something different."

Sebastian rubbed his stubbled chin as he tilted his head, staring at the space in the corner of the room. "That is very generous of you. I think she should appreciate that. She just sent me statements for your clients so I could review them. She put the wrong names on the forms. I don't know how that's possible, as all of the statement information is automatically populated based on the name entered. Had I not found the mistake, we could have been releasing some seriously confidential information to the wrong people." The statement hung heavily in the air.

Harmon's heart beat erratically. He hadn't heard about that mistake until now. His face heated with embarrassment. But he couldn't find a reason for how it could have happened. There was no excuse. Harmon uploaded any information for those statements into the system, so all Mandy would have had to do was run the reports. "I will adjust her system permissions."

Sebastian brought his old, tired eyes back to Harmon's. "Make sure she knows if anything like that happens again, she is out of here immediately, and it will not reflect well on you either, Harmon."

He felt the threat in the words, but he kept his mouth shut; no sense digging himself a grave alongside Mandy. He walked back to his office as if wearing blinders, not noticing anyone else, and when he reached his sitting area, Mandy was nowhere to be seen.

He would talk with her just before the end of the day. It would give her the evening to think about it all. Harmon spent the rest of his shift with his door closed, fixing everything that Mandy had screwed up. With fifteen minutes left, he called Naudia.

"Harmon? Everything okay?"

"Yeah, do you think you could come be a witness to my conversation with Mandy? I don't fully trust her."

"Be right there. I'll ask her to come in with me on my way."

The papers had published several articles over the last few years about people claiming sexual harassment because they were unhappy. Because of it, their offices had installed cameras in the assistants' office space. None of the main offices had them, however, so he wanted Naudia present to avoid any potential for false claims.

Harmon hated this part of his job; firing people never felt good, even if he had the reputation of being the prick of the building. It wasn't intentional. He didn't take joy in terminating people. Each second that passed as he waited for Naudia and Mandy, his heart beat faster. When his door opened and the two women stepped in, he released a long, slow breath.

"Thank you for coming. Mandy, please have a seat."

The woman who never appeared to have a care in the world now seemed to be made of porcelain that could break the minute Harmon breathed too hard. Mandy sat directly in front of his desk, while Naudia took the love seat against the far wall.

"Mandy, as I am sure you know, you have made several major mistakes over your year and a half here." He said it as a question to give her a chance to speak for herself.

Instead, she fidgeted with the hem of her floral blouse.

"So, it is with great sadness that I tell you your last working day with SOS Accounting and Investing will be the Wednesday before Christmas."

That anxiety built into empathy as Mandy's breaths became faster and more labored. "I can do better. I will do better." She swallowed rapidly as if trying to keep her fear buried deep rather than speak it.

He hoped to hell she wouldn't spew her lunch all over his desk.

"It's a done deal, Mandy. That will be your last day of work. But I also must inform you that if you have any other big mistakes before then, your termination will be immediate."

The fear quickly shifted to something else as Mandy's face hardened into a deep frown. "What, you don't want to pay me for the two days of Christmas? Is that why you're letting me go so early?"

"Early? That's two months!" Harmon ran a hand over his face. "We will give you the holiday pay for the remainder of that week."

She scoffed. "What, am I supposed to thank you for that? Oh wow, thank you *so* much, Harmon, for letting me go the week of a major holiday."

Her grip on the arm of the chair turned her knuckles white; Harmon was nearly at the same level of anger.

"I was set and ready to fire you *today*. This extended period is so you can go out and start job hunting sooner rather than later. I suggest you do so. Unless you would like to finish your employment here straight-away," he nearly growled. "Now, unless you plan to give me a letter of resignation, you are free to go." Harmon's breaths quickened, and he didn't want to get any closer to that edge of anger hazing his vision.

CHAPTER FOUR

SKYLAR

"Happy Halloween!" Lara shouted as she skipped through the diner's front door.

Skylar was at the counter, preparing to close out her last tab. It had been a surprisingly good night. Halloween could be hit or miss. It was broaching three, and she liked to have dinner finished before they set up their Halloween table. The park near Skylar and Zelda's apartment building encouraged people to set up tables, almost like a craft fair for the kids to take turns stopping at. Some people brought pop-up tents and created themed spaces inside. The event started at six and was open until ten. It kept the trick-or-treaters off the streets.

"Lara, just get over here and sit, you fool," Zelda called from her seat at the counter. It ran from one end of the diner to the other. The high stools seemed to be Zelda's favorite spot because that was where Skylar almost always found her.

Lara shrugged at her sister's harshness and sat next to her. "So, I got a bag of Reese's, Kit Kats, and some Yorks."

"Is that all?" Skylar counted out change for the couple at the table in the corner.

"Of course not. Those are all of *our* favorites. We'll keep those bags under the table and give out the other junk to the kids."

Zelda laughed and shook her head at her sister. Skylar giggled as she made her way to the table of regulars, giving them their change and wishing them a good night. They, too, would be getting ready to set up their Halloween table. When she got back to the front counter, Zelda and Lara were arguing.

"Can't we just get dinner here? Then we'll eat in the car and start decorating right off." Lara's favorite holiday was Halloween, and she was not one to skimp on the decorations. "Also, next year, we're doing a tent. No more of this half-assed decorating."

"Our table always looks great," Zelda argued.

"It looks *okay*, but did you see the Grant twins' tent last year? The damn thing looked like people were stepping into a horror movie set."

Lara had been friends with the Grant twins all through school. Zelda was convinced Lara would eventually end up with one of the boys, but it seemed they were all happily sticking to the friend zone, though they had always been competitive.

"You're still friends with them, right? Why don't you help them?"

Lara looked as if Skylar had tried to punch her. "Yes, we're friends. But it's like a rivalry. The four of us"—she motioned to Zelda—"used to play *very* competitive games of kickball and wiffle ball on weekends. If I help them, they will think they won!"

She was nearly shouting, and Skylar had to cover her mouth as she started to lose it. Lara took it far more seriously than she'd ever imagined.

"Okay, I get it..."

"Everything okay, girls?" Connie asked as she filled a soda glass at the machine.

"They're taking our Halloween table a little too seriously." Skylar placed a stray tray back on the counter next to Connie.

Zelda scoffed and held up her hands as if in surrender. "I have zero problems with continuing to use our Beetlejuice-themed table from now until the end of time."

"Well... it's not going to be Beetlejuice this year." Lara smiled sneakily.

"What?"

"Oh boy," Skylar muttered. This was bound to be an argument between the sisters.

Connie shook her head, turning back to clear a table her customers had vacated. "Good luck with those two tonight," she muttered on her way past. "Also, I put in some burgers for you girls. There is no reason for you to go home and cook." The arched brow let Skylar know she couldn't argue.

As Lara and Zelda continued their debate over the pros and cons of changing their table to a *Hocus Pocus* theme, Skylar finished her end-of-shift duties. The burgers were ready just as Skylar took off her apron. This evening's dress was black with white polka dots and a wide belt. It was fun to wear and swirled around her legs in a way that made her feel like a princess.

***

Since Lara had conveniently left all the usual decorations at home, it seemed their table would indeed be set up like the old Sanderson sister museum in the *Hocus Pocus* movie. And each of them dressed up as one of the Sanderson sisters—another layer to the theme Skylar wouldn't have thought of, complete with an itchy-as-hell wig. Skylar had to admit, if she needed a themed party, Lara could take care of it.

"Okay, Lara. I'll give it to you, you sneaky little shit. This does look good. But I hate the wig." Zelda shook her head as if she could get it to settle into a more comfortable position.

"Well, none of them have blue hair..." Lara shrugged.

When Lara turned to get the bowl of candy ready, Zelda stuck her tongue out at the back of her head. Skylar loved watching the two banter. Not for the first time, she wished she and *her* sister could have the same relationship.

"I am going to find the Grant boys. I need to know what they're doing for their tent this year. Also, I have one more surprise for you girls." Lara waved over her shoulder as she took off to find her friends.

The event was set to start in less than five minutes, and Skylar was excited to see what the kids would dress as this year. She adjusted her red wig, which was far heavier than she had anticipated. Thankfully, the costumes Lara had picked up were shorter than the dresses from the movies—it was too hot for a full-length dress.

"What do you suppose the other surprise is?" Skylar asked as she fidgeted with the candy bowl. She screamed when the black cat on their table hissed as her hand reached for it. The bowl was designed to look like the damn spell book from the movie, and the robotic cat seemed just as hell-bent on protecting it.

Zelda threw her head back and cackled.

"Did you know it was going to do that?" Skylar asked with an accusatory tone.

"Not at all," Zelda said between gasps for air.

Before Zelda's cackles subsided, her older brother stepped up behind her. Skylar raised a brow at him and his costume. He leaned in close to Zelda's ear and did the best impression of Billy's moan from *Hocus Pocus*. Zelda screamed, and it was Skylar's turn to laugh manically.

Zelda turned, took in her brother, then started laughing all over again.

Jerry rolled his eyes, straightened his cravat, and took a seat behind their table.

"She roped you into this too?" Skylar took the seat next to him.

"Yeah." The resignation in his voice made Skylar think that having his face painted to look like a dead man had not been his idea.

"You should really learn how to tell her no."

"Trust me, I know." Jerry reached for one of the Twizzlers in the candy bowl. "Fucker," he mumbled at the hissing black cat.

Their table was a hit; several of the kids and even parents had taken pictures with them. The cat was another big win because all the kids loved that it was motion sensing and would only react when someone reached for a candy. Lara was all but patting herself on the back as the evening ended. Their Halloween was spent laughing, exchanging stories, and reminding Skylar why she loved Zelda's family. They had always welcomed her into their group. She felt like one of them. Even their parents had accepted her with open arms. They'd even included her in the last three Christmases since she and Zelda had moved in together.

She hoped they would always be close.

Chapter Five

HARMON

The last week had been a mess. Harmon felt like Mandy was trying to push him over the edge. Her mistakes were less drastic than some she'd made in the past, but he still found himself working late to correct her fuckups. But it was almost the weekend, and he was happy to be getting away from her. He intended to hold to his promise and allow her to stay until Christmas. Twice since he'd told her she was done, she had left for interviews. Selfishly, he hoped she would find something sooner rather than later. The advertisement for a new assistant wouldn't be posted until two weeks before Mandy's last day. The job posting was already waiting in his email drafts, ready to hit the papers.

He had gone to Retro twice and had seen Skylar through the windows, but he couldn't muster the courage to go inside. He worried that the evening at the grocery store had been a fluke. That night, he had been a walking disaster and didn't know if he should trust his memory of how their first meeting had gone. Besides, he hadn't dated anyone since Jackie. Sure, he'd hooked up, but never with the same woman more than once, and he wasn't sure if he was capable of dating again. His wandering mind came back to reality when his phone buzzed on his desk.

Porter: *You ever find your princess?*

It was as if the fool could read his mind. Harmon shook his head as he responded with a succinct no. Then he leaned back in his chair as he searched the diner on Google. It would be open for another few hours. He could run home, change, then see if she was working and if he could find his nerve and actually go inside. After his marriage failed, he'd sworn off relationships, and this was the first time he'd wanted to get to know someone new.

Resolve in place, he finished his work and vowed he wouldn't second-guess himself—he was going in tonight.

As he stepped into the small diner, he felt as though he'd been transported back to the fifties. A jukebox occupied one corner. The floor was made of black and white tiles. Stools lined the bar, all with red vinyl cushions that matched the countertop. If he had seen it anywhere else, he would have said that red and light blue didn't go together, but somehow, the robin's-egg-blue walls went great with the red booths and countertops. The polished chrome accents tied the space together.

An older woman stepped out from behind the counter, wearing a red dress with black polka dots that looked like it came from the fifties as well. "Just one?"

Harmon wasn't sure exactly where it stemmed from, but for some reason, that question grated on him today more than usual. Just one. Just him. After his divorce, he had always been alone, afraid of being with anyone else. *I don't deserve someone else. What am I doing here looking for Skylar?*

"Hon?"

"Yes, just me."

"Okay, dear, would you like a seat at the bar or a table?"

"At the bar, if that's all right."

"Anywhere you'd like." The woman nodded to the seats as she weaved through the gap in the counter, holding a tray overhead.

She brought the food to a couple at the far end of the dining room. They looked to be so in love, he didn't know if he should be disgusted or jealous.

"Good afternoon, my name is Skylar, and I'll be..." Skylar's face registered shock, a smile, then the smile was replaced by what Harmon assumed was her professional facade. She cleared her throat. "Can I start you off with something to drink?"

He couldn't help but wonder if he'd made a monumental mistake by coming here. This was not the welcome he'd expected.

"Just a Coke, please."

"We serve Pepsi products."

Her response was short, and he couldn't help the feeling of whiplash. Maybe the connection he'd felt a few nights ago had been one-sided.

"Pepsi's fine."

She nodded and turned away.

Shit. Shit. Shit.

He wanted to run. But now that he was there, he had to stick it out. It was too late to tuck tail. He tried to focus on the menu as he watched Skylar out of the corner of his eye as she filled a plastic cup with the restaurant's logo on the side. Twice she pulled her phone from her pocket and looked more and more displeased each time. That could certainly be part of her strange attitude, or because he'd ambushed her at her place of work. He should have known better.

Skylar returned, placing the soda in front of him. "Do you know what you'd like to order?"

"Anything on the menu you think I should try as a first-timer?" He wanted to get back to the banter they'd shared the other night.

She sighed. "You can't go wrong with one of Benji's signature burgers."

Assuming Benji was the chef, he nodded. "I'll take one of those, medium rare, please."

"Fries?"

"Yes, please."

She spun and headed into the kitchen, where the older woman had exited only a few minutes before. The door swung silently as she disappeared.

"She's a bit stressed today. Not really herself." The woman from earlier stood at his shoulder with a now-empty tray.

Part of him wanted to ask, but the other part of him knew he needed to wait and see if Skylar would tell him on her own—or tell him to fuck off. But opening up to him would be too much to ask, wouldn't it? They'd met once, and the last thing she needed was to have some creep not only show up at her work but also start prying into her personal life.

The older woman looked like she planned to head to the kitchen when she paused, opened her mouth as if she to speak, shook her head, then proceeded through the swinging door.

The feeling that this was a mistake grew heavier for some reason. His stomach churned with anxiety. Through the small window in the kitchen door, he watched the woman embrace Skylar and rub her upper arms. It felt like spying. Granted, he wasn't trying to watch them; he just happened to notice their movements. The moment they stepped apart, Skylar's arms flew around as she talked animatedly. He couldn't make out her words, but she definitely looked upset. And just when he was about to look away, she looked up and motioned in his direction.

They made eye contact. Her eyes narrowed, causing that feeling of invading her space to inflate. He dropped his gaze and pulled out his phone.

Harmon: *I think I screwed up.*

Porter: *You'll need to be more specific than that... Did you fire Mandy?*

Harmon: *Well, kind of, but this isn't about her. It's that girl from the grocery store I told you about.*

Porter: *I'm not sure how you can "kind of" fire someone... How could you already screw that up? You've met once.*

Porter: *Shit, did you show up at that diner?*

Harmon: *Yeah... I didn't ask for her number the other day.*

Porter: **Laughing crying emoji**

Porter: *She probably thinks you're a psycho.*

Harmon hovered over the keyboard, intending to type back that not everyone got to marry their college sweetheart, but he'd had that chance and had ruined it. Porter had no idea what it was like to date. He'd been married far too long to remember trying to meet someone. Then again, Harmon hadn't tried to go on a date with anyone in nearly a decade. Hookups were far from dates. Besides, none of them meant anything, and now he'd met a woman he wanted to get to know, and he was messing it up before it started.

The kitchen door swung open as another text from Porter came through. Without checking the message, he tucked his phone back in his pocket. When he looked up, Skylar stood before him, sadness etched into her features.

"I'm sorry if I'm coming across as rude. It's been a rough week."

With her standing so close, he could see the bags under her eyes. "Don't feel like you owe me anything, Skylar. I'm sorry if I freaked you out by showing up."

She laughed, and he wanted to surround himself with the sound on his rough days.

"Honestly, if you'd shown up any other day, I think I would have been myself. I just, today is... is a hard day for me." Her voice caught at the same time as a bell rang from the kitchen. "That'll be your burger."

Her dress twirled around her knees as she headed back through the swinging door. She wore another one very reminiscent of Snow White. He wanted to smile, but the hurt in her voice broke something in him. When Skylar came back out, she forced a smile, but the sadness lingered in her eyes.

As she placed the plate before him, Harmon leaned in. "Can I try to give you a better day tomorrow? Or maybe next week?"

"And how do you plan to do that?" The skepticism in her voice made him feel small.

"By taking you on a date."

She smiled. "Okay, Romeo. What does your perfect date look like?" With narrowed eyes, she put one hand on her hip.

Harmon opened his mouth to respond, but was at a loss. In the past, his perfect date would have been simple, dinner and a movie. But something told him Skylar would not find that response acceptable. "That depends."

"On what?"

"Who I'm taking out. I mean, what's your favorite thing to do? Where do you feel most like yourself?"

Skylar raised a brow. "Answering a question with a question?" More skepticism dripped from her words.

"Well," he hedged, "if I take someone on a date, I want it to be something we can both enjoy."

Skylar smirked. "I'm pretty easygoing. I'm up for just about anything, usually. I haven't been on a real date in over two years."

Harmon chuckled. "It's been a few years for me too." He didn't want to reveal how long just yet. "Can I have your number, and we can chat about it when you're ready?"

Chapter Six

SKYLAR

"Z, I'm home."

"In here." Zelda's voice came from the kitchen and caused a sinking feeling in Skylar's gut. When she stepped through the doorway, she was relieved to see Zelda sitting at the counter, eating a sandwich. "You don't have to race into the kitchen every time you hear me in here. I *can* manage a sandwich."

Skylar's face heated with guilt. "Sorry," she groaned. If ever there were a day where she couldn't stop seeming like an ass at every turn, apparently, today was the day. The memories of her mother floating around her brain, her sister's incessant texting, treating Harmon like shit, and now hurting Zelda's feelings were making Skylar feel like she was worth less than the forgotten dust bunnies under her couch. She'd been trying to escape these emotions for years, and they just wouldn't go away.

"Sky, I was kidding. I hate to see that look on your face. What's going on?"

Unbidden and unwanted, the tears she'd been fighting most of the day finally broke free. "It's the anniversary, Z."

Zelda sat back as if she'd been slapped, then she pulled her phone from her pocket, seemingly to verify the date. Her face paled when she lit up the screen. "Sky, why didn't you say something this morning? Or text me today?"

Skylar shrugged. "I thought this would be the year I could get through the day without thinking about her. About what I did to her." She fiddled with her purse strap.

"That was not your fault; it would have happened regardless."

"You don't know that. I certainly don't know that."

Zelda left her seat at the island, pushing her blue bangs out of her eyes. When she reached Skylar, she held her by the upper arms. "Look at me. That girl would have been texting and driving regardless of your mom being on that road. Your mom and her drinking would have caught up with her at some point. Lastly, she could have gone to a closer store to get you those damn tampons, pads, whatever the hell it was." Zelda's hand left Skylar's shoulder to wave in a way to let her know the detail didn't matter and not to bother correcting her on what her mother had been going to get. "She went to that store because that was where she liked to get her booze. She probably would have gone to that store no matter what. So, I want you to stop blaming yourself."

Skylar wiped at her eyes. "She did care about me, you know. Sure, she drank—a lot—but she was always there when I needed her. She always went out of her way to make sure I got what I needed. I just, I don't know. I sometimes wonder if I had said something to her about how much she drank, maybe she would have cut back. You know?" The way Zelda had so easily summed up her mother made Skylar feel she needed to defend her memory.

Zelda held Skylar's gaze and shook her head. "Sky, it would have taken so much willpower and determination for her to quit. A fourteen-year-old was not going to convince her to stop drinking. That had to be something she wanted to do."

Skylar nodded. "Tonya blames me too."

"Tonya, the crazy bitch who also tried to break into your car for the change in your cupholder while you were at work? Tonya, the woman who could have done so much with her life but settled on being a drug addict? Tonya, the one who moved across the country just to make your life miserable? She cannot put all that on you, and I don't want you to either."

Her points were logical, but something inside Skylar wouldn't allow her to write off her sister's decisions as not her fault. If their mother had survived, things would have been different. Before their mother passed, Tonya *was* different. Better.

"Tonya has been texting me all day. I just don't know how to fix things with her."

Zelda nodded with a sad smile. "You can't be the only one who wants to fix your relationship. And some things just couldn't be fixed. Tonya has to want it too. She uses this to control you and make you feel guilty. I mean, it's been..."

"Fourteen years."

"Exactly, fourteen years, and she still wants you to feel like it was your fault."

"She did take care of me so I didn't have to go into the foster system."

"Yeah, she's a real saint. Collecting money from the state to spend on herself and her addictions sure did you a lot of good. I'm *positive* any family you could have ended up with would have been ten times worse than that." Zelda's words dripped with sarcasm.

Part of Skylar wanted to make excuses for her sister, but another part knew Zelda was right. Tonya had gotten in with the wrong crowd as a young teenager and hadn't left that group until Skylar had moved away. She was never someone Skylar wanted to look up to. But Tonya was her older sister, and she'd made sure Skylar graduated high school.

"I mean, really, how old *were* you, Sky?"

"Fifteen."

Zelda's lips formed a firm line, and her brows pressed together as if to push home the fact that Skylar had still been young when it all happened. "She's five years older than you, Sky. She should have known better." She squeezed Skylar's upper arms then dropped her hands. "You go get changed and sit on the couch, then we'll apply for some jobs. Got it?"

A smile pulled at Skylar's mouth. "And you'll make me one of your cold turkey sandwiches?"

Zelda rolled her eyes, feigning annoyance. "I guess."

After changing into some pajamas, Skylar settled onto the couch. In one of her rarest shows of love, Zelda offered her the remote. Skylar scrolled through the movie selection and picked a Sandra Bullock movie that she'd seen far too many times and would not be giving up anytime soon.

"That cute guy I told you about stopped in at the diner today."

"No shit?" Zelda sat up straighter, more interested in the conversation than the characters on the screen. "Was he there for you?"

"Well, I think so. I didn't come out and ask. I feel like that would have been weird. Hey, you want fries with that burger or just me?"

Zelda tipped her head back and laughed. "I wish you would have said that! You need to get that sleaze-ass player out of your mind."

"Sleaze-ass?"

Zelda shrugged. "Just made it up. It sounded like it would fit the tattooed devil. Anyway, is Grocery Guy going to take you out to dinner at some point?"

Skylar tipped her head from side to side. Indecision churned in her middle. "I haven't made up my mind, but I did give him my number... and we talked about maybe going on a date."

"Has he texted you yet?"

The more they talked, the straighter Zelda sat. She was the first one to push Skylar to go on a date but seemed opposed to dating herself. Skylar would need to get to the bottom of that one. Then again, Zelda had been around for what had happened with Christopher then with CJ. Men whose names started with C were off-limits from now on. It was the only logical response.

A blush warmed Skylar's cheeks as she thought of the absence of texts. "No, not yet."

Chapter Seven

Harmon

Harmon: *I know yesterday was a rough day for you, but I thought we could go on a date? Maybe see a movie.*

It had been several hours since he'd sent the text, and he wished he could take it back. As he reread the message for no less than the tenth time, he was disgusted by how desperate it sounded. There should be an option to recall messages that hadn't been opened yet. They could call it the boomerang effect; he would start on the patent as long as someone else was smart enough to make it work. But given the time that might take, he would continue to suffer in the misery of limbo coated in hope.

When lunch rolled around and he still hadn't heard back from Skylar, he was convinced she no longer had an interest in him. Dating was too much for his old heart.

"I finished the Donovan statement," Mandy chirped from his doorway.

He had taken to leaving the door open again. Despite how Mandy irritated him, it was more annoying to try remembering to close his door just so he didn't have to look at her.

"Send it to me for proofreading before it goes to the client." Since Sebastian's vague threat, Harmon preferred to determine if a statement was complete, accurate, and ready to be mailed out. The woman had already cost herself her job. He wouldn't let her cost him his as well.

The statement had minor issues. She'd forgotten to update the date range of the statement as well as the last page with the summary of the different investments. That was a manual statement Harmon had made and sent to her, but it was an easy fix. As he finished it up and prepared it to go out, his phone burned like hot coals in his pocket. His hand kept reaching for it. He wasn't used to constantly checking his phone. Hell, usually, he could go all day without even thinking about looking at his cell. But since he'd sent that damn text, he couldn't stop himself.

"Here's that statement. You forgot to update the dates at the top of the letter, letting them know what quarter it was from, and you didn't include the overall investment summary that I emailed you last week."

Mandy's shoulders slumped. The job just wasn't a good fit for her. She needed to find something laxer, perhaps where she wasn't preparing paperwork. "Sorry," she mumbled as she clicked around on her computer.

"Other than that, it looked good." It felt strange not to berate her for something, but he couldn't ignore the pity settling in his gut. She would be gone in seven more weeks. It wasn't the nicest way to view their remaining time together, but it was the best he could do.

Mandy's brows shot up, and she gave Harmon a half smile. As he turned to go back to his office, he realized that in the time they'd been working together, he had never really told her when she was doing her job well. The only time he'd given her feedback was when she'd screwed something up. As he sat back down, he swore he would do better.

The vibration in his pocket nearly made him jump out of his chair.

Skylar: *I think you have the wrong number, man.*

Harmon grimaced.

Harmon: *I'm guessing this is not Skylar?*

Little dots appeared right after he sent the message. Anxious anticipation had him holding his breath for the response.

Skylar: *Nope, name's Finn.*

Harmon flopped back in his chair. Either she'd intentionally given him the wrong number, or he'd misunderstood her. Her indifference at his presence the night before made him lean toward her not wanting to spend time with him. But she did apologize for it. Their banter had eventually come back to the surface. Sick of allowing his worry to control his life, he grabbed his keys from his desk and headed out. He hadn't taken a lunch—a perfect excuse to go to the diner.

The drive went by remarkably fast; usually when he went out for lunch, traffic was a monster he didn't want to tackle. But it was later than usual, and he was walking through the door of the diner before he'd come up with a full plan.

"Hey, what are you doing here?" Skylar smiled at him.

That was the reaction he'd been hoping for the day before.

"I wanted to ask if you might go to the movies tonight. I know, not the most creative of dates."

With one hand Skylar tucked the tray under her arm and cocked her hip to the side. "Why didn't you just text me?"

"I entered your number wrong in my phone. I tried to text you earlier this morning, and the person responding was adamant their name was Finn and that he lives in Wyoming but used to live here in Arizona."

Skylar laughed.

"I assure you it was quite the conversation. At first, I thought maybe you were messing with me. I ended up getting most of this guy's life history. Far more than I needed."

"We'll fix that, unless you'd rather talk with Finn?"

"Who says I have to choose?"

Skylar tipped her head back and laughed. This woman was drastically different from the woman he'd talked with the night before. "Fair enough, and yes, I would love to go to a movie."

The older woman from the night before came out from the kitchen. "Hello again, dining in?" The way she asked the question made Harmon feel like she found this all too amusing.

"I'm just on lunch, probably get something to go."

"Skylar can handle that. I'm Connie, by the way." She winked at Skylar as she walked away, causing Skylar's cheeks to tinge an adorable shade of pink. It only took them a moment to decide what movie they would go see that night. They'd agreed to meet at seven. Then he was on his way with the same burger he'd ordered the night before. The only thing that struck him as odd was the fact that she insisted she drive herself to the theater. Then again, his recent dating experience was limited, and most of the women he went home with, he met at a bar.

He wasn't used to the giddy anticipation that followed. He only had an hour or two left in his day, and the plan mapped itself out in his mind as he drove back to the office. He would go home, change out of his work attire, then head to the theater.

It was the first night in a while that he decided work could wait until the next day, and he left on time. As he stepped outside, the air was stifling. His shirt stuck to his torso as he made his way across the lot. After dropping into his car, he headed home, hurried to get ready, and left for his date. *Date. Well, here goes nothing.*

The theater was only a fifteen-minute drive from his house, so he arrived twenty minutes early. As he waited, the anticipation began to fizzle, and the nerves settled into his bones. They'd picked a romantic comedy, hopefully safe for a first date. He rubbed his hand up and down his jean-clad legs as he waited. He didn't even know what kind of car she drove, so he texted her.

Harmon: *I'm here. Let me know when you arrive, and I'll come find you.*

The little check marks showed it had been delivered but had yet to be read. That was fine. She was probably driving.

"Snap out of it, Harmon." He shook himself. His nerves were getting the best of him. Turning to his usual form of distraction, he picked a random social media app and started scrolling. As he did, he was reminded of the house down the street from Porter. He searched until he found the listing again. The price wasn't on the website; they wanted interested parties to call their realtor. He figured it was a trap. If that house and price didn't work for him, they would give a slew of other options. It almost made him think about the run-ins he would have on a car lot. Everyone knew *exactly* what he needed.

Switching back to scrolling, he fell into the rabbit hole of watching videos of people cooking. He loved to cook, so he often got lost in the endless abyss of people sharing different recipes. A notification dropped onto the screen.

Skylar: *I'm here. Meet at the door?*

Harmon: *Sure, should I expect to see you dressed as Snow White?*

Skylar: *Not today, it's a special occasion. I broke out my Cinderella ball gown.*

Chuckling, Harmon stepped out of his car. Knowing Skylar had actually shown up eased some of his nerves. As he made his way to the front door, he fidgeted with the hem of his shirt. The theater was one of the biggest in the state, and he was happy it was so close to his house. He loved to watch movies here and there. Sometimes, he and Porter would catch the newest sci-fi release.

Skylar stood just outside the glass doors in a pair of high-waisted jeans and a crop top. A sliver of skin showed between the two. The emerald-green top seemed to make her hair shine brighter, and she clasped her hands over her middle. As he got closer, Harmon realized she was holding her phone. One of her legs bounced, and he wondered if she was just as nervous as he felt.

When her gaze finally landed on him, a spark lit up her face. Her smile was wide and genuine, and somehow, this felt right.

"Hey." She tucked a strand of hair behind her ear as she blushed.

"You look beautiful." The outfit was simple, but it suited her well—the jeans hugging her curves, and the top, well, it gave him a *very* good idea of what was underneath.

"Thanks. So, what are we seeing again?"

Harmon shrugged before putting his hand on her lower back to lead her into the theater. She kept looking toward the parking lot, almost as if searching for someone. She easily dislodged the idea as she turned to smile up at him.

"Honestly, I don't remember. It's a rom-com, though."

She giggled, and it was like a shot straight to his gut. He was falling too easily into this. She seemed like a genuine person. They stepped inside and were immediately hit with the smell of buttered popcorn and sugar. It was familiar and comforting in a way. They got their tickets. Harmon stopped at the bar to get their snacks, and Skylar got a lemonade. The seats in theater B were leather recliners, or at least they appeared to be, with footrests. This theater was always expensive, but Harmon thought being comfortable was more important than getting cheap tickets. Tonight was about the company. As they walked, their arms brushed, and he wished he had an empty hand to take hers.

They found their seats, and Skylar's face lit up with excitement again.

"I haven't been in a movie theater since I was a kid."

Harmon's eyes widened, his brows rising. "No shit?"

She shook her head. "Growing up, it was just my mom, my sister, and me. We didn't usually have much money for extra activities." She shrugged as if it were no big deal.

Harmon wanted to ask about her father. "And now that you're an adult?" When she looked confused, he expanded on his question. "I just mean, why haven't you gone as an adult?"

"Oh, I don't know. Never really thought about it, I guess. No one to go with. My last boyfriend was... He liked to go to establishments of a different caliber."

The way she phrased it left Harmon with far more questions than answers about this woman and her past. Talking about an ex on the first date was not what he would hope for, so he filed that question away in the back of his mind.

The movie gave plenty of laughs, a few serious moments, and a lot of tension. They watched comfortably in silence. When the credits rolled, they waited in their seats to allow most of the other patrons to leave. Crowds were one of Harmon's least favorite things to get caught up in. It was just as easy to wait while sitting as to wait jammed next to or against another person.

Skylar turned to him, her brows furrowed. "I still don't know exactly what you do for a living."

"It's nothing exciting." He shrugged. "I'm a financial advisor. I help people figure out where they should invest their money, when to be conservative, where to be aggressive. Things like that. Sometimes, I just help people come up with ways to ensure their assets are insured, and I've even helped a few clients create budgets to put them in a better financial position."

"You must *really* like numbers..." Skylar said, almost cringing.

"You don't?"

"I mean, I'm good with numbers, but..." She shrugged, seeming to search for the right word. "I just get bored easily."

"In other words, you think my job sounds dull." He feigned hurt as he sat up straighter and put his hand over his heart.

"That's not what I'm saying at all." Another of her laughs chimed in his ears. She placed her hand to his knee and gave it a squeeze.

Dropping his hand from his chest, he put his over hers, where it rested on his leg. "Ready?"

Skylar nodded. They held hands as they exited the theater into the setting sun. It was still warm out, but not nearly what it had been.

"Thank you." She gave his hand a squeeze as if to show her appreciation for the evening.

"I had a great time. I'll walk you to your car."

"You don't have to do that. Really. I'm on the other side of the lot. Talk to you tomorrow?" Her sudden dismissal felt unnatural. Her gaze shifted around the parking lot, as she'd done before.

"Okay." Harmon's stomach sank to his toes, rooting him to the spot as she walked away. He lost sight of her as she rounded the side of the building toward the additional parking.

Making his way to his car, he was swamped by the feeling that something was off the moment they exited the theater. He worried that he made her uncomfortable when they were alone together. He sat in his car replaying their last few minutes together. He'd stopped at the trash by the door to take care of their wrappers while she waited off to the side. She'd been on her phone...

He shook his head. Overthinking it would do nothing but drive him insane.

Harmon: *Please let me know when you get home.*

Tucking his phone into the compartment by the radio, he started his car and headed out. Once he got home, the first thing he did was check his phone. This woman was turning him into a smartphone zombie. But he released a breath of relief to see she'd texted him back.

Skylar: *Just got home. Thank you again for such a great night.*

"If it was so great, why did you all but run away from me?" With a sigh, he headed into his dark, empty condo.

Chapter Eight

SKYLAR

Skylar rolled her head around her shoulders as she input the order through the computer to be printed out in the kitchen. It had been a couple of days since her first date with Harmon, and she wasn't sure how she should feel. The date had gone well, and she'd had fun, but CJ had somehow seen her at the theater. A text had come through as she was walking across the lot asking who she was dressed up for. She'd ignored it, which had only spurred him on more.

The rest of her night was spent stressing, especially after CJ told her there were cameras in the private rooms above the club and that, if she didn't cool things down with Harmon, then she would *leave him no choice but to share the video to show who she belonged to.* The idea of there being a video of them having sex made her head spin. While searching for a new job, she didn't need some illicit video of her floating around the world.

"I thought I saw your car." A chill ran up Skylar's spine at the sound of his voice.

Keeping her back turned, she ignored him as she finished then sent the order for the family she was waiting on.

"It doesn't take you long to jump from one bed to another, does it?"

Skylar's hands shook. The emotions running rampant through her body attacked one another, not knowing which should hold dominance. "What do you want?"

"Not much, it's simple really. I want you to stop seeing your lover boy," CJ whispered. It contradicted the boldness of him showing up at her workplace. "Come outside for a moment. I would hate for our conversation to be overheard. And trust me when I say, I don't think your boss would be happy to hear about what you like to do in public places."

Skylar's cheeks flushed. She looked around the diner, but it was slow—she had one table, and Connie was in the back prepping for the dinner rush with Benji. Stepping to the side, Skylar called into the kitchen, "Connie, I have one table. I'm just going to run out to my car for a few minutes."

Connie's gaze shifted from the vegetables on her cutting board up to Skylar. "Okay, dear."

"Three minutes," Skylar muttered to CJ as she brushed past him. He was on her heels, and she had barely gotten through the door before his hand was wrapped around her braid, tugging her head back.

"I am the one in control of this situation." His hot breath skimmed her face, and it took all she had not to cringe. "So, like I said, you will get rid of lover boy and you will be at my beck and call whenever I want. Or that little video of you pressed against the glass may get leaked to a few places."

Tears pricked Skylar's eyes at his threat. Her bravado from earlier was quickly dissipating, and she didn't know what she should do. Just as abruptly as it had all started, CJ released her and was heading back to the SUV, driven by the brute Nick from Club Ten.

***

"Z, I'm stressing."

Zelda turned down the volume on her game and shifted her attention to Skylar. "What's up?"

"I have barely three weeks left at the diner. I've only been called for one interview, and I don't think it went very well. *And* CJ, the creep, came to the diner today and has been texting me nonstop since that day I went to the movies with Harmon."

"Still? Why don't you just block him?"

It was a valid question. She had seriously thought about it, but Skylar worried that if she did, he would do as he promised. She was too embarrassed to share those details. His messages were odd. At first, he'd just asked what she was up to. But his texts quickly turned darker after he found out about her movie date with Harmon. "I... I don't want him coming in and making a scene."

Zelda nodded thoughtfully. "You know Jerry just got transferred to our area. I could ask him to do something about it."

"I don't want to put Jerry in a weird position at work."

"One would think with his mother being an attorney, he'd know a few things about avoiding bad press. Plus, from what I've seen of her in the courtroom, she's ruthless. I've been the reporter on a few cases where she's the defense attorney, and she goes for the opposition's weak points every time."

"His mother is an attorney?"

"Did I not tell you that? I swear I did. I think that's why nothing's ever stuck to the slimy fuck."

Skylar groaned as she dropped onto their couch. "Fuck me."

Zelda nodded and cringed. "Sorry…"

Skylar waved her off, then draped her arm over her eyes. "Can life ever just be simple? Easy? I don't know, just something that isn't this hurricane of drama everywhere I turn?"

Zelda was quiet for a moment, and Skylar wondered if she'd gone back to playing her game. When she lifted her arm to take a peek at her best friend, Zelda's lips were pursed as she stared at who knew what.

"What are you thinking?"

"I'm just wondering if maybe we can find you a job at the courthouse. They're almost always looking for people in the recording offices. You would just be filing papers, auditing the files for accuracy, things like that. But I don't think I've seen any openings lately."

"At this point, I would take anything." *A resolution to one problem is better than continuing to add to my hoard.*

Skylar's phone vibrated on the kitchen counter. Worry that it was CJ bubbled in her stomach. But it could also be Harmon.

"I need another energy drink, so I'll grab it while I'm in the kitchen," Zelda offered.

"You really need to stop consuming so much caffeine. It can't be good for you."

Zelda lifted off the couch, making Skylar settle closer to the middle. When she returned with Skylar's phone, her brow was raised.

"What?" Skylar groaned and held out her hand.

"Do you two always exchange dirty pictures?"

Skylar's eye bugged. "What? No. Never."

Zelda made another face and pulled her lips to the side.

Snatching her phone, Skylar unlocked it and checked the messages that had come through. The one image with it was of a bowling alley, and she furrowed her brows at Zelda. "There's no dirty picture."

"Kidding. I just wanted to see what your reaction would be. And might I say, you seemed very interested in seeing some dirty pictures of Grocery Guy..."

Skylar laughed. "You're impossible." She dropped her gaze to the text again.

Harmon: *New bowling alley, can I take you?*

Skylar: *Today?*

Harmon: *Any day you'll allow me.*

Skylar was finding it all too hard to distance herself from this man. *Why wasn't he the one I met in the bar all those weeks ago?* Then she wouldn't have crazy-ass CJ messaging her all the time. If it was a newer place, it wouldn't be easy for CJ to know where she was. The question stared back at her as she struggled with the idea of CJ finding out. If he did, she was fucked. The connection she felt with Harmon was one she hadn't experience in a long time.

Skylar: *Tonight, would be great.*

Harmon: *Can I pick you up? Or would you prefer to drive yourself?*

It was an innocent question, but Skylar had a hard time allowing other people to drive her around. *What if they got distracted?* It only took a moment to make a deadly mistake. Hell, she was surprised she'd decided to get a license. Trauma could do that to a person. Before her mother's accident, she'd always wanted her license, but when it had come time, she'd only gotten it out of necessity.

Skylar: *You can pick me up if you want.*

Harmon: *Let me know where, and I'll be there.*

"Since you're smiling like a fool, I'm guessing you're going to see him?"

"We're going bowling." Another activity it had been years since she'd done. Most activities she did because they were free—hiking, going to the beach.

Zelda smiled. "I hope you have a good time. I'm going to go kick some little kid's ass who keeps talking shit."

"I'm assuming this will be a virtual ass beating?"

Zelda laughed. "Yeah, they were just hovering off to the side in one of my online games the other day, running their mouths. So, I proposed a challenge."

Skylar shook her head. She wasn't sure what Zelda's plan entailed, and she certainly didn't want to find out. "Well, I'm going to get changed."

Skylar had just finished getting ready when her phone vibrated on her dresser.

Harmon: *I'm outside.*

Skylar fluffed her hair one more time, released a long, slow breath, and headed for the door. But before she could make it out, her phone went off again. Assuming it was Harmon, she checked the lock screen.

CJ: *Now, I know after what I said, you wouldn't be going out with someone else... again.*

Skylar's hands turned clammy, and her heart began to race. This couldn't be happening. She raced to the living room window to see if she could spot wherever the dick was posted. She saw nothing out of the ordinary. No one seemed to be watching her apartment. There was no way he could know Harmon was there to get her. As she scanned the parking lot again, she still came up empty.

Skylar: *I want nothing more to do with you. Stop messaging me.*

As she made her way down to the lot, that seed of doubt that someone was watching her sat heavy in her limbs. CJ was clearly stalking her. She just hadn't figured out how yet. Besides, if he leaked the video, it would damage his reputation and his mother's more than hers. She wasn't well known in the area at all. There would be more consequences for him and his family than for her—or so she told herself as she took a steadying breath.

When she stepped out into the early-evening air, she scanned the parking lot again. Ready to bolt back upstairs if the need arose, she kept one hand on the door. Again, nothing looked out of the ordinary. The crunch of small stones under her shoes echoed off every surface. When she peered around the lot one last time, she spotted Harmon stepping out of a black sports car.

Of course he has a nice car. She wasn't sure why it was so annoying that Harmon might have his entire life together while she was dealing with craziness from all sides.

"Hey, beautiful."

She couldn't stay annoyed when she saw his genuine smile. Most of her situation was her fault. She shouldn't have hooked up with CJ—that was becoming more and more apparent.

"Hey."

She stepped closer to Harmon and took his hand as he walked her around the other side of his car and opened the door for her. It was odd. She didn't think anyone had done that for her before. It was so sweet.

"Thank you," she murmured before settling into the leather.

Harmon slid into the driver's seat. "So, you hadn't been to the movies in a long time. How long has it been since you went bowling?"

A flush filled Skylar's cheeks. She wasn't sure why, but it embarrassed her to think how little she'd done in her life. "Probably longer than going to the movies. I used to try getting my ex to go with me, but he didn't seem to have much interest, and Zelda prefers her video games."

As they pulled out of the lot, Harmon rested a hand on her knee. Warm comfort spread through her body at the contact. It made her feel wanted, cherished in a way. It was terrifying to let someone new into her life when things were so far from what she wanted them to be.

"We'll fix that tonight. So, is there anything else you would like to do that you haven't done in a while?"

It almost felt like an inuendo was hiding in there somewhere, but Harmon didn't seem the type. He wasn't pushy.

"Well, like I said before, it was just me, my mom, and sister. She couldn't take us to do much. Most of the time as a kid, if I did anything, it was for a school field trip."

Harmon added pressure on her knee. He gave her a sad smile. "We'll change that."

She was afraid to cling to such a promise. With everything in her life so uncertain, she couldn't make plans with someone beyond the current moment. Instead of voicing her concerns, she said, "I would like that." It wasn't a lie; she would enjoy spending more time with him. She was just skeptical if their relationship would last after she lost her job. *Nobody wants to date an unemployed woman.*

The remainder of the drive was comfortable as they chatted about their school days. Harmon talked about college and the best friend he would be visiting for Thanksgiving. By the time they reached the bowling alley, Skylar felt she knew him in a way that warmed her heart.

"Shit, it looks like they're closed." He pulled up next to the front door, where a bright-orange paper was taped.

Closed due to water line break. Sorry for any inconvenience.

"That sucks," Skylar said as she deflated into her seat. She had really been looking forward to bowling.

"We'll find something else to do." Harmon pulled back out onto the road. "How about we find a place to sit and chat?"

"Sure." Skylar smiled at him.

"There's a club I've only been to a few times in town. Go there?"

The joy on her face dropped when she realized where he intended to take them. There was no graceful way for her to tell him why she didn't want to go to Club Ten, and being right under CJ's nose was the last place she wanted to be. "If you want," she found herself saying, though she didn't mean it.

"Okay, we can go, have a couple drinks, and think of an alternate plan." He pulled away from the traffic light just as it turned green, bringing Skylar closer to the place she had no desire to return to. But the words were hard to find, and before she could, they were parking, then finding a table in the far corner of the club.

"So, do you have any good stories about you and your sister?" Harmon sipped on his club soda. He'd said when they arrived that he would only have one beer, and an hour into their night of chatting and people watching, he'd stayed true to his word.

But his question had anxiety building inside her. It started at her ankles and seemed to snake its way up her legs, burrowing into her stomach. She swallowed hard. "Not really, we're not close."

Harmon nodded as if he understood. Prying questions usually came next. She was already plotting ways to deflect a discussion about the dysfunction in the hatred Tonya felt for her.

"So, what do you do when you're not waitressing or grocery shopping?"

His question was so far removed from what she had expected that Skylar sat back against her chair. Her posture had gone rigid as she'd prepared for the onslaught of his interrogation. But instead, he'd changed the subject and given her an out. Either he was good at reading people, or she was about as transparent as the cellophane wrapping on the packages of cookies she'd annihilated earlier from the local bakery.

"Umm, I like to do puzzles—when we have the space."

He cocked his head in a more adorable way than anything she'd seen recently.

"You know, like jigsaw puzzles, usually ones by my favorite painter. He has a collection of Disney puzzles."

Harmon chuckled, a rumble that nearly vibrated the entire table. "Snow White?" he asked with a cheeky grin.

She rolled her eyes. "Well, yes, actually, I do have one of Snow White, if you must know."

Harmon's grin brought butterflies to her stomach. "I am going to run and grab one more soda. Do you want anything?"

"No, I'm all set, but I can get it." Harmon shifted to the edge of his seat.

"You've been getting them all. I'll get it." Skylar slid from her stool. She wanted to use the restroom as well as get herself one last drink. She just didn't want to tell Harmon she needed to pee. Not that it was a huge secret that she would, but still. The club wasn't nearly as busy as it had been the last time she'd been there. As she sidestepped a couple getting quite handsy in the hall, she noticed a shadow behind her as she approached the bathroom door. Skylar's heart began to hammer as she looked over her shoulder. It was Liza, the bartender she'd seen a couple of months ago.

"Hey, Skylar, right?"

Shocked, the woman knew her name Skylar narrowed her eyes and nodded.

"I need to talk to you." Liza followed her into the bathroom then bent at the waist, checking under the stalls. "If you go to the bar to get a drink, only come see me."

Skylar was taken aback by the demand.

"CJ isn't here tonight, but for some reason, he gave all the bartenders your name, and they've been instructed to call him if any of us see you."

Skylar shook her head. "Why?"

"I don't know, but I can tell you, CJ having anything over you is unbearable. Trust me."

"I don't understand."

"He's a manipulator. If he can control you, he will do anything in his power to make you bend to his will. Do. Not. Bend. If he senses weakness, he never gives up."

Skylar hesitated only a moment before sharing. "He's shown up at my work to tell me he has a video of the time he and I spent together in the room above the club."

Liza scoffed. "Of course he did. There are *no* cameras up there. He's full of shit. That's where he likes to do his drugs and all sorts of other less savory things."

Anger and relief washed over Skylar in equal measure.

"Usually he loses interest quickly, but something about you has him hooked. Just be careful, and if you see Nick, his henchman, turn the other way."

"I will, thank you."

Liza waved to the stall. "Do your business, then I'll walk back out with you."

Skylar had never had a shy bladder, but knowing someone was waiting just outside the door made it difficult for her to go. Once she was done and had washed her hands, she followed Liza to the door.

"Why do you work here if you know how terrible he is?"

Liza gave her a small, sad half smile. "His dad pays well, and unfortunately, CJ has something on me that could cause me to lose my kids." She shrugged then led Skylar out of the bathroom and back to the bar. After getting her soda, she headed back to Harmon's table. She was relieved to have confirmation that there were no cameras in those rooms to worry about.

When she got back to their table, she matched the grin spreading across Harmon's face. He took another sip from his soda, never taking his gaze off hers. People's eyes had never been something Skylar paid attention to. Sure, she'd liked the ice-blue color of CJ's, but Harmon's were different; they were soulful. Something in them made her think he could understand her heartache.

"So, what do you do when you're not playing with numbers?" She picked up their conversation again as if she hadn't been to the bathroom, as if a massive weight hadn't just been lifted from her shoulders.

"I love puzzles... *number* puzzles. Not quite the same thing. But..." He shrugged.

"Like those damn one-through-nine puzzles? I can never solve those," she said, nearly vibrating in her seat.

"Yes, Sudoku?"

"Sure?" She quirked a brow to relay the fact that she didn't know what they were called, just that they always seemed too hard. One wrong move, and it was doomed. One piece in the wrong spot for her puzzles was damn easy to recognize almost immediately.

"Yeah, I do the one in the newspaper every day."

"In pen?" she asked aghast.

With a chuckle, Harmon nodded.

"You must be some kind of nerd." She smirked slyly.

His cheeks flushed, and he changed the subject. They seemed to find an easy rhythm in that way. They would pick a topic to discuss, and though they liked many different activities, they enjoyed some of the same interests as well. Harmon liked running; she liked going for evening walks. Harmon liked his nerd puzzles, and she liked her picture ones. She liked that they covered more substantial stuff, yet they were still simple things that anyone could chat about.

Skylar's only problem with the night was getting in her head, watching over her shoulder. Her last relationship had been over for more than two years, and she figured it was time to move the fuck on. Her hookup with CJ had happened almost two months ago—it was time she forgot his existence. A shiver wormed its way up her spine when she thought about him—and his wife. But it was hard to push that text message out of her mind. If he had followed them from her house, he would know where they were. Even if Liza hadn't given her away.

Being attracted to two different men in such a short span of time felt strange, almost wrong. Throughout the night, she had to remind herself that she was not to blame, but still, her stomach felt unsettled in the same club where she'd been with CJ not long ago.

At the end of the night, Skylar walked closer to Harmon than was necessary as they headed for the exit. He gave off a protective aura that drew her in. Even as they walked out, she dreaded the thought that CJ could be lurking around one of the corners, waiting to come after her. She couldn't suppress the feeling that CJ had been watching her and everything she did from high above. It was a horrid sensation to suspect someone she thought she could trust might be watching her every move.

I don't think I really trusted him. We hardly spoke. He was just supposed to scratch an itch, she told herself, but she wasn't entirely sure she believed it.

"Are you okay?"

Skylar smiled up at Harmon and nodded. "I am. I was just thinking about the last time I was here."

"Oh?" He smirked, quirking his brow.

This with Harmon was vastly different from the connection she'd briefly shared with CJ. This was real. That had been nothing.

"It was nothing to write home about," she said, brushing off his curiosity.

His eyes narrowed slightly, as if he didn't believe her nonchalance. But then he smiled and pressed on as they stepped out into the early-November night.

All evening, she'd stalled about discussing some points of her life. Family, more than anything. Some things were too hard to share with someone, no matter how long she'd known them. She couldn't help but wonder if her avoidance annoyed him, though. If it did, he showed no inkling of it. *This is only a second date. He doesn't expect the moon and stars.*

The scent of cigarette smoke accosted her, and she nearly gagged. She had always hated the smell, but never to the point of nausea before. Coughing, she covered the reaction. Harmon opened her door for her, pressed a kiss to her temple, and guided her into her seat before rounding the car to his side. When he was settled in the driver's seat, Skylar leaned over the center console.

"Where to now?" High from the knowledge that CJ had been lying and they'd made it out of the club without seeing him, Skylar felt so happy, she didn't want the night to end. Perhaps blocking CJ's number would be worthwhile.

"I just bought *Roadhouse*. Would you want to come back to my place and watch it?"

Skylar looked up from buckling her seat belt to fully face him. "You *just* bought a movie that was released like thirty years ago?"

Harmon chuckled. "Well, yeah." He rubbed the back of his neck. "It's always been one of my favorite movies." He shrugged.

"I suppose it's one of mine too. Sam Elliott is one of my favorite actors."

"Me too." Harmon pressed a soft kiss to her temple just before he started the car.

Their drive back to his house was filled with comfortable conversation, this time about Skylar's unique roommate, who rarely took things seriously. Despite her silly nature, she gave some of the best advice. She wondered what Harmon would make of her and Zelda together. They always had such unique conversations.

Skylar studied Harmon's profile as he drove. His dark hair was cleanly trimmed, and his eyes almost looked golden in the setting sun. He reached across the center console to place a hand on Skylar's thigh. Within seconds, she brought her hand to his to interlace their fingers. The feel of his strong fingers interlacing with hers made her want more. How much more, she wasn't entirely sure yet, but she wanted more nonetheless. Something inside her kept saying she needed to pump the brakes—to think about this more, but her body had already set its sights on him.

"Well, this is me."

Skylar looked up at the stucco building that housed his condo. "It looks nice," she said as she opened her door.

"I love it here. The minimal shared walls and the fact that the units are soundproof makes it feel like I don't even have neighbors. Most of the time."

That would be nice indeed. She didn't dislike her neighbors, but it was always awkward when one of them heard some intimate action. It made her cringe. Harmon led Skylar through a door and down the hall of shared spaces. A pool, fitness room, and what appeared to be a game room were some of the rooms they passed.

She walked quietly beside him, taking in the clean lines of the building. The stairwell was simple and effective. He opened the door for her, gesturing for her to head up first. She brushed past him and made every point of contact last a few extra seconds. Decidedly, she was going to drive him insane. As she walked, she swayed her hips just a little more than necessary. It would be hard for him to miss the way the material brushed against her thighs. She'd been sweet and kind all night, but all she could think about was the opportunity to kiss him. They'd been dancing around one another, sharing small touches to the point of driving her mad.

It was strange, but she trusted that he would not push her into anything she didn't want to do.

When they reached his door, he unlocked it, and before they were over the threshold, Harmon was invading her space. Kicking the door closed behind them, he wrapped her up in his arms. Pressing her up against the wall of the entry, he finally sealed his lips to hers. It would be so easy for him to take her right here. He groaned as their kiss deepened. Her thoughts wandered.

Sliding his hand up her thighs, he gripped her ass, pulling her body flush against his, pressing his erection against the place she so desperately wanted it. Skylar whimpered, and she could feel it pulse against her.

"Tell me you want this. If you don't, we need to stop before I burst."

His deep, gravelly voice made her crave him inside of her.

Skylar's eyes widened despite the fluorescent light of his entryway. "I want this, probably more than I should." A blush heated her cheeks.

Not needing further coaxing, Harmon created a little distance between them as he continued to cage her against the wall and skimmed one hand around to her front. He slipped two fingers beneath the edge of her thong and pressed them to her clit, releasing another cry from her lips when he added pressure and painted her clit with small circles. When she seemed ready to burst, he pressed both fingers inside of her. The sensation was almost too much. His thumb took up the duty of engaging her clit, and fuck if she wasn't putty in his hands. Only a moment or two passed before her walls fluttered around his fingers.

"Harmon." His name was a low, breathy whisper, and from the look in his eyes, she guessed he would do just about anything to make her say his name like that at least a few million more times.

"Yeah, darling?"

"I'm, I'm, oh my…"

With a groan, Harmon pressed his lips to hers, silencing her. Her body was already telling him everything her words couldn't convey. Her tongue pressed into his mouth, and she tasted the lingering flavor of beer. They kissed, and he slowed his pumping until her shaking and fluttering subsided.

"You are fucking gorgeous," Harmon whispered in her ear as he eased his fingers out of her.

They still stood in the entryway, both wearing their shoes. Goddamn.

"I want you inside of me." Her plea released a new wave of yearning inside her.

Fumbling with his wallet, he struggled to take out a condom. Then he lifted Skylar around the waist and carried her to one of the stools at his breakfast bar. If they were lucky, it would put her at just the right height.

And oh fuck if it didn't. With her elbows braced on the counter behind her, chest heaving and underwear soaked, she could only imagine what a wanton picture she was painting. The cool stone felt phenomenal against her flushed skin.

When he unbuttoned his pants and released his cock, Skylar shimmied out of her panties. She felt shy at first, and he made it known he wanted no part of that. Taking her knees, he spread her legs wide. As he pressed his dick to her clit, her eyes fluttered with pleasure. Shifting down, he brought himself to her entrance. She was so ready, it was damn near impossible for her not to rock forward and take him inside of her. When he did finally take her, he slid easily inside her. The moans continued to fall from her lips. By the time he was buried to the hilt, her walls were fluttering around him. She was going to come again embarrassingly fast.

As he pumped in and out of her, the whimpers he coaxed from her coupled with his groans, and the way his dark eyes bored into hers was too much. Her pussy tried to squeeze the life out of him, and his grip tightened audibly on the counter behind her. But she could tell he was holding himself back until she was on the brink with him.

"Oh damn, Harmon."

Taking that as his cue, he fucked her faster, bringing her to her orgasm just as he whispered, "Goddamn it, darling, I'm coming."

When they were both spent, Harmon rested his forearms on the counter on either side of her. She looked up at him, biting the corner of her lip.

"Sorry, that was so... fast." His gaze shifted, presumably taking in the fact that they were both still nearly fully dressed.

"Next time," she whispered and pressed a kiss to his lips.

CHAPTER NINE

HARMON

It had been two weeks, two blissful weeks of him and Skylar exploring whatever this was between them. No matter how it was sliced, they were certainly compatible in bed. They still hadn't shared too much about either of their pasts, and they hadn't come up with a label for anything yet. Harmon groaned as he thought about Jackie and how things had ended. He resolved to tell Skylar the next chance he got.

Porter: *You still coming to Turkey Time tomorrow?*

Harmon laughed at Porter's way of referring to Thanksgiving. Harmon responded in the affirmative and started getting ready for his coffee break. Luckily, his office always made the day before a holiday a half day, so no one accomplished much anyway. The appreciation he felt for the company and everything they did for their employees made him proud to work where he did. They were so good to their employees. "And clients," he muttered, thinking about the way he'd been crammed into a too-small seat for a meeting several weeks prior.

As he exited his office, his jaw clenched at the sight of Mandy. She wasn't doing anything wrong at the moment, but just her presence instigated the fiery inferno of irritation. He hated how short his fuse had been over the last several years. And lately, it had gotten worse. After finding out about Jackie's wedding, he'd been less than thrilled. He didn't know if he wanted to hear about his ex-wife's new life or if he wanted to remain ignorant for the rest of *his* life. *Ignorance is bliss, right? Why torture myself when I could pretend she doesn't exist?* Something sad stoked the volcano already at the brink of eruption inside him; it happened around every holiday. He wondered what his life could have been when his traitorous brain played the *what-if* game. It didn't matter how many years passed since their divorce; he still couldn't extricate himself from the torture. Forcing out a long slow exhale, he tried to be positive. He had Skylar now. No need to think about Jackie and her life. Still, Thanksgiving with Porter and Verity was more difficult since Verity was still one of Jackie's best friends.

"Morning, Mr. Westerly."

He grunted in response, afraid that if he opened his mouth, it would be less than a cordial greeting for the happy-go-lucky woman.

The day went by quickly, and as he left, he was tempted to head to Retro to find Skylar, but that seemed a bit much. They'd been on a few dates. Thanksgiving was coming, and Skylar would be working the rest of the weekend. It dampened the holiday, but Harmon was determined to have a good time. He'd already texted to check on her. The last thing he wanted was for her to think it was a fleeting thing between them—for him, anyway. It seemed he needed to convince her otherwise. Each evening they spent together, when they went their separate ways, it was as if Skylar couldn't get home quick enough. As if she was outrunning something.

As he made his way out of his office at the end of the day, Mandy stepped in front of him.

"So, I saw that Sebastian gave his assistant a bonus for Thanksgiving." She looked at him expectantly, tapping her toes on the carpet.

"Naudia has been his assistant for a long time."

Mandy planted her hands on her hips. "So what? You're saying that because I've only been here—" She paused and started counting the months on her fingers.

It took all his willpower to keep his mouth shut.

"Nineteen months, I don't get a bonus?"

"That was something Sebastian paid out of his pocket because she is a *superb* employee." He almost felt bad for the implied dig.

Mandy either didn't notice or had no idea she was an A-plus pain in his ass because she kept talking, even after their discussion the month before. "If you can't appreciate me, my mom said I shouldn't stay here." Her head bobbed in a way that looked very unnatural and potentially sharp enough to snap her neck.

Harmon ran a hand over his face then matched her stance with his hands on his hips. He wasn't the tallest of men, but he was definitely taller than his assistant. "Mandy, I thought I made it pretty clear last month that I don't want you to stay here." *And if you leave sooner, it will be better for me.* He was proud of himself for keeping the second part *inside* his head.

"Are you kidding me? You were serious? You think you would last without me?"

"Mandy." He pressed a thumb and forefinger into his eyes. "Are you delusional? I mean that in the most literal way possible. How can you possibly think I would miss you when you mess up my schedule once a week at least, double-booking meetings, or the fact that you almost flew me into the entirely wrong state?" He was close to seething, so he cut himself off.

"Well, since you're so perfect, I guess you don't need me." She stomped around her desk, picked up her purse, and started for the door.

"Mandy, wait," Harmon called, and she had a slight smile on her lips as if she'd won something. "If you're quitting, you need to give me your keys before you leave."

She made some strange, animalistic sound that was almost a growl, a scream, and a hiss in the same breath. Before he knew what was happening, she hurled the keys at his face, then she all but ran from the building.

He almost caught the keys before they collided with his nose. Almost. The large magnetic fob for the building's front door landed heavily on the bridge of his nose, instigating an instant nosebleed. *Fuck.*

He cupped one hand under his nose to prevent ruining the white carpet. Why his boss had selected white was beyond him. He pushed his way through the break room door and onto the thankfully tiled floor.

"Goodness, Harmon, what happened?" Naudia asked as he started tearing paper towels from the roll.

Holding the paper towels under his nose to catch most of the blood, he called over his shoulder, "Damn Mandy." His response was muffled, but he figured she would get the idea.

"I saw her running from the building. I assumed you ended up firing her early, but now I'm guessing that's not the case?"

"Not quite," he said in a nasally voice.

***

Harmon relayed Mandy's tirade to Naudia and Sebastian, then Porter, who couldn't stop giggling on the other end of the line. Standing in his bathroom at home, Harmon pressed a finger gingerly against the angry red bridge of his nose.

"Okay, let me make sure I got this right. Fuck-It-Up Franny not only didn't believe you that she was fired, but she also thought you should pay her a bonus out of pocket?"

Harmon didn't often regret telling Porter something, but this was one of those times. "It would appear so..."

"Shit, she's crazier than you let on."

Harmon nodded as he left his ensuite bathroom. "Trust me, I know. It doesn't make sense. I almost wonder if it was some kind of game to her. I don't know. It just seemed strange. She was upset she was still getting fired, but she didn't want to stay."

"You think she'll try getting something out of you with this?"

"That's the thing. I don't know."

"Huh."

The silence stretched as they considered what Mandy might try. But any logical possibility escaped him. He didn't want it to ruin his long weekend.

"Anyway, I just wanted to let you know in case I show up with a black eye tomorrow." His phone pinged in his ear with a text notification.

Mandy: *Will I still get the holiday pay?*

The phone nearly clattered to the ground as he read the message over a few times. This was ridiculous. *How could she possibly think that, after everything, I would do anything to benefit her?*

"Un-fucking-believable."

Chapter Ten

SKYLAR

"Two shifts, that's all I have left." Skylar moaned as she hefted their turkey out of the oven. She'd only been an hour late getting it in, so it finished at half past one. She was exhausted that morning; she had worked late the night before, and the night before that, she'd been out late with Harmon. The reminder of her evenings with him never failed to filled her cheeks with heat.

Peeking up from the bird, she found Zelda and Lara sitting at opposite ends of their tiny dining table. Lara was busy demolishing deviled eggs like an Olympic sport and only seemed to be half listening.

"We updated your resume weeks ago," Zelda said as she typed away on her phone.

"I know, but I don't think I'm qualified for much of anything." Skylar's evenings were spent scouring the newspapers and various websites for job openings. The worst part was the abundant scams, and she tried to be careful not to fall into their traps. The jobs she'd submitted her resume to didn't seem to be interested in her. The one interview she'd had did not prove fruitful.

"Jush shen it," Lara said around a couple of eggs.

"Slow the hell down, Lara. You're the only one who eats those nasty things. I think she said, 'Just send it'?" Zelda looked at her sister with a raised brow.

The older sister's role of translating never went away. Zelda was the middle child of their sibling trio. Jerry, their older brother, named after their great-uncle, was the only one not named after a video game character.

Lara nodded as she exaggerated chewing and swallowing her eggs. "I just mean, what's the worst that can happen? They don't call you for an interview? They use your resume as toilet paper?"

Skylar needed a laugh; she'd been taking it so seriously and was getting herself too worked up. So much so, she had been short with Harmon a few times, and her walls were rigidly in place some days. "I'm not dropping it off in person. Most places want them emailed anyway."

"All I'm saying is that if you send it anywhere you're even remotely qualified to work, that increases your chances of getting a call."

Skylar debated the point. It was valid. If companies didn't think she was capable or qualified, then they would file her application in their virtual recycling bin. She had seen a few administrative assistant jobs that wanted a few years of office experience, but maybe she could give it a shot. *How different could it be from taking reservations and creating schedules?* Those tasks had been her responsibility for the last year. Connie had liked getting the time back, not having to worry about who would cover what shift and if it would create any drama between the servers.

"Okay, I'll send it to everyone."

"Plush, you know," Lara said, swallowing another mouthful of eggs, "most places can't find good employees to save themselves."

Zelda nodded as her sister spoke. "She has a point."

As Skylar pulled the stuffing out of the turkey, she was hit with the aroma of what Thanksgiving used to be when she was a kid. She made the stuffing just like her mother and her grandmother used to make it. The nostalgia consumed her mind. She wished she could go back to those holidays when she had no responsibilities other than helping with dishes when food was gone. A pang of sadness settled into her stomach, dissipating her hunger.

"Sky, you all right?" Zelda asked from her side.

Skylar hadn't even noticed her leave her seat. She had frozen in thought with her spoon of stuffing halfway to the serving dish. Blinking rapidly, she tried to clear the tears that welled in her eyes. "Yeah, I'm good."

"You go sit with Lara, and I'll finish this."

"Sure you can handle it?"

Zelda tossed her head back in laughter. "Luckily, heat is no longer required, and *I've* always been good with a knife." She raised a brow.

Lara slammed her hand on the table. "Don't you bring that up again!"

"What am I missing?"

Zelda shrugged and removed the last of the stuffing, then began to carve the turkey.

As they ate their Thanksgiving dinner, Skylar couldn't help but look around at her and Zelda's cozy, little apartment and feel that she should have been further ahead in life by now. Sure, she'd tried college—couldn't stand it. She'd tried to have a serious job in a medical office, but again, couldn't stand it. The drama, coupled with all the rules about confidentiality and the fact that it felt like people were trying to trip her up made her leave that career quickly. Then there was Christopher, who she'd thought she had found her forever with. And after discovering just how wrong she'd been, she'd become stagnant. No new guys, no new job, and now those things were coming back to bite her. The diner was closing, and of the last guys she'd been with, two had been total snakes. But then there was Harmon. When it felt as if she were driving the wrong way down the highway, she thought of him. Perhaps he would help her avoid getting hit.

"Yooo hooo, Earth to Skylar." Lara waved a hand in front of Skylar's face.

Skylar shook her head. "Sorry, I was... thinking."

Lara and Zelda pinned her with scowls. The sisters didn't often look alike, but in that moment, they could pass for twins.

"No more stressing today!" Lara demanded.

Zelda threw a napkin at her sister. "We will figure it all out tomorrow. We can't do anything about it today."

Giving the sisters a small smile, Skylar cleared her throat as they loaded their plates with dessert. "Fine, I'll stop stressing if you guys help me take my mind off things."

"Duh," Lara said in her usual sarcastic way.

Skylar's smile turned devilish. "In that case, tell me the knife story—or whatever that was about carving the turkey."

At the mention of what Skylar was sure would be a good story, Lara's head dropped back against her chair with a dull thud.

Given the opportunity to clue Skylar in, Zelda sat up a little straighter. "So, it was the Christmas right before we all met, so nearly five years ago now. I'm surprised we never told you this."

"We *surely* don't have to now…" Lara continued to stare at the ceiling.

"Oh, I'll make it quick." Zelda smirked.

That familiar jealousy coursed through Skylar. She and her sister had never had such an easy relationship.

"So, we had all just finished opening gifts. I was struggling to open something, and I asked Jerry if I could borrow his pocketknife. Lara, being the ever-helpful little sister, jumped at the chance to help. At the ripe old age of seventeen, she was convinced she could do it better than I could. I don't even remember what it was. The—"

"It was a bathroom set, those ones that Nanna got us every year." Lara still stared at the ceiling but refused to allow an inaccuracy.

"Yes! It was. Okay, so there were these little plastic tabs wrapped around it, and I couldn't get it out, so Lara came over with Jerry's knife to saw through the plastic. One broke, and she lost her grip on the knife. I was sitting on the couch. The knife dropped, and the tip landed between two of my toes, slicing the side of one. Jerry always keeps it insanely sharp. So, I'm lucky it landed between them and didn't fall directly on top of my foot or something."

"You make it sound so dramatic," Lara complained, shoveling a large bite of her pumpkin pie into her mouth.

"I literally could have lost a toe."

Their good-natured arguing lasted for the rest of the night, even as they played some of their favorite games. They discussed how it sucked that Jerry was working, and Lara loaded up a container of leftovers to drop off at the police station for him on her way home. Their parents were enjoying a Caribbean cruise and would be home in just under a week. They would all be spending Christmas together.

CHAPTER ELEVEN

HARMON

"MY HEAVENS! WHY ARE you here, Harmon?" Naudia asked from his doorway, one hand over her heart.

He raised a brow. "Did I startle you? I could ask you the same thing."

"I forgot my gym pass." She cocked one hip to the side and moved her hand from her heart to her hip as if challenging him to have a better reason for being there.

He sighed. "You do remember I no longer have an assistant, right? I have to be out of town all next week. Between holidays and meetings, I'll be lucky to have a new assistant in place before the end of January. Who wants to start a new job just before Christmas?" He ran a hand through his hair, no doubt making it stand on end. It was longer than he would have liked, but to go along with the rest of his life, it had been neglected.

Naudia nodded. "How about this? You post the job today, stating we are taking applicants until the second week of December. As they come in, I will interview those who are most qualified. Then I will go over the interviews with you. You can make your selection at the end of the third week of December, and your new assistant can start January first?"

Harmon smirked. "Or you can be my assistant instead of—"

"Don't even think about it. I am perfectly happy in my position, and this is the only offer of assistance you'll get from me," she said with a mock glare—at least Harmon hoped it was all in good fun.

"Okay, I would actually really appreciate your help. I also came in today to double-check my bookings for this upcoming week. I'm glad I did, or I would be facing a replay of the trip to meet with Mr. Wilton."

Naudia cringed, then her eyes softened. "Get that ad posted today, state we will begin interviews with qualified candidates and that the position will remain posted until filled. This way, if we find someone we like, we can hire them sooner rather than later."

Harmon released a sigh of relief. "I will, and thank you."

Naudia nodded as she finished making her way down the hall to her office.

After another two hours, Harmon had his bookings corrected and the job posted for the new position. "And now we wait," he muttered as he shut down his computer and headed home.

As he drove, he was tempted to stop and see Skylar. Her shift at the diner would be over in several hours, and he needed a distraction. They had plans to spend Saturday evening together after her shift, but he didn't want to wait another day.

The walk across the parking lot of his condo building had never made him feel so alone. He was still struggling with the idea of being with someone. But Skylar made that thought easier to bear.

Harmon: *I hope your shift goes well. I can't wait to see you tomorrow.*

The rest of the day went by with hardly any responses from Skylar, just short texts here and there.

Pacing in his kitchen, he had more to think about than he wanted to at nearly ten at night. Refreshing the page on his job ad, he found that only one person had applied to be his assistant. And from what he could see, they were nowhere near qualified. He would be working out of town again for a few days, and he could only hope that after the weekend, more people would apply. When his phone vibrated, he snatched it up.

Porter: *I didn't get the chance to ask yesterday, did your waitress warm up to you?*

Harmon: *Yeah, but she almost seems afraid to date, in a way. I don't know, man, it's weird. That first day I visited her, she had personal shit going on. Some days, it's like she can't get away from me fast enough.*

Porter: *The fuck does that mean?*

Once again, Harmon was hit with an annoyance he didn't usually feel toward his oldest friend. From his perspective, Porter and Verity had few struggles. Getting pregnant seemed to be easy for them. They had three kids, a nice house, good jobs, and a seemingly happy marriage. Harmon's life had been the opposite. Porter couldn't understand. Before he said something he would regret, Harmon set his phone down and slid on his sneakers, leaving his phone on the kitchen counter.

As he waited for the elevator to take him to the first floor of his building, he thought more and more about the house he'd seen for sale near Porter and Verity. The next weekday he had mostly open, he would take the opportunity to check it out. For some reason, every time he thought about the house, Jackie came to mind. Verity and Porter had been careful to make sure Harmon and Jackie wouldn't be at their house at the same time over the years. *But if I lived just down the road, would their avoidance be able to continue?*

I bet Jackie would want it to continue. Things had ended so abruptly in some ways and had been doomed from the start in others. He was finally at a place where he could recognize that they wouldn't work out now. Hindsight and all.

The elevator wasn't necessary in the building, but it was a welcome luxury, even if it took far too long for the car to move up and down.

As he stepped into the elevator, his mind wandered back to the woman he couldn't stop thinking about for more than a few hours at a time. He was so lost in his thoughts about Skylar that he was already jogging down the road before he realized how far he'd gone. It was moments like this that made him wonder how he never got hurt. The days that he couldn't remember anything along the drive from one place to another made him wonder how he could function in such a way.

Just as he rounded a corner, the Do Not Walk sign lit up. Harmon took the opportunity to stretch while waiting for it to change. Sweat trickled down his back under his T-shirt. The noises from the club next to him made him wish he'd brought his phone and headphones just to drown out the sounds of the busy street. Being past ten in the evening didn't stop people from their activities. He racked his brain as to why it would be so busy that late at night.

"Fucking Black Friday," he mumbled. The last thing he ever wanted to do was join the hordes of people who felt it necessary to race to a store the moment they finished their Thanksgiving meal and stampede through the door to get all the best deals before anyone else could snag them. A chill rushed over him as he remembered how, one year, a man had been trampled to death. *No, thank you.*

The light changed, and he continued jogging across the street. As he finished his loop, his mind continued turning back to Skylar. The level of anxiety that settled in his gut annoyed him.

Harmon took the stairs back up to his condo rather than wait a few minutes for the elevator. The long weekend was going to drop him into an even longer week. The end of the year was always chaotic.

Pushing open his door, he took in the space around him. The entryway held the washer and dryer. Just beyond stood the living room then the open-concept kitchen to the left. To the right was the hall leading to the bedrooms. The condo had been such a good price, Harmon couldn't pass it up when he saw it for sale seven years ago. It was three bedrooms—definitely more than he needed, but something in him had always hoped he might end up with someone.

Chapter Twelve

SKYLAR

"I submitted my resume to eight companies!" she shouted to Zelda as she got the last of her work uniform buttoned up. They'd applied to three together the night before, but Skylar was determined, especially since today was the end of an era.

"Good, I know someone will call you. I have faith—ah, you bastard!"

Skylar laughed as she pulled her purse down from the hook by the door. Zelda could do many things, but holding a coherent conversation while gaming wasn't one. Most insults made no sense, so when they did, Skylar took that as a good day.

"I'm assuming that last part wasn't about me."

Zelda chuckled from her room just off the living room. "Well..." She let the word drag out longer than necessary.

"Yeah, yeah. Whatever. I'm heading to Retro."

"Can you bring me home something for dinner?"

"Sure, text me your order, and I'll put it in so you get first dibs. You know it will be slim pickings as the night goes on."

"You got it. Fucking shit stick!"

Skylar shook her head and stepped out of their apartment. She checked her phone as she took the stairs down to the main street. Disappointment dampened her mood. Harmon hadn't texted her at all. Granted, he knew she was working today, and the last few days, she hadn't been able to sneak away and text him during her shifts. But still, she'd hoped he would check in on her at the very least. The assumption that he would text stung a little. Maybe she should have reached out to him. Thoughts ran rampant, stressing her more than necessary. Her stomach churned with anxiety.

Her drive to work was filled with overanalyzing everything she'd said to Harmon the last few days. They'd been seeing one another for a few weeks. They'd slept together multiple times, and she worried because they hadn't determined what they were. Harmon had come across as genuinely interested, but now, she couldn't help but worry he no longer was. Perhaps he was getting bored already. That would be a new record for her. At least Christopher had lasted two years.

As she parked her car and looked up at the front of the restaurant, she couldn't help but succumb to the horrible ache in her chest. She was losing the place that had become her second home over the years. Not only was the restaurant an important part of her life, but so were the people inside—namely, the owners, Connie and Leon. She would miss them more than she could imagine possible. Taking a calming breath, she forced herself to get out of her car and make her way inside.

"Oh, I'm glad you're here, dear," Connie said from behind the counter, her signature black-and-red polka-dot dress in place. "Wendy called in sick. She feels terrible missing our last day, but she hasn't been feeling well and didn't want to cause any issues on our last night."

Skylar cringed. "I hope none of the kids are sick."

"That's probably where it came from. Kids are a germ's best friend. The little incubators touch everything."

Hearing the way Connie talked about children, no one would guess she'd had four of her own. Much to her and Leon's dismay, they'd all moved around the country. So, when Skylar started working for them during some of her darkest days, they'd taken her in as a surrogate daughter, and she couldn't appreciate them more.

"Well, I guess that's one way to describe kids. Makes me really want some," she deadpanned.

Connie waved her off. "You know what I mean."

Skylar stepped around the back of the counter to put her purse on the shelf and pull out her apron, tying it around her waist. She, too, wasn't feeling well. The smell of the grease heating in the fryers wafted from the kitchen. And though she tried to avoid fried food as much as possible, she knew she would come to miss that scent. But today, it churned her stomach as her anxiety reared its ugly head. It also reminded her of visiting her family in Maine during late summers, when they would have their county fairs.

Once her apron was secured, she set up the last of the kitchen items the waitresses were in charge of. Side salads were ready. Soups were in the warmer, and Zelda's meal had been set aside to be cooked at the end of the night.

The seats were packed with all the regulars, along with many people who wanted to try out the small diner before it closed its doors for good. Perhaps someone else would reopen it, but it would be the end of the Retro Skylar knew, and she wasn't sure she could participate in an imitation. It would surely feel wrong.

"You've got one more at the counter."

"Really? I thought we said no more." Skylar wasn't complaining. The tips today had been far better than those she'd gotten for the last few weeks. That was one thing; most people knew she would be losing her job in the next few hours, and they wanted to help. They hadn't advertised the closure, but word of mouth had far-reaching arms. She'd been running all day, and she was exhausted.

"I think you'll want to take this one."

Connie gave a sly smirk, and Skylar's heart hammered in her chest. Taking the ranch she needed out of the fridge, she craned her neck to see out the small window in the kitchen door. Sitting at the bar, facing the door, was a man with dark hair and milk-chocolate eyes.

A smile spread across her lips before she could hold it back. Stepping up in front of Harmon, she leaned on the counter, bringing their eyes level. "Back so soon?"

Harmon's gaze left the menu to meet hers. "If it meant I got to see you every day, I would go broke eating out."

Skylar rolled her eyes but was more than a little flattered by his comment. It soothed some of the edges of her self-doubt—cracking her protective walls.

He was being sweet, charming, and funny. Still, some part of her brain told her to proceed with caution. It was difficult to ignore the nagging thought that people never truly wanted to be around her, and anxiety over the possibility swirled in her gut. "What would you like for dinner?"

"Honestly, I already ate. I came to see you. I know we were going to meet after your shift, but I couldn't wait." His voice got progressively quieter as it filled with yearning.

Before she could respond, Connie came racing out of the kitchen. "She would love to."

Skylar's mouth fell open. "Subtle." She ran a hand down her face, careful not to smudge her mascara. "I have to bring Zelda her dinner after my shift."

"That will take all of five minutes, hon."

"It wasn't an excuse, Connie."

Harmon's eyes darted between the women. "I should have waited for you to text me. Sorry."

There it was again; she was being short with him for no reason. They already had plans. Skylar looked between Harmon's clear discomfort and Connie's expectant expression. "What did you have in mind?" Skylar hedged. She had figured they would just hang out at his place.

Harmon sat up straighter in his deep-gray button-down that fit him perfectly. "That bowling place we tried a few weeks ago. They're doing a black light night."

"That sounds great!"

"The kitchen's closing, so Skylar's tables should be emptying out soon. Once they've paid, she's free to go."

"I can't do that. What about all the closing duties?"

Connie waved her off again and walked away to take care of her tables.

"She's something else," Harmon said around a laugh.

"That she is. I have to go check on my tables. Can I at least get you something to drink?"

"Sure, a Pepsi please." Judging by his smirk, he was mighty proud of himself for remembering they didn't serve Coke.

Skylar nodded and took off for the table of regulars who'd been nursing their after-dinner coffees longer than anyone should. They wanted to see the place close about as much as Skylar did. She could sympathize with their reluctance to leave. As the diner emptied, she tried to think of all the good nights she'd had there. Those were the memories she wanted to keep—the stories of how patrons had found the place and who came back and how often. She wanted a candle that would remind her of Connie's cherry cheesecake or, oddly enough, the smell of the diner after the floors had been freshly waxed.

Between waiting on the last of her tables, she finished as many of her closing duties as she could. She didn't want Connie and Leon to do it all on their own. From Harmon's behavior, she wasn't sure if he knew it was the place's final night.

CHAPTER THIRTEEN

HARMON

HARMON FOLLOWED SKYLAR TO her apartment while listening to the flashback night on the radio station. Nerves crept up on him while he waited outside for her so they could take one car. They'd been on a handful of dates already, but it felt as if he could so easily screw this up. And if things went as they usually did, he would.

The evening had passed faster than he'd expected. He'd had a great time watching Skylar work.

As he waited for Skylar to reemerge from her apartment building, Harmon decided that he would do whatever he could to get the house near Porter. He needed to stop allowing his life to sit in some strange limbo. What had happened between him and Jackie had been an isolated incident. He could hardly believe what had happened had. The shame and self-hatred had been strong—something that hadn't faded in the many years since.

Harmon nearly jumped out of his skin when Skylar dropped into the passenger seat, just as Kenny Loggins started to sing. The song unlocked a nostalgic memory in his mind's eye. He, Porter, Verity, and Jackie used to love watching *Footloose*. Hell, he still liked the movie despite the memories it dredged up. That had been their thing. Once a week, the four of them would get together, and one person picked a movie they would watch. The girls seemed to favor movies from the eighties and nineties.

Blinking a few times, Harmon tried to clear the thoughts of his ex-wife and everything that had gone wrong between them from his mind. He turned to face Skylar. She looked good in a pair of jeans and a cropped black T-shirt.

"Sorry that took so long. I wanted to get out of my dress."

As she settled into the seat, she wiggled to the music, and something in his heart swelled at the sight. She was so carefree, something that had been missing from Harmon's life far too long.

"So, think you can beat me?"

"I haven't played in quite a while." He rubbed the back of his neck.

Skylar played with the chest strap of her seat belt as he drove. "Um, yeah, it's probably been longer for me."

He was sure he would be rusty and didn't anticipate impressing her with his skills. "We'll both get reacquainted and support a local business. It'll be fun."

"Trust me when I say, sports of any kind have never been my thing. I do not have much natural athletic ability."

Harmon chuckled. "I love to play sports. Doesn't mean I'm always good at them. It's just fun to try."

"I'll take your word for it." Skylar almost seemed uncomfortable. He hoped that would fade once they arrived and began playing.

They spent the rest of the drive discussing how their Thanksgiving holidays had gone, and Harmon talked about his impending business trip. The end of the year was always a chaotic mess of flights, hotels, and meetings—all of which, in his opinion, could be emails or video conferences. But no one cared what he thought.

As he pulled into the parking lot, the bowling alley was busier than expected. The glowing effects of the black lights must be a big pull.

As he shut off his Stingray, a car he'd saved for five years to afford, he turned to Skylar. "Ready to go in?"

"Yeah, I just don't want to embarrass myself." She looked at the building as if it would chase her away.

"Skylar." Harmon hooked a finger under her chin and turned her to face him. "There is nothing wrong with trying something new. Plus, this isn't a competition. No one else will care how you do. I just wanted to do this so we could spend time together before I leave for most of next week."

Skylar nodded then got a determined twinkle in her eyes. "All right, prepare to be amazed." She giggled as she pushed her door open.

Harmon hesitated only a moment. She almost always seemed so confident. Then, when she was dropped into something out of the ordinary, she shifted, became self-conscious. He didn't want that for her.

Chapter Fourteen

SKYLAR

When Harmon met her around the front of the car, he pulled her to him, their lips mere inches apart. "I would really like to kiss you right now." His breath tickled her lips.

The simple words revved up the desire that was always near at his presence. "I wish you would."

Before she could think about closing the space between them, Harmon snaked one arm around her back, his other hand combing through her hair at the base of her skull. Their lips met, and she pushed up onto her toes to bring them impossibly closer. By the time Harmon finally pulled away, Skylar was breathless.

He cleared his throat. "We, should, ah, head inside if we're going to bowl."

If she didn't know better, she would think he was a little embarrassed to be making out in public. "Probably."

Opening the trunk of his car, Harmon returned with a small black bag.

"You have your own ball?" Skylar asked incredulously.

"I competed a little in high school. So, it's been an eternity since I played regularly, but yes, I do."

"Great," Skylar muttered. "Let's go." She waved him to the door. "Maybe we need separate lanes so I can ask for bumpers."

When they stepped inside music was blaring, and it was darker that Skylar had expected.

"Damn." Harmon took in the sights around them too.

There was a small arcade off to one side, behind the lanes. And then there were at least a dozen lanes. It looked as if there was a birthday or some other type of party at one end, which would explain the number of cars they'd seen outside. The starry pattern on the carpet glowed in the black lights. The shooting stars appeared to be racing across the floor. Behind the shoe counter was a small bar and lounge area.

"I had not expected all this. I think last time I went bowling in like fourth grade, the lanes were old and cracking and the balls were all chipped." Skylar laughed with excitement. The nervousness she'd felt about coming evaporated as she watched the large party at the end shift through their players. When someone got a gutter ball, they all seemed to experience it together, and when someone did well, they cheered as one.

Harmon's hand fell to her lower back, and she loved the contact. They stepped up to the counter to get their shoes and be assigned a lane. While Harmon went to get their names set up, Skylar searched the racks on the wall outside the lounge area. She had no idea what made a ball a good choice. Some had holes that were too small, others were the opposite, and she wasn't sure what would be a good weight. In the end she selected a yellow ball that glowed in the lights.

"Do you want to go first?" Harmon was lacing up his shoes.

Skylar sat next to him, shucking off her booties. "You can. I want to see how a pro throws the ball."

Harmon chuckled. "I am far from a pro."

Skylar wrinkled her nose as she thought of the other people who may have worn the shoes she was about to slide on. It made her a little nauseous. She hated feet, so to think about putting hers in after someone else caused a shiver to run over her body.

"They clean these, right?"

"The shoes? I would assume so. Usually places spray them out after each use. Does it bother you?"

"I just don't like the idea of my feet being where someone else's has been... You know?"

Harmon squeezed her shoulder. "If it bothers you, then we can get you your own shoes if you find you like coming."

"Okay." She leaned into his touch. It had been foolish to think that Harmon was just going to disappear on her, she realized as he got them set up and gave her a few tips before he went up and threw his first ball. He knocked down seven pins. Then when his ball returned, he got two more. If that was how he was going to do, she imagined his score was going to be vastly higher than hers.

"You're up."

Skylar nodded, wiggling her fingers in her bowling ball. She tried to find a comfortable grip. The swooping leg lunge thing Harmon did, she was not going to attempt. Stepping up to the lane she lined herself up, took a deep breath and dropped her ball on a forward swing. It landed with a thud then moved at a snail's pace down the lane, and Skylar worried it would stop before it reached the end. But as it rolled, it kept inching to the left side. Skylar leaned as if she could coax it into rolling the other way instead. It didn't. It dropped into the gutter and a big fat zero populated on her first frame. She didn't want to turn and face Harmon but didn't have a choice as her ball came out of the return. She was not so confident to think she could back up to get it.

"Sky, come on. Get your ball, try again. This time get a little lower when you roll it. Swing your arm all the way back and then release it on the way forward again. It will give it better momentum."

As Harmon spoke she finally turned to meet his eyes. His expression was encouraging, and his smile was soft. Probably so she wouldn't think he was laughing at her. "Okay," she said as she took her ball back to the edge of the lane. While she released a long slow breath, she tried again, squatting rather awkwardly. She swung her right hand back, and when her hand was perpendicular to the ground, she let it go. It didn't land nearly as hard as before, and it managed to stay on the lane clear to the end, taking down two pins. Skylar gave a little squeal, and Harmon clapped for her and stood, giving her a hug.

"That was great," he whispered into her hair.

She flushed at his praise.

They took their turns, and each frame Harmon gave Skylar one more tip. By the last frame, she knocked down four pins on her first throw and then three more. Making it her second best of the game.

Skylar hadn't been joking when she said she hadn't bowled much. But she didn't complain each time her ball seemed magnetized to the gutter, and Harmon vowed they would come back so she could get in some more practice.

She was surprised to find she was excited about that idea.

As they walked to the car, she thought about the way they'd kissed a few times while playing, and it was getting to the point where she was struggling to keep her hands to herself. Each time she walked past him, she'd caught herself making an excuse to touch him in some way.

Harmon opened her door for her and gave her a kiss before she took her seat. "What are we going to do now?" She wanted the distraction of the night to continue.

The car revved to life, and Harmon rubbed the back of his neck. "I need to get home. I have that flight early in the morning."

"Oh, right." Skylar had to tamp down the sting of rejection.

He hadn't actually rejected her. He was being sensible—just like he had been all night. He'd only allowed himself one alcoholic beverage. She'd had so many men tell her they would only have one drink, which naturally turned into six or more. For once, she found herself with a man who might be able to keep his word. It made her want to trust him, but past experiences told her to give it time. Everyone waited a few months to show their true colors. Some longer than that.

"I'll only be gone for four days. Maybe we could get dinner Wednesday night, when I'm back in town?" As he asked, he busied himself unnecessarily with the car's digital screen.

He was nervous. In a way, it felt good to make a man like Harmon nervous. He'd been calm all night, and to know she could impact him boosted her confidence and pushed the sense of rejection aside.

"I'd like that."

"Yeah?" He looked up from the screen, and a half smile crossed his lips.

Chapter Fifteen

HARMON

SUNDAY MORNING CAME TOO fast, and Harmon had to drag himself out of bed. Usually, he reveled in the idea of an adventure, seeing a new city. But lately, the cities all seemed the same. He couldn't find the small beauty in life anymore. The feeling that something was wrong with him lingered at the back of every thought lately. It was as if anytime he was away from Skylar, life felt wrong somehow. Having his emotions so tied up in another person unnerved him. Hiking, being in nature, or trying new things used to be at the top of his wants and desires. Now, though, he wondered what he was supposed to do. He'd only acknowledged something missing after seeing the evidence that Jackie had moved on. She no longer clung to their failed marriage like he did. The what-ifs played on a loop in his mind. The two biggest being *What if I didn't lose my temper?* and *What if we hadn't lost Cecelia?*

With an irritable groan, he forced himself out of bed. It would only be a few days away. His brain's constant revolution around his past wrongs and the ways he could improve exhausted him—intensified by fear that he would do something wrong again. It was as if Skylar had entered his life at both the most inconvenient and perfect time.

As he brewed his coffee, he lost himself in thought as he watched it drip from the portafilter. He wanted to get to know Skylar better but didn't know how to tell her what *he'd* done. How he'd ruined his marriage. *I have to tell her the monster I am.* His stomach ached at the thought. She would never want to be with him once she found out what type of man he was.

His flight, Uber ride, and dinner that night were uneventful. He found himself in Boston, usually one of his favorite cities. The amount of history all around drew him to new areas. Hell, he'd walked the Freedom Trail on several occasions. But today, all he could think about was Skylar and all the ways he could fuck this up before it even truly began. *Issues, I have severe issues.*

He had two meetings scheduled for Monday with two different investors. When the hotel and flights had originally been booked, he'd chosen to stay an extra day, hoping to get out and find an adventure either Monday evening or Tuesday night. That no longer seemed appealing.

Skylar: *I hope you had a great flight.*

The air left his lungs as he reread the text. He was reading too much into it. It was getting ridiculous. He didn't want to respond too quickly and seem like the lovesick puppy he worried he was becoming. After the walk back to the hotel from the restaurant, he would text her back. As he made his way into the elevator, he could no longer ignore the response sitting at his fingertips.

Harmon: *It was good. I had the window seat and loved the view. I hope you have a good couple of days at work.*

Right before hitting send, he, for some stupid reason, added a heart emoji, and before he could change his mind, the message was on its way through space. *Am I a teenager? That was probably too soon for anything like that.*

Skylar never messaged back, and he figured that was just as well, as he went to sleep Sunday night. Maybe he needed some kind of closure after what had happened with Jackie, which was the last thing he thought about before he fell asleep.

When Harmon checked his phone before his first meeting, a rumble of excitement rose to life in his gut when he saw an unread text from Skylar waiting for him.

Skylar: *What time are you getting back on Wednesday? Do we want to make dinner reservations?*

This time, he didn't hesitate to message her back, confirming immediately.

Monday and Tuesday, in some twisted sense of fate, happened at both a snail's pace and far faster than he'd expected. Then again, he wasn't having to correct flights, hotels, and other travel issues as he went. The plane had landed, and he would be able to disembark in just a moment. He and Skylar had solidified their plans for dinner. They'd been texting every evening, and his brain had drifted to thoughts of her every moment of the day. Skylar was someone he could see spending time with for a while.

As he rolled his luggage through the airport, thankful he didn't have to wait for a checked bag, his phone rang in his pocket. Hope that it was Skylar blossomed in his chest. He had to press the disappointment down when he saw it was Naudia.

"Afternoon," he said by way of greeting as he wove through the busy airport.

"I have interviewed three people so far."

Harmon stopped in his tracks, earning a few harsh words. "Really?" His disbelief oozed into the words.

"Yes. The first two were duds, but the one I just finished really seems like she would be a good fit. No office experience, but she seems very willing to learn and I think would be a good choice." Silence stretched across the phone as Naudia waited for his response.

"Does she at least seem like she has more brain cells than Mandy?"

"Harmon," Naudia snapped like she was his mother. "Everything comes down to will and skill. This woman may not have all the skills that we're looking for yet, but she is certainly willing to learn."

He began to walk again. "When can she start?"

"Immediately."

"She doesn't need to give notice?"

"No." Naudia continued to speak, but a group of young women yelling drowned out what she said.

He didn't have time to be picky, so he would just have to deal with whatever he was given. "Okay, tell her she can start tomorrow."

"You want her to start in the middle of the week?"

"You just said she could start anytime. Drop her in, and let's see how she fares."

Naudia was quiet for a moment before she badgered him into allowing her to start Monday, then warned Harmon that he needed to be nice to the woman when she started. Shaking his head, he ended the call just as he stepped through the automatic glass doors into the Arizona sun. Before redepositing his phone in his pocket, he texted Skylar that he would pick her up after he had a chance to get home and change.

The flight had been packed, and he was happy to be getting back to his regular life. Boston had felt overpopulated and just plain claustrophobic. It seemed everywhere was just bursting to capacity.

Almost every minute of the flight, Harmon had gone back and forth about whether pursuing Skylar was a good idea. He'd sensed that feeling of unpredictable rage at the club, if only for a moment, and it terrified him. Canceling their date would be the best thing he could do for both of them. But he couldn't bring himself to make that call. Something primal inside him was drawn to her.

He didn't even know if he was capable of giving someone what they deserved. Skylar seemed to have a way of making him more comfortable in his own skin—more than anyone else had. He found himself wanting to open up to her, even if it was just over the phone. He'd been sharing parts of his life with her that he hadn't talked about in years.

The biggest hurdle would be talking to her about Jackie and Cecelia. To be fair to her, he had to share what had caused his marriage to end—the monster he'd allowed himself to become while trying to resurrect what was already decaying. It had done nothing but hurt them both.

His mind had been running so quickly, he was almost surprised to find himself in his shower. The trip from the airport home had been a blur of overthinking. "This is just another date, Harmon, not a damn marriage proposal or a lifetime commitment," he growled in the shower while trying to prepare himself for a night with the woman who had taken up residence in his brain.

Chapter Sixteen

SKYLAR

Skylar had finished her grocery shopping for the week and just wanted to head home and get ready for dinner with Harmon. The outfit she'd picked out hung waiting in her bathroom. She'd selected a formfitting olive-green dress, one she'd last worn when she, Zelda, and Lara had gone out for a girls' night. It had been a month or so before the night she'd decided she needed a one-night stand.

She was unlocking her car when she heard a familiar voice behind her. It elicited a shiver down her spine. "So, you can't be bothered to respond to my texts? I see you have a phone." Tonya's special skills had always included making Skylar feel like a failure.

"Tonya, I don't see a reason to text you back when all you do is run me into the ground." Skylar did her best to hold herself together. *Why do I always seem to run into people at the grocery store?*

Shifting her gaze from her car to her sister, Skylar was overcome with disappointment. They had once been close, when they were really young. Tonya had always seemed so cool, but then, once Tonya reached high school, she no longer had time for Skylar. She'd surrounded herself with a crowd who had liked nothing more than to get drunk and party every night. And that had left Skylar on the outskirts of her life.

Tonya was slim, slimmer than was healthy, and Skylar feared drugs were still an everyday occurrence in her sister's life. Dark circles hung under her bloodshot eyes. Her hair was blond like Skylar's, but it was unkempt and tossed up in a high bun.

"You deserved every word. It's your fault Mom is gone."

"It's not, and you know that." Skylar turned back around and dropped her grocery bags into the trunk of her car. "I wish we could get past this." Some part of her always wanted to fix what had gone wrong between her and Tonya. It had been her default setting since she was a child. They'd fought often, and no matter who was in the wrong, Skylar would apologize to keep things good between them. When Tonya started using drugs after their mother's death, Skylar had made excuses for her. Zelda had told Skylar many times to get some distance from her sister, and she acknowledged that Tonya was not good for her. But Skylar couldn't push away the only family she had left.

"Grow up, Skylar. You need to take responsibility for your actions."

"My actions? My *actions*? Are you for real right now?"

Skylar rarely yelled, so her raised voice caused one of Tonya's brows to lift, almost in challenge. It silently asked if she was really going to get into a verbal sparring match in the middle of a parking lot on a random Wednesday afternoon.

Skylar's last talk with Zelda about her sister had emboldened her, or it was the confidence she was gaining after spending time with Harmon, so she dove in. "Look at Mom's actions," Skylar said. "She was such a desperate alcoholic that she *drove drunk* all the way across town when all she had to do was drive one block for the tampons I asked for. And now look at you! You can't go a day without some kind of substance racing through your veins, can you?" The moment the words passed her lips, she felt terrible. She shouldn't judge her sister. Quitting was one of the hardest things a person could do, and there she was berating Tonya. Instead of criticizing her, Skylar should be offering her help.

"That's all you see when you look at me? An addict?"

"No!" Skylar cried. "I see a sister who I want a better life for. One who shut me out the day our mother died. The same sister I used to have living room sleepovers with... I see that sister, but she's buried under the one who's afraid to acknowledge her feelings." Her throat and nose burned with the need to cry, but she held back the tears, knowing Tonya would make fun of her emotional side.

Tonya opened her mouth, but nothing came out. Instead of giving a response, she turned on her heel and stomped across the parking lot. That feeling of being a terrible sister sank in Skylar's stomach, bringing back the anxious nausea that hadn't been far from reach lately.

As she buckled herself into her car, her phone vibrated in her back pocket. Pulling it out, she was greeted with a new message from Harmon about dinner. She didn't see how she could make this work when the only relationships she hadn't ruined over the years were with Zelda and Lara. Even then, she had put them all on a strange footing a few times. As she drove home, she continued to swallow down her tears. The argument with Tonya replayed in her mind on a loop. Each time it played back, Skylar considered what she could have or should have said. Each one ended on a better note than reality. When she parked, she sat in her car a moment, giving herself some time to push away the damned emotions clogging her thoughts.

I will have to try harder to get through to Tonya. I cannot lose my nerve. Tonight, I have a date...

Being someone who hated to make more than one trip after shopping, she loaded her arms up with groceries. It was the closest she came to weight lifting, and it never ceased to make her feel like a weakling by the time she was done. When she reached her front door, her arms ached, and she had to set the bags down to unlock her front door. Zelda was likely working, and she didn't want to disturb her.

After taking care of the groceries, she changed into the dress she'd selected. She smoothed it down over her middle. That was another difference between her and Tonya that she'd never been able to ignore. While Tonya had always been slim, Skylar was curvy. The extra weight around her middle had always made her a little self-conscious. The color did great things for her complexion, and it also made her hair appear more coppery. Using her curling wand, which she never failed to burn herself with, Skylar curled her hair into small waves.

As she was applying clear gloss over her lips, her phone buzzed on the counter. She preferred to keep her lips natural rather than use tinted gloss or lipstick, which never failed to make her look washed out.

Harmon: *I'm out front. Do you want me to come up and get you?*

Skylar was quick to respond. The resolution to keep her apartment in better order wasn't fully in effect, and she didn't want him to witness the disaster that was her living situation.

Skylar: *No need, on my way down.*

Harmon had parked right out front of the building, and the sight of him and his car sent a shiver of excitement over her. The way his gaze drifted over her body made her feel exposed in the tight dress. She felt the urge to suck in her stomach, something her ex had encouraged her to do. Some wounds healed more slowly than others. But then Harmon's eyes took on a hooded look, and she knew he liked what he saw.

When she opened the car door, she was hit by the manly, almost woodsy scent she had come to associate with him. It reminded her of the bergamot candle sitting on her nightstand.

"You look stunning." Harmon's voice was low and raspy. He cleared his throat before he continued. "I'm glad dinner worked out tonight."

Plastering a smile on her face that she wouldn't be able to scrape off without a scalpel, she nodded. "Me too."

Harmon had said he wanted to surprise her with dinner at one of his favorite places to eat. He maneuvered them through the streets with ease. He looked humble but great in a simple black polo with a pair of dark jeans. Before long, they were pulling into a parking lot shared by a few different businesses—a consignment clothing shop, a nail salon, and a genuine Mexican restaurant. She loved tacos but had never had real Mexican fare.

As they pushed through the front door, a young man behind the counter addressed Harmon by name. *I guess he wasn't exaggerating about how often he came here if they knew him by name.* They went to the counter to place their order.

"What would you like?" Harmon asked after she'd flipped the menu over a few times.

"It all sounds good. I'm not sure what to get."

He chuckled. "Oh, it is good."

"Why don't you pick a few of your favorites, and we can share?"

Her idea was met with a broad grin. "Deal. How do you feel about spice?"

She nodded and tipped her head from side to side. "Well, I like buffalo sauce but not usually anything spicier than that, if that helps."

"I got this."

Harmon's confidence calmed her nerves, but not enough to assuage the butterflies in her middle. That fear that she would mess this all up sat like lead in her feet. Her run-in with Tonya was affecting her more than she wanted to acknowledge. He placed their order then led her to what he deemed the best table in the place.

"So, that's Olivia and her son Juan. Olivia and her husband moved to the US before any of their kids were born. They've had this restaurant for the last several years." Harmon squinted, staring at the ceiling as if the information were etched into the metal ceiling tiles. "I think it was four years ago? Anyway, I stumbled across the place a little over two years ago, and I've been coming to it at least once a week since." He shrugged.

"So, this is all family run?" she asked, taking it in.

The scrollwork in the copper ceiling tiles gave them depth. Three of the walls were red; the one across the restaurant showcased a mural depicting what Skylar had been taught was the Day of the Dead. Beautiful blossoms and people covered the wall, blending into portraits of women dancing, then finally what looked like a family eating together. Each scene was so different, yet the mural shifted effortlessly from one part of their history to the next.

"Yeah, Olivia's husband, Mateo, painted that." He tipped his head to indicate the wall she took in.

"It's amazing."

"It is. He has a contract to do one on the exterior of a building soon."

She loved the way Harmon had taken the time to get to know this family. Their food arrived—enchiladas, pork tacos, and quesadillas—and it smelled amazing. It all looked too good. She was ravenously hungry, and she wanted to taste them all.

"What do you want to try first?"

"All of it?" She smiled sheepishly.

Harmon laughed, and the sound warmed her. He started cutting each of the portions in half, slid one portion onto a plate, and pushed it toward her with some salsa verde, sour cream, and a red salsa. He explained that the red salsa was the hottest and she should start with the salsa verde.

When they'd eaten as much as they could, Juan came by to clear their plates.

"Thank you," Skylar said as he took away the dirty dishes.

"I'm just going to run to the bathroom." Harmon stood from their table.

She took in the restaurant again. The place had filled quickly. They'd arrived for an early dinner, and now, there wasn't an empty table in the house.

"Okay, I might wait outside. It's starting to feel a little stifling here. Plus, it looks like some people by the door are waiting to be seated."

Harmon nodded, handed her the keys to his car, then stepped away. It was a small gesture, but it meant he trusted her. She left their table, giving the woman behind the counter a wave as she headed outside. The evening was warm, but not unbearable. It was reaching that time of year when she didn't feel like she was boiling most of the time.

She was nearly to Harmon's car when her heart jumped into her throat. She'd blocked CJ's number and had successfully avoided him for two weeks.

"You spread your legs for him like you did me?"

Skylar's head reeled back almost as if CJ had struck her. "You have no right to speak to me that way." She spun to face him, and his ever-present shadow, Nick. "This coming from the man who's married and didn't bother to tell me that the night we met." Her tone was angry even as she tried to keep their conversation quiet.

CJ shrugged, and the tattoos that had seemed sexy before appeared ominous as she looked at them more closely. They depicted what looked like death and despair. His arms flexed with his annoyance, and he leaned closer. "My wife knows the score. You, however, need to learn a few things. I don't like when people touch what's mine."

He stepped into Skylar's personal space, and she instinctively backed away from him, her shoe catching on the old asphalt.

"You're fucked in the head if you think I'm yours in any way. I want nothing to do with a married man."

CJ's jaw flexed, and Nick shifted. Apparently, neither of them liked it when he was put in his place, but she had been with someone who tried to manipulate her before. She refused to let this ass scare her into whatever it was he thought he wanted from her. Besides, he had lied. There was no video, and if there had been, it surely would have been leaked by now.

Before she could take another step away from them, CJ's hand was around her bicep, painfully holding her in place. "You're going to listen, and you're going to listen well. We're not done with one another until I decide we are. I don't want you going on any more dates. And if you can't stick to my rules, little Zelda might have to pay for your selfishness. She seemed like a good friend. You don't want to be the reason someone gets hurt, do you?"

The pressure of his grip had steadily increased as he spoke. Her body told her to run, but she was frozen. Her bravado from moments ago was gone. Moisture stuck to her skin, though whether it was sweat or the spittle leaving CJ's mouth with every hissed word, she wasn't sure.

"Do you understand me?" he asked, shaking her.

She tried to nod, but her body refused to move. She didn't think she could even try to fight, knowing it would be one of the least wise things she could do when he had one of his giant minions at his elbow. This version of CJ was different from the man she'd met at the club all those months ago. She wanted to shout as much at him. *He's changed since he showed up at the diner.* Dark circles ringed his eyes. They were red with anger and who knew what else.

"Good," he seethed. "I was looking for you a couple of weeks ago. Then, someone told me Liza rushed to the bathrooms when some woman matching the description I gave them went. You've been ignoring my texts, so we're going to rectify that now. Take your phone out of your pocket. I want to see if you've blocked my number. If the call doesn't go through, I will be forced to teach you another lesson."

He swiped away a tear she'd unwittingly released, the touch so tender and in such drastic contrast to the way he was manhandling her. It opened her eyes to how deranged he really was.

Given she had few other options, she pulled her phone from her pocket. Something rattled in the distance, stealing the men's attention. CJ appeared paranoid as Nick raced off to determine the source of the noise. Skylar only had a moment to make the change, and she hoped she'd done it right. Her heart hammered as she lay her phone flat in her palm. When Nick returned, he muttered something about a dumpster. CJ's grip hadn't loosed on her arm, and her fingers began to go numb. Phone in hand, CJ raised an eyebrow at her in challenge. She nearly dropped to the ground in relief when hers rang. She would rather him think she was ignoring him than know she had blocked him. She didn't want to find out the punishment he might have had in mind.

"Good girl."

The phrase sent a chill running down her spine. Adrenaline surged through her muscles, ready to kick in whenever she needed it. She'd never liked that kind of praise, and it felt even more disgusting coming from CJ's lips.

"Since I'm a reasonable man," he said as he released her arm and tugged his jacket sleeves back down, covering his forearms and tattoos, "if I call you and you don't answer, I will call again in exactly five minutes to give you time to get to the phone. If you don't answer a second time, I will have to show you what happens when my girls misbehave."

She shook her head, not even realizing her body was denying his demands without her consent. Like a lightning strike, he had her jaw in his hand, holding her face so she couldn't move it. A squeak of fear leaped from her lips as she slammed her eyes shut.

"Open your damn eyes!"

The shuffling of rocks on the sidewalk told her his minion had stepped closer. She did as she was told, meeting CJ's cold, hollow gaze.

"And before you think you're clever and decide to call the police, you should know my father is best friends with the police captain and my mother is the district attorney."

He brought his face close to hers, and she could smell his breath. It churned her dinner in her stomach. What had begun as a great day was quickly losing its luster. First Tonya and now CJ. He released her just as quickly as he'd grabbed her.

"I'll be in touch." He stalked toward his SUV parked outside the nail salon.

Their position had been blocked from view by a large white van. On the sidewalk, watching their confrontation, was a woman with vibrant red hair. As the men approached her, her angry gaze remained on Skylar.

The roiling in Skylar's middle turned into a cyclone as CJ climbed into the back of the SUV. The minion took the front seat, and the woman sulkily climbed into the back on the far side. As they disappeared from sight, Skylar's dinner made its reappearance. This could not be happening. Her life had just started to fall back into place. She'd received a job offer earlier that day, and she'd just had her fourth date with Harmon. It was supposed to be when her life took a turn in the right direction. But now, things couldn't get worse.

Chapter Seventeen

Harmon

"Sorry, I took so long." Harmon dropped into the driver's seat. "Olivia wanted to talk to me about..." The look on Skylar's face gave him pause. "Are you okay?"

She nodded and gave him a weak smile. "Yeah, just not feeling the best at the moment."

He was about to ask if she thought it was the food, but they'd eaten all the same things, and he felt fine. "Okay, let's get you home." He reached over the center console and placed his hand on her thigh.

She stiffened under his touch, so as casually as possible, he pulled his hand back and fidgeted with the radio, then settled his hand on the shifter instead. His gut festered with the feeling of unease; he just wasn't sure where the change had come from. Their date had been going well—or so he'd thought.

As they drove back to her apartment, he couldn't think of anything to say that wouldn't sound stupid, so he settled on silence. But it wasn't the comfortable silence they'd fallen into before. It was strained, and he felt like she was hiding something.

What could have happened in the seven minutes it took me to piss and talk to Olivia? He glanced at Skylar out of the corner of his eye as he stopped at a red light. She was still tense, her eyes glazed over as if she was about to cry.

When the light changed and he began to drive again, he racked his brain for anything he could have said that would have come across the wrong way. Nothing came to mind.

As they found a parking spot at her apartment building, he shifted in his seat to face her. Reaching out as gently as he could, he took her hand in his. He was terrified he would spook her and she would take off.

"Sky, please look at me."

With only a moment's hesitation, she met his gaze, and her vibrant green eyes looked sad.

"What happened while I was in the bathroom?"

Her eyes widened marginally, just enough for the gesture to be visible. "I... I ran into someone I hoped I would never see again."

Harmon's eyes roved over her body, taking in every bit of her, looking for signs of wounds or who knew what. He didn't know why, but something made him feel he needed to look her over. "What did they say? What did they do?" he all but growled. Something in his gut told him this was likely an ex. The thought brought jealousy revving to life, extending to every nerve in his body. He hated the idea of any other man spending time with her. He took a deep breath to calm himself before succumbing to his strained patience.

"Let's just say he thinks the fleeting connection we had is still relevant." She dropped her gaze from his. "I'm sorry, Harmon. I didn't mean to ruin our dinner. I had a great time. And I promise I *want* nothing to do with this guy."

Her voice cracked, and it felt like a punch to his gut.

His jealousy faded, replaced by a need to comfort her. "Hey, someone else's actions have nothing to do with you, darling." He reached to cup her cheek, bringing her eyes back to his.

She tipped her head to let her face rest more heavily in his palm.

"Do you want me to walk you up?"

She gave him a small smile and nodded while her cheek remained in his palm. With a tentative sigh, she closed her eyes. He leaned in, pressing his forehead to hers. Their lips hovered a breath away from each other. He, too, closed his eyes, reveling in the feel of her body and his connecting in such a simple way. With no sexual tension or yearning behind it, just the two of them comforting one another. He doubted she even knew what her presence did for him. They sat like that for several minutes.

When Skylar pulled away, she seemed more at ease. It was much better to see than the sadness, but he wanted to take their time. With her tremulous emotions outside the restaurant, he didn't want to be too much for her. Skylar was special, and he wanted to treat her as such, even if he couldn't pinpoint any one thing that made her so unique. "Dinner this weekend?" he asked.

Again, she nodded.

"Are you okay?"

A light blush filled her cheeks. "Much better than before."

Harmon smiled and pressed a kiss to her forehead before opening his door and making his way around to walk her up to her apartment. He'd only ever waited outside for her, so he needed her guidance to get to the correct door.

On her threshold, she fidgeted with her purse strap. "Do you want to maybe come in?" she asked so quietly it was nearly a whisper.

But he heard every word of it down into his soul. "More than anything. But I promised myself I wouldn't do something that felt like taking advantage of you. I want to get to know you. I really like you, and I don't want to risk ruining things. I know if I come in, I will be battling the devil inside of me the entire time to keep my hands off you."

Skylar looked torn by his response as her gaze shifted from one of his eyes to the other—as if she were searching for a lie. "Okay, in that case, this weekend?"

Something in him wondered if that one question had more than one meaning laced in it. His heart and dick stood in opposing corners. "This weekend," he agreed then leaned forward to give her one more small peck on the lips.

A moment later, her apartment door softly closed in his face.

***

The work situation without an assistant was getting a bit overwhelming. Granted, he could do it, but that also required him to work later than usual—and that was altogether too much. From Wednesday on, he had worked no less than twelve-hour days to get everything done for the week.

He'd only been able to call Skylar once, and that didn't feel like nearly enough. She deserved more. She deserved someone who could put her first—and he would. His new assistant would start Monday, and he could breathe a little easier as he shut down his computer for the weekend. Saying goodbye to the office for a few days would be good for him. For his mind and soul. He intended to come in calm and ready to train his new assistant on Monday. He would show her everything that needed to be done. In his haste to get everything completed on time, he'd never taken the time to sit down with Naudia like he'd wanted to discuss his new assistant. Granted, he trusted Naudia's opinion, but that didn't mean he should walk into the new week totally blind. His phone rattled against his keys in his pocket.

Porter: *Have you been kidnapped? I'm starting to worry.*

Harmon laughed as he read the text before locking the office door behind him. It was nice to know his best friend had noticed his silence. The lack of communication had felt strange—they never went more than two or three days without speaking, but Harmon had been so busy since the Sunday before that his responses had been sporadic at best, and nonexistent at worst.

Harmon: *Just finished working. On my way out now.*

He jogged down the steps and out into the late evening. He had plans with Skylar the next day, and he simply could not wait. It was thrilling to have someone new in his life—a *friend* he wanted to become more with and know for a long time.

Porter: *Shit, man, it's nearly nine.*

Porter: *Still no assistant?*

If Porter ever managed to put all his thoughts in one text, it would be the day Harmon played the lottery because that would be the proof he needed that life was out of whack and his numbers would definitely be drawn.

Harmon: *Monday. Thankfully.*

Mandy's presence had been exhausting, but this was an entirely new level of run-down. She had managed most of his calendar and meetings as well as fielded and screened his calls, and trying to do it all himself left him feeling like he was drowning with no lifeline—or that it had simply bobbed just out of reach as the ocean pulled it farther away.

This time, when a text came through as he started his car, he smiled at the screen like a goon.

Skylar: *Can't wait to see you tomorrow.*

The kissing emoji at the end amped up his heart rate. He liked something about her emojis far too much. The thought had him dropping his phone. He wasn't sure how old Skylar was. They'd gone on a few dates, but he'd never seen her drink alcohol.

As he pondered the appropriate age gap—because he knew they must have a few years separating them—he drove home. The thought of home and his bed had never sounded so enticing.

Chapter Eighteen

SKYLAR

"Not that I am complaining, but why have you been on a witch hunt for every dust bunny that has ever even thought of coming into existence?" Zelda asked as she walked into their sparkling, fully clean living room.

Their Christmas tree no longer occupied a box against the wall. It now stood in the corner of the living room—a little crooked—but it was upright, and after the battle Skylar had had with the damn thing, that was good enough. The clothes were all folded and put in the correct places, or at least in the proper rooms. What happened to Zelda's clothes after they got folded and neatly stacked on her bed wasn't Skylar's problem. She'd disposed of the magazines they were never going to look at again, and Skylar felt good about all she'd accomplished over the last few days.

She shrugged. "I had the time. Might as well get it done, seeing as I'm *not* working." It was a fact she had been struggling with all week. The feeling of worthlessness was too much to stomach if she sat still for more than a few minutes. So, to keep that nagging emotion at bay, she had cleaned the apartment top to bottom. Literally. Every floor, baseboard, wall, and ceiling she could reach were cleaner than when they'd moved in. The trick would be getting it to remain in such a state after she went back to work. It was all too easy to say she was too tired and would get up early to take care of something tomorrow. The getting up early part never happened. A morning person she was not.

"You know, there is nothing wrong with you being unemployed for a few days," Zelda said calmly and leaned into Skylar's direct line of sight. "I don't think any less of you for taking a few days off. I know how you think. You were holding out hope."

Skylar's eyes teared. "Why you gotta be all wise after being sassy?"

Zelda cackled, dropping her head back. The way she laughed was so infectious, it never failed to make Skylar lose her composure. The tears she'd been holding back vanished as she laughed alongside her friend.

"What's for dinner?" Zelda asked after she'd calmed herself. She dropped her work bag on the kitchen island.

"You're like a child."

"Hey, you *remember* the last time I tried to cook, right? We nearly got evicted." Tapping her nails on the counter, she stood on her toes, apparently trying to see what was in the frying pan on the stove. However, given her height, she likely didn't need the height boost.

"Just some omelets. I'm damn tired."

Zelda shrugged. "I could eat eggs any time of day." She retrieved her work bag from the counter and disappeared down the hall, likely to change into her sci-fi movie pajamas. They were pretty much a staple for every evening at their place. If Zelda wasn't wearing them, they were either lost or she had finally decided to wash them.

Skylar had the table set and dinner ready by the time Zelda sauntered back out. As expected, she wore her fleece pajama bottoms with little green aliens all over them.

"It smells amazing!" Zelda said as she dropped her skinny ass into the chair. The woman could eat anything, and she never seemed to gain an ounce.

Skylar suspected Zelda had some kind of thyroid condition. Between the amount of junk she ingested coupled with the fact that she was always exhausted, it would make sense. But her clear dislike of any kind of needle prevented her from getting tested.

"Thank you. They're tomato, spinach, and mozzarella."

Zelda lifted a brow, looking at the omelet like it would be the final meal of her life—because the contents would poison her.

"Oh, stop." Skylar playfully rolled her eyes. "Eating a few vegetables will do you good."

"So, when are you seeing Mr. Ham-Ham again?"

Skylar coughed as she just about choked on her dinner. "Harmon?"

"Close enough." Zelda shrugged mischievously.

It was Skylar's turn to drop her head back and laugh. When she looked across the table again, Zelda was still waiting with one brow raised in question.

"Ugh, fine... tomorrow night."

Zelda wiggled her brows. "You gonna put him out of his misery?"

"Don't give me that... I asked him if he wanted to come in the other night. *He* said no, and that it would be 'too tempting,'" she said, using air quotes. "He wants to take things slow, for your information." She just left out the part where they'd been together once before.

"Ooo-ooo." Zelda's voice could reach octaves no normal human should be capable of unless they starred in a horror film.

***

Saturday afternoon arrived faster than Skylar had anticipated. It was the beginning of December, and people couldn't get out of their own way, never mind Skylar's as she drove to Harmon's condo. As she did, she constantly checked her mirrors for any sign of CJ. It had been several days since she'd seen him at the Mexican restaurant. And so far, nothing, no calls, no texts. Part of her felt as if she shouldn't go against him. The other part was adamant that this was her life and she needed to live it her way. Releasing a long, slow breath, she stopped at a traffic light and peered around. The deal was that she would pick Harmon up this time since he had done so the last few times. She also felt better when she was the one behind the wheel—a trait she referred to as passenger anxiety.

She followed her phone's GPS through town in her freshly cleaned car. Since the apartment had gotten the full treatment, she figured old Thelma could use some love too. The fabric seats were in the best condition ever, and the windshield was much easier to see out of—something to stay up with. The car was several years old, but the best part was that Skylar no longer owed anything on it. And because *Thelma and Louise* had been Skylar and her mother's favorite movie, the teal car had earned its name rather easily.

Harmon's building was far nicer than hers, and she couldn't suppress that feeling of embarrassment for nearly letting him into her apartment earlier in the week. She was almost relieved to see Harmon already waiting outside. She had texted him before leaving, but she flushed a deeper shade of red than could be found on the color wheel as he approached her. It wasn't the first instance he had seen her car, but for some reason, she hadn't really cared what he thought the first time. She loved her car.

All her feelings of inadequacy more than likely stemmed from her fight with Tonya—and the fact that she didn't have a job. Oh, and because she wasn't as put together as she had envisioned herself being at the ripe old age of twenty-eight. She had assumed she would be happily married, living in her first house by now.

"Hey," Harmon said as he dropped into the passenger seat. His dark eyes twinkled in the dome light and the high sun. "Mm, your car smells good."

Skylar swung her hand at the little black tree hanging from the shifter on the steering column like she was the model in an infomercial. Harmon laughed that deep rumble that sent too many nerves skittering down to her toes. Then, with only the look in his eyes to warn her, he pressed his lips to hers. They were soft but confident. He pulled back before they got carried away.

"How was your week?" she asked breathlessly.

Again, Harmon laughed. "It was okay. Far busier than I'd expected. How about you?"

She swallowed hard. She hated feeling like she was lying, but she still didn't know how to tell him he was dating someone semi-unemployed. She'd found out earlier in the week that she'd gotten one of the jobs she'd interviewed for, but she was afraid to tell anyone in case she jinxed it. She would wait to see how the first week went before saying too much.

"It was all right." She needed a subject change fast before she did lie. "I was thinking we could get Chinese takeout then go to this park I stumbled across when I first moved here…" Her heart started to hammer in her chest. She'd moved to Arizona in part to find somewhere new but also as a way to escape her sister and the memories of her mother. Neither plan had worked.

"Sure, I love to be outside."

Skylar swallowed hard. "Perfect." The word came out as a squeak, and she cleared her throat to make it seem less like a dog's chew toy. "What kind of Chinese food do you like?" She tacked on quickly.

Harmon's dark eyes narrowed momentarily. He was perceptive, and she needed to remember that. He would easily catch onto all of her anxieties if she wasn't careful. "Nothing too exciting, usually lo mein or some teriyaki chicken and steak. You?"

She hummed in the back of her throat because she could eat just about anything from her favorite spot. "Do you want to get a few different things and share? It worked out pretty well last time. Plus, I mean, I like just about everything at Beijing Bistro. Have you been?" *Ugh. I'm rambling…*

Harmon groaned, and a smile slid across her lips as she started her car. "Of course I have. They have the best food around. I'm game to share."

They ordered as they drove and only had to wait a few minutes after arriving. Their conversation, much like the other nights, was easy and flowed naturally. Any pauses were comfortable, and Skylar could breathe easily. Even the few years she'd spent with her last boyfriend hadn't been so smooth. It was a nice change of pace. Even when she'd thought things were going well with Christopher, there had been an undercurrent of discomfort. More than just the way his mother disapproved of her.

As they set off again for one of Skylar's favorite parks, she tried to focus in on Harmon's story about work. He seemed to have a great relationship with everyone in his office. He was so well put together, and she felt so... not. She was broken, with some of the pieces still missing and only half glued back together. This was probably a bad idea. He was older, by at least seven years, she would guess. The job he held could afford to send him on different trips for work around the country. And he owned his own condo.

Skylar owned her car. That was all she had to her name besides her clothes. She had fewer friends than she had fingers, and she had no college degree.

"So, you said earlier you found this place after you moved to the area?"

Skylar nodded just as her stomach grumbled, demanding to be satiated by the tantalizing aromas mocking her from the back seat. Her cheeks burned hotter than Thelma in the Arizona sun.

Harmon chuckled. "What made you move to Prescott Valley?"

She delayed answering as she stopped and turned at a light, pretending to ensure their turn would be safe. "I needed a change of pace, scenery, and well, people, I guess." It was honest but vague. *How can I casually say my sister blames me for my mother's death and ran me out of town?*

When Harmon said nothing, she panicked, and she kept talking to ensure he didn't ask too many more questions about the reason behind the move.

"So, I found a tiny—and I mean minuscule—apartment. I could reach the refrigerator from my pullout futon bed... Anyway, I was down to almost my last dime, and I happened to be driving around town. Kind of aimlessly, really, because when your arm span is almost as big as your apartment"—she shrugged—"it's better to be anywhere else. And that was when I stumbled across this park, then Retro." As she mentioned the place, her stomach pinched, and she was ashamed of her lack of honesty. "And as they say, the rest is history."

Harmon asked a few questions about how she'd come to live with Zelda as they finally made it to the parking lot. It gave them an excuse to stop talking about her history. The way she had to dance around her past, only touching on the things she felt were safe, was exhausting. But their relationship was still new, and she feared revealing anything too soon would doom them. She would tell him everything. Eventually.

"Damn, this place is beautiful."

"Isn't it?" Skylar took a deep breath. The fresh forest air—or as close to a forest as they could get at the moment—in her lungs made her feel alive. "If we pass this picnic area and go across that bridge, there are more tables on the other side."

"Is that where you'd like to go?" Harmon was already pulling their bags of food from the car.

"Mm-hmm." Skylar leaned in to grab their waters before they took off.

By the time they reached the bridge, Harmon no longer looked so certain about crossing it. It was old, and while it looked deadly, it wasn't. At least from what she had experienced.

"That looks like it could collapse into the water at any moment."

Something in Harmon's voice sounded off, just enough to make Skylar wonder if he had a thing about water. Or heights.

"It's fine. It's not going anywhere. Are you afraid of heights?" *Bridges? Water?* She didn't want to embarrass him, so she kept her questions to a minimum.

Harmon tipped his head, considering his answer. "Well, maybe bridges that look as though they could drop into the water at any moment and take me with them."

Skylar couldn't help it; she burst out laughing. This man was nervous to walk across a bridge that had held thousands of people over the years. Catching the look of slight annoyance on Harmon's face, she calmed her hysterics. "Sorry. We can eat on this side if you want." She motioned to the closest picnic table, which would still give them a good view of the water.

Harmon huffed and shook his head. "Lead on."

The resignation in his voice had her fighting back another fit of giggles. He sounded like he was accepting his fate as he made his way to the gallows.

Once safely on the other side of the decrepit old bridge, their meal had been easy. They fell into the same easy rhythm of sharing stories about growing up. It sounded as if Harmon had been lucky enough to remain friends with one of his college friends, who he'd visited for Thanksgiving and who didn't live far. It gave her hope; she'd never had a friend stand the test of time. Or distance. Or drama for that matter.

"So," Harmon said as they held hands, making their way back to her car.

It felt nice to simply hold someone's hand. She couldn't help but look forward to each connection they shared.

"So?" she asked.

"Would you want to come back to my place? Hang out a bit? No pressure," he hastily added when Skylar stopped walking.

She hadn't made the conscious thought to stop; it was more that she wanted to check his expression, make sure it was really what he wanted. They'd already slept together once, but he'd seemed skittish about it after their last date. He was the one who'd denied her the other night. Nothing in his expression gave any indication of his thoughts, just hope. His dark eyes seemed to beg her to spend more time with him, to take him up on his rare offer.

"I think I'd like that." Even as she said it, that niggling anxiety of not being good enough wiggled to the surface.

Chapter Nineteen

HARMON

As Skylar drove back to his place, he couldn't help but wonder if she felt obligated to come inside. She literally had to go to his place to drop him off. *I should have waited to ask once we were there, but I probably would have lost my nerve.*

"So, you said you own your condo?"

"Yeah, my building has seven other units. Three upstairs, three on the middle floor, and one on the far end that takes up two floors."

Skylar nodded as he explained the layout and the amenities.

"It was a steal, really, when I bought it."

He was over-explaining everything now that they were here. She would think he was a total mansplainer, but he couldn't shut up. He cared about Skylar. He'd cared about the other women, as well, but he cared about Skylar differently. *Pacing,* he reminded himself. He was just so damn worried about rushing things. She was clearly younger than him. Now that they'd talked more, he thought she was between seven and ten years younger than him, which would make her mid to late twenties, while he was closer to forty.

"Elevator or stairs?"

"You have an elevator? I've been here how many times? You have never once mentioned an elevator."

Harmon huffed a laugh. "Yeah, but it's not always the best."

"You'll get into a questionable metal cage that could drop you to your death, but that perfectly fine bridge made you nervous?"

"That *perfectly fine* bridge was almost entirely rust. The wooden boards looked like they could snap in half, *and* it freaking creaked the moment I stepped on it. I swear it swayed." He knew he sounded like a little bitch, but he'd definitely felt that thing sway. The elevator here was slow, but not ready to fall apart.

Shrugging, with mischief twinkling in her eyes, Skylar suggested, "Why don't we just take the stairs? They're better for us anyway."

"Scared?"

She arched a brow. "I'm not afraid of much, Harmon."

The teasing way she said his name had him wishing for things he wasn't convinced he should want yet. But the phrase gave him pause. He wondered what she'd been through. At times, he could swear she was holding back. His mind was a tangled mess.

"Stairs it is." He took her hand in his, leading her through the lobby, to the left, and up the stairs closest to his door. The condos were big; the standard six had three bedrooms each. He used one room as a spare bedroom for guests and the third as his home office. He rarely put it to use, and it essentially just housed his laptop.

When he unlocked the door, he was glad he'd remembered to not only take out the trash that morning but replace the fragrance plug-ins. The woodsy scent was just potent enough to give the space an undertone.

"Everything here is so... clean," Skylar said from behind him as she unzipped her little boots.

"Thanks. " As he took the space in from a newcomer's point of view, it seemed plain. A framed photo of Porter, Verity, and their kids occupied one wall along with a picture of him and his parents and one of him and Porter at their college graduation. They made his life look so simple and succinct—as if everything that mattered to him could be neatly captured in those three little frames. But there was so much more to him.

The rest of the living room was furnished for comfort, and Skylar headed straight for the leather couch. She moaned as she sat down, and the sound sent an extra pulse to his dick. Great.

"Do you, ah, want to watch a movie?"

She raised a brow at him. "Sure."

All he could think about was her coming back to his place and mostly watching *Roadhouse* the last time she was here. "What would you like to watch?" He looked anywhere but at her on his couch. Suddenly, having her here was far worse than he'd thought it would be. He wanted her. But she was hiding a few things, and so was he.

"Mm, I'll watch pretty much anything but horror. I don't need to watch people make stupid choices and die..."

Her assessment of horror movies wasn't totally warranted; he'd seen more than a couple that could be described in just that way.

He turned on the television, finding a streaming service with some of his favorite movies. "This one?" he asked, hovering over his newest obsession. It wasn't a movie, but he'd only watched the first three episodes of the show, and he would love to have someone to discuss it with.

Again, Skylar shrugged. "Sure."

Harmon sat next to her, the plush cushion all but sending her toppling onto his lap. But she didn't try to move away. So, he put his arm over her shoulders, and all he could smell now was her floral scent.

After sitting like that for several minutes, Skylar shifted, and he realized he'd been rolling her hair between the pads of his thumb and forefinger. Something told him he should stop, but the devil on his other shoulder encouraged him to continue.

The first episode ended, and Skylar made no move to leave.

She turned, and her green eyes looked ready to swallow him whole. Harmon leaned in an inch, and Skylar must have noticed because she shifted just enough to bring their lips closer. He was a goner as he pressed his lips to hers. Just like every time before, hers were giving and soft. The kiss escalated quickly, and his tongue danced with hers as he released a low rumble deep in his chest.

That was all the encouragement Skylar needed. Next thing he knew, she was straddling his lap. His hands went to her hips, squeezing the flesh and pushing her down against his growing erection through his jeans. He wanted her to know what she did to him. Following his lead, she ground into him. The friction made him growl as she moaned. He sank his fingers into the waistband of her leggings, ready to strip them off her.

***

Monday morning came around, and Harmon couldn't wait to see Skylar again, but since he needed to train his new assistant, it would probably be a few more long days.

Still, he had a new spring in his step as he got ready for work—either due to spending a couple of evenings with Skylar, or the knowledge that work would, hopefully, be getting a bit easier. He was excited to meet his new assistant. Naudia had spent the last few days of the prior week communicating with her and making sure all her paperwork was done. He would have some full-time help again. One could only hope the new woman was more detail-oriented than Mandy. He felt like a dick for continuing to bring up how terrible she had been.

As he pushed the glass door open into his office, he met Naudia on her way out.

"She's here. I set her up with an email, and I have her looking over the disaster of a calendar you've been trying to navigate on your own. I don't know what that crap is, Harmon."

He frowned. "Nothing is wrong with my calendar."

Naudia jutted out a hip. "None of those appointments were in order. How did you intend to keep things straight?"

He shook his head and waved her off as he pushed through the door, calling over his shoulder, "Thank you for everything, Naudia. I wouldn't have been able to hire anyone so quickly."

"You're welcome, and I know. Just don't scare her off."

The joke hit closer to home than he would ever admit, but that was what he was best at—scaring people away. Hell, he frightened himself sometimes. His anger rarely unfurled into an insatiable inferno, and he did his best to avoid it. Laughing off her comment, he stepped into his office to find a woman sitting at his assistant's desk. Even with her back to him, he recognized her immediately. The soft curves, that long light-brown hair braided in a neat plait. It had been down and laced between his fingers two nights ago, and again the night before.

No. He hadn't realized he'd spoken aloud until she jumped and spun around. The smile affixed to her face slowly dropped from her rosy cheeks. He shook his head. It couldn't be. He shouldn't be noticing things like that about his assistant.

"Harmon?" she gasped in disbelief.

He blinked a few times, as if she would disappear and his real assistant would materialize in her place. "You're a waitress." It was stupid to say, but it was the first thing that came to mind, and it seemed he no longer had control over what left his mouth.

She shifted from one foot to the other and folded her hands in front of her. "I was." She nodded.

"Skylar, what's going on?" His breathing accelerated as he tried to wrap his mind around the expected situation.

Again, she fidgeted uncomfortably. "The thing is, Retro closed down for good the Saturday night after Thanksgiving. That was why it was so busy. It's also why I haven't been working when you've texted lately. I... I didn't know I would be your assistant." Her gaze dropped to her shoes as she moved the toe of one foot back and forth on the white carpet. It had been cleaned of any trace of blood from his encounter with Mandy.

He shook his head again. It seemed to be the only thing his body was capable of. "You can't be my assistant. I can't be *sleeping* with my..." He stepped back to the door, closing it to give them a modicum of privacy. The glass walls would let anyone see in, but they would muffle some of the sound. "I cannot fuck my employees."

Skylar flinched. She stepped forward, bringing her gaze back to his. "Harmon, please. I need this job. I don't have anything else. You can't fire me." Tears glistened in her deep-green eyes.

Something twisted heavily in his stomach. He knew things were too good to last. There had to be something coming for him; he was finally happy for the first time in years. Nothing in his life ever worked out well for long.

Here was the punch line.

CHAPTER TWENTY

SKYLAR

SKYLAR NEARLY DROPPED EVERYTHING in her arms as she crossed the threshold into her apartment and found Zelda excitedly bouncing just inside the entry. She looked like a puppy waiting for their owner to get home.

"Fuck, Z, you scared the shit out of me. Don't do that."

Zelda reached forward, taking the grocery bag out of Skylar's hands. "I'm just so thrilled for you. I wanted to know how your first day went."

"You won't be for long," Skylar muttered, as she let the ballet flats she'd worn for work drop to the floor. For about two seconds, she had considered wearing heels while she was getting ready that morning. But she wanted to make a good first impression on her new boss and not look like a child playing dress-up in her mother's closet. Because that was exactly how Skylar felt every time she wore heels—like an imposter.

"Why's that?"

Skylar groaned as she leaned over the back of the couch to retrieve the remote and turned the television down. Zelda must have been playing her video games in the living room while waiting for Skylar to get home because the home screen of a game blared an obnoxiously loud theme song. When she turned for the counter, she found Zelda had already unpacked the fixings for their usual Monday-night tacos. Instead of taco Tuesdays, they reserved that meal for Mondays, simply because neither of them ever fit into a mold, so they wanted to do things their way.

"Soooo?" Zelda asked, dragging out the word.

Skylar took her time answering, pretending to be engrossed in the frying pan she took out of the cupboard. "It was good, after I convinced him not to dismiss me immediately after he saw me."

Zelda gasped, and her head reeled back. Then she frowned, looking Skylar up and down. "Did you not follow some strict dress code?"

"Nope. You know that guy you've been calling Ham-Ham that I was getting to know?"

Zelda nodded and rolled her eyes as she mutilated the tomato. She wasn't allowed to use Skylar's good knives, considering she had almost cut off a finger trying out a chopping technique she'd seen on some cooking competition show. "Obviously, I kinda know who he is. You just haven't introduced us yet. What does he have to do with anything?"

"He's my new boss."

Zelda's mouth dropped open, complete with a small popping sound. "No way. You've got to be fucking with me right now."

"I wish I were."

"This is the guy you slept with this weekend?"

Skylar nodded as she stirred the hamburger around the pan. Something about the ground beef's smell churned her stomach. The longer she stood over the pan, the fouler the scent got. "Does this hamburger smell bad to you?"

Zelda cocked her head. "Are you just trying to get out of talking about this?"

Skylar shook her head.

Dropping the knife onto her cutting board, Zelda wiped her hands off on the towel sitting on the counter then tossed it down next to her cutting board. She leaned over the pan and took a deep inhale. Just imagining the scent of the hamburger filling her nostrils sent Skylar over the edge. She raced out of the kitchen and to the bathroom off the entryway. Barely making it to the toilet in time, she vomited everything in her stomach.

"You all right?" Zelda asked from the doorway.

Skylar pressed a hand to her stomach as she tried to calm the raging ache.

"Have you been sick all day?"

Skylar rinsed her mouth at the sink, ignoring her audience. When it became apparent Zelda wasn't leaving, Skylar said, "No, I've been having serious anxiety lately. It's been making me feel like trash. I'm just usually better at hiding it."

"I mean, you've been through a lot lately. The anniversary, losing your job, CJ."

The mention of CJ had another round of nausea flooding her system. She hadn't told Zelda about his impromptu visit about dating Harmon.

"And then your sister texting you, being her usual bitchy self. I can't believe she's in the area. It was bad enough when she was a dozen or so states away."

Skylar's eyes widened as she couldn't help but agree. Her life had been easier before Tonya decided to track her down in Arizona the year before.

"Could be the culmination of everything. I have been under a bit of strain."

Zelda lifted a brow as if to say "duh" then turned, stating, "I'll finish dinner. Just tell me what to do" over her shoulder.

Skylar nodded. Walking Zelda through the rest of the dinner preparations while she made sure Zelda didn't let the hamburger burn. Skylar's stomach settled, and by the time she sat down to eat, she felt normal.

"So, what did Hunka-Hunka Ham-Ham say when he saw you?"

Skylar wasn't sure if she should laugh, cry, or throw her greasy napkin at Zelda's face. "He was sorta dumbfounded... I never told him Retro closed."

"Excuse me?" Zelda's eyes nearly bugged out of her head. She was honest to a fault, so any kind of omission or lie drove her insane. Truth, first and foremost, was one of her hard rules. Sure, she liked to joke around, be sarcastic, and play a prank here and there, but she always told the truth. Consequences be damned.

Zelda's mother had drilled into her kids that honesty always would do more for them. Which might explain why Zelda was a court reporter, her older brother was a cop, and while Lara was starting her dream job as a pediatric nurse, she, too, was honest to a fault.

"You're telling me you've spent how many hours with this man and your job never came up?"

Skylar fidgeted with her hair. "Well, he didn't ask me any specific questions about work."

Zelda made a noise of disbelief and shot Skylar a glare. "Fuck, Sky, that right there could be enough to make someone not trust you."

"Ugh. I know, I know. I just couldn't find a way to say it. I mean, there is no good time to be like, 'Hey, I know we've only been talking and seeing one another for a few weeks, but just so you know, I'm unemployed. My bosses gave me six months' notice, but I was just too stupid to take them seriously and go find a new job.'"

"Stop. If this man was serious about wanting to get to know you, do you think he would have turned you away because you lost your job through no fault of your own? Seriously!"

"Don't get mad at me."

Zelda sighed. "You know how lies bother me. My dad lied to me for years, to all of us."

Whenever Zelda mentioned her parents, it was her mother and stepfather she was referring to. Skylar had a general understanding of how things had ended between her parents but not all the sordid details. Zelda was rarely willing to bring up such a touchy topic, and Skylar did not feel like encouraging the discussion.

After a few minutes of quiet, Zelda asked, "So, what happened when he recognized you, other than letting his jaw hit the floor?"

"He dumped me, essentially." As she said the words, she realized how much it had hurt. He'd cast her aside so easily. It was obvious how much Harmon cared about his job, and though they were still getting to know one another, he had been quick to end their... whatever this was, once they'd met any resistance.

"I'm sorry, Sky."

Skylar nodded. "It was probably for the best. I mean, you should have seen his place. He has his life all figured out. I'd just fuck it up, like I do most other things in life."

"We're not doing that tonight. No pity parties. You are a smart, capable woman. And you don't know that he has everything figured out. He could be a mess about this whole thing too."

Chapter Twenty-One

HARMON

Sitting alone at his dining table, Harmon stared at the tumbler of amber liquid in front of him. It seemed to stare back at him, taunting him, daring him to drink the entire bottle. When he first split from Jackie, he had turned to drinking, but now he never allowed himself more than one drink a night. Even that last year with Jackie he'd spent half in the bag most of the time. The drinking could have been a contender for why he'd lost his patience with Jackie that night. Another reason not to allow himself to drink too much. Part of him knew he needed to cut back more. Quitting entirely sounded even better, yet impossible. Tomorrow. Tomorrow he wouldn't have anything to drink. But today... this glass...

When his phone vibrated across the table, he answered it without looking at the caller ID. "Hey," he said somberly.

He'd already drank his one glass. This second one was a test.

"What the hell are you thinking?"

"About what?"

Porter huffed on the other end of the line. "About what the hell you said to that poor woman. You literally told her you couldn't fuck your assistant? You couldn't think of any better way to say it?" Porter, ever the patient, fix-it man.

Harmon swirled the temptation, creating a whirlpool in its center. Mouth watering, he knew he could down the whiskey in one gulp. "I don't know, man." He watched the whirling liquid slow.

"I thought you really wanted this chick."

Harmon narrowed his eyes. He hated when anyone referred to someone as a chick, and he didn't even know why. "I do... or I did. Fuck me. I don't know." He picked up the glass, smelling the spicy aroma. It was barely an inch from his lips.

"Well, you better figure it out before you confuse her any more. Shit, you'll be lucky if she stays. And if she leaves... you may have already fucked that up too." Porter rarely held back. This was no different.

"I know." Harmon brought the glass to the sink and dumped the contents down the drain. Rinsing the tumbler, he sighed then put it in the dishwasher. "Why the hell is my life never easy?"

"No one's is."

The denial was on the tip of his tongue. He wanted to throw Porter's and Verity's marriage back at him. They always seemed happy. But he, more than anyone, should realize that what happened behind closed doors was an entirely different matter.

"Just think about it. I've gotta go. Talk to you later, man."

After saying his goodbyes, Harmon hung up and dropped his phone into his pocket. It was getting late, and he needed to lie down. Instead, he stood in his kitchen staring into space. *If he could make a workplace romance work, would it be worth the headache it could induce? Who would want to go home with the person they were stuck around all day?*

Making his way to the living room, he dropped into his recliner and took out his phone. Four times he composed a text only to immediately delete it. Dating a coworker would be iffy. Someone who reported directly to him was definitely not an option. No matter how many times he reminded himself of that, he couldn't push away the thoughts of being with Skylar, spending time with her. He wanted to get to know her even more on every level. Now that he had intimate knowledge of her and the way her body felt pressed against his in all the best ways, he couldn't get her out of his mind—he wasn't sure he wanted to. Which was an issue all on its own.

Each time his phone screen dimmed, he tapped the center of his reflection, even if it was just to view the lock screen. Every time, he was met with the sad fact that he had no new notifications. He wasn't sure if he should be relieved or not. He had hoped in some fiber of his being that Skylar would reach out to him. *But why would she?* He had made it quite clear they could not be together. Hell, he was almost certain she'd cried. They had just been getting to know one another, but to have that chance snuffed out was hard to swallow—even for him, when he was the one to end things.

He bounced his head off the back cushion of his chair a few times, unsure if he was trying to knock sense into himself or just punish his stupidity.

He needed a distraction and pulled out one of his puzzle books. As if mocking him, it opened to a Sudoku game he'd been stumped on. Not only was it tough to solve, but now, when he saw a Sudoku puzzle, he thought of Skylar. The way she'd laughed at his love of the game. That brought about all kinds of unwanted thoughts—the way she'd felt against him the night before. The way she made him laugh. It was something he could grow accustomed to.

"No, Harmon, you can't." He snapped down his recliner's footrest.

Trudging to his bedroom, he searched for his running gear. It was one of the best ways he had found to expel emotions that threatened to swallow him whole. His running shorts and T-shirt were draped over the end of his footboard. He'd worn the set that morning when he'd run before work. They were still relatively clean, so he decided to wear them again.

As he stretched, the setting sun was at the perfect angle to cast what looked almost like a spotlight into his bedroom through the parted navy curtains. All his furnishings were dark, so he kept the walls and the accents light. He loved the contrast between light and dark. The rich chocolate brown of his walnut dresser and bed frame seemed nearly black against the pale-gray walls and white sheets. Harmon's curtains and blanket were almost the same dark-blue hue. The look was simple, and he didn't have much in the way of embellishments. He was usually the only one in the space, so decorating it seemed unnecessary. When he had sufficiently stretched, he made his way out onto his preferred running route.

The sky was blue, but the clouds looked like they could be on fire. The setting sun created a glow on their underside. Getting out of his condo was one of the best ways to remind himself that there was more to life, things far bigger than him, things that—no matter what happened to him—would continue to occur. It was both sobering and depressing.

The burn in his muscles eased the ache in his chest. He'd hated the look on Skylar's face when he'd ended things between them before it really had a chance to grow into anything more than a smoldering ember. But he couldn't be selfish and fire her to pursue a relationship. They wouldn't have stood a chance together after that. The one thing that kept burrowing into his thoughts was why she hadn't felt comfortable to tell him what was going on for her. She'd never once mentioned the diner's closure. Heck, he had been so busy and consumed by all the drama of his work life, he hadn't noticed she wasn't working—or that she was texting him back right away.

This could be proof of what I can't give her. Attention. Presence.

By the time it felt like his legs couldn't carry him any farther, all traces of the sun had vanished from the sky. The air had cooled, and his lungs greedily took in each breath. The clouds were no longer visible in the absence of the sun and moon. Watching all the good vanishing around him broke him. Again.

Chapter Twenty-Two

SKYLAR

The strange tension between her and Harmon at work ate away at her as she drove to the office. Anxiety plagued her every morning. When she got out of bed, it nearly made her physically ill. Almost ten days had passed since she'd started working for him. And every morning, much like this one, she worried that today would be the day he said he couldn't work with her, that she would have to find a new job.

In her mind, she relentlessly practiced the conversation where she would beg him to let her continue working until she found a new job. It was emotionally and physically draining. When she got home in the evenings, she could barely stay awake past dinner. Zelda was starting to worry and seemed to check on her far too regularly. Skylar entered the office building just as her phone began to vibrate in her pocket.

"Hey, Z, what's up?"

"Morning," Zelda mumbled. She wasn't usually awake so early in the morning. Her job allowed her to work from home some days. When the cases were via virtual hearings, she could stay home and attend the meetings online. Most mornings, she stayed in bed later than most people who worked a nine-to-five.

"Are you all right? It's a bit early for you to be calling."

"I just remembered something, and it woke me up out of a dead sleep. Not fully awake, though, so I'll go back to sleep after this."

It was barely before seven. Skylar liked getting to the office early, and Harmon hadn't told her not to. Yet. Skylar smiled as she unlocked the glass door leading to the sitting area outside of Harmon's office, which also housed her desk and one small armchair against the entry wall, and directly across from her desk was their bathroom. To the right of her desk was Harmon's office, separated by a frosted-glass door. "Okay," Skylar said, dragging out the word.

"Would you be able to stop by the pharmacy on your way home?"

"Sure. What do you need?"

There was a strangely long pause. "Now, don't freak out."

Well, if there was anything that could ratchet up Skylar's anxiety a few more notches, it was someone telling her not to panic, "freak out," or any other variation of telling her to stay calm. It was like telling someone to relax when they were about to get a shot. Or not to touch a wall because the paint was still wet. They had to test it. Anytime a person was told not to do something, it was almost as if their common sense vanished and their curiosity and anxiety took control. So Skylar's already-serrated nerves were fraying at their brittle tips.

Zelda let out a long sigh. "I should have waited until later to call you, but I didn't want to forget."

Frazzled, Skylar dropped her keys and handbag onto her desk. "Damn it, Z, just spit it out." Her hands were clammy, her heart raced, and her breathing was ragged. *Is Zelda seriously ill? Did she run out of her refills for her inhaler?*

"I need you to pick up a pregnancy test."

The words were rushed, and Skylar's relief was almost palpable.

She laughed humorlessly as she dropped into her chair just as Harmon made his way down the hall with Naudia. They walked side by side drinking their coffees. Jealousy rose inside her, replacing her earlier panic.

"Don't scare me like that. I thought you were terminal or something. Also, I didn't even know you had a boyfriend."

Another long pause.

"Well, I mean you don't have to have a boyfriend, I guess. I'm not trying to make you feel bad. I think this is all coming out wrong..."

"Skylar, are you sitting down?"

"Yes."

"The test isn't for me," Zelda said as Harmon opened the glass door and Naudia continued past, presumably to her office, waving at Skylar as she went. "It's for you."

Skylar's eyes jumped to Harmon as her breath hitched. "What did you just say?"

He must have sensed her trepidation because his steps faltered. He paused by the corner of her desk.

"The way you've been so nauseous and tired... Also, our cycles are usually synced. I finished my period over a week ago."

Skylar grabbed the small desk calendar and began studying the dates as she chanted, "No. No-no-no," in rapid succession.

"Damn. I'm sorry. I knew I should have said something to you in person. I just... I've been meaning to talk to you about it, but every night, you go to bed right after dinner..."

Zelda's voice became white noise as Skylar failed to understand anything she said. The numbers on the calendar looked as if they were floating on the white background. Blinking a few times, she tried to force the dates into focus.

"Skylar!" Harmon snapped. She'd forgotten he was standing at her desk.

"Z, I've gotta go."

"Skylar, just come home early. Tell Harmon you're not feeling well. Get a test on your way."

"Z, I said I have to go. I'll see you tonight, when I get *done* with work." It felt as if every emotion were building up inside her—anger at Zelda for saying something like this to her so early in the morning, fear of the possibility she might be right, anxiety over not knowing. And a small sliver of joy at the possibility. Lastly, confusion at how that could be possible. She couldn't remember when she'd had her last period. And unfortunately, it wasn't rare for her to skip a month.

She blinked rapidly as she hung up her phone, not listening to Zelda's goodbye.

"Skylar," Harmon snapped again, but this time, he was kneeling on the floor by her feet, trying to force himself into her line of sight. "What's going on?"

She shook her head. With her hands still clammy, she clasped them in her lap. She couldn't tell him. Their working relationship was already rocky as hell. *Now what can I say? "Well, you know, I might be pregnant with either your baby or some insane asshole's who I hooked up with at a club about two and a half months ago."*

Before she could get a single word out of her mouth, she was racing for the bathroom. She barely made it through the door before she was throwing up her entire breakfast. Warm hands rubbed slow, calming circles on her back.

Oh, god, Harmon just witnessed me puking up my guts.

He gathered her hair into one hand to keep it out of the way as she continued to retch. In her eyes, this couldn't get much worse.

When she finally stopped, he released her hair but continued his calming touch. "Can I get you some water?"

"Please," she croaked as tears streamed down her face. The exact reason for the tears was a mystery. Shame. Fear. Fatigue. It could have been any of them.

When Harmon left to fetch the water, she rose to her feet. She hadn't even noticed she'd sat down. The room was silent. The only sound came from the clock just outside the bathroom door.

Turning on the faucet, she splashed cold water on her face and rinsed her mouth. By the time Harmon returned, she had just finished patting her face dry.

"Sorry, Benji was at the cooler filling that damn gallon-size water bottle he carries around."

She gave Harmon a feeble smile as she accepted the disposable cup. "Thanks."

"You're welcome. Do you want to lie down? I have that love seat in my office."

She hesitated. After tossing her cookies in such an elegant way, it would be the perfect moment to go home. Then again, if she was pregnant, she couldn't afford to miss work. She would need to save up as much money as she could to prepare.

"Just for a moment," she said at the same time as Harmon said, "Or I can drive you home." The concern in his eyes was going to shred every bit of dignity she had left.

"I'll just lie down. If I don't feel better in a few minutes, I'll go home."

Harmon nodded and placed his hand on her lower back, leading her into his office and over to the dull beige velvet love seat with matching throw pillows on each end. "Sorry, I bought it more for decoration than anything. I'm afraid it's not very comfortable."

She held up a hand to stop his rambling. "I'm sure it will be fine."

As she lay down, she found it was stiff and smelled as if it had just been dropped off from the store. He wasn't kidding about it being purely for decoration. She was far from caring; her head pounded with all her mixed emotions. Closing her eyes, she told herself she would just rest for a few minutes, then she would get up and get some work done.

A light brush along her arm woke her from her nap, and it took her blinking a few times to remember where she was. When the room came into focus, Harmon was kneeling in front of her again.

"Why don't I take you home? You've been sleeping for nearly four hours, and it's lunchtime anyway." His breath was warm on her face, and it smelled of spearmint.

It was unfair how put together he could be when she was constantly falling apart. She probably smelled of bad milk and old eggs.

She shot up to a sitting position. "I what? I just meant to close my eyes for five minutes. I can't believe I fell asleep. Why did you let me fall asleep?" Her tone was harsh and accusatory, as she wondered if she was headed for a constant state of embarrassment. Skylar rubbed her hands over her face. "I am actually feeling much better."

Harmon remained kneeling in his black slacks and white button-down. He'd taken off his jacket and wore suspenders today. Why that seemed so enticing, she wasn't sure, but the man had just cranked up her hot-ometer about five paces. She wanted to groan, and she must have let it slip out if his quirked brow was any indication.

It was so unfair. She just wanted to get her life together, and here she was looking like a fool again. *It might be about to get worse, Skylar,* she reminded herself.

"You all right?" Harmon brushed some of her hair out of her face.

Damn this man, he was making it nearly impossible not to throw herself at him. On the bright side, her office was the only one with glass walls. Harmon had real walls, and she didn't have to worry about anyone seeing the intimacy of their moment. It would take next to nothing for her to lean forward and bring their lips together. She inched forward.

Harmon closed his eyes and sighed. "Skylar."

Her name was a whispered plea, whether to stop her or continue, she wasn't sure. When he opened his eyes again, he took her face in his hands, but it wasn't to pull her to him. It was to halt her progress, and sadness settled in her middle at the realization.

"Skylar, I want to comfort you. But this is all so complicated. I can't date someone I'm working with, especially not someone working *for* me."

She nodded, but the rejection still stung. Essentially, if she wanted the man, she had to give up the job. Sitting up straight, she pressed her back into the love seat. "I'm sorry. You're right." She swallowed hard as she tried to blink back the tears stinging the back of her eyes.

Harmon shook his head. "Goddamn this is ridiculous." He rubbed a hand down his perfectly shaved face.

His actions did nothing to dissuade the desire building inside her.

"I think it's pretty obvious I wanted to date you when I showed up at your work a few weeks ago. But you working here, it complicates things."

"Is there a policy against employees dating?"

"Well, no, but…" He shook his head and stood, extending his hand to help her up. "Let's go get some lunch and talk about it a more."

With few other options, she followed him from the building and got into the passenger seat of his car, but not before noticing the blacked-out SUV. As if to test her, Skylar's phone vibrated in her purse. The pressure behind her eyes dropped into her throat as she struggled to swallow.

CJ's text was simple yet set a ripple of fear skittering through her.

CJ: *I thought I told you not to date him.*

Skylar: *We're working together now, just getting lunch.*

Chapter Twenty-Three

HARMON

As they pulled away from the office building, he couldn't help but notice a stiffness in Skylar's posture that hadn't been there before. It was amazing how one could become so attuned to the people they spent time with. Regardless of how long they'd known one another. He was hyperaware of the little nuances and changes to people's behavior. Now, he just needed to figure out what had caused the shift.

Skylar leaned forward, almost as if to adjust her pants, but her gaze focused on the side-view mirror. An obnoxiously dark SUV pulled out behind them. It looked like the one that had been outside her apartment when he'd dropped her off a few weeks ago. It could be a coincidence, but based on the way her eyes locked on the mirror, his gut told him it wasn't.

"Skylar," he hedged gently, trying not to spook her more than she already was. "Is everything okay?"

In the periphery of his vision, he saw her sit up straighter as she cleared her throat. "Yeah, just tired."

If he had a dollar for every time a woman had told him she was "just tired" when really she felt like her world was caving in on her, he could afford to buy their entire state. He would probably still be married. He may even have a kid. The last thought twisted like a dagger in his gut.

He shook his head. None of those thoughts were helpful. He wanted to find a way to ask her without pressing too hard. But first he wanted to get this SUV off his ass. They were definitely being followed. The realization made the hairs on the back of his neck stand on end.

Skylar's phone buzzed. They stopped at a red light, so he took a moment to watch her. She leaned forward, looking in the mirror again. Then she typed out a message. It went off again almost immediately, and she began to shake. Their light turned green before he had time to question her.

"Where are we going for lunch?" she asked, her hands poised over the keypad of her phone.

"Anywhere you want." His grip tightened on the steering wheel.

"I'm actually not hungry. Can we just go back to the office?"

His fingers were nearly numb from gripping the wheel so tightly. "Sure" was all he could muster, and he all but growled it at her. Something was wrong, and it had to do with that asshole behind them. He was willing to bet his job that was who kept texting her. As he turned to circle the block to their right, he saw his opportunity.

The light was already yellow. He pressed the accelerator and sped through just after the light turned red and traffic began moving from the other side. Their tail was stalled long enough for Harmon to turn down a lesser-known side street then stop at a small convenience store he'd discovered when he'd mistakenly turned down this particular street a few years ago. Their deli had some of the best sandwiches and pizzas he'd ever tried.

"I know someone was following us, and I am almost certain you know exactly who it is." With that, he got out of the car and headed into the store. He could feel himself approaching that edge, the one that would drop him into a rage he didn't want to unleash. He'd left the car running. Part of him wondered if both the car and the woman would be there when he returned.

"Mr. Westerly," Mr. Hipton said from the behind the counter. He was an older gentleman who had inherited the store from his family nearly twenty years prior. He didn't have any surviving family and stuck to strict formalities.

"Afternoon, Mr. Hipton."

The man nodded then indicated the pizza case with questioning eyes.

"Can I get two of your turkey subs?" Harmon had picked them up for himself and Skylar on multiple occasions over the last week. It was strange how easy it had been to integrate her into his life. It had become a habit to let her know where he was going for lunch and ask if she wanted anything. He couldn't recall ever doing so for Mandy. Then again, she hadn't given him the warm and fuzzies.

"You got it," the older man said, the lights glaring off the top of his balding head.

Harmon took a step back so he could see through the glass to his car. It was still there. That was a plus. As he watched Skylar fidget, his anger dissipated. He needed to cut her some slack. She was clearly going through a lot. He let out a long breath as he tried to make himself take a step back from his insecurities and the fears he kept locked away.

"Is she the one you've been bringing those extra sandwiches to?"

Harmon nodded and smiled.

Mr. Hipton nodded. "Don't be like me."

Harmon tipped his head in question.

"The way you stormed in here, the fact that you've been getting her meals—which you've never ordered more than one of anything before—and since you keep looking out at her, I can see you care."

"I do. It's just... complicated." That was the word of the day for him, apparently. He would need to look up a few synonyms.

Mr. Hipton nodded again. "Okay, I'll uncomplicate things for you." The older man held up a finger to halt the arguments on the tip of Harmon's tongue. "Do you like her?"

"Well, yes. Bu—"

That wrinkled hand shot up again as he held up two fingers. "Does she make your days more enjoyable?"

That question gave Harmon pause. Sure, she made his days easier. She did her job eons better than any other assistant he'd had. But even before she had become an employee, he found that she was easy to talk to, easy to spend time with. She was quirky, sassy, and intelligent. He looked over his shoulder again to find her looking into the store directly at him, and he was struck in the gut by how beautiful she really was.

"I will take those puppy dog eyes as a yes." Mr. Hipton slapped the two subs on the counter.

The toasted bread and turkey made Harmon's mouth water.

"Don't fudge it up."

Harmon frowned. "I haven't paid yet."

Mr. Hipton shrugged. "Frequent flyer discount."

Arguing with Mr. Hipton was like expecting rain to come for more than a short spurt in their lovely state of Arizona—fruitless.

"Thanks."

"Thank me by taking my advice," he harrumphed as the phone began to ring.

Taking that as his cue to leave, Harmon took the sandwiches from the counter and made his way back out to Skylar. She was checking her phone again when he sat down.

"That took a while."

"No longer than usual. This is where I get our lunches all the time."

She nodded, seeming agitated.

"I'm sorry for what I said before I went in. I know you're hiding something from me, and I was getting annoyed."

"You're annoyed?" She opened her mouth to say something more but then shut it with a resounding snap. "Can we please get back to the office?" She clicked on her phone screen again.

What is it people always say, pick your battles? It wasn't that he wasn't picking this one. It was more that he intended to wait for the appropriate time to strike.

"Sure."

Chapter Twenty-Four

SKYLAR

Skylar spent the rest of the day brooding in silence. When Harmon had evaded CJ and his goon, it had pissed CJ off. The man had demanded to know where they were, and she could honestly say she didn't have a clue. She could have described the building. She could have checked her phone's location or done a multitude of other things. But they just weren't going to happen.

She would respond to CJ to keep him away from Zelda, but she refused to do anything more, even if she was still a little nervous for Zelda. She was working from home that day, and Skylar would text her and check on her. Just as she thought it, her phone buzzed on the desk next to her mouse. CJ's name flashed on the screen.

CJ: *Dinner tonight.*

It wasn't a question. He'd made the consequences of not responding obvious, and she imagined they would be much the same if she refused him.

Skylar: *Where?*

CJ: *I'll pick you up.*

He was more delusional than she remembered if he thought she would willingly get in a car with him. Just planning to meet up with him made her question her sanity. Obviously, it was evacuating her body one cell at a time—or perhaps it was more a mass exodus.

Skylar: *I have some things I need to do. I'll meet you.*

The three little dots appeared and disappeared several times, making her heart beat in an irregular pattern. So engrossed in her anxiety, she nearly jumped out of her chair when Harmon knocked on the corner of her desk to draw her attention.

"Time to go."

That sinking feeling settled into her middle again. She didn't want to admit that he was right to be annoyed with her. She was keeping so much from him. Even if she wanted to tell him, she didn't have a clue where to start. *Where is Zelda when I need her honesty?*

"Right, closing things up now." When she reached for her mouse to close out of her emails, her phone buzzed again. She wanted to shout for CJ to shut up but didn't want to seem even more unstable. Her life was completely out of control—vomiting, a potential pregnancy, a psycho she'd slept with once, and a boss she couldn't have. *What a life I'm living. Everyone else around the world would be jealous.*

CJ: *Surf 'N' Turf at 5:30. That gives you just enough time if you leave now.*

She shook her head, knowing the only way she could get there on time was if she did some heavy speeding.

Skylar: *Fine.*

She rushed to close out of her computer and toss everything into her bag that she needed to take home with her.

Harmon caught her hand. His touch was gentle, just as it had been that morning, but she didn't have time. "Are you okay?"

She nodded. His concern ripped her apart. No one other than Zelda and Lara had cared for her feelings in a long time. And the fact that this man had been nothing but kind to her unleashed an ache in her chest that threatened to burst.

"Dinner plans, gotta go, sorry. Thanks for everything today."

Harmon released her and nodded.

Racing out of the building and jumping into her car, she knew the only place she could make up time was on the highway. As she merged into traffic, she dialed Zelda.

"Hey, Z, sorry, something came up. I'm going to be late tonight." She was afraid to tell Zelda exactly where she was headed, but she had to work out whatever CJ wanted from her. Why he wanted to go to Phoenix for dinner was another issue altogether.

"Harmon can't just take care of it on his own?"

Skylar swallowed around the discomfort lodging in her throat. "This isn't work related."

"Okay... Do you want to tell me what it is related to? Because now you're making me nervous."

"CJ." It was all she could get out. She had no other information to give, and speculating would be plain dangerous.

Zelda gave a long, measured pause before speaking again. "Whatever it is, I don't think it's a good idea. I told you how he acted in court, never mind the way his wife behaved."

"I know. I have to try and get him off my back, and I don't think ignoring him will do the trick... Just let me try this."

"Have you thought about calling the police?"

Skylar nodded as she accelerated. "I have, but just think about who he is. The connections he and his family have... Plus I don't have proof."

Zelda sounded like a raging lion. "Mm... I'll run to the pharmacy then grab some takeout for dinner." There was another odd pause. "What time do you think you'll be back?"

"Around nine?"

"Damn, you've been passing out by seven lately. Where are you going? I don't want you falling asleep behind the wheel."

Thanks, Z. More to worry about.

***

She pulled into the parking lot of Surf 'N' Turf three minutes early. She'd never been so nervous.

Skylar: *Just arrived at Surf 'N' Turf in Phoenix.*

After texting Zelda their dinner location, just in case they needed to establish a timeline, she hovered over the text thread with Harmon. Part of her wished she'd come clean to him about their lunch break companion. The part of her trying to temper the amount of crazy he got exposed to was getting overwhelmed. Too many people seemed to want to make her life more difficult lately.

Part of her had hoped he would text her, demanding to know who had been following them earlier. It was disgusting how she wanted his concern for her to build to a point that he couldn't stand being away from her. He did care. She knew he did. But no message came in the two minutes it took her to gather the courage to head inside. After what felt like an eternity, she made her way to the front door and checked her phone one last time before tucking it into her purse and trudging into the restaurant.

Pushing through the heavy black doors, she was relieved to see how busy the restaurant was. If she had to meet this psycho, she wanted to do it in a public place. She didn't recognize any faces, which was both terrifying and comforting.

The hostess smiled at her as she stepped across the threshold. "Good evening, do you have a reservation?"

"I'm meeting," she paused and cleared her throat, "CJ."

The woman in a black button-down with the restaurant's S&T logo on her chest checked her list. Everything in this place was black—even the exposed pipes along the black ceiling. The walls were made of what looked like cedar shakes.

"Could it be under another name?" the hostess asked.

"Oh, sorry, his full name is Cannon Adams or just Adams maybe?" Nerves turned her palms clammy, and her chest ached.

The hostess looked at her list then smiled. "Ah, here we are. Your party is already waiting. Follow me."

Already waiting. Two words, and Skylar's world seemed to shrink down to the space between her eyes. It was hard to register what she passed as they walked. She was glad she'd stayed in her work attire; otherwise, she would have been vastly underdressed in her usual after-work outfit of sweats and a T-shirt. They weaved around tables with varying numbers of people. It was as if all their faces were missing—she couldn't make out a single feature. On the back wall of the restaurant was a large bar that spanned almost the entire length of the space, but it was all a blur. It ended at a small wall where she assumed the bathrooms would be.

"Here you are," the woman said with another of her smiles—or perhaps she'd never stopped.

Skylar squared her shoulders and brought her gaze up to meet CJ's, only it wasn't CJ at the table. It wasn't even someone she'd met before. Sitting with fingers interlaced and an angry scowl was who, based on the fiery head of hair, Skylar assumed was CJ's wife. It was as if her brain froze for a moment because she just stood there with her mouth open. No words came out. Her muscles had stiffened, and she couldn't move from where she'd stopped.

"Not who you were expecting?" the woman asked, a sinister smile spreading over her features. The bright red of her lipstick clashed with her hair in a way that made her seem just as menacing as her husband.

Then it hit Skylar. She had seen this woman before, outside the Mexican restaurant Harmon had taken her to. "Not at all," Skylar said when her voice finally returned. Still, her body was not entirely sure what she should do, so she remained rooted to the spot just behind what should be her chair.

"My *husband* should be back to pick me up in an hour. That should give us a few minutes to get to know each other before his return."

"And if I don't stay?"

Again, she smiled. "CJ and I are both nightmares, just... different. If you would like to know the kind of hell I can rain down on you, feel free to march back out that door. Just remember the name Grace Snyder if you do. Your fates may end up similar..."

The name was vaguely familiar, but nothing immediately came to mind. The urge to pull her phone out of her pocket and search the internet for the name tempted Skylar. Instead, she pulled out the chair opposite the redhead. "What do you want from me? I don't even know you."

"Perhaps not, but I know your type. You fuck a married man then likely try to extricate funds from him for hush money." Her black nails tapped on the tabletop as she spoke.

She was beautiful, but wore more makeup than Skylar thought she'd worn over her entire life. The woman's clothes were brand name and looked either new or well maintained. Knowing the money CJ's family had, Skylar wouldn't be surprised by either.

"I have no intention of coming after CJ for money. I didn't even know he was married until weeks after I met him," she hissed at the woman across the table.

"What can I get y'all to drink?" The waitress seemed to appear out of nowhere.

Her Southern drawl had Skylar wondering where the waitress was originally from.

Her companion continued the incessant tap of her nails on the table. It put Skylar on edge. The sound, combined with the stress of the situation and the people around her, was almost enough to overstimulate and shut her down.

"I will have the lemon lavender martini," the redhead said.

The waitress smiled and nodded. "And you?" she asked, turning to Skylar.

"Just a lemonade, please." A drink was out of the question when she feared she might be pregnant, and she definitely wanted to keep her wits about her. When the waitress was out of earshot, Skylar looked across the table and demanded what she'd been wanting to know since she arrived. "Who are you?"

"Myra."

"Okay, Myra. Why in the world did you ask me to come out here?"

"Well, I was with CJ this afternoon, more specifically at your office building. I guess you could say I was curious about the bitch that had him tailing her all through town then raging when he lost track of her."

She spoke so calmly, it didn't match the way Zelda had described the woman from a few weeks ago. The cool way she talked about her husband incessantly messaging and following another woman in her presence unnerved Skylar.

"I want nothing to do with your husband."

One of Myra's perfectly plucked eyebrows quirked. "Funny. For someone who doesn't want anything to do with him, you accepted a dinner invitation rather quickly."

"Only because he threatened me if I ever didn't reply to him."

Myra tipped her head as her gaze narrowed on Skylar as if trying to decide whether to trust her words. They remained quiet as their waitress returned to bring them their drinks. Myra let the waitress know they were only staying for drinks.

"I don't care what CJ has threatened you with... I want you to shut down any of his advances next time. He tries to meet up with you, you decline. He shows up at your work, you decline. He calls you?"

"I would be happy to decline the call." The ice in Skylar's tone caught the attention of the couple at the table next to them. "And what am I to do if he comes after me?"

Myra shrugged. "That's not my problem."

Skylar scoffed. "And if I don't *decline*?"

"As I said before, look up the name Grace Snyder. You may decide crossing me isn't worth your time. I'm calm now. Push me, and I won't be the next time we meet." She lifted her glass as if cheersing Skylar just before she downed her drink.

Fear, anger, and brittle frustration brought Skylar shooting to her feet. After tossing a few dollars on the table, she made her way to the door. Myra didn't say another word. Skylar wasn't sure which of them had won this round. But she was almost certain it was not the end of whatever that had been.

***

Skylar wasted no time getting onto the highway to head home after meeting Myra. The woman had to be just as fucked up, if not more so, than her husband. Her brain wouldn't allow the meeting to be pushed from her mind. It was on a constant loop. She couldn't see how she would appease both insane people. By the time she parked outside her apartment, she still didn't have an answer.

Zelda had, indeed, stopped at the pharmacy on her way home. When Zelda handed Skylar the bag, it was as if the test inside weighed more than Skylar. Its implications made her want to vanish into the ground beneath her feet. Sure, she'd assumed she would have children one day. But not today. Not this year.

With a long, slow exhale, she took the bag into her bathroom. She dropped it onto the crowded countertop and told herself she would take the test after she got a glass of water. She was not in a good place mentally. The last thing she wanted to do was take the test when she was already feeling down. If the results were not what she wanted, she would sink deeper into that depression she'd worked so hard for years to claw her way out of.

After retrieving a water from the kitchen and drinking nearly half the bottle, she went back to her bedroom. Instead of heading into the bathroom, she dropped onto her bed.

Her stomach churned at the thought of the test revealing two little pink lines rather than one. But as she thought about it, she realized she wouldn't be too upset either way. That couldn't be right. *How could I even consider being a single mother? What about Zelda?* Their apartment was barely big enough for the two of them.

Her phone pinged with a notification.

Tonya: *I see you're too good to visit our mother around the anniversary of her death... I always knew you were beyond selfish.*

Skylar typed a scathing reply just to delete it. Her sister could spin herself into the victim, no matter the situation. And Skylar wasn't delusional enough to think it would be the day that didn't happen. Their mother had been buried in New Hampshire, and the anniversary had been weeks ago. Tonya couldn't have flown back either. To expect someone to take a flight just to look at a headstone was asinine.

Tonya: *She'd probably still be alive if she never had you.*

Two minutes later, another text arrived.

Tonya: *I hope the guilt eats at you every day.*

Skylar swiped a tear from her eye as she realized what a fool she would look like if she were pregnant. Tonya wasn't wrong; she did blame herself. No matter how many times she'd been told it was not her fault, it didn't sink in, because if it hadn't been for her, her mother wouldn't have been out on that road.

Squeezing her eyes shut, she took a deep breath in through her nose and tried to focus on her surroundings. The apartment smelled of lilacs and warm spring rain, or so Zelda's candle claimed. There was silence other than the steady breaths Skylar released, and the air was still. Once she was calm, she tried to process all that had been brought into her life over the last few months.

"Sky, you good?" Zelda called from what sounded like the living room. She was close but not right outside the door.

"In my room."

Zelda peered in at her. "You take it?" She nodded at the bag on the counter.

Skylar shook her head. "Not yet. Tonya's been texting me."

Zelda groaned, knowing how terrible Skylar's sister could be. "I wish you'd let me block that twat cake."

Skylar burst into laughter, which was better than the tears she wanted to let out. Wiping the tears from her eyes, she released a long, slow breath. When she finished, she propped herself up on her elbows. Zelda retrieved the bag with the test in it from the bathroom, and Skylar accepted it with such care, one might think a bomb were in it, ready to detonate at the slightest shake. Pulling out the box, she flipped it end over end and tapped her finger against the cellophane wrapping. It felt like once she opened it, there was no going back, no playing oblivious to what might be happening.

"What if we wait until the weekend?"

"Sky, you don't need to ask me. I'll be here for you either way—even if I am not very kid friendly."

Skylar snorted a sound that could be construed as "Ya don't say," but Skylar kept the words to herself.

"Buuut," Zelda dragged out the word. "I'm sure any crotch goblins you have will be tolerable. I'll help you in any way I can. And you know Lara would do anything she could too. She's all about babies."

"I should hope so. She's a pediatric nurse."

Zelda waved her off as if that made no difference in how a person might view a child. "So, you'll rain on that stick Saturday morning, and we'll either celebrate with mimosas or by going out to those goblin stores and finding your style."

Skylar couldn't hold back the tears now.

Zelda leaned in and pulled her close. "It will be okay."

"I think I'm crying because I just realized you're right." She shrugged. "Do I just do it now and get it over with?"

"Your call."

Chapter Twenty-Five

HARMON

"Harmon, I swear, if you're calling me to complain again about the fact that you broke up with a woman you have to see every damn day at work, I might reach through this phone and strangle you." Porter wasn't usually one to snap at someone, so either he really was fed up with Harmon's whining, or he was overtired, overstimulated, or just over life. A stomach bug was going through their house, and Verity had also succumbed to the illness. So, that left Porter to run everything by himself.

"Well, it's not really that," Harmon hedged. Yes, he was calling about Skylar, but this time, it was because he was worried about her. It was different from what he'd called Porter about nearly every other day these last few weeks.

"Yup." Porter's tone informed Harmon he didn't believe a word of it. "Are you calling about Skylar?"

"Yes, but—"

"And are you still upset that *you* told her you couldn't be together?"

Harmon groaned in response.

"And do you still wish you could fuck her again?"

"Fuck you, Porter."

"I'm a little tired at the moment, but you're also not my type."

"Ha ha, so clever."

"You better hurry up and fill me in on today's drama, because the vomiting bouts have been coming in waves. You probably have me for another ten minutes before my mop, sponge, or other cleaning supplies and I are needed."

Harmon cringed. "Sorry, man, I didn't realize how bad it was."

Porter made a sound that triggered an image of him shaking his head and waving off his concern. "Just spill. Verity likes to hear the updates."

Harmon shook his head. Verity likely enjoyed hearing about his struggles. "Two things happened today, and I don't know what to do about them."

"Hmm," Porter grunted to show he was listening.

"First, Skylar puked like crazy this morning then napped for nearly four hours."

"She probably has whatever hell germs have been released in our house."

Harmon chuckled. He couldn't help but appreciate the way Porter could make anything into a joke and feel less dramatic than it was—something he and Verity seemed to have in common. That was one of the things Harmon thought made them so good together. Neither seemed to take too much personally.

"If my internal clock is working properly, you've got eight more minutes in your therapy session."

"Okay, okay." Harmon got up from his recliner to pace around his living room. "So when, I woke her up, we went to get lunch. An SUV was tailing us almost the entire way. At first, I thought I was just imagining it, but then I caught Skylar constantly checking her side mirror. She was tracking this guy."

"Huh," Porter supplied thoughtfully. "You asked her who it was?"

"Yeah." Harmon rubbed the back of his neck. "I may have been a dick about it. She wouldn't tell me, and I got a little pissed."

"A little?"

"Well, quite frustrated, but I didn't yell at her. I just got us away from the SUV then left her in the car to get us some lunch."

The other end of the phone line was silent for longer than Harmon liked.

"That is strange," Porter finally admitted. "Do you have any idea who it was?"

"No, but what was worse was that they were waiting in the parking lot at work for her. It was just too coincidental, you know?"

"I do, and I would probably walk her in and out of the building from here—shit—" Porter finished on a shout.

A vast amount of shuffling followed on the other end of the line, and just when Harmon heard what sounded like a dinosaur roaring, the call cut out. Harmon shivered at the thought of dealing with a house full of people with the stomach bug. The amount of vomit one person could expel was insane, never mind four. Harmon checked the text strain between him and Skylar. There was nothing new, but he couldn't help himself.

Harmon: *I hope you're feeling better.*

It was a poor excuse to text her, but good enough as far as he was concerned. Watching the screen, he both hoped more and grew resigned that she wouldn't reply. He fell asleep in his recliner, waiting for a reply. When he awoke at four in the morning, he had a strange crick in his neck, and he swore he was made of crumbling mortar.

"Fuck me," Harmon muttered as he shuffled to the bathroom. A hot shower was all he needed. That would make it better, he tried to assure himself. When he got out, he felt minorly improved. His neck muscles were still tender but not bad.

When he arrived at the office, Skylar was already at her desk. She had dark circles under her eyes and looked to be on the verge of tears. Her expression caused some of that mortar to disintegrate at his feet. She never did reply to his text. It was one of the first things he'd checked when he woke that morning. So, walking through his office this morning, he felt not only out of place but awkward because he wasn't sure what to say to her.

As he came level with the edge of her desk, her green eyes met his, but they were bloodshot and held the weight of demons he wasn't privy to. Yet. He didn't know yet, but he would. Eventually. He hoped.

"Mornin'," she said, dropping her gaze to her keyboard.

"Hey, are you okay?"

Skylar nodded. "I am. I'm just tired. I hardly slept last night."

It was right on the tip of his tongue. The urge to ask her why, to demand to know who their shadow had been the day before. But he couldn't force the words out. He was the one putting a stop to each of their almost intimate moments, and so much more. Instead, he nodded like a fool and continued to his office.

As he worked, he couldn't suppress thoughts about what Porter and Mr. Hipton had not-so-subtly been getting at these past few weeks. He was the only stupid, stubborn person standing in the way of his and, if he was so arrogant as to believe, Skylar's happiness too.

Keeping his office door open wasn't uncommon, but it definitely wasn't his usual way of working, especially after Skylar started. He needed that barrier between them, but that day, he kept it open. After their lunch break the day before and her clear state of sadness, he didn't want to leave her alone. Didn't want her to *feel* alone.

"I have to make a call. I'm just going to step outside," Skylar said.

Checking the time, Harmon wasn't too foolish to ascertain the intentional overlap between her phone call and his next phone meeting. He dipped his chin in acknowledgment. "When you're done, I want to talk with you about yesterday."

Her face paled, but she gave him a small, hesitant smile.

Just as she stepped out of his office, his desk phone rang, and he was soon immersed in the call from hell. Once he finally got off the phone with one of his most pain-in-the-ass clients, he looked up to find Skylar watching him. That nervous undertone still laced her features. It was embedded in the quiver of her lip, the way her brows drew together ever so slightly, and the way her lips pressed into a thin line.

After briefing her on the call he'd just finished, he dove into the real reason he wanted to talk with her.

"So, yesterday. Who was in that SUV?"

Skylar visibly swallowed. "His name is CJ. I went on one date with him several months ago, before we met," she hastened to add. "And he seems to think I shouldn't be seeing anyone else. So, when we went out to lunch together yesterday, he kind of lost his mind."

Harmon's jaw tightened in that familiar well of anger. He hated that some man thought he had the right to tell Skylar who she could spend time with. That after one date, this prick thought he... Harmon stopped that train of thought and took a deep breath.

"Do you want to be with him?" The words tasted bitter and almost hurt to get out.

Before he finished the question, Skylar was shaking her head. "No, the worst part is... a couple of weeks after our date, I found out he's married..." Tears shimmered in her eyes.

Harmon was torn between pulling her close and keeping her at an arm's length.

She must have seen the battle on his face and mistaken his hesitation, because she rushed to add, "I had no idea. If I had known, I never would have... I never would have spent the evening with him."

Harmon stepped forward, pulling her to his chest. She melted into him as fresh tears soaked into his shirt. Before he could consciously make the decision, he was pressing a kiss to the crown of her head. Her hair smelled sweet and floral. He held her until her grip loosened around him. Only then did he allow his hold on her to slacken.

"Are you okay?" he pressed again.

She nodded. "Sorry about your shirt." She grimaced.

Peering down at the sodden fabric, Harmon shrugged. "It's fine. The day is almost over anyway." Before he took another step away from her, he cupped her cheek and swiped his thumb across the smooth skin. Then he dropped his hand to her shoulder and slid it down her arm to her small, delicate hand. Their fingers intertwined for a moment, and he gave her hand a squeeze, then released her.

Chapter Twenty-Six

SKYLAR

Work went by quickly, but not as fast as she would have liked. Any smells flipped her stomach. Her emotions were on a Ferris wheel, sometimes stopping at the top, others at the bottom, releasing all the emotions she usually kept bottled up. It felt like a foreshadowing of what her pregnancy test would reveal when she finally found the nerve to take it. She hadn't lied to Harmon when she'd said she couldn't sleep. The possibility of being pregnant had kept her up all night. She'd gone from not sleeping with anyone for nearly two years, which was why she'd stopped her birth control—*why pay for something I didn't need?*—to having two possible fathers to her potential child.

Watching Harmon as he locked his office door, she knew—given the choice of men she'd slept with in the last two months—she would pick him as her sperm donor. He'd kept his door open that day, when typically, it was shut tight. Whether he'd done it to keep an eye on her or make sure she was all right, she wasn't sure. Either way, she felt comforted by it. Her email pinged with an incoming message, one from a particularly difficult client who had been giving Harmon the runaround for the better part of the afternoon. When he'd ended the call, after hearing his side of things, she'd asked why the client didn't do their own investing if they were going to be so difficult. He'd simply stated, "They don't do anything themselves." Not knowing the people, she'd just nodded.

In her almost two full weeks of employment, she had learned some people called every week, even if the stock market hadn't changed much. Some people preferred to have annual meetings, and of course, a slew of people fell in the middle.

She closed out of her email without viewing the message. She would deal with that one in the morning. The last thing she wanted to do was get into an argument with someone over email. If Harmon couldn't assuage their concerns, the odds of her being able to after only being hired weeks ago was like swimming with crocodiles and thinking they wouldn't bite.

"Ready to head out?" Harmon held out a hand to her.

She hesitated for a handful of awkward seconds before accepting it and standing. They walked from the building in companionable silence. It was comforting not to feel that urge to terminate the quiet.

"Heading home?"

Skylar tilted her head as if it would help her read him. The man was terribly confusing. One moment, he was pushing her away, creating physical and metaphorical distance between them, and the next, he was holding her like she was the most precious thing in the world. So, his continued concern did nothing but increase that confusion.

"Yeah, I don't have much else to do tonight."

Harmon inclined his head. "Let me walk you to your car." The parking lot was near empty, but they fell into step together. The evening air was cool and soothing against her skin. The day had been exhausting, and she felt it more with each step. Harmon seemed to be scanning the parking lot, something she should be doing. After everything that had happened with Myra, she should feel more on edge. The fact that CJ had been waiting at her job only the day before should have been at the forefront of her mind. But all she could think about was getting home and hopefully sleeping the rest of the night away.

As if voicing her thoughts, Harmon said, "The fact that that CJ character showed up yesterday—here—makes me worry for you."

"I think he's done with me anyway." She laughed, but it didn't feel remotely genuine. The words tasted of lies, and from the concern painted across Harmon's face, he didn't believe it. "Anyway, I'll see you in the morning." She turned and got into her car before she allowed herself to do anything foolish, like throw herself at her boss. Because that was becoming more and more tempting, and she'd already embarrassed herself once at work thinking he wanted her. He didn't—she would do well to remember that.

As she drove home, she replayed all the little things he'd done for her that day. He'd gotten her lunch, water, checked on her without prompting. That hug, it was such a simple way to comfort a person, and yet, it felt like so much more. If she were foolish, she could almost think it meant he cared. He was strangely attuned to her, which should be annoying. But it didn't feel smothering or as if he was hovering over her. He was simply letting her know he'd been thinking about her. He tried—which was more than what others had done. She shook her head as she waited at a red light. She needed to stop fantasizing about her boss. He'd made it abundantly clear that they would not be venturing into relationship territory.

After she got home, she started on dinner. Zelda sat close by, chatting about the events of her day. Zelda also kept an eye on Skylar, as if she feared Skylar would fall into a puddle at the stove. Skylar couldn't help but chuckle at her friend's clear concern. The only thing she should be worried about were the onions Skylar was chopping for dinner. They were particularly brutal. Not only because they made her damn eyes water, but also because she absolutely despised them. But Zelda loved onions in her omelets, and breakfast for dinner was on the top of Skylar's list of favorites. Broccoli, spinach, tomato, and cheddar—that was all Skylar needed, while other than the onions, Zelda would no longer allow vegetables within throwing distance of her omelet.

"Heard from that snotty sister of yours since yesterday?"

Skylar shook her head. "Not yet, but she always seems to sneak up on me." She gave a humorless laugh. "She's good at sending painful words my way when I least expect it. Hell, yesterday she was ranting about me not visiting my mom's grave on the anniversary. I doubt Tonya made it back to visit. It's so weird."

Zelda seemed to be studying Skylar's face, but it was hard to tell with tears streaming from her eyes. The damn onion. She should have only chopped what Zelda needed. But no, that wasn't who Skylar was, so now she was dicing an onion that clearly had a vendetta against her, because the damn thing was trying to burn her eyes out.

"Are we still on for this weekend?"

Skylar nodded as she tried to swipe the tears from her eyes with her forearm.

"I was thinking we should start..." The doorbell cut off the last of what Zelda was about to say. "Expecting someone?" Her eyebrows pinched in confusion. They rarely had company, and Zelda knew about CJ and his threats.

Skylar scrambled to find her phone in case he had tried to call. She couldn't find it anywhere. She must have left it at work. Her heart pounding at a near-deadly pace, she took her knife with her to the door. She feared he might have found out about her meeting with his wife the night before. How he would react to that news was a mystery she didn't want solved.

Checking the peephole, she almost dropped to the floor in relief. Standing just outside her door, Harmon raised his hand to knock. Before he could make contact, she swung the door open. A smile chased away the fear that had nearly brought her to her knees.

"Hey, you left your..." Harmon trailed off as his eye dropped to the knife in her hand. "Phone."

"Sorry, I was working on dinner. Do you want to come in?" She hoped he would say no, say it would put them in a compromising position and wouldn't be appropriate because they worked together.

But he didn't. Instead, he smiled, nodded, and stepped through the door, forcing her to take a step back.

"I had to run back into the office and send an email I forgot to send out in the new quarter... You don't care about that... What are you making?" He slid his shoes off as she stood watching him like a fool. It was the first time he'd been inside her apartment.

Skylar turned and scanned the area around them. Her deep clean hadn't lasted. Junk lay stacked on the end table. Her laundry basket sat full in the living room, like usual, and something smelled funny. *Shit.* What she smelled was certainly the sausage beginning to burn in the pan. "Omelets," she called over her shoulder as she scrambled back to the kitchen.

Harmon followed at a leisurely pace.

Zelda, who had been watching their exchange just around the corner of the kitchen, dropped back into her chair at the dining table.

"Will you be joining us for dinner...?" She tipped her head, pretending to be confused about who he could possibly be.

"Harmon," he said, answering her unasked question.

That was Zelda's go-to way of getting information out of people. It seemed to work for her. When people thought they were giving her information she didn't already know, they seemed to take pleasure in anticipating those questions.

"I don't want to impose." His gaze shifted back to Skylar, and she tensed. His searching eyes told her he was waiting for her approval.

"Of course you can stay, if you'd like," she said as she checked the screen of her phone for missed calls or texts. The screen was blessedly blank.

Harmon paused before shifting from the dining area with Zelda to the kitchen with Skylar. Without a word, he picked up the spatula and started stirring the sausage then switched to flipping the bacon.

She hadn't had to ask. The urge to slap herself to make sure she wasn't dreaming surged inside her. It was such a simple thing to do—she didn't need to celebrate his choice. Any decent person should help, so long as it wasn't Zelda. Frowning, she shook her head. She was comparing him to her ex, and that wasn't fair.

"Onion bothering you?" Harmon asked from his place at the stove. Again he was wearing those damn suspenders, and she had no idea why she found them so attractive. It was stupid.

Clearing her throat and turning back to the damn vegetable she hated with a passion, she responded, "No, not really."

Zelda sat at the table watching their exchange. She smiled, batting her eyes at Skylar while Harmon had his back turned. Skylar had half a mind to throw the second half of the onion at Zelda's smug smirk.

Skylar made a face at Zelda then finished chopping the onion. When they had dinner nearly done, Zelda set the table and brought over the condiments. They had a good routine. Skylar made their meals, and Zelda cleaned up afterward.

"So, Harmon, I hear you and Skylar work together."

Skylar narrowed her eyes at her friend. She wasn't sure where Zelda was going with this, but she didn't think he needed the reminder that they worked together, that he was her boss.

"We do..." The way he said it made it clear he was suspicious of her friend.

"Oh my gosh, did I forget to introduce you two?" Skylar dragged one hand down her face.

"Harmon, this is Zelda, Z for short. We've been friends and roommates for a few years."

Harmon smiled at Zelda. "Nice to officially meet you. I've heard lots about you."

Something twinkled in Zelda's eyes, and Skylar wished she could launch herself across the table to prevent Zelda from saying whatever was on the tip of her tongue. "Same, my friend, I have heard *a lot* about you too." She tapped her chin as if deep in thought.

Their dinner went blessedly smooth; nothing too bad came out of Zelda's mouth. The worst of it was Zelda hinting that she didn't think Harmon treated Skylar very well. And there was the sly remark about that being typical for people in Skylar's life. Skylar tried to kick her under the table at that comment—turned out her legs were too short. After that comment, something in Harmon's gaze softened when he looked at Skylar, and it looked too much like pity for her comfort.

Chapter Twenty-Seven

HARMON

It had been a few days since Skylar got sick. She still seemed on edge, but she certainly was better. Twice over the last two days, he'd seen that SUV hovering around her. Whoever this CJ prick was, Harmon wanted to introduce himself. Something about his behavior felt familiar; he just couldn't place it.

Harmon and Skylar fell into an easy rhythm. Lunches were spent together, and they shared small, innocuous touches here and there. The thin thread of control, restraint, or foolishness he'd been holding onto was burning away. Soon, he would have nothing left to hold him back from her.

Skylar knocked on his door and peered in. "I hate to say this, but Anne is on hold for you. I tried to assuage her, but she is convinced something is wrong with her last statement."

Harmon rubbed his hand over his face. If one person could drive him to drink, it would be Anne Sargent. She was a unique kind of pain in his ass. And worse, she was an attorney.

"Thanks, Sky." That, too, had changed; he hadn't made the conscious decision to use the nickname Zelda had for her, but it had stuck in his brain. And there was something perfect about it, as if, with Skylar, his life was full of warmth and broad possibilities.

She gave him a wan smile. He wished he'd kissed her the night he'd brought her phone to her. She and her interesting roommate had been fun company, and he'd enjoyed their banter and antics. As Skylar went back to her desk, he hated himself for admiring the way her gray skirt fell over her soft curves. *Shit.*

When the call rang on his phone, he inwardly cringed as he picked up. "This is Harmon." Keeping to his best customer service voice, he talked Anne down and got her to understand that what she saw as a discrepancy was just a difference in the timing of deposits and the statement. The joys of working with people who always thought they were right.

As soon as he hung up, he went out to Skylar's desk, where a man leaned on the edge of it. The man's back was to Harmon, and he leaned in, his face far too close to hers for Harmon's liking. Before he could make sense of it, that switch flipped, and jealous rage burned inside him. He ate up the distance between himself and this other man in three quick strides. Breaths now coming in ragged, angry pants, it took all his self-control to not grab the man's throat and toss him out of her space. Skylar's eyes shot to his and showed alarm as they widened.

"Yeah, and this is the three of us at Dani's first birthday. She was so sweet," Jeremiah said as he leaned in again, showing Skylar a photo on his phone. His daughter—she'd just had a birthday two weeks ago.

Harmon froze. It was innocent. *You're overreacting, you dickhead. Back off.* Harmon swallowed hard, turned on his heel, and headed back to his office, shutting the door with a resounding click. His brain knew it was nothing to get worked up about, but his heart and adrenaline hadn't gotten the memo. He was still ready to beat the shit out of someone. Hands trembling, he tried to shake them out as he slowed his breathing. "This is madness," he muttered on a huffed breath.

After a few minutes, Skylar peered into his office. Her smile was slow to grace her lips, as if she was unsure if she should be grimacing to commiserate with the Russian roulette results of a conversation with Anne. She likely thought his earlier rage had been about the damn woman. He didn't know how to tell her it had nothing to do with the bitch and everything to do with his, at times, unfettered emotions.

"Lunch?" she asked from her spot in the doorway.

Usually, it was Harmon who asked.

It would be so easy to fall for this woman. And if he were being honest with either of them, he'd probably done so before he left the grocery store the night they met. He swallowed down the urge to break his own rules. The way she bit her bottom lip made the growing voice in the back of his mind say, *Fuck the rules.*

He was surprised to see it was already three; they were usually better about taking lunch at noon. "Damn, it's late."

"Yeah, I was going to say something earlier, but you were on that conference call, and then Anne was calling every few minutes, so I knew if she went to voicemail, she would lose her mind." Skylar cringed.

Harmon ran a hand down over his face. "Shit, Sky."

Skylar gasped, and he dropped his hand, ready to stand and confront what had startled her, until she giggled. Drawing his brows together, he looked at her in question.

"I've never heard you swear at work before, Mr. Perfect. I mean, it took you a couple of weeks, a long meeting, and talking with Miss Crazy to drive you to that point."

Harmon chuckled and shook his head. It also took him getting insanely jealous... "Hey, I cuss," he teased defensively.

She put her hands up, palms out. "I'm just saying it's nice to know you're human. You make mistakes."

He huffed. "You have no idea."

It was Skylar's turn to look confused.

He hadn't meant to say that, but shit, she wasn't wrong. It had been a long day. "Go close up, and we'll get lunch. No sense in coming back for half an hour."

Skylar withdrew from his doorway, her flowy skirt twisting around her thighs as she spun. He nearly groaned at the thought of her thighs being bare against him. Nope. Not a work-appropriate thought. But technically, they were going to lunch, and he clocked out for that, or he would if he weren't paid salary.

When Skylar was ready, and after he'd let everyone know they wouldn't be returning, they walked out together. Their hands brushed as they walked, and neither of them pulled away. As they rounded the building, his hackles rose when he found that damn SUV sitting in their parking lot. Skylar took a big step away from him, giving him an almost pleading look as she veered toward her car. Across the parking lot. When she reached her car, she just stopped. She didn't do anything—she just hovered.

His brain felt like mush as he strode across the parking lot to where she stood frozen, her hand on her door handle.

"Why is he always hovering around you?" Jealousy tinged Harmon's tone.

He watched as Skylar swallowed—hard. It was at that moment he was reminded of how much older he was.

"It's, ah, a bit complicated." She fidgeted under his gaze. She never fidgeted, not even when she screwed something up at work. She'd made it sound like he would leave her alone.

Something sour bubbled in Harmon's gut, about to overflow like the damn sourdough starters his mother kept around their house when he was a kid. It threatened to make a mess everywhere. "Who is he to you? Really?" he asked between clenched teeth. He was beginning to doubt this was the repercussions of a one-night stand.

Skylar's eyes shifted between him and the man he knew without looking was approaching her. "Please, get us out of here. I promise I'll tell you everything. Just get me away from him," she begged.

One curt nod, and he had her hand in his as he virtually dragged her back through the parking lot, careful not to let her bump into anything in her dazed state.

"Skylar!" the other man shouted, anger clear in his voice.

Pulling his keys from his pocket, Harmon pressed them into Skylar's palm and kissed her forehead. "Go get in my car. Lock the doors. I'll be there in a moment."

Her eyes widened. "Don't talk to him, please."

Her request added fire to the already-erupting volcano in his gut. He wouldn't ask the prick anything. He would simply tell him to stay away. The rest was her story to tell.

"Go," he said again.

She swallowed visibly as the other man called her name again. Harmon waited a moment to make sure she listened before he turned around. Harmon nearly stumbled as he recognized the man. If Harmon hadn't just spoken to the spoiled prick's mother, he probably wouldn't have put two and two together. But there, in front of him, was Cannon Adams, one of the worst men he'd ever met. He hadn't seen the man in years, but somehow, he was tied to Skylar.

"Skylar's busy," Harmon called back.

Cannon's jaw tensed. His eye darted to a spot over Harmon's shoulder, and Harmon hoped like hell Skylar had made it to his car. Hands clenched at his sides, Harmon prepared for a fight, but nothing happened. Cannon simply shifted his jaw from side to side and sniffed hard.

God, is he on something? The thought of a drug addict going after Skylar filled Harmon with a fear he didn't know he could feel for another person—not again, anyway.

"You need to leave. Skylar wants nothing to do with you." He wasn't entirely sure that was true, but from the way she'd reacted, it was close enough. *She'd said as much, but then, why does he seem to keep appearing?*

Cannon tipped his head back and let out a cold, calculated laugh. "Call me when Pencil Dick here can't get you off like I can," Cannon called across the lot.

Harmon stood his ground until Cannon got back into the waiting car, then he made his way over to his own. Skylar sat in the passenger seat, her leg bouncing at nearly ninety times a minute.

Harmon dropped into his own seat and sighed. "Skylar, the man following you… is that Cannon Adams? CJ for short?"

She nodded.

"Fuck me," Harmon murmured, running his hand through his hair. He'd known but needed the confirmation.

Skylar's throat bobbed as she struggled to say what was on her mind. "You know him?"

Harmon nodded. "Damn." He wasn't angry—disappointed perhaps. The undertone in his words were too much for even him to decipher. "Sky, you know Malcom and *Anne*?" He emphasized her name since they'd both dealt with her too much that day. "Who are always such a pain in my ass?"

She nodded solemnly.

"CJ is their son. They own that club we went to one night. Well, technically Malcom does. Anne is an attorney and likes to keep that connection under wraps as much as she can. That's why she goes by her maiden name, not her married name. Their son, CJ, or Cannon James, is their greatest pride and disappointment. Malcom has, on more than one occasion, told me how much he screws things up—how much CJ has cost them." Harmon slid his thumbs up and down his suspenders. "They're my biggest client."

"Harmon, I'm sorry. I had no idea who he was to you when I got the job. He just won't go away. I've tried." She bit her bottom lip, hesitating to continue. "He's hell-bent on harassing me." She swallowed hard. "I understand if me working here is too much."

Harmon shook his head before she'd finished her thought. It was as if his mind had finally worked out what his heart had known for weeks, and before he could hold the words back, they spilled out. "Skylar, I don't care if I lose them as a client. For the chance to love you, I would lose it all. I would let them grind my name to a single grain of sand and turn my reputation into nothing but whispers of dust floating in the air." Relief flooded him as the weight of his stubbornness lifted. He hoped it would take away his misery from the past few weeks.

Chapter Twenty-Eight

SKYLAR

Tears flooded her eyes. No one had ever spoken to her so lovingly, and that broke her. Heavy sobs racked her body. Harmon brought her to his chest over the center console. Rubbing soft circles on her back, as he had done many times, he brought her the calm she needed.

When the hiccups subsided, she peered into his eyes. "I thought you couldn't love me. That we couldn't be together."

Harmon shook his head as he ran a hand through his hair, releasing his hold on her. "I know. But if you want to try, we can. We can be professional at work then be ourselves outside of work. I can't stand the idea of some other man being with you. I hate the thought of CJ putting his hands on you. But I do have stuff from my past I need to tell you before you agree to be with me."

She nodded, afraid of where this might go as she wondered if she should bring up her own traumas. She agreed to follow Harmon to his condo to discuss their pasts and potential relationship. She had to fight talking herself out of it before she'd even pulled out of the parking lot. Not for the first time, she wondered if she should have already taken the pregnancy test.

Her desire for Harmon hadn't lessened over the last few weeks. While they were working together, she saw only a slim chance of being able to get over him. So, after what he'd said, she would give him a shot.

She pulled up next to Harmon outside his building. As soon as she parked, she felt numb. Her hands didn't want to move, and prickles covered her entire body. It was not the time for her anxiety to take over. Closing her eyes, she breathed in deeply through her nose and pushed out a calming breath. After a few breaths, she was able to shut off her car, release her seat belt, and get out.

"Are you okay?" Harmon asked, his brows pulled tight together. He stood waiting at the back of her car.

She nodded, afraid her voice would reveal her nerves. This was silly. She wanted to be with Harmon; she wanted to spend time with him and see what they could be together. Harmon held out his free hand. It was such a simple gesture, but she felt the sincerity in his touch. It was as if he knew she needed that reassurance that he was there for her.

When they entered his condo, he excused himself to make them something quick for lunch—or dinner. Part of her wanted to follow him into the kitchen, but a larger part wanted to give herself some breathing room. Turning on the television with the remote Harmon had given her, she was surprised to find it on a game show. She liked trivia, so she left it. Occupying her brain would help. As she set down the remote, she saw one of Harmon's puzzle books, and she couldn't help but smile. She could do this—she could tell him.

Harmon came back with two plates, placed them on the coffee table before her, then disappeared again. Moments later, the floor creaked with his return. He'd brought back a bowl of chips and two bottled waters.

As she picked up her sandwich, she was hyperaware of the bread's texture against her fingers, the smell of the bitter cheddar cheese, and the turkey's seasoning. The desire to calm her anxiety and her inability to do so frustrated her. It didn't matter some days. She couldn't get her heart or the cold sweat that covered her body to recede. Anything could trigger it. It was strange how it worked. If an angry customer yelled at her, she was fine. But if something in her personal life got upended, she was an absolute wreck.

Harmon took a bite of his sandwich, chewed it, then set it down. "I was married once."

The sound of the television dissipated. Before she could ask any of the questions on the tip of her tongue, he continued.

"We got divorced over ten years ago. It ended because of me. We had lost a baby the year before." He uncapped his water and took a long swig, his eyes trained somewhere at their feet.

Guilt churned in her stomach. The fact that she may be carrying his baby and hadn't told him made the nausea hovering in the wings leap back to life—or maybe it was her apprehension.

After he carefully recapped the water, he continued. "Right after we lost the baby, my wife became a shell of a person. She didn't speak unless spoken to, and she didn't seem to enjoy anything she had before. I was sad, too, and I didn't know what to do. So, I tried to push her out of the depression she had fallen into. When she stopped the grief counseling, everything disintegrated. She was released to have another baby, and I thought that would help her. To have something else to look forward to. Because the woman in front of me was not the one I had fallen in love with all those years ago. We began trying again, and it was terrible. She didn't engage at all. She never said no, but she never seemed excited either."

Skylar swallowed hard, watching him speak. Tears stung the back of her eyes and the bridge of her nose, while strangely, a part of her was jealous to think of this woman who had a sweet man doing whatever he thought would fix her—help her. Skylar had never had that.

"I was so tired. I was working, going to school, and trying to help Jackie every day. Then, one night, when I was completely exhausted, she told me she didn't want to try for a baby anymore. Something inside me snapped." He paused looking down at his hands. "I slapped her. I immediately regretted it. I hated the way my skin against hers sounded. My self-hatred was immediate and intense. I was already sick of myself for being so mad at her for not wanting to know what had happened to the baby. She didn't want an autopsy. After I hit her, she ran to the bathroom, and I just leaned back against the fridge and slumped to the floor."

His story was harder to hear than she ever could have imagined. It wasn't her pain to bear, but she could feel Harmon's sadness seeping into her.

"I don't know how long I sat on the floor that night. But I soon realized I hadn't heard anything from Jackie in a while. I pounded on the bathroom door—nothing. I tried turning the handle and realized it was locked. When her silence continued, I broke into the bathroom. I found her on the floor, unconscious, with pill bottles all over the place." His voice cracked, but he didn't stop. "I called 911, but I was afraid they wouldn't get there in time, so I brought her down to my car. She'd lost so much weight since the baby. I couldn't believe how light she felt. I got her to the hospital, and they rushed her to a room. When she woke up, she didn't want to see me. Not that I could blame her. I'd slapped her." His gaze dropped to his hands again as if they were branded to show what a terrible person he was.

"We divorced months later. I have only seen her once since then, and I didn't speak to her, didn't even approach her. I don't think she saw me. We were at the same grocery store where I met you." He paused to flash her a sad smile. "I haven't allowed myself to date anyone since Jackie. I'm... I'm terrified. What if I lose my cool and hit someone else? I couldn't live with myself." He pressed his hands together as if he could squeeze the memories out through his fingertips. "I sent her flowers on the anniversary of the baby's birthday to let her know I wouldn't forget, but she never reached out after I sent them. So, two years ago, I stopped. I tried to call her and tell her I would let her be, but she ignored my call."

Harmon's eyes remained averted, and a moment of silence passed as she considered her response. "Harmon, I won't tell you that you did nothing wrong, because we both know that would be a lie. But do you think it was the stress that led to that situation? Had you ever hit anyone before?"

"I don't know. And no, but I was drinking a lot at that time too. I wasn't a good husband. But I know I get ridiculously jealous of you, and that scares me. I've never been the jealous type. I mean, it's stupid shit I'm jealous over. Just today, when I came out of my office and Jeremiah was at your desk, I saw red. He was standing so close to you." He shook his head.

Skylar put a hand on his leg. "He just wanted to show me pictures from his daughter's birthday party."

Skylar sat in silence for a while. Part of her wondered if this was a sign that they shouldn't be together. *Could it have been an isolated incident?* Pondering all he had told her, she turned to face him. "Regret for a regret?"

Harmon gave a hint of a smile. "I don't want you to feel like you owe me something in return for that story. I just want you to know about me, even the parts of me I wish I could cut from my chest. The ones I want to forget and never see again."

"I want to share something about myself that will give you insight into why I am the person I am. Why I hate talking to my sister or having anything to do with her really. Or talking about my family in general, I guess..."

Harmon just nodded and took one of her hands in his. The touch was as gentle as ever, and she thought back to each time they'd been together. Never once had she felt unsafe with him. Perhaps that spoke more to her foolishness than it did his anger. She still wanted to trust him.

After releasing a long, slow breath, she started, "I was fifteen, and I got my period."

She cringed. She'd forgotten how awkward it could be to talk to a man about these things. But Harmon didn't even flinch. Then again, he was more mature than any of the other men she'd tried to date.

"I always have terrible cramps. And I was in so much pain, I asked my mother to go to the store to get supplies for me. I shouldn't have asked her. It wasn't yet noon, and she'd already started drinking. But my sister was at work, and the pain was so extreme, I could barely stand up straight."

Harmon gave her hand a squeeze.

"The drug store was literally three doors down from our apartment. She could have walked. Instead of going there, she went to the convenience store across town that sold her preferred booze. I don't even remember exactly what that was." Skylar shook her head, and her light hair flitted in front of her eyes. "She got me what I needed and her chosen numbing agent, then when she was leaving the store, for some reason, she walked behind her car to put everything in the trunk. That's what I don't get. No one else was in the car with her. She could have just put it in the passenger seat." Skylar's brows furrowed as she spoke, as if saying it should make everything make sense, but it had been years, and she was no closer to understanding. "While she was behind the car, a young woman was driving down the same street. She was texting and driving and not wearing a seat belt. She veered and sideswiped the back of my mother's car, pinning my mother, then hit the pickup truck parked next to my mom's shitty sedan. My mom was trapped. The girl went through the windshield of her car and into the bed of that truck, and there was little people could do. I'm not sure how it worked, but I guess there was no tailgate. The teenager sustained minor injuries, and my mother died of internal bleeding outside her favorite liquor stop." Skylar shook her head.

"Was the girl charged with anything?"

Skylar gave him a sad half smile. "No, she—"

"That's crazy. She—"

Skylar held up a hand to halt his next words. "She tried to end it all one day. She gave herself severe brain damage. Last I knew, she still couldn't speak, walk, anything a young woman should be able to do. She's only a year older than me."

"Shit," Harmon muttered.

"Part of me wanted to hate her, but I knew that the guilt must have been insurmountable for her to try taking her own life. She tried to relieve the pain over what she'd done, and now she's trapped in a vegetative state. And I have to live with the thought that if I hadn't sent my mom on that errand, they would both be here still. Would the girl have still gotten in that car accident? Yes, but she only sustained minor injuries." Skylar shook as the torment rolled through her every muscle. It was as if she had just received the call again about her mother. Her breaths came in short, labored pants. "Sorry, I try not to get this emotional." Her speech was choppy from her ragged breaths.

"Skylar." Harmon's voice was a caress over the scars she'd borne for far too long. "Look at me." He tipped her chin up to force her gaze to his. The touch was gentle and filled with so much tenderness and love that she had to choke back a sob. "I would think something was wrong if you didn't get emotional about such a traumatic event. But—and I know this will be hard—I don't think you should blame yourself. How could you know your mother would go to that particular store? How could you have known that teenager would be texting and driving?"

She shrugged; nothing in her arsenal could bring down his words. She knew in the back of her mind that it was not her fault. But also sitting in that small corner was her sister's constant reminders, the hurtful words that never strayed far from her mind. All the what-ifs that would plague her till her last breath sat there in the silence, waiting for their moment to come forward.

"My sister blames me."

CHAPTER TWENTY-NINE

HARMON

THEY FINISHED THEIR EXTREMELY late lunch in virtual silence. Every now and then, one of them would shout out the answer to the trivia question posed on the show.

Harmon could go into a boardroom and push for companies he thought people should invest in, talk frustrated investors off the edge when they saw a dip in the stock market, but getting up the courage to ask Skylar if she wanted to give their relationship a real shot now that she knew about his past was nearly impossible. His biggest fear and shame sat on the couch in the small space between them.

When the chip bowl was empty, he took it to the kitchen, a good excuse to remove himself from her alluring presence. He rolled his shoulders then released a long, slow breath, the best way he could think of to mentally prepare himself for the possible rejection waiting in the living room.

When he reentered the room, he found it empty. His breathing hitched as he rounded the couch, and his steps faltered when he realized Skylar had lain down, not left. She was sleeping. He'd never seen someone fall asleep so quickly. Taking a seat in his recliner, he split his attention between Skylar and the television as more of his favorite shows aired. Almost an hour and a half later, Skylar rolled over, opened her eyes, and bolted into a sitting position. The room was fairly dark, and the evening sun had begun to set.

"Hey sleepyhead," he said, unable to keep the laughter out of his voice.

Using her palms, she rubbed her eyes. "I am so sorry. And slightly mortified that I just passed out like that. How long was I asleep?" she asked around a yawn.

"A little over an hour."

"My word, why didn't you wake me?"

He shrugged. "You've been quite tired lately, so I didn't want to take that away from you. Plus, you looked so peaceful and sweet."

She groaned as she dropped her head forward, and she braced herself on her elbows.

"Come here." Harmon curled an index finger at her.

She arched an eyebrow.

He chuckled lightly. "Get over here. There is no need to be embarrassed."

With a sigh, she rose from the couch and picked her way around the coffee table and over to where he sat in the wide recliner. Taking her hand, he pulled her down to sit next to him. They were touching from knee to shoulder, and he loved each point of contact. As he leaned the chair back, she shifted onto her side, and he tucked her under his arm. With his other hand, he traced lazy lines up and down her arm.

"I'm sure what I told you earlier was a lot to absorb. I don't want to push you into an answer, but would you want to give whatever this is between us a chance, or would you rather think about it?"

Skylar nodded, but he wasn't sure what she was agreeing to. Considering she was lying with him, he knew it was either an agreement to date or to think about it.

"I think I want to try," she whispered.

Harmon let out a long, slow breath.

"But, Harmon?"

"Yes?"

"I understand what happened between you and your ex-wife happened over a decade ago, but I won't be able to stay if you ever put your hands on me like that."

His heart stuttered in his chest. "I would never expect you to. And I wouldn't want you to. The baby we lost was a little girl, and had she survived—" His voice broke. Some things never got easier. "I would never have wanted her to be with someone who would hit her. I meant it when I said I have been terrified of dating anyone else, with the fear of losing control again. So, I want you to know I don't ever want to be that man. I will do everything in my power to *never* be that man again."

He'd never told anyone other than Porter the full story of that night. To his knowledge, Jackie had never told anyone either. On multiple occasions, Harmon had thought her brother, Tony, knew. He had been the one to tell Harmon he wasn't wanted in Jackie's hospital room. Then and now, he felt so raw, split wide open, and he worried that the one woman he might be interested in could rip out his intestines.

"I'm sorry, by the way. For your loss."

Harmon pressed a kiss to the top of Skylar's head. "Thank you."

They sat like that for several more hours, now watching television shows from the nineties that still aired on several channels. He couldn't help but think of them as classics.

Skylar burst into a fit of giggles while one show played. Nothing particularly funny had happened, so Harmon was a bit confused by her outburst.

"Are you okay?"

Still, she giggled. "I think I know now why you wear suspenders." She pointed to the television, where Steve Urkel adjusted his suspender straps.

"Fuck you." Harmon chuckled, and as if it was always meant to be, he leaned down and pressed another kiss to Skylar's forehead. "I like my suspenders. I actually started wearing them while I was really young. My grandfather always wore them, and when I was little, I wanted to be just like him." He shrugged. "I stopped for a while in high school and college because people thought they were weird, and I just wanted to fit in. You know? But once I was working again, I realized how much I hated wearing belts and brought back the suspenders."

Skylar shifted to look up at him, her green eyes pulling him in. "I want to see a little Harmon wearing suspenders! I bet you were adorable."

He shook his head, smiling at her easy excitement. "One day," he promised.

Shifting, he pressed a kiss to her lips as one hand snaked up over her side. "I've missed you like this."

"Me too," she whispered as she pressed her ass against his quickly growing erection.

"I don't just mean the sex, Sky. I mean all of it—when you're relaxed like this, when we spend time together without feeling like—I don't know. I'm not good at putting my emotions into words. I just mean, it feels easy when it's just the two of us and we don't have to worry about anyone else, you know? We get to just be us."

"I think you're better at explaining your emotions than you think." Skylar twisted to meet his gaze. "I may need a little work in that department, though." She shrugged.

Harmon wondered if there was more to that statement than she was letting on.

Before he could ask, her ass ground against him. He gripped her hip and pulled her tight against him. This was different than their last times together. It felt rawer, like there was a deeper connection between them this time.

"You drive me crazy," Harmon groaned into her ear, caught up in the friction building through their clothes.

Skylar giggled, and it was so sweet and borderline innocent. Breaking out of his embrace, she slid to the floor and stripped out of the damn skirt he had been fantasizing about stripping off her for far too long. When it pooled around her ankles, she was left wearing lacey panties that gave little glimpses of her perfect flesh beneath.

"Darling, you kill me." He had to adjust himself to get up out of his chair.

Just the way they undressed in front of one another was different this time. It wasn't a race. They watched one another as they peeled off each article of clothing. And when they stood bare in front of one another, it was with a better understanding. They'd both been damaged by the regrets of their pasts, but together, they would get through it.

They walked toward one another with measured steps, and when they were finally close enough, Harmon threaded his fingers through her hair. The silky strands were tantalizing against his fingers, the way her soft flesh molded to his. Their lips met in an unhurried kiss, deepening at an even pace.

Harmon pulled Skylar back to his recliner. When he sat and looked up at her, she quirked a brow as if to ask if the chair could survive. She hesitated only a moment longer. She was stunning, and Harmon had a new appreciation for her. All her supple curves called for him to caress them. Her breasts teased him from where she stood, just out of reach.

"Come on." He crooked a finger at her, beckoning her to join him.

She straddled him, and he could hardly hold back to keep the tempo they'd set. Starting at her knees, he slid his hands up her soft, smooth flesh. When he reached the apex of her thighs, she groaned before he touched her center. And when he pressed a finger to her clit, she gave a breathy moan. His dick stood at attention, but she kept herself just far enough away.

With a finger swirling around her entrance, he took one breast in his other hand. She shifted to let him take her peak into his mouth. She fluttered around his finger in time with the flicks of his tongue.

"Oh my god, they're so sensitive." Skylar writhed above him.

Leaning forward, she pressed her lips to his and wrapped a hand around his cock. He let his head fall back against the chair. Skylar smirked at him in triumph. Her grip was tight and rhythmic. The way she twisted her fist as she moved brought him to the edge too quickly. With another deep kiss, she brought him to her entrance.

"Sky, I'm not..." His next words died on his lips as she encased him. The rawness of being bare together in every sense of the word was going to send him over the edge. Each rotation of her hips created that perfect friction. Taking her other breast in hand, he gave that one the same attention as the first as she rode him. Her pussy clenched, and her whimpers of pleasure made his orgasm build along his spine.

"I'm coming," she said, and it took everything in him to keep from spilling inside of her.

"I am so goddamn close, Sky."

Her eyes widened at his words. Pulling up off him, she pumped him a few times, and he came all over his stomach and her small fist.

Chapter Thirty

SKYLAR

The obnoxious rapping on her bedroom door caused Skylar to roll and nearly fall out of bed. "What?" she half groaned, half shouted.

"Girl, it's Saturday. I've heard the best time to get an accurate test result is to take it first thing in the morning." Zelda, the woman who hardly got out of bed on time for work, was up at the ass crack of dawn, forcing Skylar to pry her eyes open.

At those words, Skylar's heart began to race. "Okay, I'm getting up."

Her feet had just hit the floor when her bedroom door flew open, and Zelda shoved a box into her chest before dropping onto her bed.

"Please, make yourself comfortable."

"I am. Now go." She shooed Skylar toward the bathroom.

"This was in my bathroom last I knew... Why do you have it?"

Zelda shrugged. "I was doing research."

Skylar didn't even want to ask as she released a calming breath. She walked to the bathroom as if heading for the gallows. Unwrapping the plastic, she took the time to carefully read the instructions. As she read, she was surprised Zelda didn't shout questions or demands through the closed door.

After finding that peeing on a small stick was more difficult than it sounded, Skylar washed her hands and dropped onto the bed next to Zelda. It said to pee into a cup, but she figured peeing directly on the stick would be good enough.

"How long do we have to wait?"

Zelda was nearly vibrating with excitement or anticipation, while Skylar felt like she couldn't pull enough oxygen into her lungs.

"Three minutes. Shouldn't you already know that with all the *research* you've done?"

Zelda checked the time then nodded. "I was only researching if that was a good brand. I got worried after I bought it."

Skylar scoffed. "What were you going to do—return it?"

Zeldra shrugged, and they seemed to have nothing else to talk about.

Three minutes had never felt so long, though she had a very strong feeling she already knew what the test would say. The desire to remain ignorant was tempting, but likely not the safest. *Where would I even put a baby?* As her eyes roamed her bedroom, she took stock of everything that could be moved, consolidated, or eliminated. There wasn't much in her closet. Perhaps she could hang more of her clothes and put the baby's stuff in her dresser. It sounded silly to hang tiny clothes. Then there was the question of the old papasan chair that sat in the corner and served no purpose other than as a catchall. That could—would need to—be replaced with a crib. Her heart raced a little faster as she wondered where she would put all the diapers a baby would need. This was not a large enough apartment for a baby.

"Time's up," Zelda announced, looking at Skylar expectantly.

If her heart weren't already tempting fate by beating vastly faster than it should, Skylar might worry she was dead, with how numb the rest of her body felt. When Skylar didn't move, Zelda offered to check the test.

"It's okay. I'll check it." As she walked to the bathroom, Skylar knew this would be the defining moment of her adult life. Her feet were heavy as she barely shuffled to the bathroom. The results stood out against the result window's white background. Tears pricked the corners of her eyes. "It's positive," she whispered.

Zelda jumped up from the bed and raced to Skylar's side. "It'll be okay. We'll figure it out." Zelda rubbed Skylar's arms.

"You're acting like the father."

Zelda dropped her head back and laughed. "Well, if it's CJ's, I don't think he'll be at the top of the list of people offering to help. If it's Harmon's, that will put a strain on your already-tenuous working relationship. And in the end, people say it takes a village, right?"

Skylar's tears ramped up as Zelda's support sank in. "I guess I need to make a doctor's appointment." She hadn't told Zelda just yet that she and Harmon were trying a relationship again.

Zelda nodded. "Do you want to call Lara and have a little dinner party? I know she would be all over celebrating."

"I think I want to wait until I know who the father is. I feel like he should be the next person to know."

Zelda nodded. "Will you tell your sister?"

The idea of telling Tonya made Skylar's stomach pinch painfully. "I don't think so. She isn't exactly the loving type. But... we're all we have for blood relations. I would want to know if I was going to be an aunt. Ugh. I wish we had a better relationship."

Zelda tipped her head from side to side as she considered it. "I know you're probably right. You should tell her at some point. Just don't rush it. I don't want her to be a bitch."

With Skylar's promise to think about it, Zelda left to give her a few minutes to think about everything. Skylar dropped onto the lid of the toilet and cradled the test in her hands. The beginning of a new life—for more than just herself. Something deep inside her hoped beyond all else that the baby was Harmon's, but for the life of her, she couldn't remember when her last period had been. The last thing she wanted was to have to reach out to CJ. A lifelong connection to the man would be a worst-case scenario.

As she looked at the two lines, she imagined herself holding a baby then watching a toddler race through a park. The idea of a child to share her life with warmed her heart. It was doable. She would find a way. If she had to get a second job until the baby arrived to afford everything, she would do what needed to be done. Then, hopefully the savings would help with maternity leave and getting all the little things he or she would need.

Just as she sat back down on her bed, her phone went off with a text notification.

Harmon: *Good morning. Dinner tonight?*

A smile tugged at her lips. She needed to tread carefully. This would be delicate no matter what she ended up telling him. He clearly wanted kids, but probably not with his assistant-slash-new-girlfriend. Hell, they'd only known each other a couple of months.

Skylar: *Love to.*

Harmon: *I'll pick you up at 5? Go to Antonio's?*

Skylar: *Sounds good.*

Skylar spent the rest of the morning with Zelda creating a list of necessary items for a baby. Both their knowledge of babies and everything they required was limited. Lara would definitely have been beneficial in the discussion. They decided to postpone their shopping trip until she could join them.

"So, do I get any votes in what you name this little crotch goblin? Or can I make suggestions?"

"Oh my god, do not call it a crotch goblin anymore. It was one thing when I wasn't sure if I was pregnant. It's another now that I know." But even as she said it, she knew deep in her heart that she'd already known. There had been too many signs.

"Why not? It's a cute name—nickname."

Skylar burst out laughing and shook her head. "I assure you, it's not. And you can certainly come up with suggestions, but I will not pick a video game name." She arched one brow; she knew the route Zelda's parents had taken and refused to impose the same on her own child.

"Fair. I got picked on a lot..."

"Did you really?"

"Are you fucking kidding me? Of course I did. But I decided early on that I didn't give a shit what other people thought. I love my name." Zelda shrugged as if it was the simplest thing in the world.

The idea of knowing at a young age that what other people thought of you didn't matter sounded like something Skylar could have used. Even as they grew up, she felt like her older sister couldn't stand her. She was always worried about doing something that might annoy Tonya. It was stressful. "I wish I'd met you when we were younger."

Zelda smiled sadly. "Me too. Now, go shower and get ready for your date." She wiggled her brows at Skylar as she shooed her away again.

Skylar hadn't been able to keep the news of her and Harmon trying a relationship to herself for long. "Harmon isn't due to get here for another two hours."

"I know. Hopefully, that's enough time."

Skylar scoffed. "Shut up. I don't take that long."

Zelda shrugged as if to say, *We'll see.*

Antonio's was an upscale Italian restaurant that Skylar loved. As she pulled a strappy romper from one of the few hangers in her closet, she couldn't help but examine her stomach in the full-length mirror on the door for any signs of change. It didn't look any different. Shrugging, she pulled on the romper but found it was a bit too snug on her chest. *My boobs can't be changing already.* Swapping out her push-up bra for one with minimal padding, she managed to get the side zipper up. She looked cute—felt it too. It looked like it should be two separate pieces. The top went straight across her chest with three straps from each side that crisscrossed in the back, and at the waist, it had a band making it appear as if she were wearing black slacks. She loved the way it accentuated her curves. She'd never been accused of being skinny, but she loved the silhouette this outfit gave her. She pulled her hair back into a chignon. It had been her go-to hairstyle as a waitress, and she was happy for an excuse to resume the practice.

Coming out of her bedroom, Skylar found Zelda bent over to peer inside the fridge.

"If you're looking for dinner, there should be some leftover lasagna from a couple of days ago."

Zelda jumped and hit her head on the underside of the freezer door. "Shit, make some noise next time. But yes, I'm scavenging for food. I finished the lasagna." She rubbed the no-doubt throbbing point on her head.

"Well, do you want me to make something before I go?"

Zelda scoffed. "I think I can manage one night on my own, *Mom*."

The nickname didn't feel as strange as Skylar had expected it to. But still, she raised a brow in question. "You know they said if we set off the fire alarm from cooking again, we're out of here, right?"

"Fuck off. I'll make an egg and have some cottage cheese or something."

"Just let me do it."

Skylar pushed Zelda out of the way and retrieved the eggs and cottage cheese from the back of the fridge. The date on the cottage cheese indicated it had expired the week before. Taking off the lid, Skylar didn't see any mold, so she tipped the container and sniffed the contents. Never in her life had she regretted a decision so quickly. The curds had her gagging just as the doorbell rang.

"I'll get the door," Zelda said with a grimace and took off.

Skylar held in her heaving as best she could as she raced to her bathroom. She had never had such a visceral reaction to the smell of something before. As she lost the contents of her stomach, she heard Harmon's deep voice trailing in from the other room. Unsure what he and Z were saying, all she could do was hope Zelda would keep him occupied for a few minutes.

When she heard Zelda repeatedly saying, "No," she knew Harmon would once again find her with her head in a toilet. *Wonderful.*

She didn't have to turn to know he was behind her. Warmth settled across her back, then one of Harmon's hands rubbed his signature small, calming circles. "Sky, are you all right?"

"I'm just stupid."

Harmon pressed a kiss to her forehead when the vomiting subsided. "We can postpone dinner if you'd like to stay in. I can make you soup or something."

"No, I'm not sick. I stuck my nose in a container of expired cottage cheese to see if it smelled like it was expired."

Harmon grinned. "I'm going to guess it did."

"Don't laugh at me."

Chapter Thirty-One

HARMON

"So, does that mean you still...?" As he pivoted to search the cabinet for a washcloth to wipe Skylar's face, he froze. On the corner of her sink was a pregnancy test. The last one he'd seen was negative with the stark single line telling him that he wouldn't be a father.

"Still what?" Skylar turned, still kneeling on the floor. "Oh my god."

Her face paled as he reached for the positive pregnancy test sitting on the counter.

"Is this yours?"

"Harmon, wait."

"Is it yours?" His voice came out broken and choppy. He hated how weak it made him sound. Every cell in his body felt as if it balanced on the edge of a precipice, ready to vault him over the edge and into the darkness below if she said no.

She pressed her lips into a firm line as she nodded.

With the confirmation, his heart began to hammer. He swallowed hard. Tears welled in his eyes as he looked back down at the test. Two lines, it was definitely positive. That would explain why she'd been so sick the last few days. After he placed the test back on the counter, he pulled Skylar up off the floor and into a hug. His chest ached with the excitement of becoming a father. Granted, he would have liked to be in a more concrete relationship. They'd only slept together a handful of times, but they'd decided to give things a shot, and now...

"Skylar, I swear to you I will be a good father. I promise. I will be here for you every step of the way." He held her at arm's length to look at her better.

Her eyes grew wide and shimmered with a watery sheen. She opened her mouth as if to say something but couldn't if the emotions swimming in her eyes were any indication.

"It's okay. We'll figure things out as we go." He tucked a strand of wayward hair behind her ear then pressed a kiss to her forehead.

Tears spilled from her eyes, and he swiped them away with his thumb.

"When did you find out?"

"Today," she croaked. "Just this morning."

"Are you nervous?"

She nodded, and he pulled her close again, reveling in the way it felt to hold her, to know she was growing a life inside of her.

Before he got too emotional, he took a step back. "Would you like to stay home to eat?"

She shook her head. "No, I put on this cute outfit and did my hair. I don't want to waste it."

Harmon chuckled as he pressed another kiss to her forehead. He couldn't stop kissing her. "You finish getting ready, and I'll meet you in the entryway."

As he made his way out to the kitchen, he tried to remember if they'd used protection the first nights they'd spent together. He thought they had, but nothing was foolproof. He'd wanted a baby for so long, and while this was all out of order, he couldn't suppress the giddy excitement ready to burst from him. He wondered if he had ruined her surprise. Perhaps she was planning to tell him at dinner tonight. He would make it up to her.

When Skylar emerged from her room and came out to the entry, he was enraptured by her. When he'd found her in the bathroom, she'd been kneeling on the floor, so it had been difficult to see what she was wearing, but now he found her stunning. With her caramel hair pulled back, he could see the slim lines of her neck. And her jumpsuit hugged her curves in all the best ways.

"You look beautiful."

"Yes, she looks great. Now before you two make me sick with all your sweet words, I have a date with a little shit online who thinks I can't beat his ass within five minutes. I don't want them hearing you two in the background making kissy faces at each other."

Harmon's mouth dropped open, and he shifted his gaze to Skylar. She shrugged like this was an everyday occurrence and slid on a pair of wedged heels. It was the first time Harmon had seen Skylar in heels, and it was strange to have her at almost eye level with him.

"Now that will make it easier for me to make kissy faces at you," he said loudly enough for the words to carry to Zelda in the living room.

Zelda tipped her head back and laughed. "I hope you guys have a good night," she said over her shoulder.

Harmon extended his hand to Skylar, and they made their way out to Harmon's car. As they walked, he quickly realized why Skylar didn't seem to wear heels very often. She wobbled constantly. He'd heard somewhere that balance was difficult sometimes for pregnant women, but he thought that was later on in the pregnancy.

"Did you, ah, bring some flats or anything? Just in case?"

Skylar scowled up at him, and he flinched inwardly. He just didn't want her to trip and get hurt. "I have some in my car. I'll grab them on the way by." She didn't sound angry per se, but she was definitely upset.

"I'm sorry. I wasn't trying to hurt your feelings." Damn, it constantly felt like he was saying the wrong thing in one way or another.

"I just wanted to feel sexy and not like an Oompa Loompa for a day."

Her comparison made him snort. "You are a far cry from an Oompa Loompa. You always look beautiful. Now, go get those flats. I'm not saying you have to change. I just want you to have them in case those hurt your feet. Deal?"

"Fine," she said, and before she could turn and walk away, he pulled her into a hug, pressing a kiss to her soft lips.

Harmon flinched as she clumsily made her way to her car. The thought of her falling made him wonder if he should have offered to get them for her. He tried to push the pregnancy out of his mind. As excited as he was for a baby, he needed to remember to put Skylar first. He wouldn't be having a child without her.

As they drove, they talked about what they would like their Christmases to look like. It was only a couple of weeks away. Harmon wondered if it was too early to propose they spend the holiday together. With the additional knowledge of the baby on the horizon, it was hard to tell what was too fast and what was appropriate. Skylar seemed hesitant to talk about the pregnancy, so he did his best to talk about anything else but found his mind constantly rotating back to thoughts of it.

"Have you been here before?" Harmon parked the car as close to the front as they could get.

"A few years ago."

Jealousy swirled through his veins. He wanted to ask who she'd come with. That would only make him seem jealous. After shutting off the car, he rounded it to Skylar's side to open the door for her.

"I think you're the only person who has ever done that for me."

"Open the door for you?" he asked, a little surprised by her admission.

She nodded. "My last boyfriend was... I don't know how to put it. All about images and making himself seem as important as possible, and doing something for someone else, he apparently thought would make him look... weak?"

That way of thinking made Harmon shake his head. "I like doing things for you," he reassured her.

Placing a hand on the small of her back, Harmon led her up to the front door. The hostess wore a starched white button-down and black slacks, as did the waitstaff. The restaurant was one of the more formal dining places in town.

"How many?" The hostess smiled at them.

"Two, please." It felt good to say they were dining for two rather than just one.

"Right this way." They followed her to a table at the edge of the dining room. The tables were stained a dark ebony, and the chairs were black. The walls were packed with what looked like photos from Italy. Antonio, the owner, had lived in Italy until he met an American tourist who eventually became his wife. Harmon had only met the couple a handful of times, and those had usually been for dinners the office put on for employee appreciation outings.

"Your server will be right with you."

The hostess left as Harmon pulled out Skylar's chair for her. She smiled up at him, and the flutter in his chest began again.

"Do you have any idea what you might want?"

Skylar flushed and dipped her head. "I may have looked up the menu earlier, after we made plans. I think I'll do the chicken alfredo."

Harmon's lip quirked in a small smirk. "I usually do the Trip Around Italy. It's like a small tasting platter of a few entrees. You just pick three you want."

"That does sound good, but I really want garlic." She grimaced. "Sorry, my breath will be horrendous..."

A tall man with a great tan sidled up next to their table, and when he smiled down at Skylar, that familiar jealousy heated Harmon's neck.

"I'm Enzo, and I'll be your server this evening. Would you like to hear our specials?"

Skylar beamed up at him and nodded.

As *Enzo* listed off the specials, Harmon did his best to push the ridiculous emotions aside. When he was finished, Skylar asked for a water and ordered her alfredo as she had initially planned. Harmon ordered his Trip Around Italy, asking for the spaghetti, white lasagna, and chicken parmesan over linguine. After hearing about Skylar's mother's struggles with drinking, Harmon didn't want to be the cause of her to worry about someone else, so he, too, ordered a water.

Almost immediately after their waiter left, someone else stopped at the corner of their table. Harmon looked up to see Malcom Adams.

"Mr. Adams, how are you today?" Harmon stood to shake the other man's hand.

"Good. I thought I saw you over here. Anne is on the phone." Malcom rolled his eyes as if to say, *You know how it is.* He pointed over his shoulder to a table in the middle of the dining room.

Anne had her back to them, but the unmistakable bob was definitely the woman who enjoyed making his days miserable.

"And who do you have here?" Malcom asked, shifting his attention to Skylar.

Her eyes widened before she forced a smile and stood as well. "Skylar," she said, extending her hand.

"You look lovely, my dear. I hope Harmon treats you well."

The stiff smile stayed fixed to her face as she nodded. Malcom seemed ignorant of her discomfort. She knew exactly who the man was. After he and Harmon shared more small talk, he headed back to his table when his food was delivered despite Anne's continued phone call.

Tension remained in Skylar's posture for the remainder of the meal, and Harmon was at a loss for how to make her feel better.

CHAPTER THIRTY-TWO

SKYLAR

As Monday morning rolled around, Skylar was terrified to call the doctor's office to set up her first appointment. Harmon had been so enthusiastic about the baby, she'd never found the right words to tell him it might not be his. *What's the point in raining on his parade if there's a chance it's his? Oh, I don't know, Skylar, maybe that it would crush him to find out later.*

She only hoped he was the father.

Eight in the morning had never felt so far yet so close. She spent the morning doing laundry, organizing, and cleaning the kitchen counters, all sprinkled with nervous pacing. When the time finally rolled around, she dropped onto the couch and pulled out her phone. *I can do this. No matter the outcome, I will be fine. The baby will be fine.* With her mini pep talk complete, she dialed her doctor's office.

"Good morning, Irene Memorial Hospital."

"Hi, my name is Skylar Gilmore, and I recently took an at-home pregnancy test and would like to make an appointment." Other than that, she had no idea what to say.

"Mm-hmm, do you have any preferred days of the week you'd like to come in?"

Something heavy and disappointing dropped into her gut. For some reason, she'd assumed they would want to see her immediately, not schedule something out. "No, any day will work."

"Mm-hmm, okay, it looks like I have an opening with Dr. Pearson on Tuesday, December twenty-third at ten."

That was over a week away. "I had thought you'd want to see me sooner."

"Mm-hmm."

The woman's constant response was going to send Skylar over the edge.

"Is there any reason for concern? Have you been spotting or having severe cramps?"

The urge to lie abated almost immediately. Her desire for answers was no reason to take away an emergency time slot from someone else. With a sigh, she admitted, "No, I haven't."

"Mm-hmm, how about this? I will put you on a wait list. If anyone cancels, I will give you a call and move your appointment up. I can't guarantee you'll get a call, and if you do, it may be with only an hour or two's notice."

Skylar was nodding before the woman finished. "That would be great, please."

After confirming her phone number, she hung up and headed for the door to go to work. Harmon had told her to come in whenever she was ready today. He had been so understanding of her wanting to make the call alone. She wondered if she should ask him to come to the appointment. Anxiety twisted through her system as she considered the idea on her way to work.

As she pushed through the glass doors and headed toward her desk, Harmon rose from his chair, and a woman seated opposite him followed suit.

"Morning, I didn't think you'd be in this early."

Seeing another woman in Harmon's office caused an irrational wave of fear, hurt, and anger to course through Skylar. She knew the feelings were likely due to her hormones, but she couldn't help the heat that filled her cheeks. She gave Harmon and his guest a tight smile.

"Skylar, this is Mandy. She was my assistant before you." The way he said her name with such distaste made Skylar feel vaguely better.

She remembered Harmon talking briefly about the woman who had constantly messed things up at work. For some reason, she had pictured the woman to be unattractive. Now looking at the leggy, thin, radiant woman before him, she couldn't help pulling her cardigan tighter around her body, hiding herself. At the motion, Harmon's brows drew together. She had always been a shapely woman, but she'd never felt the need to fit into the mold of what society called a beautiful woman. Well, not since she and her ex broke up. He and his mother had made it a point to bring up her body to her.

She cleared her throat. "Nice to meet you."

Mandy eyed Skylar up and down with a look of disgust.

"Mandy was just leaving."

The harshness in Harmon's voice had Skylar peering at him. He looked angry, and that alone made her feel less bad about her insecurities.

"Surely, I can do better than her," Mandy said in a whiny voice that would have sounded more at home coming from a toddler than a grown woman.

"I assure you, you cannot, *and* you had the opportunity. Now, please leave before I have you escorted out."

With a pout in Harmon's direction, Mandy stomped from the office. The carpet muffled the impact of her tantrum.

Skylar wanted to laugh at her behavior, though she felt childish for immediately assuming something was going on. *Is this what pregnancy is going to be like?* If so, she knew she was in for a wild ride. Before Mandy was fully out of sight, Harmon held Skylar at an arm's length, caressing her shoulders and looking her over. Something in the way he did it made her feel safe—cherished.

"You don't look happy." He squinted slightly, then his eyes flew wide. "Is everything okay? Do you feel all right?"

"Yeah, everything's fine. It's just, I couldn't get an appointment until over a week out."

Harmon rubbed her biceps. "That's all right. It will give the baby more time to develop." He said the last in a whisper, and she appreciated his discretion. Being new at the company, she didn't know how everyone would take to the new girl being pregnant.

She wanted to stand on her tiptoes and kiss him. The urge to inhale his spicy scent was almost too much. She needed to take a step back. They were at work, and their deal was that they could give this a shot so long as they could act professional at the office. And her mind was drifting far from professional.

"Is there anything else?"

Damn this man, it was as if he could peer through a window straight into her heart and mind at times. She groaned then admitted, "I just got a little jealous. I mean, I walked through the door, and you had a woman at your desk, then you both jumped up the minute I arrived. It felt... I don't know, like you were trying to be secretive."

Harmon shook his head about halfway through her ramblings. "Never, she had just arrived. She ambushed me, really. My door was open so I could see if anyone came in. I was so focused on my computer, I didn't even realize she was here until she started talking."

His earnest eyes implored her to believe him, and she did.

She cleared her throat. "Anyway, what are we up against today?"

Harmon shot her a half smile. "Well, you will get your first chance to officially meet Anne in person. Not sure if that's a test or an initiation of sorts."

At the mention of CJ's mother, Skylar's fingers went numb as anxiety crawled up her arms. She wasn't sure how, but she managed to smile up at Harmon as if it was no big deal, then she dropped into her chair.

All morning, she studied the clock, waiting for Anne to arrive. With only ten minutes left until Anne's appointment, Skylar couldn't hold off stealing another moment. Racing across the carpeted floor, she dropped onto the toilet, hoping Anne wouldn't arrive while she was indisposed.

When Skylar emerged from the bathroom, a woman with ice-blue eyes wrinkled her nose and gave Skylar a once-over.

Shit.

CHAPTER THIRTY-THREE

HARMON

It was finally time for Skylar's initial checkup, and the night before, Harmon had convinced her to let him attend. Much to their excitement, they had called her to reschedule the appointment, so she—they—would be getting in about four days early. As they drove, she picked at her fingernails, something he had identified as one of her nervous tells. She had been on edge for the last few days; he assumed it was nerves and that, once she heard the baby's heartbeat, she would calm down.

His own anxieties would be eased too. The never-ending fear of losing the baby, even in her first trimester, was killing him. The image of a perfect yet unbreathing baby played on in his mind every night. He'd been rid of the haunting dreams for a couple of years now. But as the reality of their situation settled in, so did the very real feelings that he had been holding back. He didn't know if he could survive another loss like that. He wasn't even sure his first few years without Cecelia could be considered living. He'd existed.

After he parked at the doctor's office, he took Skylar's hand in his, swallowing down his fears. "Ready?"

She let out a long, slow breath. "I think so."

"Let's do this." Before dropping her hand, he pressed a kiss to her knuckles then came around to open the door for her.

His heart hammered as they made their way to the front door. Skylar was so quick to blush, Harmon found it difficult not to make her blush at every opportunity. They entered the building, and he was surprised to find he didn't feel accosted by the scent of antiseptic cleaners. Most places had that distinct smell to let people know the facility had been cleaned, sterilized. While this facility looked clean, it didn't carry that hospital tang. *That's one plus.* Harmon held Skylar's hand as he followed her down a hall filled with paintings and other works of art available for purchase. They boarded the elevator and headed for the third floor. He had never been to this section of this particular hospital.

The doors opened, and he followed Skylar to the check-in counter. They'd barely been dating for a week. He wasn't sure if it should be considered "again," since they'd put up their walls with one another once he'd found out Skylar was his new assistant, but they hadn't really been dating the first time. They had still been in the getting-to-know-you stage then. So, he wasn't sure if standing right with her at the counter was the right thing to do or if he should stay back and give her some privacy.

"Mm-hmm, okay." The woman behind the glass made a tsking sound as she tapped her obnoxiously long fingernails on the counter. "So, do you know when you will have insurance again?"

"I just started a new job. I think I need to be there ninety days to get the insurance." Skylar fidgeted with the hem of her shirt.

"Mm-hmm."

Harmon had forgotten the position didn't allow people to sign up for insurance until they surpassed their ninety-day trial period. *Shit.* No wonder Skylar had seemed so agitated and nervous. She probably didn't know how she would pay for the appointments.

"Okay, I'll need you to update these forms. Go ahead and take a seat, and a nurse will be out to get you shortly." The woman closed the glass window.

Skylar pored over the forms and filled out everything rather quickly. Harmon sat in the chair beside her, bouncing his leg.

"If you don't stop jackhammering your leg, you're going to take the building down."

Harmon gave her a chagrined smile. "Sorry, I don't do well when I have nothing to do."

"Don't you have some app to play with on your phone or some doomscrolling to do on social media?"

Harmon shrugged. "I don't really care for social media. I have them. I just don't go on them unless I have absolutely nothing else to do."

"And right now, what else do you need to do?"

"Support you. I don't want to be on my phone if you want to talk about anything." He shrugged again. "I always feel like being on my phone puts up a wall telling people I'm not interested in them."

Skylar drew her brows together. "I guess I never thought too much about it. That's a good point."

Harmon leaned in and kissed her. She smelled of something sweet and refreshing. If they weren't in public, he would do far more than kiss her. The skin-tight maxi dress she was wearing made his brain go places it shouldn't.

She cleared her throat. "So, what did they think at work when you said we would both be out for an appointment?" She looked ready to cringe.

"Nothing really. I did tell Sebastian that we knew each other before you started working and have been seeing where our relationship would go."

Skylar stilled, and he wondered how monumentally he'd fucked up.

"You did what?"

"Don't get mad." He put his hands up, palms out in surrender. "He sensed something, and I wasn't going to lie. That always tends to make things worse in the end. Better to be honest up front."

Skylar swallowed hard and looked as though she were about to say something.

"Don't worry. The company doesn't have policies about dating coworkers. It was more my preference. I've been told I can be quite the dick at work." He rubbed the back of his neck.

A few people could attest to that fact, Mandy being the most prevalent of those people. Although, in his opinion, she'd deserved most of what he'd dished out.

"I haven't seen it yet." She nudged his elbow with hers where it rested on his armrest.

"You seem to calm me when I feel like I'm cresting that hill of anger."

Skylar tangled her fingers with his and gave his hand a squeeze.

"Skylar Gilmore," a nurse in pale-purple scrubs called from the edge of the waiting room.

No other couples had come in while they'd waited. Harmon kept hold of Skylar's hand as they stood to follow the nurse down the hall. The light reflecting off the tile floor made it look as if there were a sheen of water on the tiles, almost like ice.

As they asked and answered the general questions and Skylar talked with the nurse about her symptoms and concerns, and Harmon sat quietly in his chair. He wasn't sure how involved Skylar wanted him to be in these appointments. It was so strange to feel out of place. When the nurse asked Skylar to step onto the scale, Skylar's cheeks flushed, and she bowed her head and nodded. It was one of the first moments she'd seemed self-conscious about her weight, other than with Mandy in the office. He rubbed her back to let her know not to be ashamed—at least, he hoped that was the way it came across. He didn't care what numbers appeared on the damn scale. She was gorgeous, kind, and someone he could have a real conversation with. That was all he cared about.

Twice as she walked to the scale across the room, she glanced at him over her shoulder. This was awful. He hated to see her feel this way. The nurse waited as Skylar stepped up then took down the measurement.

Skylar and the nurse returned, and Harmon put her hand in his, rubbing his thumb over hers. After a few more questions, the nurse let them know the doctor would be in soon and left.

As he moved into Skylar's space, he inhaled her perfume. Again, it was something floral he couldn't define. Harmon released her hand and took her face between his palms to press a kiss to her soft lips. Dropping his hands, he brought their foreheads together. It was such an intimate moment, he felt the one thing he'd avoided for so long swirling inside him.

"Skylar, you know I think you're beautiful, right?"

She nodded, her nose bumping his.

"Good," he whispered and pressed another kiss to her lips.

When a knock sounded at the door, he shifted to sit up again.

The door swung open, and a doctor who looked to be in her midfifties entered. "I hear we're having a baby." The woman was all smiles and brought an ease to the room.

Skylar nodded.

"All right, I'm Doctor Pearson. I will be your doctor unless you prefer a midwife." She paused for a moment as if waiting to see if Skylar would jump in.

"So, you must be Skylar, and I'm assuming you're Dad?"

Harmon smiled and nodded, then extended his hand to the doctor. "Harmon."

Doctor Pearson took his hand and gave it a firm shake. "Good to see you here. I love when dads come to the appointments. Based on what you told the nurse, it sounds like you would be due in July or the end of August." She said it almost like a question.

Pink filled Skylar's cheeks again. "That's kind of why I'm here. I'm not entirely sure when I'm due."

"Not to worry, hon. We will go over a few things, do an ultrasound, get you some pictures of that little one while I take some measurements, then you will be on your way."

As they discussed everything Skylar should be doing and what activities she should stop or continue, Harmon took the time to really look around the room while still listening.

***

Skylar

"When you arrived, did the nurse ask you to give a urine sample?"

"No, she didn't." Skylar was making her way to the bathroom as she answered.

"All right. If you can leave a urine sample in the cup in the bathroom then remove everything on your lower half once you get back to the room, I will get the ultrasound cart while you do that."

Skylar nodded. She wasn't sure if she should feel awkward or not with Harmon in the room. She'd heard of people getting internal ultrasounds but hadn't expected that. After she did her best to urinate in a cup that seemed far too small, she lay down on the exam table, pulling a small white sheet over her lap to give herself a semblance of modesty. She supposed she would need to get comfortable with people being down there—no matter how much that thought made her stomach clench with anxiety.

Harmon moved the chair to her left. He offered her his hand, and she immediately felt better with his presence. She could get used to having him around. The steadying caress of his thumb over the top of her hand made her relax into the table. The nurse they'd seen earlier ducked into the room after knocking, took the urine sample, and left again without a word. She wondered if they had to verify if she was indeed pregnant before they did the ultrasound.

After what felt like an eternity and the top of her hand started to feel raw from Harmon's insistent rubbing, she both wanted to keep his touch and tell him to stop. It seemed she'd been in a constant state of contradiction lately. When people talked, she wanted them to shut up.

When it was too quiet in the apartment, she wanted someone to talk her through her anxiety. It was getting ridiculous.

An obnoxious rattling approached the room, followed by a light knock on Skylar's door. It was the doctor returning with the promised ultrasound machine. To Skylar, it looked like a computer on a cart. The only things that hinted at its purpose were the two wands on the machine. Dr. Pearson wheeled it into place on Skylar's other side. She plugged the machine in and pressed a few buttons on the screen.

"Are we ready?" the doctor asked, letting her gaze settle on Skylar.

She nodded, but her anxiety was of a different opinion. Her heart hammered its way up into her throat, and she tried to swallow it back down.

Then Dr. Pearson squeezed what looked like lube all over the end of the condomed wand and lifted the sheet, inserting the device inside of Skylar. It was a bit strange but only slightly uncomfortable. With her other hand focused on the keypad of the ultrasound machine, the doctor rapidly pressed buttons. The doctor would shift it, type some more, then make some humming noises that did little to ease Skylar's discomfort.

Skylar focused on the screen, but she couldn't tell what anything was. She couldn't differentiate one thing from another. The doctor was definitely taking measurements of some kind.

Without warning, a loud sound filled the room. It was almost like something she'd seen on a ghost hunter show. It made Skylar nearly jump out of her skin.

"That's your baby's heartbeat."

Harmon visibly relaxed in her periphery. Skylar felt slightly guilty; she should have considered how he would take this after losing his baby all those years ago. If what he'd said was true, he hadn't been in a serious relationship since his divorce. Their hands were still intertwined, and she tightened her grip. It was the best way she could think of to show him that she saw him, saw the pain. He sent a teary-eyed look in her direction then gave her a weak smile.

"So, I'm taking some measurements to help us pinpoint how far along you are." The doctor shifted the monitor of her machine so Skylar and Harmon could better see the screen.

Skylar was shocked at how adept the doctor seemed at tapping on the machine while moving the wand to get the proper angles. The little tadpole was wiggling all over the palace. As she watched the black-and-white screen, letting the sound of her unborn child's heartbeat fill the air around her, she was in a state of bliss. At that moment, she knew she could do this. She would do anything for that tiny being.

"So, it looks like the baby is measuring at almost twelve weeks. You are nearly through your first trimester. Congratulations."

Harmon smiled at her. She did her best to keep a smile plastered to her face. The man at her side who desperately wanted a child couldn't be the father. And now, she had to figure out the most graceful way to obliterate his dreams.

Her chest ached with the impending revelation. It needed to be taken care of sooner rather than later, but she didn't know the best way to say it. Terror filled her that the truth of the matter might push them apart.

And now, she had to decide if she would tell CJ. *Would it be better not to tell him? Or would he catch on?*

Chapter Thirty-Four

HARMON

He'd dropped Skylar off at home after the appointment. It was only a few days until Christmas, and he hoped he could convince Skylar to tell his parents about the baby. He didn't want to do anything sooner than she was ready for. He looked at the photos again, tracing his finger over the outline of the tiny human Skylar was growing as he sat in his condo. The miscarriage mark was almost behind them. He could distinguish little more than the baby's skull, spine, and what he thought were the arms.

Skylar had been strangely silent on the way home. It was a lot to take in. She had told him she wanted to talk with Zelda about the appointment and was tired. She'd been falling asleep quite early. Many times, she'd fallen asleep as they were texting each other in the evenings. So, he could understand her exhaustion.

He peered into the room at the end of the hall. It was supposed to be an in-home office, but he rarely used it. The walls could easily be painted, and there was plenty of room for a crib, dresser, and maybe a rocking chair. Searching his pockets, he wanted to finally call about the house near Porter. If they had their own yard, that would probably be best for the baby. "You're getting ahead of yourself, Harmon." Finding his pockets empty, he made his way back out to the living room.

His phone rang, where it sat on the glass coffee table. Leaping up to answer the call, he nearly slammed his knee into the corner of the table in his haste. Hoping to find Skylar's name lighting up the display, he held back a curse when instead it was Porter.

"Hey."

"Just wanted to call and check in about Christmas. Verity wanted to get an idea of who would be coming. You've come every year for the last several, so we thought we'd check with you first."

Harmon looked down at the ultrasound again. "I think I'll spend the holiday with Skylar."

A beat of silence followed. "Things are getting serious?" Porter's tone held a strong smattering of surprise.

With a nod, Harmon said, "Yeah, we are... If I tell you something, will you swear not to tell. I mean it. You can't tell anyone."

It sounded like Porter moved to a different room. "We're solid. What is it?"

"We're having a baby."

Porter gave a slight pause. "No shit?"

Harmon laughed with nervous excitement. "Yeah, I can't believe it."

"Congrats, man, when is she due?"

"End of June, the thirtieth."

Porter chuckled. "Seriously, I'm so happy for you. You sure I can't tell Ver? If she finds out I knew before her and kept it a secret, she might castrate me."

"Just make sure she doesn't tell anyone." Harmon knew that keeping a secret from a significant other was nearly impossible. The urge to share all the good news in life with them was nearly impossible to ignore—as was the desire to commiserate when bad news came.

The two men spent a few more minutes chatting and catching up. When they ended the call, Harmon pulled up the photo he'd taken with Skylar the first night he'd surprised her at Retro. And in that moment, it hit him. He opened the details on the photo, doubting his memory.

The photo had been taken on November second, which meant they hadn't had sex for the first time until a couple of days later. As he counted out the weeks on his fingers, a wrecking ball slammed into his gut, bringing with it a searing pain.

He traced his finger over Skylar's baby's image again. It was her baby. Not his.

Fuck, CJ...

As the disappointment settled into his bones, he decided he would wait to see if Skylar would tell him. He didn't want to go into it accusing her of anything, so he would wait and see what she might say about it. Perhaps she hadn't noticed. But the way she had withdrawn from him after learning how far along she was seemed revealing; he had a hard time believing she was unaware of the timeline.

He stared at the tiny critter that was about half the size of a lime, based on some of his online research. As he looked up all the information that he could about the baby's development, he realized he wasn't nearly as upset that the baby wasn't his biologically. He had even played with the idea of adopting or fostering for a while. So this would be similar.

As he downloaded an app that would let him know what the baby was doing each week, he could only hope that Skylar would eventually notice the timing discrepancy or, if she already knew, that she would find the courage to tell him so he could, in turn, tell her none of that mattered. Love didn't require genetics.

Chapter Thirty-Five

SKYLAR

"Zelda, how in the hell can I just casually bring this up?" Skylar paced the dark area rug in their cramped living room. "Hey, Harmon, sorry to say it, but this baby"—she pointed at her middle—"isn't yours. I decided I finally needed to get over my ex, who I broke up with two years ago! So, I went to a nightclub one night and fucked some random guy in a private room. Oh yeah, and come to find out he's fucking married. *And* in case you forgot, his parents are also your biggest client. You think that's how I should tell him?"

Zelda tipped her chin as if thinking hard. "I may suggest altering it just a smidge."

Skylar lunged for a throw pillow on the couch and threw it at her friend's face.

Zelda lifted a hand, easily deflecting the blow. "You had a feeling it wasn't his from the beginning, didn't you?"

Skylar shrugged. "I guess. I hoped my gut instinct was wrong. That if I brought him with me, if we made a go of things... I don't know. That maybe it would just kinda work out. You know?"

Blue hair swayed as Zelda nodded. "I get that. But you can't just wish a situation into fruition, and Harmon deserves to know the truth. Do you plan to tell CJ?"

Skylar groaned because, no matter how it appeared, Zelda would always slice to the center of it all. "I have no idea what to do. You know his wife tricked me a few weeks ago. I don't want to deal with her crazy for the rest of my life too."

"Okay, if Harmon wasn't in the picture and you were facing doing this on your own, would you want CJ to be part of it?"

"Hell no. He is clearly a creep, and I don't want him coparenting with me. I would rather do it on my own."

"And do you think Harmon would want to be there either way?"

That gave her pause. "Honestly, I have no idea. With how desperately he wants a baby, maybe. But I need to tell him so it's his decision. I'm just scared."

Zelda gave her a half smile. "I understand why you're nervous, but I agree that he needs to have all the facts. Do you want to call him?"

Skylar halted her pacing. "I can't tell him over the phone!"

Zelda rolled her eyes. "I didn't mean for you to blurt it over the phone and then ask him if he still wants to be baby daddy numero uno. I want you to call him, invite him over or go to his place, and explain everything and how it happened."

"I will. I just need to let it sink in a little."

Zelda stood from the couch, stretching. "Well, I'll let you come up with your plan. I need to head to bed. I have an early meeting in the morning. But just know, the longer you wait, the bigger the potential hurt. For both of you."

"You don't want to help me make a plan?"

"I just did. From here, you need to figure out which way you want to tell him. I can't write you a script, Sky."

Skylar groaned again as Zelda left her to her own devices and, worse yet, her own thoughts.

***

After a few days of thinking, Skylar was no closer to figuring out how to tell Harmon the baby wasn't his. As she watched him move around his desk, loosening his tie after a particularly difficult client, she felt that connection to him. She'd chickened out at every opportunity she'd had. She was afraid of not only losing him but also her job. She needed this position. She would get the needed insurance about halfway through her pregnancy, so going somewhere else wouldn't work. Surely, he wouldn't fire her over it.

They were planning to spend the holiday together. Zelda was heading to her parents' house with her sister and brother. Usually, Skylar would go with them, but she wanted to spend Christmas with Harmon. It might be the best opportunity to tell him, when it was just the two of them.

She ran a hand over her abdomen. She felt the slight swell that hadn't been there before. It wasn't much, but her clothes were starting to fit a little too tight, and she'd taken to wearing loose dresses to work. She was only a few days away from the end of her first trimester, then she would be out of the miscarriage danger zone.

"And that's a wrap until after Christmas," Harmon said, extending a hand to help her out of her chair.

She hadn't even noticed the time. She had been so much more spacey lately. Focusing was becoming a foreign concept.

"Sorry, I still need to close down my computer. I'll meet you in the parking lot?"

Harmon nodded. "Sure, I need to wish everyone a happy holiday anyway." He pressed a kiss to the top of her head. He was infinitely sweet, which did little more than make her feel like trash.

Tonya: *What is Miss Perfect doing for Christmas?*

Skylar grimaced at the message; she wanted to work things out with Tonya. It would be good for them both, and her sister deserved to know about her future niece or nephew. With a sigh, she tried to respond in the most appropriate way possible.

Skylar: *Spending the holiday with my boyfriend. I would like to see you at some point.*

Good enough. She figured that was the best olive branch, or fir branch, she could offer at the moment. If Tonya agreed, it would be a Christmas miracle.

Once she'd shut down her computer and tidied her desk, she headed to the reception area. She hadn't seen Harmon go down the stairs to the lobby, but that didn't mean he hadn't yet. With her purse tossed over her shoulder, she made her way out to the parking lot. The temperature had been hovering around forty-five degrees. It wasn't necessarily cold, but it never failed to send a chill over her body. A shiver scuttled up her spine.

As she approached her car, movement across the lot caught her eye. Expecting to see someone from work heading out to enjoy the holiday break, she smiled as she turned, but her lips fell just as quickly.

"Skylar," CJ called across the asphalt in a singsong voice as he stretched her name to fill the span of several seconds.

She didn't want to talk to him, so she turned to her car.

"A little birdy told me you're pregnant." His swagger, which had made him sexy and appealing only months before, revolted her. "And I can't help but wonder if perhaps..." He eyed her up and down. "It's mine."

She shook her head. How he'd found out, she wasn't sure. The only people she'd told were Harmon, Zelda, and Lara—and Harmon had told their boss.

Shit.

Maybe the owner of the company had mentioned it in passing to CJ's parents. They wouldn't have known it could be their grandchild she was carrying. They didn't even know who she was, so none of this made sense to her. *How did he find out?*

"No, you're not pregnant, or no it's not mine?"

She swallowed hard. "It's not yours."

CJ's eyes narrowed. "Don't lie to me," he seethed, taking a step closer to her.

"Skylar?" Harmon's voice carried to her. It was a caress to her skin and a balm to the anxiety coating her palms. Harmon wouldn't allow this piece of shit to touch her.

His presence emboldened her. "CJ, you need to leave. I don't want anything to do with you," she said as she stood taller.

He leaned in close, and his warm, clammy breath caused the hairs at the base of her neck to rise. "I'll find out. If it's mine, it will be mine to take."

His threat sank under her skin. She would be stupid to think he wouldn't act on it.

Chapter Thirty-Six

HARMON

THAT BOILING JEALOUSY BUBBLED up in him the moment he saw Skylar standing with CJ, who hovered over her by her car. But her body language clearly demonstrated that she was not interested in his leering gaze that trailed over her body. His quick strides across the lot brought Harmon to her side in moments. Skylar visibly relaxed when he reached her. The adrenaline of his mixed emotions swirled through his limbs.

"What did he want?" Harmon asked, fearing he already knew the answer. He was the only person that Harmon knew of who could be the baby's biological father. Even without being the other half of the baby's genetic makeup, Harmon didn't care. He would be a better father than CJ ever could. That thought had only continued to develop over the last few days.

"N-nothing." Shaking her head, she watched the blacked-out vehicle as it rumbled out of the parking lot.

The fact that she wasn't sharing what CJ wanted broke something inside of Harmon. *How many other secrets is she holding onto?* If they were going to do this, she needed to be honest with him. Then again, there might be more to the situation than he knew. Relationships couldn't be built on lies, and he had been nothing but honest with her. So, she needed to extend him the same courtesy. It had been several days since they'd learned her due date. That was more than enough time for Skylar to bring up the baby's parentage, and she hadn't—if she'd done the math. Harmon looked down at her, his brows furrowed, as if he could read her mind to determine what she did or didn't know.

Harmon forced a calming breath in and out through his nose. His anger was already dissipating now that CJ was gone. It was strange the way his rage seemed to fizzle out the moment Skylar was within reach, as if her presence had some kind of calming effect on the inferno beneath his skin. She was a salve he couldn't live without.

"Did you want to stay at my place tonight? Then we can spend Christmas morning together." His voice was gruff, and he worried it came out more like a command than a question. *Goddamn, do I need to tell her I'm not the father?*

Skylar nodded and blushed. "I'd like that."

"Meet you there?" he asked then pressed a kiss to her lips. Most of the office was now aware they were seeing each other, and he was astounded to find that he wasn't freaking out about it. It was just so easy for them to be together.

While Skylar ran home to get some clothes, Harmon pulled out everything he would need to make their Christmas dinner. He was used to his parents making a large ham each year, but since he wouldn't be traveling back to see them, he'd improvised with some ham steaks. Just as he was getting the bag of apples out to start peeling, the doorbell startled him out of his mindless preparations.

Opening the door, he was hit with that familiar ping of how beautiful he found the woman on the other side. She held a tote bag to her chest, a small gift peeking from the top with tiny Grinches all over the paper.

"Hey." Holding out a hand to take the bag, he brought it into the kitchen with him so Skylar could take off her shoes.

All Christmas Eve, Harmon was on the edge of his seat wondering if he should just tell her what he'd discovered during his mental calculations. It felt as if he was the one keeping a damning secret. As they went to bed that night, he vowed he would say something the following day if she didn't.

***

Skylar's phone rang early Christmas morning. She was sleeping so soundly, Harmon picked it up, intending to silence the ringer, but when CJ's name lit up on the screen, that jealous monster within had him swiping to answer the call.

"What do you want?"

CJ's cocky laugh sounded from the other end of the line. Skylar stirred. Harmon slipped out of bed, taking the call to the living room.

"How are my leftovers? Or should I ask how my baby is?"

Harmon's jaw clenched in time with his heart. "Shut the hell up, CJ. Now, tell me what you want."

"No, I think I'll wait until Skylar can talk with me. You interrupted us yesterday. Today, I have a... proposal for her."

The way CJ said it sent snakes slithering in Harmon's gut.

"Don't interrupt us next time," CJ said, venom in his voice.

"You need to stay the hell away from her," Harmon snapped, his vision narrowing as dark anger threatened to take over.

"Maybe I'll wait until she goes back to her apartment—you know, the third door on the second floor?"

"What are you doing?" Skylar shrieked from the living room.

"Ah, sounds like my baby mama is there now. Why don't you hand the phone over to her so—"

Harmon hung up before CJ could finish. His breaths were ragged. He wanted to throw Skylar's phone out the damn window, into the road below. Instead, he tossed it onto the couch.

Her eyes widened when she snatched it up, presumably checking the call log. "What were you doing?"

"Why does he keep contacting you?" Harmon held his entire body rigid as he gave her a final chance to tell him the truth.

Her hand immediately went to her middle, an instinct to protect her unborn child. Those snakes formed a knot of panic, rage, and terror within him. He didn't want to lose her, but he may have crossed a line he couldn't return from, because now he had to tell her he knew.

"Whose baby are you carrying, Skylar?" He spoke at nearly a whisper, but every thread of anger laced his words.

Skylar shifted from one foot to the other then looked back down at her phone. "CJ's," she said just as quietly, but the answer rang through the condo as if she'd screamed it at him.

Though he'd already known the truth, it didn't fail to crack his heart.

"I'm sorry. I wish the baby was yours."

"Why didn't you tell me that day?" When she seemed confused about what day he was referring to, he amended, "After your doctor's appointment. Why let me drone on and on about how excited I was when you knew the baby wasn't mine?"

Skylar shook her head. "I didn't know how to tell you…"

"But you've known since that day?"

She nodded.

"So, if I wasn't smart enough to do some simple math, you intended to let me brag to everyone that I was going to be a dad. Did you consider how stupid I would feel if someone else did the math and put it together?" He was so angry, yet he wasn't shouting like he thought he would. His words had an icy edge, but they came out smooth and measured.

"It wasn't like that. I wasn't trying to hurt you. I was trying not to. I was going to tell you."

Each of her sentences came out in quick, broken sobs, and his anger fizzled out. He hated seeing her in pain—even if it was her choices that had led to their argument.

"When? When were you going to tell me?"

"I—I don't know."

"Damn it, Sky. How will this ever work if we can't tell each other the truth?"

She shrugged and began picking at her fingernails. "I wanted to tell you today."

Chapter Thirty-Seven

SKYLAR

With her hands shaking, she dropped them to her sides. Her fear quickly morphed into rage. "Harmon, I don't know why you think you have the right to answer my phone." The terror battled with her anger. She'd been planning to tell him the truth today. CJ might have stolen that chance from her. Then again, it appeared Harmon had known since the doctor's visit. CJ had just moved their confrontation forward.

"Sky, if something is going on between you two, please tell me now."

His breathing quickened. When she opened her mouth to speak, he tensed, as if hanging on her every word.

But somehow, she wasn't afraid of *him*. Something inside her told her he may get angry, but he wouldn't hurt her. "I told you that was a one-night thing. I don't know what his problem is. He just... he just won't go away!"

Harmon closed his eyes and let out a long, slow breath. "Why haven't you done more to stop him? Block his number. Call the police. *Do something.*"

When his eyes opened again, she could see his pain.

"Zelda told me how ruthless his mother is in the courtroom. So I didn't figure anything I tried to say or do would stick. I blocked his number for a little while, then he showed up at that Mexican restaurant we went to. And it's just been a revolving door of him somehow knowing where I am. He's been threatening me and Zelda. Then I started to worry I was pregnant and didn't want to give him a reason to come after me."

He nodded then swallowed hard. "Anything else?"

"His wife, Myra, is just as crazy as he is. She tricked me into going to dinner one night. She was messaging me from CJ's phone. Remember that day we were driving, and someone was tailing us?" Harmon nodded. "Well, that afternoon, she messaged me, and I went to Surf 'N' Turf thinking it would be CJ at the table, but it was her."

"Is that it?"

The way he asked it filled her with dread. It was as if he was resigned, but she didn't know what about. Unbidden, her head and lower lip began to tremble. "No, nothing more. But if you've known the baby isn't yours, why didn't you tell *me*?"

Harmon nodded again then dropped into the recliner across from her. He ran a hand down his face. "I wanted you to trust me enough to tell me." His voice was hoarse as if he was holding back emotion. "But you kept it from me. You never even mentioned the possibility that it could be someone else's the day I saw the pregnancy test."

Tears stung her eyes as she tried to blink them away. "You were so excited." She knew that was just about the worst argument. If anything, it should have pushed her to tell the truth more quickly.

His eyes snapped to hers, pain swimming beneath the unshed tears. "The baby isn't mine." He pushed out a long, slow breath. "Not biologically anyway, but I would've been happy to call him or her mine."

"What?"

"Skylar, I already wanted to be with you, and I thought that the baby was mine. It feels like it should be. But how can we keep moving forward if you have such a hard time telling me anything?"

Skylar's breaths came in short, fast pants. "I still don't understand why you didn't say anything sooner..." She knew she was being difficult, but it stung to know he'd been aware of it for days and hadn't said a thing. The fact that he'd put it all together so quickly made her feel like a fool. She didn't know which was worse. Probably her own deceit. He was right. She should have said something the day he found the test.

"Are you serious? Why didn't *I* say anything? Why didn't you? You knew how excited I was when I found out you were pregnant. You knew what happened to my daughter." His voice cracked. "And *you* didn't tell *me*..." he whispered.

It broke her heart. Skylar clenched her fists at her sides. She was overwhelmed. The knowledge that he had known all along sat like concrete in her middle, ready to sink her to the bottom of the ocean. Maybe neither of them was capable of being honest with the other. She needed space to think. *Could he still want to be with me? Or does he just want to be with me for the baby? Is he looking to replace the one he lost?*

"I think I need to go." She made her way to the front door, where her shoes waited. Tugging them on and retrieving her jacket, she felt his presence behind her. The smell of his cologne surrounded her, and she wished she had the courage to finish the conversation.

"I don't want you to go, Skylar. I want you to know that I care about you. And I know how unhinged CJ can be. Do you trust me?"

"Damn it, Harmon! I don't know. I have no idea what I'm doing anymore. CJ keeps popping up. I want nothing to do with him, yet I'm carrying his child. His fucking wife came after me one night. I'm trying to fix things with my sister, but my family is a mess." She shook her head again. "Why would you want to be with me?"

Harmon gently took hold of her shoulders, spinning her around to face him. "Because I found a woman who I finally want to talk to at the end of my workdays. Someone I want to explain my past to. A woman who makes me want more again."

Her heart continued to break, shattering into small pieces that she could never put back together. *Saying he'll support me and my child now is one thing, but what about when things get hard? Will he want to continue to be here?* Her worst fear was that CJ might want some sort of custody of her child.

"Please talk to me. Tell me what you're struggling with. I want to work this out. To... to talk it out." Harmon's pleading tone was too much. This man, who'd been through so much, was too kind, while she was running from the devil.

"Do you want this baby as... as a replacement?"

Harmon reared back as if she'd slapped him. "What?"

"I feel like you never got closure with your ex-wife, and now, you have this chance to have a new baby..."

"I can't believe you would ask that." Harmon took a step back. "Skylar, I asked you to give me another shot at a relationship *before* I knew you were pregnant."

Everything was getting all jumbled up. She was ruining things like she always did, she just didn't know how to stop. "I think I need a day to think." She snatched her purse from the counter and headed out his front door without another word.

As the door shut, he said her name on a broken whisper. It echoed through her head as she sat behind the wheel of her car, staring out the windshield. She wasn't entirely sure how long she sat like that, but she was brought back to the present by tapping on her driver's-side window. The sound nearly made her jump out of her skin.

Harmon stood outside her car, his face an expressionless mask. The look in his eyes made her think of someone staring off and not seeing anything before them. Her gaze left his when something in her periphery moved. Her phone was in his hand. She didn't remember setting it down.

Starting her car, she tried to think of what she would say as she lowered the window, but nothing came to her.

"I don't want you to go." He extended her phone to her through the window. "But I won't press you to stay. I hope you have a Merry Christmas, Skylar." Sadness flashed over his features.

"Harmon, I-I don't know what to do." It was hard to admit, but there was no denying the way her life had steadily fallen apart since she met CJ. From there forward, she could see each day like a descent toward this moment. *It didn't have to lead to this, you selfish bitch...* If she'd been thinking that night, if she'd paid attention to make sure he wore a condom, make sure he complied to her request, she would be in an entirely different situation. Or so she thought.

"It's okay. No one has to have everything figured out. Just know I will be here to talk when you're ready. This isn't it for us." He gave her a small, sad smile. "Take all the time you need to think." He patted the roof of her car then stepped away, heading back to his building.

Part of her wished he had tried to haul her back inside. After always coming in second best, she couldn't suppress that familiar feeling now. But she wasn't sure who she was coming in second to. Exhaling, she shifted into reverse and headed back to her apartment. She regretted leaving Harmon almost as soon as she pulled out onto the main road.

Chapter Thirty-Eight

HARMON

It was shaping up to be the worst Christmas he'd ever had. In most recent years, he'd spent Christmas at either his parents' house or, more often than not, Porter's. The clock seemed to mock him each hour as it chimed the advancing time. He was still alone. He'd finally found a woman he wanted to be with, and she'd run at the first opportunity. *What did I do wrong? I said I wanted to be there for them both.*

As the clock finished chiming eleven, he rolled off the couch and figured if he left now, he could at least make it to Porter's for lunch. Verity always served lunch by noon. He took out his phone, debating checking on Skylar, but he put it back. He'd said he would give her space. No matter how badly he wanted to go back on that promise right now, he wouldn't.

Crawling under the tree, he unplugged the lights, looking over the few gifts he and Skylar had gotten for one another that remained unopened. And they would until she came back. He knew she would.

Harmon rifled through his walk-in closet, locating the envelopes with the gifts he'd gotten for Porter and Verity's children. He always got them gift cards. He didn't know what the girls would want, and Hunter was still so young, he figured they could use it for diapers if they needed.

Unable to deny himself any longer, he sent Skylar one message.

Harmon: *I'm going to visit Porter unless you want to come back.*

The little dots of anticipation appeared before he could close the app, as if she had been waiting to hear from him.

Skylar: *Tomorrow.*

One word gave him both hope and a large dose of despair.

With a sad look at the pie they'd made for dessert, he tried to ignore the sweet fragrance emanating from it as he pulled a bottle of wine from the rack next to the refrigerator. He and Skylar would eat it tomorrow, he promised himself.

With the bottle of wine tucked under one arm and the cards in hand, he locked the door with the opposite hand. After taking the stairs down, he stepped out into the cool Christmas day. He was excited to see his friends in just a few minutes. Porter would be the perfect person to bounce everything off of.

The half-hour drive seemed to both drag and fly by. Skylar, the baby, CJ, and how they could possibly move forward swirled around his frazzled mind. The more he thought about it, the more he didn't care if the baby was his by blood. Heck, he'd considered fostering on his own, but he'd worried about his temper. At least with Skylar, he could share the love, frustration, and everything between with her. He groaned as he hit his head against the headrest a few times.

He would tell her as much when he saw her the next day. There had to be some way to prove he hadn't come back to her over the baby. He was drawn to the way she could be herself most of the time, regardless of her past.

Pulling up outside Porter's home, Harmon tried to see if the house at the end of the street was still for sale. Unable to see a sign, he made a mental note to drive down to the end of the street on his way home. Getting away from CJ literally might not be a bad idea. The commute to work would be about the same. He could rent out his condo, make a little extra money to offset whatever the mortgage ended up being on the house.

He shook his head to clear the thoughts as he registered that he was already at the front door. Since lunch would be starting soon and he'd originally planned to stay home, he suddenly felt strange just showing up. Granted, he'd spent the last several Christmases with them, but this year, he'd specifically said he wouldn't be coming. Knocking on the door, he waited to make sure he wasn't intruding. There was a car in the drive next to Porter's parents' car that he didn't recognize.

Verity opened the door, her bright smile faltering for a moment as she looked behind her. Why he hadn't thought of it, he wasn't sure. He didn't know which part was more surprising—seeing his ex-wife, or her protruding belly. He recognized the man next to her on the love seat in the living room from the wedding photos on social media. One of his hands rested on her abdomen. It was as if, this Christmas, the world wanted to rub in his face everything he still didn't have.

"I-I wanted to drop off the kids' cards," Harmon said, already backing down the front steps.

"Harmon, wait," Verity called after him as he turned to head for the curb.

"I don't want to ruin your Christmas."

As he reached for his car door, he realized he'd never given Verity the cards for the kids. "Shit." He peered back up at the house with its perfect exterior and even more perfect little family and their perfect best friends. Something he didn't want to think about swirled in his middle. It was sour and childish.

"Harmon, hold up." Porter jaunted down the steps. He was wearing a ridiculous set of holiday pajamas. No doubt Verity had made him wear them.

Harmon huffed, holding the cards out for Porter to take.

"I didn't come out here for the damn cards." Porter rubbed the back of his neck. "You said you weren't coming. So, when Verity said Jackie was going to be around, I figured it would be nice to invite them."

Harmon nodded, the feeling of botching their holiday already sinking in his gut. But what didn't make sense was that the anger always simmering somewhere close to the surface was nowhere to be found. It was as if being around Skylar had allowed him to open up to a well of emotions he hadn't experienced before.

"No, it's fine. I should have called first."

"Wait, why aren't you with your girl?"

Harmon released a bitter laugh. "Long story."

Porter raised a brow and tucked the cards in his back pocket, then crossed his arms over his chest. "If I can avoid a conversation about breast pumps and delivery room plans, I'm more than happy."

Harmon's gut wrenched at the thought of what had happened to Jackie in the delivery room when they were together—the way neither of them could understand at first, then the concrete wall that had erected between them, one he'd never been able to scale after they got home from the hospital. And it only got worse after Jackie refused to continue her counseling.

Shaking his head, Harmon cringed as he told Porter about their morning.

"So, she wanted space?"

"Essentially."

Porter nodded. "I thought once that Verity and I would break up."

As if he'd been slapped, Harmon's head snapped back. "What did you just say? You two have always been perfect together."

With a snort, Porter said, "There's more to the story of us getting married than you know. But that doesn't matter now." Porter shook his head. "Now, what are you going to do about Skylar and the baby?"

"Nothing, I'm going to give her some space and see what happens."

"Just remember she's loaded with hormones. Make sure she knows you care. And if she's afraid you want the baby as a replacement for Cecelia, you may have to work hard to prove otherwise."

"I will." Harmon dropped onto the driver's seat of his car. "Merry Christmas." His gaze shifted back to the house. "Do you think we'll all be able to hang out again ever?"

"Honestly?" Porter scrunched his face as if thinking far too hard. "I do. Darrin has been good for her. She's more herself."

Something pinched in Harmon's chest. "Tell everyone I said Merry Christmas."

Porter smiled and nodded. "Merry Christmas, you can come in."

"I don't think we're there yet."

Harmon looked over Porter's shoulder to where Jackie stood with her husband. He pressed a kiss to her forehead, one hand protectively cradling her baby bump. Harmon couldn't shake the feeling that it was to protect the baby from him. Jackie stepped away from Darrin and started down the steps toward them.

"Maybe we're getting close," Porter said as he turned away.

Harmon stepped back out of his car to meet Jackie halfway. It looked as if it took Porter a minute to convince her husband to go back inside with him. Harmon hated that his past actions had caused such distrust.

"Hey," Jackie said as she stood a few feet away. She looked good. A healthy flush filled her cheeks. As he took in her pregnancy glow, he found he wasn't jealous, like he'd felt when he first arrived. He was... happy for her, for them.

"Merry Christmas," he said, feeling awkward. It was strange to finally have someone he'd wanted to talk to for over ten years standing in front of him. He could no longer recall what words he'd wanted to say.

"I just wanted to say I'm sorry about how things ended between us." Jackie's eyes fell to the ground.

Harmon swallowed hard around the lump in his throat. "Of the two of us, you have nothing to apologize for. I-I have never forgiven myself for that night."

"Harmon, wait." Jackie held up her hands. The sun reflected off the large diamond on her hand, emphasizing that she had fully moved on and that it was time he did too. "We both made mistakes after losing Cecelia. I should have talked to you, but I didn't. I had so much bottled up inside me."

Harmon let her words sink in. "I think we were both too young and naive to really process what had happened. I only ever wanted to apologize. I am so sorry for everything I put you through at the end of our relationship. I was too dumb to figure out that pushing you into having another baby was one of my most ridiculous ideas." He shrugged. "I just wanted you back—the Jackie I knew when we first started dating."

She smiled and looked back at Verity's house as if she could see her husband. "I know you did. That girl disappeared in the delivery room. Trust me, I wanted her back too."

"I'm glad you've found someone new," Harmon said, needing to bring the topic to something less heavy. The day had already been full of that.

"Thank you. I'm so happy," she said as she subconsciously rubbed her stomach.

"Can I... can I give you a hug?" It was such a strange thing for him to feel like he needed to ask. But it finally felt as if they were putting it all behind them.

Jackie nodded and stepped forward, arms out.

Chapter Thirty-Nine

SKYLAR

It was nearly dinnertime on Christmas, and Skylar was deeply regretting the way the day had gone. There was no way Harmon would want anything to do with her now. It had all blown up in her face, just as she'd feared. If she'd just been honest with him from the beginning, they would be together now. She could have stayed with him that morning. She could have gone back to him earlier in the day, but she'd said she wanted to wait—when really, she didn't. But her cowardice prevented her from saying anything. And her fear had been a waste.

Skylar tucked a pack of crackers into the side pocket of her purse. She'd taken to carrying them with her everywhere. If the nausea became too much, munching on one would miraculously alleviate the need to vomit. Usually. She rubbed a hand over her stomach. Her pants were tight now, but her pregnancy wasn't obvious yet. She couldn't wait until she could look in the mirror and see the proof of her baby inside her.

If the man she'd been getting to know over the last few months could really see himself with a woman who was carrying another man's child, she felt she owed it to him to give it a chance. To not be suspicious of him. Especially since just thinking about him made her heart flutter in a way that could only mean one thing. He'd made a good point. He was interested in her well before either of them knew she was pregnant. He had been willing to throw out his no-coworkers rule for her. It should have been glaringly obvious. *Can I blame it on the pregnancy brain?*

Sliding her feet into a pair of clogs, she pulled on a sweater and headed out of her apartment. She figured Harmon would like the surprise of her showing back up to see him. Stopping by his place to see if he was back sounded like a good way to distract herself. They could try their Christmas again.

But when she stepped out of her apartment, she was immediately grabbed from behind and pressed up against the opposite wall, a chest meeting her back and pinning her in place. A strong, tattooed hand wrapped around her throat. She inhaled sharply.

"You listen, and you listen good," CJ snarled.

Skylar's eyes felt as if they would bug out of her head from the pressure on her throat. She could barely take air in, and when she did, it made a strained, raspy sound.

"I have a proposition for you, and since your boyfriend isn't around, I'd guess we have a few minutes to speak. Yeah?" he asked as if she would agree if she could. "Now, don't you think you should invite me in? Doing business in a hallway isn't very becoming."

Skylar nodded. As soon as she did, the pressure around her throat lessened, and she could take a full breath. She gasped and gulped in as much air as her lungs would allow. The heart trapped in her ribs beat an erratic rhythm for an entirely new reason from before.

"I hate that I have to say this, but if you do anything stupid, I'll shoot you with the gun in my waistband." CJ pressed his pelvis against her backside as if to emphasize what he was talking about. Something hard dug into her flesh. She was torn between hoping it was or wasn't a gun.

When he stepped away, CJ turned to face her apartment door. "As I'm sure you've noticed, I'm not a patient man."

Skylar struggled with her keys, her hands shaking so hard she could barely get the key into the lock. For once, she wanted one of her nosey neighbors to report a commotion in the hall. But the fact that most of the parking lot had been empty when she'd returned that morning made her doubt she could be so lucky. Most of her neighbors were young and would be spending their holiday out of the building.

CJ's hand ripped her key ring from her hand. His cologne surrounded her like a cloud of noxious gas. The scent that had once been seductive was nothing more than nauseating now.

"You can't fucking do one simple thing, can you?" He stepped closer to her, caging her in. He easily slid the key into the lock then shoved her over the threshold as the door was still opening. He slammed it closed again, following her into the apartment.

As she stumbled toward the living room, she tried to casually slide her phone from her purse into the sleeve of her sweater.

"Don't bother. Before you have the chance to call anyone, I will kill you and *my* kid."

A hot rush of adrenaline dropped from her head to her toes. Her heart pounded harder. Her breathing came in short bursts, and her chest ached. The faster her breathing became, the harder it was for her to understand CJ's words as the world began to tilt around her.

His hand collided with her face in a kaleidoscope of pain and spinning. She dropped to the ground at CJ's feet. Her phone skittered across the floor, stopping near the refrigerator. Fingers tangled in her hair as he dragged her back upright. She cried out. Her head felt as if it were in a tornado, and pain radiated from her eye to her chin.

"Sit the fuck down," he snapped as he propelled her to the couch.

Skylar released a shaky breath as she collapsed onto the edge of the couch. Panic settled in, and her entire body vibrated with it.

CJ remained standing, and he put his hands on his hips, opening his jacket to reveal he indeed had a handgun tucked into the waistband of his jeans. With the sleeves of his jacket pushed up to his elbows, the way his arms flexed felt more menacing than sexy as his tattoos rippled with his movements.

"Let's try this one more time," he gritted out. "You will not put me on the birth certificate for the little bastard you're carrying. You won't try to get any kind of child support from me, but if I say I want something to do with the little shit in the future... that's what will happen."

His words contradicted themselves. She couldn't imagine a reality where he would want anything to do with her baby. Because that was what was growing inside her, *her* baby, not his. She knew at that moment she would forever protect this baby from him. But in the meantime, she figured agreeing would be best.

"I have no interest in putting you on the birth certificate." Her spinning mind was starting to slow, and she could think a little more clearly. Perhaps her response wasn't the best, but it was true, nonetheless.

CJ's nostrils flared, and Skylar cringed as he moved his hands from his hips to his knees, bringing his eyes to the same level as hers. "If I try to get ahold of you, you *will* answer. If I tell you to abort that fucking parasite..."

Her heart leaped into her throat at the thought of losing her baby.

"Don't shake your head at me." His hand was in her hair, holding her still. She hadn't even known she was shaking her head. She wanted this baby; she wasn't going to let someone talk her out of it.

Skylar's phone rang on the floor across the room. CJ released her hair, and she rubbed at the spot on her scalp that felt as if he'd nearly pulled the hair out.

CJ bent to pick up her phone. Turning it over in his hand, he sneered as the screen lit up his face in a way that made him look every bit the monster he was. "Your fucking boyfriend is calling." His jaw ticked with clear annoyance. "Remember what I said. *All* of it."

Her throat was too dry to speak.

"Tell him about this or try to report me to the police, and maybe he'll find himself in the ground next to his last baby." CJ tossed her phone onto the counter and walked out of her apartment, slamming the door behind him.

Sobs racked her body as she stumbled to the kitchen counter to grab her phone, then she ran to the front door, where she slid the deadbolt into place. As she looked around her apartment, dread sank into the depths of her middle as her heart ricocheted off her ribs.

Chapter Forty

HARMON

HARMON GROANED AS HE pulled off the highway. He'd tried to call Skylar no less than four times, and each time, the call had gone unanswered. She didn't hit ignore; it just rang and rang until voicemail picked up. *Well, it wasn't declined.* He hadn't been able to muster enough courage to leave a message.

"She's just sleeping, Harmon." He let out a long, slow breath. With the way they'd left things that morning—damn it, Christmas morning—he felt like the biggest dick in the world. On the off-ramp, he decided to check Skylar's apartment to see if she was home.

The streets were relatively quiet. Compared to most evenings at this time, he would have seen so many people heading home from work. The trip to see Porter and Verity sat solidly at the back of his mind. Even more so was the conversation with Jackie. His mind wandered to the flowers he used to send each year on their daughter's birthday. He worried that if they didn't keep her spirit alive, then no one would remember her. Heck, most people acted as if she'd never been a presence in their lives, however short-lived.

As Harmon turned into the lot of Skylar's building, he scanned the cars around him. Relief filled him when he spotted her car in its usual spot. Parking next to her, he took a steadying breath as he prepared to see if Skylar would talk with him about their fight.

Taking the stairs two at a time, he was suddenly hit with apprehension. He wasn't accustomed to overthinking, but the possibility of her not letting him in to work things through sat like stagnant pluff mud in his gut.

As he approached Skylar's apartment door, he forced himself to take a few calming breaths before he knocked. He waited several beats then knocked again. When he reached the third round of knocking with no answer, a more grotesque form of dread washed over him, coating every inch of his flesh. His heart spiked. It was terrifyingly reminiscent of the day he'd found Jackie in the bathroom. His heart pounded so fast, it might cause severe health complications. He pulled out his phone to call her again while he continued to pound on the door. All of his senses were on high alert. The lack of sound on the other side of the door was enough to make his vision blur.

When a door squeaked on its hinges and a disheveled woman stood in the doorway of the neighboring apartment, he didn't know what to do.

"I'm Skylar's boyfriend. Have you seen her today?"

The woman lifted a single brow at him. "Some other man was here earlier, looked like she knew him." She crossed her arms over her middle.

The thought of another man having been there sent jealousy and anxiety pumping into his every muscle. "I assure you, I'm her boyfriend. The man earlier, did he drive a blacked-out SUV?"

The older woman nodded, causing her graying hair to fall into her eyes. Heart in his throat, Harmon pounded the door harder.

"Was that guy bad news?"

"Very," Harmon gritted out between hits.

"I have a key." She turned and scurried into her apartment, shutting her door in his face. He didn't stop his assault on Skylar's apartment door while waiting for the neighbor to return. For all he knew, she was going back inside to call the cops on him.

The door groaned again, announcing the woman's return. She scurried across the hall, unlocking the door as she preceded Harmon into the apartment. With any luck, she was just as worried about Skylar as he was. They scanned the living room and kitchen. But as they worked their way farther into the apartment, they were not met with silence. Instead, ear-splitting music throbbed from behind Skylar's bedroom door. Harmon jogged down the hall. He knocked on the door but got no answer. Taking the knob in his hand, he drew in a breath and hoped for all he was worth that the door was unlocked. When the knob turned, he let out a heavy breath.

"Thank god," he muttered as he stepped into Skylar's room only to find the door to the connecting bathroom shut.

Dread iced him. Like with everything else in his life, once he thought he was in the clear, another obstacle materialized. Everything from his brain to his toes went numb. This door, he knew, would be locked. He started knocking before his hand even reached the handle. He could only hope she would hear him over the music emanating from the stereo by the door.

The neighbor eyed him wearily as she watched him pound on the door and call out to Skylar. He almost collapsed into a heap on the floor when he heard water sloshing on the other side of the barrier. *She's just taking a bath. Just a bath.* He repeated the thought like a delirious mantra. He hadn't been in this situation since Jackie. He'd never cared about another person this much. Now he worried he might lose Skylar and the baby. He hadn't known Skylar long, but he wanted to be there for them both. In the few seconds it took her to get to the door and unlock it, he knew he was in love with her.

CHAPTER FORTY-ONE

SKYLAR

THE FLOOR WAS SLICK under her wet feet. She worried she would slip. Something terrible must have happened for Harmon to burst into her apartment like that. She swung the door open and was met by a familiar chocolate gaze. His eyes were frantic.

"Skylar." His voice was a hoarse whisper, and his eyes dropped to scan the rest of her body before flicking back up to her face. "Your eye."

She opened her mouth to explain, but movement caught her attention over Harmon's shoulder. Tabitha, her nosey, ancient neighbor, stared at her with wide eyes. It was the old woman's presence that clued her in on how Harmon had gotten inside.

"Thanks for letting him in, Tabitha," Skylar said with a weak smile.

"So, you know him?" Tabitha asked, furrowing her brows at the back of Harmon's head. Her eyes held concern; it appeared she didn't want to leave Skylar alone in with him.

Harmon shook his head and leaned to the side, turning down the music. It was as if he'd been so focused on reaching Skylar that he hadn't even thought to turn it down before knocking. She was terrified to find out why he was so panicked.

"He's my boyfriend. Sorry to have bothered you. I hope you have a Merry Christmas."

Tabitha nodded and mumbled something under her breath. She was wearing some hair curlers that looked as if she'd had them since the early nineties and a robe that was older than Skylar for certain. "Mm-hmm." She muttered something else as she shuffled on her slippered feet from Skylar's bedroom and presumably out of the apartment.

"Harmon?" Skylar took in the red of his knuckles and the dampness at his hairline.

"Skylar." He took a step closer to her, cradling her face gently between his hands. His thumb caressed the mark she knew must be visible from CJ delivering his message. "What happened? Why do you have a bruise?"

His expression shifted into something terrifying, but it also caused heat to fill her, starting from her center and spreading outward over her body.

"CJ?" he growled.

"I didn't want to let him into the apartment." She shifted, feeling excruciatingly exposed in her little terry cloth towel.

"I'm sorry I wasn't here for you." Harmon's lips gently brushed across the blemish. "I'm so sorry. Did you call the police?"

Skylar scoffed. "It would be my word against his, and he told me not to. He threatened Zelda in the past and now you, saying that if I call the police—well, he essentially said he would kill you."

Harmon's jaw tensed.

"I'm worried about the baby. What if... what if he demands a paternity test?"

"He knows. I don't know how he knows, but he does."

"He told me as much tonight."

"What did he want?" The tension in Harmon's muscles and face told her just how angry he was. The way he'd barged in here—terrified.

"To let me know what his expectations were—and that, under no circumstances, unless he reached out, was I to put his name on the birth certificate." She swallowed hard, and the lump in her throat broadened as she tried to speak. "He said... He said that if he wanted it aborted, I had to comply."

"Like fucking hell!" Harmon snapped.

"I don't want to."

"You won't have to." Harmon pulled her flush against him as he continued to press kisses to her forehead and temples. "I won't let him get to you again. I promise."

Skylar smiled up at him, but she worried it was a promise he couldn't keep. The thought of getting away from CJ once and for all would be a blessing, but until something drastic happened or he found a new distraction, she wasn't sure how. And now that he had the bargaining chip of something she desperately wanted, she feared he would use it against her.

"How did he get in?" Harmon asked as he looked around her bathroom then her bedroom, as if looking for a clue in the walls.

The fury she'd glimpsed was already gone, his concern for her overshadowing his anger at CJ.

"I was trying to leave, to find you." The admission heated her cheeks, and she dropped her gaze to the floor.

The arms wrapped around her tightened, and Harmon pressed another kiss to her temple. "Were you?" He continued his trek, making his way down her throat to her shoulder.

Skylar swallowed hard, finding it difficult to think as he kissed her. She was exceptionally turned on by the way he was looking at her.

"Yes, I, ah, I wanted to talk to you about this morning... to... to..." It was as if the kisses he'd given her had severed the connection from her brain to her lips.

"To what?"

His playful tone had her struggling between annoyance and amusement at the way he affected her.

"To make sure I didn't ruin everything."

At that, Harmon nipped her neck, causing her to gasp, and he straightened. Closing his eyes, he let out an excruciatingly slow growl. "I need you to put some clothes on before I lose it."

Skylar's heart pulsed in time with the desire ramping up inside her at his admission. "And if I want you to?"

His eyes snapped open as they met hers, and one side of his mouth quirked up in a cocky smirk. "Then I suppose we could talk after. Just know, I am so sorry for this morning. I want you, first and foremost. But I also want *both* of you."

At his words, she pulled the corner of her towel out of where she'd tucked it into itself, uncovering her nakedness. His eyes widened then darkened with desire as he took her in. He was one of the first men she'd ever been with who made her feel truly beautiful.

"Fuck, Sky," he muttered as he pulled her toward her bed. Their mouths fused, and she was drowned in his desire just as much as her own. Each fervent swipe of his tongue made her all the more eager for his touch.

As if he could read her mind, as soon as she thought it, the hand cradling her head slid down her neck to her shoulder then to her breast. The friction between his palm and her nipple made her moan. These damn pregnancy hormones coupled with her lust that had been ramping up the past few days would turn her into a puddle of want in no time.

Chapter Forty-Two

HARMON

While their Christmas morning had started far worse than he ever expected, he was happy to have Skylar in his arms, blissful and sated. The three little words he'd realized were true tingled and taunted the tip of his tongue. But he knew they needed to talk first.

Skylar snuggled closer to his chest. Her hair, still damp from her bath, stuck to his bare skin. Tugging the blankets up to cover them, he threaded his fingers through her hair and tipped her face up to meet his. The softness of her lips met his, and he knew he was where he should be. Questioning if they should be together in the beginning had been foolish. He knew that now.

I cannot imagine life without you, Skylar. Now I just have to figure out how to tell you without scaring you away.

"I think you were partially right this morning..."

Skylar shifted on his shoulder, meeting his gaze. "About what?"

"You know I have always wanted a child, and I always will. But you also have to know that I wanted you well before I knew you were pregnant. Hell, I wanted you when I thought you were Snow White for Halloween. So, yes, I want this baby, but that's only because it's with you. I thought the baby was mine, and in my mind, it always will be." He paused for a moment, taking a deep breath. This next part would be difficult to say. The way she'd seemed jealous of Mandy was one thing. To talk about someone he'd thought he would spend his life with was another. "I saw Jackie today."

Skylar's brows furrowed, and her body tensed next to him.

"It wasn't intentional. I didn't seek her out. I went to Porter's house, and Jackie and her new husband were there. We talked, *really* talked, for the first time since before we lost Cecelia. I think we both needed that closure, to finally finish healing those wounds."

The jealousy in her eyes morphed into something else, compassion maybe. "Are you okay?"

Harmon gave her a half smile then kissed the tip of her nose. "I am. We both admitted we didn't do one another any favors in the final year of our relationship. But we also acknowledged that we were too young to navigate those ups and downs." It was a relief to not only have those thoughts off his chest, but somehow, he felt like less of a monster.

"I'm happy you got that."

"Me too."

They sat in companionable silence for a while.

"We need to talk about CJ."

Skylar nodded.

He extricated his fingers from the tangled mess of her hair.

"So, you know he was upset this morning."

Harmon's chest pinched at the mention of the phone call that had all but ruined their first Christmas together.

Again, she explained the events of the afternoon. He hated the way she described her panic, the way it had closed out all the sounds around her. He wondered if he'd experienced something similar when he'd found her locked in the bathroom, but he'd been able to come back from it rather quickly. She, on the other hand, had used the bath to calm herself. He wished she had felt safe to call him, to ask him to come sit with her. He said as much, and she eventually agreed that if she ever got to that point of panic again, she would.

Harmon shook his head as Skylar finished speaking. "There has to be a way to get a restraining order on him. I know his mother is an attorney, but there must be a way."

Skylar gave him a sad smile. "You've known them longer than I have. Do you really think they'd let me drag his name through the dirt? Plus, now they've met me. I don't know if I want them tracing this back to you—to work."

Harmon forced Skylar's gaze back to his. "I've told you this once, and I'll tell you a million more times. I will choose you over a business deal every time. Our fight this morning didn't change that. I think it made me realize what we really have together." His throat clogged with emotion, and he cleared it. "If anything, after today, when I was worried and I couldn't get into your apartment, then finding that bathroom door locked... I had tunnel vision. All I could think about was getting to you to make sure you were both safe."

A tear slid down Skylar's cheek to his shoulder.

"I want the two of you in my life. Always. Maybe we can just put me on the birth certificate. Could he fight that?"

Skylar shrugged, giving Harmon a sad smile.

"We'll figure it out together. Just know I will not let him take this baby from you without a fight. And I have no doubt that you will be one of the fiercest mama bears out there." Pressing a kiss to her forehead, he debated those words again. "Why in the hell did he put his hands on you? You keep glazing over that part of the story ..."

If he could ever watch a person transform into a raisin and shrink before his eyes in an instant, he figured that would be the most accurate way to describe the way Skylar folded in on herself.

"Apparently, I wasn't focusing hard enough. I don't know, really. My mind was swimming. I just couldn't comprehend what he was saying at first. So, I guess he was knocking some sense into me." Skylar frowned. "Why did you come in here so panicked? I was so scared when I saw you. I thought something had happened."

Harmon flinched. "I couldn't get into your apartment. I was panicking that something had happened to you. When you didn't answer my calls, then you didn't answer the door and your neighbor came over..."

Skylar's eyes grew wide, and she jackknifed into a sitting position.

"What's wrong?"

"When he forced me back into the apartment, he took my key out of my hand." She pulled the offending hand from under the covers as if she would find the key sitting there. "He never gave it back."

"Shit, are you sure?"

"Well, no, I guess not. Like I said, when the panic settled in, I kind of went into this haze."

After hurriedly dressing, they headed out to the ever-messy common space. They checked through the living room, kitchen, and entry but found no sign of Skylar's keys.

"I have to call Z." She scrambled down the hall and headed for the bathroom, retrieving her phone from the counter.

It was on the tip of his tongue to ask her why she was ignoring his calls when her phone was that close, but that would likely throw them back into an argument, which he was not interested in doing. Instead, he went to Skylar's closet while she dialed Zelda and headed out to the living room.

He found a suitcase in the corner and started stuffing it full of clothes. Several pairs of dress pants hung there as well as some of the blouses she regularly wore. He loaded them all into the case. There was no way she could stay here if that sadistic prick had a key.

Marching out to the living room, he found Skylar leaning against the kitchen island. Her soft curves under her silky robe mocked him.

"Z, he has a key to the damn front door. I think it's best we both stay elsewhere for a while..." Skylar paused, listening.

It would make things easier if he didn't have to force her into staying with him until the coast was clear.

"He's fucked in the head. You're not just changing the locks and *calling it good.*"

Another pause then Skylar's pleading eyes met his, and he knew he would give her whatever she wanted.

"Would you be okay if Z and I stayed with you for a little while?" She shifted from one foot to the other. "Just until I can find a way to get CJ to leave me alone. I just don't want him to come after the baby..."

Screeching came from the other end of Skylar's phone call.

"Whatever you guys need is fine by me. My place is big enough." Something conflicted in his gut, making him wonder if he should have held out. He wanted to make sure they were both safe, but maybe he wasn't ready to share his domain with someone else. He hadn't lived with a woman since Jackie. And that thought terrified him.

Chapter Forty-Three

SKYLAR

It was a week after Christmas, New Year's Eve, and Skylar had barely made it until nine in the evening, never mind midnight. As she rolled out of bed, she did her best not to disturb Harmon. Their last week together had been far easier than she'd expected. Zelda had decided to stay with Lara rather than Skylar and Harmon. She'd made a comment that sounded an awful lot like she didn't need to hear them practicing making more babies. Skylar had laughed, but selfishly, she was relieved to have the space for just the two of them.

That afternoon, they would be heading back to her apartment to pack up the last of her belongings. After several discussions—she wouldn't consider them arguments—she and Zelda had agreed they should give up the apartment entirely. Their lease would be up in February anyway, and their landlord almost seemed relieved to know they would be moving out. Likely because no more emergency services would be showing up, courtesy of Zelda's cooking.

But that morning, Skylar intended to meet up with Tonya. After taking a quick shower and putting on a flowy dress, she readied to head out. They planned on getting breakfast and coffee at a local cafe. It was one of Skylar's favorite breakfast spots, Broody Brews. She wasn't entirely sure where the name had come from, but she thought it was funny. The owner was a burly man with one of the gruffest exteriors she'd ever met. Yet he was a big softy.

As she looked in the mirror one last time, she checked for any sign of her baby bump. The small swell was more than her usual stomach, but it was so minute, she doubted anyone would notice the difference. She was a little disappointed. She was officially at the fourteen-week mark and into her second trimester. It felt as if she should be showing with that accomplishment.

With a small, disappointed huff, she headed for the door.

"Hey," Harmon said, sleep heavily lacing the word.

She blushed. "Hey, I didn't want to wake you."

"I'd rather you wake me to say goodbye than wake up alone." He strode toward her wearing nothing but a pair of low-slung sweatpants.

The sight made her wonder if she could wait to leave a little while longer. He wasn't one of those overly muscular men, but he was strong and sure of himself in a way that drew her to him.

"I'll keep that in mind."

Harmon reached her and pulled her into a deep hug. It felt so good to have him to turn to. She had stopped overthinking their relationship and wondering if they were doing everything far too quickly. This was the hand they'd been dealt, and she intended to do everything she could with it—starting with officially moving in with him.

"Good," he muttered against the top of her head. After pressing a kiss to the spot, he continued, "I hope this goes well for you."

The fact that he understood what a big undertaking this was for her flooded her heart with care and love for the man. "Me too." Though he'd made his doubts and worries known, his biggest concern was that Tonya wouldn't change and that she would find a way to take advantage of Skylar.

"Are you going to tell her about the baby?"

After a moment's pause, she said, "I think so. I want to announce it soon, and I feel she deserves to know before I post it on social media and stuff. You know?"

Harmon nodded. He'd gone to his parents' house over the past weekend to explain their situation and tell them about the baby. They hadn't cared about the fact that their newest grandchild wouldn't share a blood connection with them. Skylar's anxiety had prevented her from attending with him. He had tried to assure her they wouldn't hold anything against her, but she worried they would think she slept around. And the last time she'd spent time with a boyfriend's mother, it hadn't gone well.

"I do. I hope you know my mom has messaged me almost every day asking when she gets to meet you," he said with a light chuckle. "I won't force you to meet them, but it would mean a lot to them. And me. Just think about it. Maybe we can plan a trip in a couple of weeks."

Skylar nodded as her throat constricted. "Okay. I will. Think about it, I mean. I should be back in an hour or so." Rising onto her toes, she pressed a kiss to Harmon's stubbled cheek then his lips.

Harmon tipped his head at her, and she knew he'd caught her moment of weakness. With a squeeze of her hand, she was off.

The drive to the cafe was uneventful and, in turn, allowed her thoughts to get out of control. She feared telling Tonya about the baby would incite an argument, and she worried how that would go. With a low, slow sigh, she entered the cafe to find that Tonya was already seated at a corner table, engrossed in something on her phone. After taking a restorative breath, Skylar headed up to the counter. She ordered her usual breakfast. As she waited, she decided to wait until she talked with Tonya to choose if she would tell her sister about the baby. After the barista called her name, Skylar collected her breakfast and headed to sit with the woman who had spent years making her feel horrible about herself.

"Morning," Skylar said tentatively as she placed her coffee on the table.

Tonya looked up, nodded, then took a sip of her coffee. "Mornin'."

"Can I sit?"

The question must have triggered something in Tonya because her responding look of annoyance made Skylar feel like a child again. It never mattered what she said or did—well, not always, but many times since Tonya had become a teenager. Skylar felt inadequate, stupid. That one look brought all those feelings back to the surface.

"Yes." A delicate, forced smile spread across her sister's features.

Skylar prayed that it was a good sign Tonya, too, was trying.

"Thank you for meeting me." Settling into the old black plastic chair, Skylar tried to think of what to say next. She worried these next several minutes were going to be difficult. "So, how was your Christmas?" Even though they had texted briefly on Christmas day, it was only to exchange greetings, albeit amicable greetings. They didn't dive into the activities of the day. Skylar shivered at the remembrance of her Christmas-From-Hell.

Tonya picked at the peeling resin on the table's corner. "Lonely, it was just me."

Skylar's chest pinched at her sister's admission. They could have been there for one another, but instead, they had spent years estranged.

"Me too. Most of the day," Skylar admitted. "I really want us to have a better relationship."

"I would like that too."

Tonya couldn't say much that would surprise Skylar anymore, but that had done it. "Really?"

Tonya nodded. "We're all each other has left."

Skylar blinked away the tears that were ready to spill—damn hormones.

They spent an hour chatting in stilted spurts. Skylar had to constantly reassure herself that they could do this. They would figure it out. People mended estrangements all the time. She and Tonya could join that number.

As she headed back to Harmon's house, she loosed a sigh of relief. Breakfast had been a success. She was moving in with Harmon—officially. Things were finally working out. She was so high off the success of the morning that she didn't think twice when she answered the call coming through her car's speakers.

"Hello?"

"Skylar."

The childish way of dragging out each syllable of her name and singing it made a shiver run up her spine.

"How was breakfast?"

Her eyes shot to the rearview mirror to see if CJ was tailing her again. No one was behind her. "What are you talking about?"

"I saw you. Brooding Brews... Who were you with?"

Her throat constricted at his question, and she couldn't get any words out. Telling him what their relationship was could put a target on Tonya's back.

"Skylar," CJ said in his same smarmy way.

"What?" she ground out.

"From your silence, I'm guessing she's important to you..."

She refused to confirm or deny.

"That's fine, remain silent. I'll figure it out. As you know, I'm... resourceful."

With that, he clicked off. It had sounded an awful lot like a threat, but she wasn't sure if that was his intention. *Now he's going to go after Tonya... Oh god.*

By the time she got back to Harmon's apartment, she was a trembling mess. Harmon looked up from one of his Sudoku books with a hesitant smile. It dropped when his eyes met hers, and his turned to steel as he rose from his chair.

It was seconds before he stood before her, cradling her head in his hands. "What happened, Sky? What did she say?"

Skylar shook her head. "It wasn't her. CJ called. I didn't mean to answer it. I was just happy with how breakfast had gone. I didn't think to check who was calling."

"It's okay. What did he say?"

"He said he saw me getting breakfast with my sister, asked who she was. I refused to speak, and he said he would figure it out."

Harmon nodded, as he usually did while deep in thought. "I think we need to block his number for starters."

Skylar couldn't agree more, but she still worried about his threats to hurt Harmon or Zelda.

"Then, we need to give Tonya a heads-up. I know things between you are... delicate, and I know you want this to work out, but she needs to know to watch out for him."

Skylar nodded. She felt like a robot. *Why do things seem to constantly work against me?* She didn't know if the weight was worry, hunger, nausea from the baby, or just the baby. She swore she had been feeling strange flutters lately, but she hadn't told anyone, worried it was just gas or something foolish. She didn't want to get excited about feeling her child move if it was too early. She didn't even know when that would occur.

"Did you hear anything I just said?" Harmon stood in the doorway to his bedroom.

When he'd moved, she wasn't sure.

A flush covered Skylar's cheeks as she had to admit she'd been lost in her mind. "No, I was... thinking." That was a good catchall.

Harmon gave her a small half smile. Crooking a finger at her, he beckoned her closer. She obeyed until they were nearly toe to toe.

"I'm sorry this hasn't been the day either of us thought it would be. Not entirely, anyway, but it will still work out. We're getting the last of your stuff, remember?"

Skylar nodded against his chest. "Thank you."

Harmon rubbed the back of his neck. "You know I would do anything for you. Right?"

"Yes," Skylar admitted, knowing the same could be said for her.

He held her for a long while, rocking back and forth, and it was one of the best hugs she had ever experienced. Forehead kisses were quickly becoming one of her favorite ways Harmon showed affection.

"Let's go pack your apartment."

Smiling up at him, Skylar nodded. The plan was to meet Zelda and Lara there. Harmon would be their main source of muscle, and knowing the rest of the group, Skylar would be relegated to carrying small and insignificant things. But she wanted that apartment out of her mind. Each time she thought about it, the moment CJ's hand had connected with her cheek filled her mind. It was time to move on. She didn't want to be tied to a place associated with such a memory. She wondered if that was the same way Harmon's wife had felt. The thought had nagged at the back of her mind, and she understood now—not wanting to return to a place where someone she once would have trusted had betrayed her. CJ and Harmon were vastly different in the trust category, but still, she understood.

One of the first things that happened when they arrived at her apartment was Tabitha coming out to investigate. She had been concerned, to say the least, when Skylar had let her know CJ, the man who'd shown up at her door, was no good and that, should he reappear, Tabitha should stay inside her apartment. Harmon distracted the older woman while Skylar headed inside with her empty boxes to get started.

Chapter Forty-Four

HARMON

After extricating himself from the neighbor, who could turn out to be helpful as a witness at some point, he headed into the apartment. The concern she felt for Skylar was evident in every annoying and prying question she had, but he had to remember she was asking, hopefully, with the best intentions.

Once across the threshold, all he could hear was giggling coming from another part of the apartment. He had yet to meet Lara and was quite interested to acquaint himself the woman who had deemed herself the only person qualified to be their baby's pediatric nurse. He didn't even know if people could pick their nurses. The ladies were supposed to be packing all the clothes while he would be loading up some of the larger items. They hadn't moved any of the dressers or other bulky items yet. Smiling like a fool, he peered around the corner. It was so relieving to see Skylar in such a carefree state. Since Christmas and CJ's impromptu visit, she had been jumpy and nervous.

"Now, what could possibly be that funny?" he asked, leaning against the doorframe.

Zelda, whom he found funnier than anticipated, arched a brow at him. "Girl stuff about people you've never met, Mr. Lurks in Doorways. If you spontaneously obtain a vagina, you will be more than welcome to join us... Wait, shouldn't you be in the *kitchen*?" She shot him a devilish smirk.

He had to laugh. That was something he'd heard other men say to their girlfriends or wives, and coming from the tiny blue-haired spitfire, it was too comical.

"I get it." He raised his hands in surrender. "I'm not welcome here. Just wanted to introduce myself to Lara."

She stood from the pile of clothes she was surrounded by. It looked as if they had taken every drawer from the dressers and dumped them on the floor to refold them into boxes. He'd thought they would just bring the drawers down to the trailer, then he would bring down the shell of the dresser, but he wouldn't question their tactics when they were clearly having fun—and he was so severely outnumbered.

"Hi, I'm Lara, Zelda's *slightly* saner sister."

That one earned a giggle from Skylar and a glare from Zelda.

"Nice to meet you. I'm Harmon. Skylar's..." He looked to Skylar for guidance.

They had only been trying things again for a few weeks, and he wasn't entirely sure if Skylar wanted to label things. He'd used the label to assure the neighbor he wasn't trying to break into Skylar's apartment for devious reasons, but that was all.

"Boyfriend," she supplied with a private smile.

Lara grinned up at him. "Now, treat my girl well, because I do know how to make a murder look like an accident," she said, tapping her temple and sending him a wink.

We should set this one loose on CJ and see what happens. "Noted." Fear that he would screw things up sizzled in his stomach as he stepped back and headed for the door. "I'll be in the kitchen."

"Oh, our brother, Jerry, will be here soon to help with the big, manly things," one of the sisters called.

With his back turned, he couldn't tell which spoke. It was a bit freaky. They didn't look much alike, but their voices were identical. He didn't even know that was a thing between siblings. The sisters were small and spritely, and if their similarities carried over to their brother, he wasn't sure what to expect.

"Harmon," Skylar called.

Now that was a voice he could pick out in a cacophony of tones.

"Hey," he said, turning as she approached.

He wrapped an arm around her back, pulling her close. She'd gone from wearing dress pants most of the time to flowy, loose dresses, and he couldn't say he didn't like the change.

"So, Jerry is a cop…"

"Why didn't you tell me before? Why haven't we talked to him about CJ?"

Skylar cringed at his accusing tone. "Because he's still relatively new on the force. I made the girls promise not to say anything. It sounds like CJ's mother has a lot of clout. I don't want him to lose his job for trying to help me. Zelda has seen it in the courtroom…"

There she went, putting other people's needs above her own again. Harmon sighed, but he understood, because he knew how Anne was, and he didn't doubt she was as much of a bitch in the courtroom as she was in her personal life.

Skylar fidgeted then continued, his silence likely amping up her anxiety. "He's only been there six months; this is a better department than the last one he was in. I just don't want to screw things up for him."

Harmon nodded. "Okay, but if CJ pops back up or finds another way to contact you, I want to know immediately."

Their conversation was interrupted by the doorbell ringing.

"That will be Jerry," one of the girls called from the bedroom.

Harmon ambled to the door since he was the closest and swung it open. The man at the threshold was far from what Harmon had expected. With ice-blue eyes, dark hair, and a football player's build, he must be hiding Jerry behind his hulking size.

"Who are you?"

"Harmon. You must be Jerry."

"Yeah, still don't know who the fuck you are." The man was a bit intimidating. Harmon was in good shape, but Jerry had several inches on him and looked like he was well acquainted with all the equipment in a gym.

"Jerry, cut it out," Zelda called as she launched herself at her brother.

"Hey, rascal." He tousled Zelda's hair like she was a child.

"You'll mess it up." She swatted his hand away, laughing.

The way some siblings interacted, their playful jabs, was something he had always wished he could have. Sure, he had Porter, who could tease him relentlessly and gave him the facts when he needed it, but having someone he could just know would always be there—that was something special. But then his mind drifted to Skylar and her sister. Theirs had never been that strong sort of bond.

With a shake of his head, he brought himself back to the present. After Jerry's initial grilling, their endeavor of working together went quite well. He found out that Jerry was two years older than he was with a large age gap between him and Zelda. Their parents had had Jerry while they were quite young and Zelda and Lara later on. But once Jerry had determined if Harmon was a terrible character or not, the day had gone by in a flash. They were soon at Harmon's condo, unloading everything, and Harmon even offered to help unload Zelda's belongings at Lara's house. However, it sounded as if Lara had a neighbor who would be tripping over himself to do anything he could for Lara if her siblings' teasing was anything to go by.

"So, when are you going to post about the baby?" Lara asked, nearly vibrating as she stood by the front door, readying to leave.

"I don't know. You know I'm not huge on big look-at-me posts. If you want to post something about becoming an auntie soon, feel free." Skylar shrugged.

Harmon had rarely seen her on any kind of social media, so he wasn't surprised to see her give away the responsibility to post.

"Can I really?" Lara asked.

"Yeah, go for it. One less thing I have to deal with."

"Please make it obvious you are *not* talking about me when you make the post," Zelda demanded with her hands on her hips. "If I start getting congratulations texts, I'll lose my shit."

Skylar laughed.

No sooner had Skylar given her permission than Lara had her phone in hand. As Skylar and Harmon said their goodbyes to Zelda and Jerry, Lara continued to tap away, then proclaimed she was done and tucked her phone back into her pocket. It took another twenty minutes to finish their goodbyes, then the trio was on their way.

"I'm ready to sleep," Skylar groaned as she checked her phone. It was only six in the evening. "Shit, shit, shit."

"What's wrong?" Harmon asked, tucking a loose strand of hair behind her ear.

"I never told Tonya about the baby this morning, and she's already seen Lara's post."

"Oh, do you want to call her?"

"Yeah, I think I have to. Do you mind giving us a few minutes?"

"Sure thing." He pressed a kiss to her forehead then headed for the bedroom.

As he hung Skylar's clothes in his closet, he had a silent battle within himself about whether he wanted to eavesdrop or continue with his work. Raised voices from across the hall made Harmon pause on his way to the closet with one of Skylar's silky blouses. He couldn't discern what was said, but Skylar's raised voice continued to echo off the walls.

He tugged at the end of his hair, indecision weighing heavily on his conscience. The need to heed Skylar's wishes for privacy fought with the urge to protect her and make sure she was all right. And that included verbal assaults from her sister. While breakfast had gone well that morning, things were quickly shifting now that Tonya had found out Skylar was pregnant. Releasing his hair and a long, determined breath, he hung the shirt and pivoted to check on Skylar. When he tentatively knocked on his office door, he waited for her response.

"Tonya, it's not like that. Don't bring up Christopher. Are you kidding me?" Skylar paused and swiped at the tears running down her cheeks. "I have to go. I need to take care of a few things." Skylar hung up and tossed her phone onto Harmon's desk. It landed with a dull thud as she pressed the heels of her hands into her eyes.

"Hey, you all right?" Harmon crossed the room and pulled her to his chest.

When they were pressed together, she deflated, sinking into his hold. She was always so strong in front of others. He'd never so much as seen her shed a tear in anyone else's presence. It was odd, but it made him feel good that she was comfortable enough to let her emotions show with him.

"I'm fine. Tonya just likes to bring up things from my past." She shrugged under his arms as if it were no big deal.

"Like what?"

"Ugh. Well, I'm guessing you heard me tell her not to talk about Christopher?"

"Yeah." He nodded, his chin resting on top of her head.

"He was my last serious boyfriend. We dated for just over two years." She took a step back from him and sighed. It was clear she didn't want to tell whatever this story was, but it burned inside him to know what the man had done.

Harmon took her hand in his and led her to his desk. After settling into the chair, he lifted Skylar onto his desk, putting her legs on either side of his. "If you want to tell me, feel free. If you don't want to... I just hope one day we can get there."

Interlacing their fingers, she studied the contact as she spoke. "We started dating about four years ago. We met one night when I was taking a walk. I used to love going on walks. Anyway, he came out of a cafe in Mesa. He was on the phone, and it was like straight out of a movie. He wasn't paying attention to where he was going, walked straight into me, and dumped his fresh hot coffee all over me. I had to lose my overshirt pretty quickly to avoid getting burned, and he felt so bad, he walked with me a few blocks to get me a new shirt. We talked the entire way. And I guess you could say we hit it off."

Despite the years that had passed, Harmon couldn't deny the jealousy that coursed through him at the mention of another man in her life.

"We started dating, and things were going great. His parents owned and operated a few food trucks. They focused on organic, vegan, and vegetarian fare. Christopher was supposed to be shadowing his father, getting to know the business better, be more involved. Well, about a year into us dating, they opened a few actual restaurants. The food was good. But no matter what, his mother never seemed to approve of me. I tried. She thought I was too heavy, so I dieted. She didn't like the way I slouched, so I kept my spine straight all the time. Then it just turned into every little thing I did was wrong. I started avoiding going with Christopher to dinners at his parents' house. But then, when their family reunion came around, he really wanted me to be there. It was as if I was walking alongside a stranger as we meandered around the party. He was super critical about everything I did, said, and ate. I don't think I had ever been so uncomfortable in my own skin until that day. I just kind of shut down. I didn't know what I had done to deserve it. I worried that he would leave me and no one else would ever want me, that I would never be good enough. Then, one night, I heard his mother talking about how I would never measure up to her friend's daughter and that was who Christopher should be with. I was just coming back from using the restroom when I heard this conversation. He'd never defended me, not against one dig she made. So, that night, I decided we were done. I didn't care anymore. I hadn't been eating and was trying my damnedest to lose weight so I might be good enough to fit into their family."

Harmon couldn't help the growl that radiated up his throat. "Those assholes."

Skylar nodded. "I guess you could say that. I just didn't have the self-confidence to tell them off. So, when we got back to Christopher's place that night, I told him we were done. And all he said was 'Yeah, probably for the best.' It broke me. I was so devastated that he didn't see a single thing in me worth holding onto. So I grabbed my few belongings from his house and went home. Zelda was ready to rip him a new one."

"I am so sorry they made you feel that way, Sky. I think you're amazing just as you are."

She gave him a weak, watery smile. "Thanks. I've learned a lot over the years. I just still fall into that spot where I worry I'm never going to be enough sometimes. I guess it's important to let you know."

"Is this part of why you were so against going to visit my parents?"

She nodded, and the ache in his chest made him worry his ribs would burst apart. Placing his hands on her knees he leaned up to press a kiss to her lips.

"My parents would never treat you that way. I swear to you."

CHAPTER FORTY-FIVE

SKYLAR

SEVERAL EVENINGS OVER THE last couple of weeks, Skylar had taken to standing in the guest room, wondering what it would look like as a nursery. She always tried to leave before Harmon could catch her daydreaming, but it was a gorgeous room, and she couldn't help but wonder what color it should be. The room was bare necessities now. A full bed sat against the wall with one nightstand and lamp. The room wasn't huge but large enough to make the bed look comfortable in the room.

"You don't have to hide, you know."

Skylar jumped and slammed the door shut.

"What do you want to do with that room?"

She shook her head as her face flushed. "It's not my house. Not up to me."

Harmon gave her one of his half smiles that never failed to make her weak in the knees. "If it were..." he said, turning the knob and pushing the door open again. "What would you do?"

She fidgeted and shifted her weight from one foot to the other as it became obvious he wasn't going to let it go. And for that, she was grateful. Sometimes, letting people know what she wanted and desired was difficult. Blame it on the sister who never cared and told her that her opinions didn't matter. Or the mother who never seemed to consider giving up her drinking for her daughters. Even Christopher who didn't seem capable of supporting her.

"I won't say you're crazy unless you want to paint some sort of insane mural of a thousand cat heads or something." He quirked a brow at her. "That's not your plan, is it?"

"No, I was thinking of a nursery," she said without thinking much more about it. His joke had made her feel comfortable enough to forget her fears of not being taken seriously.

Harmon's half smile turned into a full grin. "You know, I was thinking the same thing. Is that how we're spending our long Memorial Day weekend in a couple of months?"

Harmon was acting like he had before. If she didn't know any better, she would say he had no idea the baby growing inside her wasn't his. They hadn't brought up the topic again since he'd repeatedly told her he wanted to be everything to both her and her baby. And that had sounded like the best idea she'd ever heard.

"Can we?" she asked at a near whisper.

Zelda would be going out with her sister to spend the holiday with their family. Skylar was still struggling with her strained relationship with Tonya, the texts she randomly received from CJ's wife, and the fear that CJ would turn up somewhere. She hadn't heard from him since the day she'd gone to breakfast with her sister, but his wife had seemed to take it upon herself to message Skylar. She didn't know why she hadn't blocked Myra as well. But her messages, while strange, weren't threatening. She kept asking if Skylar was trying to steal CJ away from her. The woman seemed discomfited, yet she had been so confident when they'd met. The day when Myra had ambushed Skylar, she'd been threatening and kept bringing up another woman's name. Skylar nearly choked on her next breath as she remembered the name she never seemed to have a good opportunity to look up, Grace Snyder. How she'd remembered it, she wasn't sure, but she would make a point to look up this woman.

Harmon pressed a kiss to her forehead, "Of course. I'll make some snacks. You get your computer and that pin-it site you like ready to go."

"It's called Pinterest," she corrected as knots of anxiety took root in her stomach.

"Close enough. Now move that sexy ass before I talk you into defiling this room tonight." He leaned in again, snaking an arm around her back.

She giggled and pressed a kiss to his lips. "Pin-it it is..." she said with a sassy sway to her hips as she walked away.

While Harmon got the snacks ready, she hurriedly typed Grace Snyder into her web browser. The title of the first article had her holding her breath. This couldn't be right. "Woman Found Brutally Attacked in Alley Behind Nightclub" the headline read.

Grace Snyder had survived her attack and vehemently claimed she wasn't aware who her attacker had been. When Skylar reached her list of injuries, she nearly cried out when she realized the woman had been pregnant. The beating she'd received, likely at the hands of someone contracted by Myra, had ended in several broken bones. Lacerations littered her legs, arms, and back. The article stated it appeared she'd been whipped. The article didn't mention what had become of the baby, but something in Skylar's gut told her it wasn't good.

"This can't be her." But as Skylar read the article again, dread bloomed in her stomach. She recognized the alleyway in the photo. It was the same one where she'd met CJ. She would be far more cautious of Myra going forward, and she both wished she had and hadn't looked up the damn article.

As Harmon joined her on the couch with the promised snack and a water, Skylar shifted her cursor to close out of the window. Before clicking, she hesitated. This would be just the thing she shouldn't be hiding from Harmon.

"What are you reading?" He leaned in closer as she shifted the screen so he could see better.

Skylar took a handful of blueberries as Harmon read.

"Did you know this woman?"

Skylar shook her head. "You remember how I told you Myra threatened me? She referenced this woman when she made those threats." She pointed at the name in the article.

"Fuck, Sky." Harmon ran a hand down his face.

Chapter Forty-Six

Harmon

"Anne is here," Skylar called from the doorway of his office. Her belly was just becoming obviously pregnant to anyone who looked at her, and it did something to him. It was amazing to watch someone he cared about grow a new life inside of her.

Harmon shook his head. "Send her in, please."

Skylar, nodded, retreated, and returned shortly with the woman who was a brute in most of her life. She was the definition of small dog, big personality. As she stood in the doorway with Skylar at her side, she eyed Skylar up and down with a clear look of disdain. He couldn't help but wonder if CJ had told his parents about the one-night stand that had led to the woman before him getting pregnant. He'd never brought it up because this baby was going to be his and Skylar's to care for.

"Malcom will be joining us in about twenty minutes. I'm here to kick off the meeting."

Harmon had to suppress the urge to sigh at the idea of spending almost twenty minutes with the woman before her husband arrived. "Okay, Skylar, will you bring Mr. Adams in as soon as he arrives, please?"

he asked while Anne made herself comfortable in one of the armchairs facing his desk.

Skylar nodded then exited the room, leaving the door open.

Twenty minutes was a long time to go over the same information that Harmon reviewed with Anne at least once a week. It was excruciating to say the least. Malcom arrived right on time, and as promised, Skylar brought him directly into the room.

"Harmon, how are you, my boy?"

The difference between the spouses couldn't be more glaring. "Good, thank you. How have you been?"

"Good. Good. I'm planning on renovating one of my bars to add a full kitchen…" As Malcom went into detail about the renovations he had planned, Harmon couldn't help but hope the meeting would end swiftly. The way Anne shot scathing looks over her shoulder at Skylar sitting at her desk every few minutes had him on edge. It wasn't her normal behavior. Usually, she would do everything she could to ignore people around them.

"So, I guess what I'm trying to get at with all my ramblings is do you think I can pull some money from one of my investments to help cover these costs without having to pay an astronomical amount in taxes?"

As they discussed the different pros and cons of his options, something sat at the back of Harmon's mind that he wanted to bring up. He just didn't want to discuss it in front of Anne. As if in answer to his prayer, Anne's phone began to ring, and she excused herself, stating it was a work-related matter. Out of the office and out of earshot, Harmon knew it might be his only opportunity, so he needed to make the most of it.

"Sky, I'm just going to talk with Malcom privately for a moment."

She tipped her head momentarily before nodding. The trust in those green eyes pierced right though him, and he hoped he was about to do the right thing. Only time would tell.

"I would like to discuss a personal matter," Harmon said as soon as he closed the door. "And I hope this will not impact our working relationship."

Malcom didn't do much to indicate he was listening other than give a slight incline of his head.

"Skylar, my new assistant, met CJ a few months ago at one of your clubs, Club Ten to be specific. There have been some issues with him in the last few months. It must be almost five months since they met, and he has been harassing her."

Malcom's jaw tightened. Either he was annoyed Harmon would bring up such a subject, or he, as Harmon hoped, was displeased with his son's behavior. While Anne worked in the law system, it was Malcom who took most matters more seriously—especially those concerning behavior and his son. His candid descriptions of CJ in the past led Harmon to believe he would be the better person to approach. Anne didn't like to be told that anyone she was involved with was doing anything wrong, so to accuse her own flesh and blood would be tantamount to accusing her.

"The young lady that showed me in?"

"Yes, her name is Skylar."

Malcom's brows pulled together. "I did notice she's pregnant." He leaned forward, resting his arms on his knees.

It wasn't a question, so Harmon thought it best to keep anything else to himself.

"I'm not going to ask, because I don't want to lie to my wife... but I will tell you, if it is CJ's, it would be best to stay as far from him as possible. I have always done what I can to keep him in line, but there is only so much a father can do. When a person wants to make certain choices, there is little we can do to stop them."

Harmon nodded. He worried this was where Malcom would tell him that his son was an adult and there was nothing he could do to help. "I understand."

"I will talk with both Anne and CJ." He sat back, crossing his arms over his chest, appearing to be deep in thought. "I'll tell you what. I still have ways of tracking his behavior. If I see anything... unsavory. I will intervene."

"Thank you. We would hate to have to file for a restraining order, but we will if we have to."

Harmon's relief must have shown on his face because Malcom continued, "But I will stress that even I can't prevent some of his actions. My influence over him stopped long ago."

Chapter Forty-Seven

SKYLAR

It had been two months since she moved in with Harmon. She was now twenty-two weeks along, and she would be attending her gender ultrasound in a matter of weeks. It was initially scheduled for the first day of her twenty-second week, but they had called her to reschedule because another mother was having pregnancy complications and there were only so many doctors and techs who could handle it.

It had been a few weeks since their initial discussions about what they wanted to do with the nursery, but they'd decided to wait until after the baby shower. So, again, she stood in the doorway daydreaming about the space for her little one.

Harmon came up behind her, wrapping his arms around her middle to cradle her bump. "You still upset?"

"I'm not upset." Her denial was fast and sharp, which only proved his ability to read her. "Ugh fine, I am."

Pressing a kiss to the top of her head only slightly muffled his chuckle. "It's okay to be upset, disappointed, and even annoyed. Today was supposed to be a big, special day, and life happened."

"I feel like life always just happens to me. I've been able to control so little in my life. And I'm always there, holding the construction-grade trash bag to clean up all the shit that follows." As she spoke, she got progressively louder. Once she finished her little tirade, her shoulders slumped. "Sorry."

"You're fine. Stop apologizing. I'd be lying if I said I wasn't upset, but we both know an emergency takes precedence."

She cringed at the comment. She completely agreed that emergencies needed to come first. She was grateful he couldn't see her face.

"Why don't you go pick out some comfy pajamas? I'll run you a bath, then we can watch a movie when you're done."

"I can't. I'm supposed to have dinner with Tonya tonight, remember?"

Harmon groaned in her ear, causing the hairs on her neck to lift and coating her skin with gooseflesh. She stiffened in his arms.

"Hey, don't get me wrong. I am glad you two are working on your relationship. I just... I don't know. I don't trust her yet."

Skylar scoffed. "You've never even met her." Her tone was more accusatory than she meant, but it felt as if he was always against her trying to mend their relationship—or it was the hormones getting to her again.

"You're right. I'm sorry. I just worry about you."

Skylar nodded. Sighing, she headed for their bedroom to get ready to go. The sound of footsteps behind her told her Harmon was hot on her heels.

"We're just getting dinner at Retro. I'm excited to see what the new owners have done."

A young couple in their early thirties had bought the place and were reopening it with the same menu. Skylar just hoped it would be as good as it used to be with Connie and Leon working the kitchen.

"Okay. Then, let me know when you're on your way home, and I will get a bath ready for when you return. I'm sure you'll still want that relaxation."

It had taken a few weeks to get used to it, but it was nice having someone want to take care of her. Usually, she was the one doing all the cooking, laundry, and most of the cleaning. With one last kiss, they went their separate ways for the evening. Part of her wondered if she should have asked Harmon to go with her. But she still worried that if he saw how terrible her sister was to her, he wouldn't want her to see Tonya anymore. Though she was doing better, those little digs still appeared out of nowhere.

Pushing open the front door of Retro sent a pulse of dejection through her. It only took her a moment to spot Tonya at one of the tables to the right of the front door. She looked better than usual. Since they'd started spending more time together, Skylar had noticed the small differences that one could easily miss. Tonya was putting on weight and looking healthier. Perhaps she was fully clean.

"How have you been feeling?" Tonya asked.

It was such a normal question but one she didn't think Tonya had ever asked her before. "Good. The nausea is still recurring here and there, but for the most part, I feel great."

"That's good." A lengthy pause followed, as it was still difficult to come up with conversation topics. "I just got my first sobriety chip." Tonya's cheeks flushed a deep crimson as she admitted it.

Skylar's mouth spread in a wide smile. "That's wonderful news. I'm so proud of you. How are *you* feeling? That's a big milestone."

"Some days really good. Some days not so much. I just want to go back when things feel like they're becoming too much."

Since their meetings and sister time had become more regular, she quickly realized the drugs and alcohol were what Tonya had used as a Band-Aid for their mother's poor maternal style. Skylar had been selfish in thinking she was the only one who had suffered. Tonya had so much anger and resentment for their mother, it was easiest to take it out on Skylar.

Their dinner was one of the easiest they'd shared, and when Skylar texted Harmon that she was on her way home, she was feeling so much better about the day. When she got back home, the tub was indeed filled for her, and all she had to do was retrieve her favorite, albeit hideous, old T-shirt. The shirt had once been her mother's, and it was Skylar's favorite to sleep in. It was one of the only parts of her mother she had left.

As she prepared for her bath, her phone pinged from where it was charging. The damn thing was getting older and was almost in constant need of charging. If the battery lasted half the day, she considered herself lucky. Pajamas slung over one arm and water in hand, she peered at the message on the screen.

Myra: *I heard you have something I want. Something I've always wanted.*

Skylar furrowed her brows, not wanting to believe what the woman could possibly be referring to.

Skylar: *What are you talking about?*

Several minutes passed before the three little dots appeared. She'd almost given up on the possibility that the crazy bitch would reply.

Myra: *My husband's baby.*

The air in Skylar's lungs turned to ice as she read the message over a few times. She blinked and tried to block the contact before anything more could be said, but her fingers fumbled with the anxiety numbing her reflexes.

Myra: *And we will have it.*

The message ended with a winking face. Skylar wanted to be sick. Hands shaking uncontrollably, she needed three attempts to block the number, and she tossed her phone back onto the nightstand as her heart raced. She would have to tell Harmon about this one. Myra's other texts had been those of a self-conscious woman. This one was from the woman capable of nearly beating someone to death.

Chapter Forty-Eight

HARMON

THE SENSATION OF SOMEONE watching his every move sat like sour milk in his gut. Each step made him feel like he might lose his lunch. Harmon had never experienced this strange sense of awareness, but when he peered around himself, he saw nothing out of the ordinary.

After making his way across the parking lot, he scanned the other vehicles in the area. None stood out to him as out of place. The only one he didn't recognize was an older-model silver sedan. It could be any model really, and he couldn't see anyone inside the car. It was likely just his imagination. He and Skylar hadn't seen CJ since he'd shown up at her apartment on Christmas. However, she had told Harmon about the disturbing text from Myra, which seemed to put him on high alert again.

As Harmon started his car, he noticed movement in the old sedan. Someone was in the driver's seat. Awareness prickled the back of his neck.

He dialed Skylar as he backed out of the parking spot. She was at one of her appointments, and the rescheduled ultrasound would take place in another week. Soon, they would find out the gender. He didn't care if the baby was a boy or girl. He just hoped the delivery went well. The last thing he wanted was to watch another woman he loved lose something so precious. He'd wanted to attend that day's appointment, but she assured him that he didn't need to go to every single one.

Clearing his throat, he waited for Skylar to answer. It wasn't like her to let the phone ring more than a handful of times before answering—other than Christmas, he reminded himself. They'd worked out so much over the last several weeks. They'd discussed what they wanted to do with the nursery, and Harmon had the distinct feeling Skylar wouldn't choose to get her own apartment again. That was one discussion he would wait for her to broach. He was perfectly content with her making his space hers. The way her perfume lingered in a room a few minutes after she'd left it did something to him. He still hadn't had the chance to check out the house near Porter and Verity, other than his drive by on Christmas. That may be something better left until after the baby was born. Skylar had already moved once. He didn't want to do that to her again before she was due.

"You've reached Skylar's voicemail. Leave a message."

Reaching voicemail caused the panic to expand in his gut, the spoiled-milk feeling growing to severe discomfort.

As he pulled onto the main road home the silver sedan pulled out behind him. *Just a coincidence,* he told himself over and over as the sedan followed two cars behind him.

Not wanting to lead a potential robber, or worse, back to his house, Harmon pulled into the lot of their usual grocery store. Driving to the far end, he found a spot where he could back in and face the entrance. A mixture of vindication and dread filled him as the car pulled into the lot as well. If this had been their intended destination, they could have several more direct routes.

Harmon waited for them to park. The sedan pulled into a spot one row away from him. As he waited for them to get out, he was shocked to see the driver had long black hair. She faced him, and he wasn't sure how to feel about a woman following him.

After waiting a few minutes without the woman getting out of her car, he went into the store, acting as if he hadn't seen her. On his way passed, he took note of the out-of-state license plate, make, and model. As he stepped into the store, his phone rang in his pocket. Ripping it out, he released a relieved breath to see Skylar's name.

"Sky, how was the appointment?" Harmon's heart seized when he heard sobbing on the other end of the line. His vision tunneled as the fear gripped him over what could have made her cry. "Skylar, darling," he said in a slow, measured voice so as not to betray his teetering emotions. "Is the baby, okay?"

"Yes," she said around sobs.

Closing his eyes, Harmon used one of the carts in the vestibule to keep himself standing. "Then, why are you crying?" he asked as gently as he could.

"I got to see him. It was amazing. He looks like a real baby. You know? I didn't know they were going to do an ultrasound." Hiccups broke up her words. "I-I wanted you to be there. I shouldn't have told you to go to that meeting. I should have let you come with me." Her sobs started all over again as she cried harder.

"Are you still at the doctor's office?" Harmon tried to do the time calculation.

"No, I just got home, and it was killing me that you missed it. I'm so sorry."

"Hey, it's okay. I'll be home soon. Why don't you get changed and turn on one of those home reno shows you like? What do you want for dinner?"

Skylar sniffled but remained quiet on the other side of the line. "You're not mad?"

A different ache took over his chest. "No, I'm not. Did you get any pictures?"

Skylar scoffed. It was a wet and ultimately unattractive sound, knowing she had been crying, but he couldn't help wishing he was there to wipe the tears from her face and make her feel better. "Of course I did."

"Okay, I'll make you..." Harmon paused to rack his brain for something quick and easy he could make them for dinner. "Chicken bacon ranch wraps with some fresh strawberries." The fruit had been Skylar's obsession lately, and Harmon was mindful to keep them stocked in the house. It had been blueberries only a couple of weeks before, but she was apparently making her way through each variety of fruit.

"Okay," she said slowly as if she didn't believe he wasn't angry with her.

"There's one catch," he said with faux sternness. "Zelda doesn't get to see the pictures until I do."

Skylar laughed again as she agreed. "She's going to be pissed," she said with the lightness in her voice that he preferred.

Harmon chuckled. "Good, she can wait until after I've seen this little human."

"She's on her way over now."

Skylar snort-laughed, and Harmon shook his head.

After virtually running through the grocery store, Harmon picked up everything he thought they would need, likely forgetting at least one thing.

As he raced around, he didn't see the woman with black hair nor did he see the car when he left. His mind was split between wanting to know who it was and wanting to ignore it so he could focus on Skylar.

Before leaving the parking lot, he sent a text to Jerry with the photo he'd taken of the license plate.

Harmon: *Any way you can find out who this is registered to?*

Harmon drove home anxiously, checking his phone at each traffic light and stop sign to see if Jerry had gotten back to him. The screen had remained irritatingly blank. As he stepped into the ancient elevator, his phone finally chimed with a text notification.

Jerry: *It belongs to a car rental agency. What's up?*

Harmon hesitated only a moment as the lift slowly brought him up to his floor but ultimately decided Jerry was someone Skylar trusted, so he should do the same. After he typed out the message explaining why he was questioning the car, he silenced his phone so he could enjoy the rest of the evening with Skylar.

CHAPTER FORTY-NINE

SKYLAR

SHE WAS BOUNCING OFF the walls, waiting for Harmon to get home. The thought of not being out in the living room was not an option. She paced in front of the door while he took off his shoes. Zelda was down in the baby's room, or what would become the baby's room, taking measurements for Lara.

"My word, Sky." He chuckled. "You're like a kid waiting to open a present."

"Even better than that." She bounced on her toes. Her small baby bump was becoming more visible every day, or so she felt. Absolutely nothing fit right anymore, and she had resorted to wearing stretchy dresses or yoga pants most days. The sundresses didn't have much stretch to them. "I get to show you something I'm making."

Harmon's head fell back as he laughed. "That's one way to put it." He pulled his wallet and keys out of his pocket to set them on the entry table like every other night. But something about his movements made it seem like he was taking longer than usual.

"Are you moving slower tonight?"

Harmon peered at her with a suspicious smirk. "It probably seems like I'm moving slower because you're moving around the place like the Energizer Bunny." Holding up his hands in surrender, he leaned forward to press a kiss to her forehead. He kept his hands up as if she would accuse him of something more. "Z, you better get out here quick. She's about to burst," he called.

Skylar rolled her eyes as she bounded back to the living room. The envelope she'd left the hospital with sat in the center of the table. It had been so amazing to see the child she was growing, and she wanted to share her excitement with the people who meant the most to her.

Something stung in her chest as she thought of Tonya. She wanted their relationship to improve more before she started inviting her over for these kinds of moments. They'd fallen into a routine of making weekly calls to one another and monthly dinners. It had taken a couple of weeks to calm Tonya down about keeping the baby a secret. Skylar kept certain things from their conversations to make sure she didn't feel too vulnerable too soon.

Zelda wasted no time getting to the living room, tape measure in hand. The woman who proclaimed she didn't like babies was becoming more and more excited about the prospect of meeting the one Skylar carried. "Let me see that crotch goblin now that Mr. Bossy Pants is home." After she said it, she looked at Harmon through slitted eyes. "I suppose that fits in a few different ways. You have lots of rules in this house, *and* you're my girl's boss."

"Asking you not to leave your undergarments hanging over the shower rod when you spent the night *once* wasn't such a big deal."

Skylar could hardly contain her smile. The fact that her best friend and boyfriend got along so well had been one of the biggest reliefs she'd experienced in a while.

Zelda lifted one brow then turned back to Skylar. "Let's see her!" she said, swiping her blue hair out of her eyes. She'd just had it redone, and the color was brighter than Skylar had ever seen it.

Skylar nodded as she pulled out the black-and-white images of her baby's profile. "Also, Z, it's a boy." Skylar grinned. Through the entire pregnancy so far, she'd been thinking of the baby as a girl. The thought of it being a boy hadn't crossed her mind. Initially, when the tech had explained what she was seeing on the screen, she'd worried she would feel disappointment at the baby being a boy. It never came. Instead, she started picturing Harmon playing toss with a little boy, teaching him how to swing a bat, and she felt peace. Even now, as they examined the photos, she imagined an older Harmon taking a little boy to the park, roughhousing with him, carrying him on his shoulders. Each thought brought that sting to her nose and the back of her eyes. She needed to calm down. She had never cried so much in her life.

Harmon's eyes grew wide. "A boy?"

Skylar nodded.

"That's wonderful, Sky," he said as tears filled his eyes. "You said 'he' on the phone, but I didn't think too much about it."

As she showed Zelda and Harmon the pictures, explaining what she thought each body part was in the images, she couldn't help the sinking feeling in her gut. CJ didn't show any respect to women, so thinking it was a girl had been safe. *Why would a misogynist want anything to do with a daughter?* But a son, a son could be his—everything. Myra already wanted him, without knowing the gender.

Zelda video chatted with her sister so Skylar could tell her everything she'd just told Harmon and Zelda. Lara had been working late and wanted to be there but couldn't find someone to switch her shifts. At that moment, Skylar wished this milestone was one she *could* share with her sister. The relationship between Zelda and Lara was all she wanted for herself and Tonya. Some options just weren't available unless both parties wanted the same thing. And Skylar's fear of Tonya eventually betraying her prevented too much progress. Tonya just wasn't like either of the girls before Skylar. When Zelda took her call into the other room as the sisters discussed their mother, Harmon turned to Skylar.

His fingers threaded through her hair, pulling her face to his. The press of his lips against hers felt bittersweet. That searing pain of knowing someone could ruin their joy sat heavy around her, as if it could block the happiness from fully penetrating.

"What are you thinking?" Harmon pressed one more tender kiss to her lips.

Swallowing hard, she knew keeping her fears to herself wouldn't do either of them any good. "What if he wants the baby because it's a boy?" Pain pinched her heart as she asked. The acknowledgment that the baby wasn't Harmon's didn't get any easier.

His dark eyes narrowed as he considered her question, and each second that passed felt like an eternity where she feared she would lose everything she cared about. "I won't sugarcoat it."

Another sharp pinch caused her to suck in a deep breath.

"It scares me too. I want you to know that I will do literally anything for you and this baby. I will do everything in my power to protect him from his sperm donor. But I will also respect any of your wishes. I'm not sure how this will play out."

His careful words brought tears to her eyes. She didn't like the resignation in his voice. "What do you mean?"

"I mean, I want to be this child's father in every sense of the word that matters, but I won't push my wants on you. I've seen what that does to people." His voice cracked on the last word.

Picturing Harmon with another woman was painful too. They were in such a fucked-up situation, she was at a loss for what they needed to do.

"You will be. I don't think I will ever trust CJ enough to let him take this baby anywhere." The idea of strapping her baby into a car with a man she couldn't trust brought added anxiety racing through her veins.

An unknown number flashed on Skylar's phone, where it sat next to the ultrasound photos of their son. Dread sank into every nerve ending in her body. Unknown numbers rarely called her.

Nothing good ever lasts.

"Hello?" she croaked into the phone.

"What was your appointment for today?"

Ice-cold dread coursed through her body. Her breathing accelerated as she thought of how quickly he'd found out.

"CJ?" she asked as her eyes locked on Harmon's as if asking him to save her from the call with the man dead set on ruining her life.

"Hi, *darling*. How's my baby?" The use of Harmon's pet name for her made her wonder if people close to them were watching their interactions for CJ. But their circle was small, and she didn't think anyone they'd put their trust in would betray them.

"He's not yours." Her voice was low and hesitant. The color drained from her face as she said it. Just in the last few hours, she'd discovered the baby was a boy, and she'd already let it slip. Pregnancy brain was no joke.

"He?"

Her breathing accelerated. Unsure of what to do, she looked to Harmon for help, but he was frozen in place. A pained expression crossed his features as his fingers turned white with their grip on the coffee table.

"This baby is not yours. It's mine and Harmon's. I want you to stop calling me."

"Let me let you in on a little secret…" His pause did nothing more than heighten her anxiety. "I want that baby, and I will have him. Didn't Myra already tell you that?"

The implication sat in the air around them like a dense fog. It was disorienting.

"So, you'll give me that baby, and we will no longer need to have a connection, yeah?"

"No." Skylar's voice cracked on the word.

"Let me spell this out for you. A few well-placed compliments and a couple of vague threats can do a lot for a person. So, either you will bring me that baby after its birth, or I'll hire someone to do it."

Harmon's posture stiffened further, letting Skylar know he'd heard CJ's demand. Not for the first time, she could see the anger Harmon was worried about. It was written in the way his hands fisted at his sides, the muscles in his forearms flexing. Even with all the frustration and fury radiating off him, she wasn't afraid of him. She was more afraid of the man on the other end of the phone.

Chapter Fifty

HARMON

HARMON MIXED CREAM INTO his coffee as he prepared for the day ahead of them. Skylar had become a husk of herself since her call with CJ a few weeks before. It had taken everything in him to not leave Skylar at home and find the asshole. Since CJ had said he wanted the baby, Harmon's anger had been a steady sizzle under his skin. He knew how much Skylar wanted this child, and if he was being honest with himself, Harmon did too. Everywhere she went, Skylar seemed to look over her shoulder. She didn't want to go much of anywhere without Harmon at her side. Knowing it gave her a sense of safety felt good, but to know how terrified she was made him want to find CJ and rip his limbs from his body. This newfound rage was beyond anything he'd ever felt before; he was terrified he would take it out on someone around him. Skylar could bring out the softest but also the most brutal side of him. He wanted to be the warrior who protected her—and the baby—from all the monsters of the world but also be the comforting embrace that would show them they were home. The fact that he could love an unborn being so much felt foreign. He didn't remember feeling this way about Cecelia when

Jackie was pregnant. Sure, he was excited, but something was different. *I'm not an immature twenty-year-old anymore.*

Skylar was in the other room preparing for her baby shower. She was down to the final stretch, and Harmon was torn about whether or not he was excited to get to the end. Part of him was still stuck in that delivery room with Jackie all those years ago. The moment of finding out his baby was stillborn would never leave him. He was okay with that; he just needed to find a way to separate that moment in his mind. He never wanted to forget Cecelia, but he'd already reached a point where it wasn't debilitating to think about every day, and he wanted to keep it that way. Otherwise, he would be worthless to Skylar in the delivery room.

"Can you help me with this zipper?"

Skylar stood in the hall, her back fully exposed. Looking at her from the back, no one would know she was pregnant. Stepping forward, Harmon took the tiny zipper and slid it up, peppering kisses along her spine as he went. The dress was a blue-and-white floral print. It reminded him of a tea set his grandmother used to have. It hugged Skylar's protruding bump.

Turning, she smiled up at him. "Thank you. You're coming with me today, right?" Fidgeting, with her fingernails, she avoided eye contact.

"Absolutely, darling." He tipped her chin up to meet her eyes then pressed a kiss to her lips. The subtle scent of her shampoo filled his senses. He wanted to bask in it. But he needed to get dressed and ready if he was going to go with her. They were on their way to a local hotel, which Zelda and Lara were turning into what they called the Wild Jungle of Arizona. He wasn't remotely sure what that would entail, but he knew his only duty was to make sure Skylar arrived at exactly eleven o'clock.

She looked up at him with such adoration, he couldn't help but mirror her expression. She was beautiful. He could get lost in the glow filling her.

"I love you," he whispered in her ear and chuckled as it elicited a shiver through her body.

"I love you." When she leaned forward to tuck her head under his chin, he closed his eyes, just trying to focus on the feeling of the moment, the way her baby bump rested against him.

Harmon gasped. "Did he just move?" It was the first time he'd actually felt it. He stepped back and pressed a hand to Skylar's middle, hoping the baby would move again, and he did.

"Yeah, he's been going crazy all morning," she said. "He's a regular party animal, I guess."

"Sounds fitting based on what the party is."

Skylar giggled, and he watched the way her stomach bounced with the action.

Harmon knelt before her, cradling her belly in his palms. "Hey, buddy, we can't wait to meet you."

They had just about seven weeks left. He stayed on the floor for several minutes talking to the baby, who continued to wiggle, and as the minutes passed, Harmon felt as if he would tear up. It was a moment he didn't think he would ever forget. He wouldn't want to forget it, for that matter.

***

When they walked into the hotel, Harmon found little signs with large tropical leaves around the borders directing guests to the hotel's conference room. When they reached the designated space, it looked as though Tarzan had been filmed in the room. It was ridiculous. Large animals and trees filled the space along with enough balloons to float a school bus into oblivion. Harmon's eyebrows rose. What those sisters had been able to pull off was unbelievable.

Skylar gasped as she came through the door, no doubt experiencing the same delusional thought that they had stepped onto a movie set. "It's beautiful," she whispered as tears filled her eyes.

"She's here!" Zelda or Lara shouted—he still couldn't tell their voices apart.

Harmon squeezed her hand then pushed her forward to see her friends. As he searched the space, his stomach sank as he took in all the faces—female faces. Being not only surrounded by all the baby things, and no doubt emotional women, would have been more bearable if he were at least in the company of another man. Just as his prospects of having someone to sit with were nearly depleted, a heavy hand landed on his shoulder.

"You want to go to the restaurant bar and grab a beer? They're going to be here a while."

Turning, Harmon was relieved to see Jerry.

"Those two hellions forced me to blow up about a hundred and fifty balloons, and less than half of them needed the goddamn helium tank they tricked me into dropping off. I need to escape before the party is in full swing and they decide they need a dancing monkey to complete the theme."

Harmon chuckled, but something clenched in his stomach. Skylar had been so nervous about being away from home that part of him felt guilty for even considering it. "Let me go say goodbye to Skylar," he said as he walked away. If she protested at all, he would stay.

Jerry nodded and edged closer to the door. The large, burly man clearly couldn't deny his sisters whatever they asked for. Not for the first time, Harmon wondered what it would have been like to have siblings. As he approached Skylar, he was reminded of how carefree she could be. He wished he could freeze this moment in time—the way she looked around her friends.

"Hey, darling," he said in Skylar's ear when he was close enough. "How would you feel about me getting a drink with Jerry at the bar?"

Ducking her head as if embarrassed, she flushed. "Go ahead. I hadn't thought about how many people would be here. I feel foolish for making you come."

Being her safe person would never get on his nerves. "I'm more than happy to be here for you. We'll be back." As he pressed a kiss to her neck, he was enveloped in her sweet floral fragrance.

Not wanting to delay whatever the girls had in mind for the shower, he headed back toward the door, scanning the crowd for Tonya. Skylar had been nervous about inviting her, and Harmon had yet to meet her. But none of the faces appeared to share any features with Skylar.

"Hurry up, man, before they rope me into one of the stupid games they have planned. Something about measuring shit with toilet paper. I want nothing to do with that."

Harmon shook his head as he tried to picture Jerry being forced into doing anything.

Chapter Fifty-One

SKYLAR

As she sat front and center for the baby shower, surrounded by all her friends and loved ones, Skylar couldn't help but bask in the feeling of support. Tonya had messaged her just after Harmon left saying she wouldn't be able to attend. With a promise to meet up at a later date, Skylar wasn't sure how she felt going into the party without her sister. But around her, she had her found family. Zelda, Lara, and even Connie had made the trip back to celebrate with her.

A hotel employee scurried into the room, and Skylar tracked his movements as he hurried around to the front table. The gifts were half opened, and the man looked as if he was on a mission. She hoped they weren't being evicted. He whispered something in Lara's ear then handed her something. She smiled, nodded, and headed for Skylar.

"Someone dropped this off at the front desk for you. They said they didn't have time to come to the party."

A small smile passed Skylar's lips as she thought of Tonya making sure to drop something off before she reported to her new job. It seemed as if she was finally getting her life together.

Nothing was written on the outside of the powder-blue envelope. Whatever was inside stretched the envelope to its maximum capacity. Confused, Skylar eased her finger along the edge. Pulling out the card, she nearly gasped when a small stack of photos fell into her lap. They were photos of her alone, with Harmon, Zelda, Tonya, and even Lara. Her eyes darted around the room just as a flash caught her attention from the back of the room. She didn't have to be too close to recognize the signature bright-red hair. Myra gave her a small wave over her shoulder as she walked away.

Skylar was nearly hyperventilating. She didn't know what to do. *Stop the woman?* She couldn't prove Myra or her husband had anything to do with the creepy photos in her lap. Nor did she feel as if she would gain anything from calling the police on CJ. Jerry and Harmon were just down the hall. She could call them.

Unable to stomach looking at the photos, she shoved them back inside the envelope, causing Zelda to tip her head in suspicion. She sat next to Skylar, taking notes on all the gifts so Skylar could send out thank-you cards at a later date. This was one she didn't plan on sending.

More annoyed than anything, Skylar functioned in a haze. Part of her wanted to send someone to get Harmon, but the other part told her it would do nothing but worry him. Shoving the envelope into the bottom of a bag she'd already opened, she turned back to Lara to open the next gift.

She would find a way to stop these people. She didn't care what it took. She *would* find a way. She spent the remainder of the baby shower thinking about anything she could do to stop CJ and his crazy-ass wife.

She kept coming up empty. She needed to talk with Harmon. He would come up with a plan.

Chapter Fifty-Two

HARMON

"Hey, Jerry. Were you able to get those video clips from the hotel?"

"Yeah, you should receive an email anytime now. I still can't believe they all kept this a secret from me."

Harmon still felt bad about going against Skylar's wishes and enlisting Jerry's help. But the fact that the hotel would have cameras had prompted him to see if Jerry could assist. Especially since he had also been looking into the rental car for Harmon. After a few calls to the rental agency and the added pressure of Jerry being a police officer, he managed to figure out the car had been rented by Myra Adams. They had yet to work out why she had been following Harmon with a rental car.

"It was her all right," Jerry said as Harmon waited for the email to load.

It was early on Sunday morning, and Harmon was out at the dining table while Skylar slept. The baby shower the day before had taken a lot out of her. "I think that's the woman from the grocery store. I just don't get why she was wearing a wig and following me."

"I've been doing a bit of digging. CJ had been brought in multiple times for various assault, theft, and drunkenness charges over the years.

I'm shocked nothing ever sticks. His mother clearly has some major pull."

Harmon nodded as Jerry spoke.

"But Myra has a rap sheet just as long. The woman has been arrested for harassment multiple times as well as assault. But again, nothing sticks."

Harmon let out a low growl. "These fuckers will be nearly impossible to stop."

"I'm afraid we'll need some concrete evidence against them—and an unbiased judge, attorney, and police personnel. I haven't brought this up to my partner or any of the others in the precinct. I'm still trying to acclimate and figure out who I can trust. I can confirm the chief likes to stay on Anne's good side, and most of the officers who have gone against CJ in the past find themselves without a job rather quickly."

Harmon pondered the revelation. Perhaps Skylar had been right to be wary of involving Jerry. "That right there is the reason Skylar avoided telling you."

"Damn her. She's like another sister. I don't think I'd be able to tell her no either," he added quietly almost as if it were an afterthought or new, sad revelation.

With a promise to keep Jerry updated with any new happenings, Harmon disconnected just in time to hear the bedroom door open. Skylar all but stumbled out.

"Who were you talking to?" She rubbed one of her eyes while the other hand cradled her middle.

"Jerry. He was able to get the video from the hotel. It was Myra who dropped off that envelope."

Skylar groaned. "Figures." She huffed then lowered herself into one of the dining chairs. The way she did it made it seem like she was in pain.

"You okay?" He stood to kneel in front of her, taking her hands in his.

"Everything hurts today. I apparently overdid it yesterday."

Harmon chuckled and tucked a stray hair behind her ear. "I guess we just need to have a relaxing day today."

"I wanted to get all the baby clothes washed, folded, and put away." Her voice cracked as she spoke. "I don't even know why I'm crying." She raised her hands then dropped them as if to emphasize her confusion.

"I'll wash everything, then we can sit on the couch together and fold them. Sound good?" It was the best concession he could think to offer her.

***

It had taken most of the day to get all the clothes sorted by size and ready to Skylar's satisfaction. They had also been able to get the hospital bag packed. It was the first moment all day Harmon had had to himself since Skylar awoke. Her being overtired, coupled with her hormones, meant he had been cautious with his words and actions all day. More tears were shed that day than he thought he had seen in all the months they'd been together. As Skylar napped on the couch, Harmon took the opportunity to take a call out on their small balcony off the living room. It was rarely used but a great spot to head if he wanted to have a private conversation.

The phone only rang a handful of times before being picked up.

"Harmon, what can I do for you?"

Figuring it was best to rip off the Band-Aid, Harmon dove in. "Malcom, I told you I didn't want to get a restraining order, but it seems that is the next step we need to take. I just wanted to let you know what we were planning."

There was a pause and some shuffling on Malcom's side of the call. When the background noise subsided, he finally spoke. "What's happened now? Is everyone okay?"

"We're all physically okay, but Myra and CJ have made it obvious they would like to take Skylar's baby. I'm working with someone now to pull together the evidence of them stalking her."

The silence that stretched felt as if it would last for an eternity.

"CJ was removed and banned from all my clubs over the last two weeks. I have a few last resorts I'm working on. But you need to do what you feel is right for your family."

Harmon took that as his green light to proceed.

"Thank you for understanding, Malcom."

"I only wish I could do more. I won't be mentioning this conversation to Anne."

After their call was disconnected, Harmon wondered, not for the first time, why Malcom was with Anne. Part of him wondered if he was trapped in a way. Knowing Anne, she would find a way to strip everything from him. And Malcom likely didn't want to risk losing everything he'd built over the years. Or perhaps, Anne's rose-tinted glasses had been welded on, and she would never be able to see the man she had enabled. After all, if she saw CJ for the monster he was, she might have to admit her own culpability, and that was not something Harmon could anticipate her doing.

CHAPTER FIFTY-THREE

SKYLAR

WITH ONLY FOUR WEEKS until the baby was due, Skylar had ignored the envelope of photos for the last couple of weeks. She still hadn't been able to come up with a plan to eliminate CJ. Harmon had been irate when she'd told him what had happened. She couldn't really blame him.

Harmon and his friend Porter were doing everything they could to set up the nursery. Skylar sat in the living room with Verity, Porter's wife, who just so happened to be Harmon's ex-wife's best friend. *Awkward.*

She felt as if everything she said would be judged as she watched their three children play Chutes and Ladders on the floor. They all seemed to be taking it very seriously—well, everyone but Hunter, the baby of the group. He was about two and a half, if she remembered correctly. When it was his turn to spin, he never spun it just once, much to his sisters' annoyance.

Verity sat in Harmon's recliner with her legs tucked underneath her. "Are you ready to be done?"

Skylar released a long, slow breath and nodded. "Sometimes, I feel like he's trying to break my ribs."

Verity tipped her head back, showing off her slender neck as her long blond hair cascaded down her back. If Skylar had had to guess how many children Verity had carried, she would have said none. She had never seen a person who seemed to bounce back like she must have.

"Trust me, they all feel like that in the end." Verity smiled almost wistfully at her children. "I hope you know, being Jackie's best friend doesn't mean we can't also be friends. I would never hold you being with Harmon against you."

Skylar let out her first full breath since meeting the couple that morning. "That means a lot."

Verity seemed to consider her. "There was a time I thought Jackie and Harmon were perfect for one another. But then, seeing her with Darrin, her new husband, I'm amazed she and Harmon were ever together. I'm not sure if that makes sense or makes you feel weird." She laughed in a self-deprecating way. "I guess what I'm trying to say is that, while Jackie and Harmon didn't work out, I think they both found who they were supposed to be with. And I genuinely want them both to be happy."

Skylar nodded through her tears. "How long have you and Porter been together?"

"Oh gosh, about fifteen years now. It's a little crazy to think. We were twenty on our first date, married after college graduation, then we moved here to be closer to his family." She shrugged as if surprised by how they'd gotten where they were.

Skylar nodded. She'd never had a relationship last more than two years, never mind seven times as long.

"It hasn't always been easy." Verity paused as if unsure she should continue. "We didn't have the most conventional start to our relationship. I was—"

Skylar's phone buzzed, drifting across the coffee table. The flash of her sister's name on the screen caused a knot to form in her throat. "Sorry, that's my sister."

Verity nodded with a sad smile.

"Tonya?" Skylar answered.

A strange pause followed while she waited for her sister to respond.

"I came to your apartment to offer you a gift for the baby, and you've moved?" The accusation in Tonya's tone sat like a dagger poised to make Skylar the devil she always was.

"I'm sorry. Things have been a bit crazy lately."

"Yup." Tonya's go-to form of punishment had always been to speak to a person as if they weren't worth full sentences. "So, what should I do with this shit? You say you want us to be closer but can't be bothered with the easy updates?"

Shame filled Skylar's cheeks. All of what her sister said was true. She'd pushed for her sister to be more present in her life. They'd been doing so well. Their dinners had been going on for a few months. The brilliant plan of getting closer had been her proposal. She was the only family Skylar had left, and yet, even after Tonya showed her she was getting her life back together, Skylar hadn't fully trusted to confide in her where she'd moved. She felt like shit.

"I'll come meet you. You've already driven so far out of your way to bring something for him."

"Thanks," Tonya said in a way that let Skylar know she was more annoyed than she was letting on.

With that, her sister disconnected. Releasing a long, slow breath, Skylar reminded herself that she wanted this. She wanted a sister bond like what Zelda and Lara had. "I have to run out and meet my sister. I feel terrible just leaving you here." She looked down the hall at the closed door where the two men had spent most of the day. They were trying to keep the paint fumes contained from the rest of the house.

"It's not the first time I've been here while those two wander off to do *'man things,'*" Verity said, using air quotes.

At that moment, Skylar was convinced Verity would be someone she could add to her friend group. And if the opportunity presented itself, it might be good to meet Harmon's ex-wife as well. It would likely be impossible for them all to avoid each other for the rest of their lives.

"I should be back in no more than half an hour."

The kids all waved Skylar off as she waddled to the door. That was the most accurate way to describe her walk now.

On her car ride to her old apartment, she tried to think of all the things she needed to say to her sister. Tonya was trying. Things were turning around. Skylar had a steady job she enjoyed, a supportive boyfriend, and wonderful friends around her. CJ had finally backed off, not that she was entirely sure what had prompted the change, but it had been several weeks since she'd last heard from him.

The last month had been almost blissful and easy, other than the discomforts of pregnancy. Heartburn was now her constant companion; anyone she talked to informed her that meant the baby would have hair. She didn't know if she should believe it. And every appointment concerning her baby had gone great.

As she pulled into the parking lot of her old apartment building, she scanned the lot for her sister's car. Nothing stuck out as familiar. Tonya, last she knew, was driving an olive-green late-model sedan. Skylar couldn't remember the model. Skylar was making her second turn around the parking lot when her phone rang through her speakers, interrupting the chorus of a favorite song.

"Tonya, where are you?"

"You drove past me. Twice."

"What car are you in? I don't recognize any of these."

As Skylar rounded the corner to make a third lap, she saw movement on the edge of the lot. The dark hair definitely looked like Tonya's.

"I'm standing next to an SUV. Do you see me?"

"Yeah, I see you." Skylar pulled in next to the SUV. Her phone was on the charger, so she figured she'd leave it. It had been down to single digits when she'd plugged it in.

The door of her car opened, and Skylar turned, smiling to greet her sister. Instead, she met a pair of eyes she'd hoped she would never see again.

"CJ, what are you doing? Where's Tonya?"

Skylar lunged for her phone at the same time as CJ's hand tangled into her hair. His other hand wrapped around her wrist in a grip she worried would break it. She tried to buck against him, kick him, but she couldn't get to him. When she tried to swing at him with her free hand, he grabbed her other wrist. She struggled against him as he dragged her to his SUV and shoved her into the back seat.

Chapter Fifty-Four

Harmon

"All right, Sky, we have everything painted. Now we can start moving…" He peered around the corner of the hall when Skylar didn't come to meet him. "Verity, where's Skylar?"

Verity lay on the floor, covered in children. The only bit of her he could see was her nearly white blond hair. "She went to meet her sister," Verity said in a muffled voice.

He could only guess what was blocking her from speaking properly. She said something to the children, and they dispersed, picking up the spinner to the game Skylar had insisted they buy for the children.

"To meet her sister?" The need to clarify warred with Harmon's acceptance that Skylar and her sister were finally getting along better.

Verity nodded, raising a brow. "She left about, damn nearly forty minutes ago, she said she would probably be back in half an hour."

The hope that Skylar and her sister were bonding fizzled into something sour. If Skylar was ever going to be later than she'd said, she called to give him an update. In his haste to get to his phone, which was still playing ridiculously loud music in the baby's room, he nearly tripped over Porter coming out of the bathroom.

"The hell, man? Something wrong?"

Not bothering to answer, Harmon shut off the music so he could think better. For some reason, the extra noise always made it nearly impossible to process. As he scrolled through all forms of communication he and Skylar typically used, his heart rate escalated. He'd received nothing from her. His anxiety only worsened when he tried to call her and she didn't answer.

"Verity," he called as he raced back out to the living room. "Did she say where she was meeting her sister?"

She was shaking her head before he finished talking.

"Shit," he hissed as he ran his fingers through his hair.

Annabell jumped at the chance to tattle on someone for saying a bad word.

"I could hear her sister almost yelling through the phone, though. She seemed upset about Skylar moving?"

Verity finished on a question, but Harmon would take anything as a starting point.

"Thanks." Harmon had his shoes on and was heading to his car before he'd fully thought through his plan.

Porter came jogging out of the house behind him. "I'm coming with you."

"What about Verity?"

"It was her idea." He dropped into the passenger seat.

Harmon nodded, not caring enough to argue.

"Why would it be bad that she went to see her sister?"

Harmon didn't have time to give him the in-depth story, so he settled on the quick version. "She blames Skylar for their mother's death and takes any opportunity to bring it up and make Sky feel like shit. They've never been close, and Tonya was making snide comments about Skylar dating me when the baby isn't mine biologically. I'm not sure how she found that part out. So, I find it hard to believe she changed, even though Sky's insisted she has."

Porter nodded. "So, if you see Tonya... you'll recognize her?"

Harmon shrugged, not wanting to commit to something if he was way off base. The drive to Skylar's old apartment was faster than ever before. Traffic laws seemed minimal in his haste to get to her.

Harmon scanned the parking lot but saw nothing. No one was outside. It took him a moment to spot Skylar's car in the far corner of the lot. His tires screamed as he pulled in next to it. Her car was empty but still running. Harmon dialed her phone again. Her ringtone was muffled, but he could hear it through the door.

***

Skylar

Skylar's head ached where she'd been struck when she wouldn't sit down and behave in the SUV. Lifting an arm to rub at the spot was nearly impossible. No, it was impossible. Something was restraining her arm—both arms. She tried to move her legs next. Everything was strapped down—her thighs, her ankles. Everything had been cinched tight.

She lay on something hard, cold. Metal maybe. Trying to blink her surroundings into view, she was too nauseous and disoriented to succeed. The world spun behind her eyelids. Even her head was strapped down so she couldn't turn it. Perhaps that was the cause of the pain.

The last thing she remembered was CJ yanking her out of her car. She tried to scream and thrash, but her efforts were useless once Tonya hit her over the head with something. *A tire iron?* The impact had her seeing stars then nothing but blackness.

"Waking up?" CJ asked in a singsong voice, one that someone would use with a child. "I thought you might be lucky enough to sleep through our little... *operation.*"

The way he emphasized the final word caused Skylar's stomach to roil. Her nausea ramped up as she searched the room with her eyes.

CJ released a disappointed sigh. "I tried to get you to work with me. I warned you. Do you not remember me telling you the first night we met that I always get what I want? I told you again just a few weeks ago." His shoes squeaked as he walked along the floor. Every few steps, the sound would return.

Skylar assumed he was pacing. The idea of opening her eyes again created an extra pulse in her skull.

"I told you I wanted my baby, wanted *my* son. But instead of listening, you involved my parents." He tsked. "A very foolish plan."

Despite the nausea, Skylar opened her eyes. "I never spoke to your parents." The shock in her voice was evident.

"Don't play dumb. That preppy fuck of a boyfriend said something to them." He finished on a shout. After taking a deep breath, he continued, "They may have cut me off, among other things, after you ran to them. They've always been on my side. But for some reason, they believed *you* over their own son." CJ's words carried more and more anger while simultaneously getting quieter. "So I came up with a plan." The sound of his shoes on the floor halted as he spread his arms wide to encompass their surroundings. "Do you want to venture a guess as to what the plan is?" His breath skittered over the tender flesh of her neck.

As her vision finally began to clear, she could take in more of the space around them. It appeared they were in a kitchen of sorts, almost like the one at Retro. But this one was larger. She was surrounded by stainless steel surfaces. Just as she was about to speak, the doors to the kitchen swung open, and Tonya entered.

"Tonya?" Skylar's voice was hoarse and scratchy as she spoke. "What are you doing?"

"Helping me of course. Why should the sister who ruined everyone's lives get to have everything her way? Why do you get to have the baby, the man, and the fairy-tale life? You took Tonya's mother and her dreams. And now you're trying to take my son from me," CJ said in a low growl.

"So." Tonya spoke for the first time since entering the room. "I'm going to help him get what is rightfully his." As she spoke, Tonya unrolled something in a cloth.

It reminded Skylar of the tools at the dentist's office. Now and then, the lights caught on one of the tools just right, and it sparkled ominously. Skylar's stomach and heart clenched. They were crazy if this was their plan. *They're going to cut my baby out of me.* She started struggling against her bindings. The worst cramping of her life filled her abdomen. "Oh no," she whispered.

"Oh yes," Tonya mocked, not understanding the reason for Skylar's words.

"You could hurt him."

"We won't," CJ assured her.

Skylar tried to shake her head. "You can't just cut him out of me."

Her eyes widened as Tonya lifted a pair of scissors and started cutting up the middle of Skylar's shirt. The cool metal dragged across her skin. The contact sent a rush of terror over her as the chilled air of the kitchen accosted her flesh.

"Tonya," she whispered, pleading with her sister.

It was only a moment, but Skylar saw hesitation as Tonya continued to slice open her shirt. Then her expression morphed into something hard. Resolved.

"This is your nephew. Don't you want to be a part of his life?"

Tonya leaned in to bring her face close to Skylar's. "Did you know his wife has been trying to have a baby for years? Then you turned up, fucked him, probably in some dark alley, and now you get to have his baby?"

"I didn't even know he was married until after. Tonya, I swear to you. I never wanted to get pregnant by him."

Tonya didn't even pause this time. The front of Skylar's shirt was open, and as her sister stepped back, she could no longer see Tonya's face. Only the blurred edges of her in her peripheral vision.

"Get the scalpel, and you, shut the fuck up before I gag you." CJ stood at the end of the table. The tattoos on his arms mocked her ominously. The snake that wound around his forearm and up his bicep might as well have been what was wrapped around her, pinning her to the table. "Do you know what people would do for a baby?"

Tears burned at the edges of her vision. "You don't even want him? You're doing all this just to give him away to someone else?"

"You cunt, you really think I'd *give* him away? No, I'm making sure he goes to a... prosperous home."

Skylar struggled against her bindings with renewed vigor. The idea of her son being taken away from her was so much worse knowing CJ would just auction him off. "This is all about money?"

CJ picked up one of the scalpels at Skylar's side, the ones Tonya had brought in with her. He tapped the blade on the edge of the table. The ring of metal on metal was enough to set her heart into a new, frantic pattern.

"Your plan of running to my parents had some... repercussions. You cost me my livelihood, so I'm taking what you want from you. And since your boyfriend had to get involved, I'll take it from him too." As he spoke, he continued to tap the blade on the table as if keeping time or counting down to something.

"You're going to want to gag her for this," Tonya said.

She stepped forward, a blade of her own in hand, just as another contraction wrung Skylar's thoughts and made her breaths stutter.

CJ smirked. "Why don't we just cut through the first layer real quick? I'd love to hear the bitch beg and cry for mercy."

Again, Tonya hesitated but nodded. When the blade pressed low against Skylar's hip, she did her best to hold in the scream that forced its way through all her barriers. They'd only just started when she felt as if her body was being ripped in half. A burning sensation raced to each and every nerve ending in her body, sending her brain into overdrive as it tried to filter through the pain.

Blood leaked down her sides and onto the table. It was at that moment she knew. She would never meet her son. This was the room where she would die.

All the regrets of her life swam through her head.

"Tonya, I—" The taste of chemicals coated her tongue as a rag was forced into her mouth when she made eye contact with her sister.

Chapter Fifty-Five

HARMON

Nothing in or around Skylar's car told him where she would have gone. He knelt at the driver's-side door and looked under it to see if she or anyone else had dropped something.

"Shit, man. I'll call the police." Porter took a few steps away from him.

As he relayed the details of what Skylar had been wearing that morning to the cops, Harmon's mind spun. She had gone to meet her sister—the one who had a huge issue with her. Harmon gave Porter her name. Only a small list of people could have done this, and unfortunately, Tonya was at the top of the list. Any opportunity to make Skylar feel like a failure or less was what Tonya did. She was hell-bent on ruining Skylar's life, and now she was doing it to both of them. He could have done so much to prevent Sky from falling for her sister's tricks—insisting on going with her each time she met up with Tonya, for one. Maybe then she would have checked in with him before leaving.

Harmon's attention snapped back to the moment when Tabitha, the crazy old woman who had lived across the hall from Skylar, flew into the parking lot on what looked like two wheels. The woman drove like a maniac, and Harmon had to take a step back to get out of her way.

"They took her!" Tabitha shouted before she had her window all the way down. "I followed them. I know where she is."

Harmon raised his brows. "You did what?"

Tabitha glared at him as if he were the dumbest man she'd ever met. "I don't have a cell phone, so I needed to come home to call the police."

Harmon grabbed Porter's arm, dragging him to Tabitha's car. "He's on the phone with the police. Take us back to where she is, and he will update them on the way."

Once Porter was in the back seat, Harmon raced around to the front. Before he had his seat belt latched, Tabitha jumped into her explanation and punched the accelerator.

"I was just getting back from taking Jasper for a walk. When I was heading for the front door, I noticed Skylar's car pulling into that spot. I thought it was strange. I didn't recognize the woman waiting outside for her, but when I saw the man get out of the SUV, I knew something was wrong. It was that little ass who attacked her on Christmas. Had I known what he was up to that day, I would have done something then." As she spoke, Tabitha expertly wove through the streets.

"Where did they take her?" Porter asked.

"Some bar. It's closed down for renovations. They're adding a full kitchen."

Harmon's stomach sank as realization dawned on him. He knew what building she was describing. They weren't far, but that also meant that if Tabitha had been there and back already, Skylar had been there at least fifteen minutes.

Harmon: *They took Skylar. They're at Club Ten.*

He could only hope Jerry was working and would get there in time.

"As fast as you can, Tabitha," Harmon urged as he tried to calm his breathing. Then he turned to give Porter the address where they were headed. His anger was on the brink, and Harmon was doing all he could to keep it in check. Neither of the people in the car were to blame, and he refused to lose control now. He feared it was critical for both Skylar and the baby—his son.

"Porter, tell them to bring an ambulance," Harmon said in nearly a whisper.

With a nod, Porter concluded his call with the police as they rounded the last corner. It felt like just yesterday when Harmon had taken Skylar here for drinks. It was the same place she had hooked up with CJ. He hated how everything seemed to revolve around this damn cesspool of a bar.

"I tossed Jasper into Nick's apartment on the first floor," Tabitha explained, "and I ran back out when I saw them taking off out of the parking lot. Unlucky for them, I have the handicap spot right by the door. So, I followed them here. Once I saw them taking her out of the car, unconscious, I raced back home." She hung her head as she came to an abrupt halt. "I should have just gone into a random store and asked to use their phone, but I panicked." She looked pleadingly at Harmon as if he would blame her for what had happened.

"They'll be okay." Harmon launched himself out of the car and onto the sidewalk. Hurrying to the door, he found it locked. The brick exterior had no windows. "Shit," he huffed as Porter came up next to him.

"The alley door!" Porter shouted, already taking off for the back entrance by the bathrooms. Most people used it when they wanted to have a smoke but didn't want to go back past the bouncers.

Harmon took off after him, their steps echoing down the alley as if mocking him for how long it took him to reach the door. Each step felt like the tick of a clock, one he didn't know when it would stop working.

Porter reached the door first and tugged. It didn't budge. "Shit, this one's locked too."

They each took turns trying to kick the door in, but all it did was damage the hell out of Harmon's ankle. While Porter had his go, Harmon looked around the alley as if searching for a key that might be hanging on the wall.

He wasn't sure what he was searching for. "I don't know any other way in—"

Before he could continue, Tabitha came around the corner holding something above her head. "I found this in the truck."

The old woman could move better than Harmon had thought. She drove like a maniac, shuffled around like she was two decades older, and apparently, ran like a track star. Harmon met her halfway, taking the crowbar from her. Shoving the end into the gap in the door, he tried to pry it open, but the iron fell onto the ground at their feet. With a growl, Harmon picked it back up and tried again. Porter came around to his side and helped him pull.

With a loud squeal, the door swung open just as they heard a gut-wrenching scream from inside.

Chapter Fifty-Six

SKYLAR

Nausea, dizziness, and more contractions held her body captive. They seemed to be coming closer together now. She was trying to count the time between them while Tonya and CJ argued.

"This is dangerous. She's clearly in active labor," Tonya argued.

CJ shrugged. "So? Get the fucking kid out."

"I don't remember if..."

"You were the one who suggested this. You said you could get the kid out no problem."

"I know. I guess... I just..."

Skylar's vision blurred as she tried to focus on their argument. Another stronger contraction ripped through her, and something wet and warm released inside her, covering her thighs. The liquid dripped down over the edge of the table and splattered on the floor.

"What the fuck?" CJ shouted, jumping back. He slammed into the cart of tools, sending a few clattering to the floor as the cart hit the opposite wall with a resounding crash.

Skylar blinked several times, trying to bring the scene back into focus. The pain was so intense that she was struggling to stay aware of her surroundings. Taking a deep breath, she moaned when pressure built against her pelvis.

Tonya ripped the rag from her mouth.

"He's coming," Skylar croaked. She had no other option than to put her trust in Tonya. It was that, or both she and her baby would likely die. That same flicker of emotion passed across Tonya's features. She started loosening the bindings around Skylar.

"What the hell do you think you're doing?" CJ asked, coming up behind Tonya.

She brushed him off. "She is in labor. Her water just broke."

"You said that wouldn't happen."

"Will you shut up with what I said? I was fucking wrong. I can't do this. I won't do this. I am not going to watch my sister die because you can't afford your drugs anymore."

"That's rich coming from you," CJ seethed.

Her sister stepped out of Skylar's line of sight, and she was desperate for someone, anyone to help her. Then Tonya was making quick work of the straps around Skylar's legs. A prickling sensation flooded her toes as she tried to move them. A side door to the kitchen behind Tonya swayed. There were no windows on this level of the club, so she wasn't sure what would have caused the movement. She wondered if the pain was so extreme, she was beginning to hallucinate. But when it swung open again and she saw familiar dark eyes, she wanted to cry.

CJ shoved Tonya away. In his haste, he almost slipped in the amniotic fluid on the floor.

Skylar's head was still strapped to the table. Her muscles clenched, and she swore she felt something widening inside her. On instinct, she drew her knees up. Her leggings had been rolled low on her hips but were still in place. "Tonya?" she cried as tears blurred her vision. She didn't dare call to Harmon; she didn't want CJ to notice his presence. But she focused her eyes on Harmon. He looked crazed.

She would take Tonya's help despite the situation her sister had gotten her into. A groan escaped her throat as another contraction racked her body. They were stronger now, more frequent. Each one felt as if it were tearing her abdomen open anew.

"You should be happy. He will never want for anything in his life. The family I've found for him is wealthy beyond belief." CJ walked toward Skylar again, watching his steps to avoid the wet floor. "Fucking disgusting."

Tonya's labored breathing came from over Skylar's shoulder. Skylar wished she could turn to see her.

"She needs a hospital," Tonya said.

"Like hell. They won't let me take the baby." CJ's anger was amping up, and Skylar feared it would all be taken out on her.

"I've already called—" Tonya began.

CJ's attention was split, and Skylar wondered if Tonya was distracting him on purpose.

"You did what?" CJ shouted, turning his attention to a place above Skylar's head.

"I never should have believed you. She didn't trick you into getting her pregnant, did she? She never taunted you about being pregnant with your baby. You told me you wanted the baby for you and your wife. I thought you just told Skylar you would sell the baby to upset her. You don't want him..."

CJ's smile broadened. "It was so easy to say what you longed to hear about your *evil* younger sister, so once I realized she was one and the same as my baby mama, I decided to see what I could do. That first night you were complaining about your sister at the bar? That was my wife, so when we concocted that woe-is-me plan about not being able to conceive, it was too easy to get you to flip on darling Skylar..."

"You fucking bastard!" Harmon shouted, catching CJ's attention.

It was then that Skylar noticed something in his hand. *A pry bar?* He had been silently approaching CJ from behind, while Tonya kept his attention on herself to give Harmon time. Someone else stood behind Harmon, watching his back.

Just as CJ turned to see who the intruder was, Harmon swung the object in his hands, causing CJ to drop the scalpel. It skittered across the tile floor.

CJ growled and dove for the tray full of tools, taking two more scalpels, one in each hand. "You want my baby too? You already have my leftovers. Why not take it all, right?"

"You never deserved her." Harmon kept shifting his gaze between her and CJ. She hated the fear in his eyes, but it was buddied with the anger that seemed to sizzle in the air around him.

Harmon made a swishing sound as he swung the tool again. It connected with something, and CJ growled, lunging for Harmon with the scalpels outstretched.

Skylar tried to focus on their confrontation, but her vision was growing hazy, and her contractions made her lose all sense of her surroundings for several moments at a time. She closed her eyes, wishing that she could just give birth. There was shuffling all around the room. When she opened them again, Jerry approached from her side, a finger pressed to his lips. When he nodded, the main and side doors of the kitchen flew open.

"Cannon Adams, you are under arrest. Put your hands up."

Skylar noticed the glint in CJ's eyes just as a new contraction raced over her body. On a broken groan, she shouted, "Scalpel!" It was the best warning she could give Jerry.

CJ spun, slicing the blade at Jerry's arm. Someone's gun fired, but Skylar's eyes were clenched shut. She didn't know what all the scuffling around her was about.

"Hey, darling" was the next thing she heard, and tears slipped from her eyes as the binding around her forehead released.

Her eyes shot open to find Harmon and Porter undoing the restraints around her body as EMTs entered with a stretcher. The sounds of struggling still rose from the end of the table, but she couldn't bring herself to look. Jerry was like an older brother to her, and she would most certainly break if something had happened to him. Another stronger contraction wrung her body. Right then, she knew she needed to focus on having her baby.

Just as they were transitioning her to the gurney, another clenching pain and burning filled her lower body.

"We're going to take care of you," a young woman about Skylar's age said as they seemed to run her from the building.

Everything passed in a blur.

"My baby is coming."

The woman nodded and pushed Skylar faster. Items flashed by in her periphery, making the nausea unbearable. She lost sight of Harmon, and her heart raced.

Chapter Fifty-Seven

HARMON

Sitting in the hospital waiting room felt like a death sentence. He didn't know how either Skylar or the baby were doing. There hadn't been room in the ambulance to ride with them, and the EMTs were concerned with bacteria getting into the laceration Tonya and CJ had inflicted. Tabitha had driven him to the hospital then taken Porter back to Harmon's car. He checked his phone for the millionth time to see only two more minutes had passed. He'd been waiting for over an hour already.

Never had he thought this was how his day would end.

He wished he had Zelda's phone number. Then they could commiserate together. It felt as if he'd been wavering on the brink of a cliff since finding Skylar's car. He couldn't handle losing both the woman he loved and a child again. It felt like it was the same in so many ways and different in so many more. *I will never recover.* The scene in that kitchen kept replaying in his mind. There was so much blood on the floor. Skylar's breathing had been erratic, and he'd feared they were too late.

He'd hit a man twice with a crowbar. His stomach clenched as he vividly recalled the cracking of CJ's bones as it made contact. He'd never heard a man scream at such a high octave. But it hadn't stopped him from taking a second swing when CJ had lunged for Jerry.

Resting his elbows on his knees, he held his head, trying to clear his mind.

"Harmon Westerly?" a nurse in pale-purple scrubs asked at the edge of the waiting room.

He couldn't have launched himself out of that chair any faster. She didn't speak. She just led him down a hall to a room at the end. Room 217. He stepped inside, and Skylar burst into tears when she saw him.

"Harmon," she cried, and he rushed to the edge of the bed to hold her.

Each tear felt like a dagger to his heart. There was nothing he could do to make anything better. He couldn't bring himself to ask the question he most wanted to know. He needed to take care of Skylar; if his worst fears were reality, then she would need him now more than ever. His anger vanished the moment she said his name. Now, all he had in him was sadness—sadness over what she'd endured, over how she'd been alone, the way her sister had betrayed her when she'd tried to make amends.

"Sky, I'm so sorry." Harmon slid onto the bed next to her as she cried into his chest. The way her body shook the bed and his entire being made him wonder how he could help her heal this trauma.

"I was so scared," she said through racking sobs. The words were nothing but a broken memory. "I thought they would take him, hurt him. I thought I would die."

The last part caused that ache in his chest to return. "I know." He rubbed slow, delicate circles around her back.

"Do... do you know what happened to Tonya?"

"She's down in the emergency room along with CJ."

Skylar stiffened under his touch. He hastily added, "They are both heavily guarded. They won't be able to get to you. CJ's parents have already made a public announcement that he is out of control. They're pleading with the police to seek justice for what he did to you and the baby." His voice broke.

"He tricked her…" Skylar said, unblinking as she stared at the wall over his shoulder.

"How so?"

"She thought I'd lied to him. She thought I'd tricked him into getting me pregnant. That I was holding the baby just out of his reach." Her brows furrowed, and she shook her head as she spoke.

Harmon swallowed hard. "I'm so sorry about the baby," he finally said, pressing a kiss to the top of her head.

"About the baby?" she asked, confusion etched on her face. "He didn't hurt him. It caused me to go into early labor, but he didn't hurt him."

The crashing relief that flowed through Harmon had him holding her at arm's length to check her face. "He's okay?"

Skylar nodded. "Oh, Harmon, I'm sorry. I assumed you knew." She swiped the tears from her cheeks. "They took him to give him his first bath and do some kind of hearing test. They just left with him before you came in."

Harmon pressed his forehead into hers. "Oh, thank god." He rubbed the tip of his nose against hers. Holding her made all the terror of the last few hours ebb away.

Skylar seemed to be soaking in everything just as he was.

After a few silent minutes, the door to her room squeaked open. A nurse in floral scrubs stepped through, holding a small bundle with a little knitted hat. "He's all clean, Mom."

The little bundle was transferred to Skylar, and Harmon didn't think he'd ever seen anything so wonderful in his life. The smile that graced Skylar's lips had never looked so genuine, or perhaps it was just her relief.

"Hi, baby," Skylar cooed. She pressed a tender kiss to the tip of his nose. They all sat like that for a while, Skylar seeming to soak in the sight of him. "Do you want to meet him?"

The moment turned all of Harmon's emotions into a tangled web of joy, excitement, and something that made his chest ache. He scooted up to the top of the bed to sit directly next to Skylar, and his breath caught as he got to see the baby's perfect face.

"I'll let you have a moment. The lactation consultant will be in to see you in a few minutes. But remember, you need to let your stitches heal, so if he needs to be changed, buzz for me. Or Dad here can change him. Diapers are there." The nurse directed that last part to Harmon, and neither he nor Skylar corrected her on the baby's parentage.

"So, what's his name?" Harmon asked, pressing a kiss to Skylar's forehead.

She gave him a shy half smile. "Novak." She paused. "Ridley."

This would definitely be a day Harmon would never forget. "You gave him my middle name?" Emotion prickled in the bridge of his nose.

"I haven't filled out the birth certificate, so if you don't like it, I can change—"

Harmon pressed a kiss to her lips before she could finish the offer. "I love it, more than you will ever know." He swallowed hard, not knowing how to appropriately phrase the next bit. "I would be honored to be a part of both your lives for as long as you're willing."

"We would be lucky to have you until the end of our days."

EPILOGUE - SIX MONTHS LATER

SKYLAR

IF SHE HAD EVER said she believed she would get to walk down the aisle on her wedding day, she would have been lying. She had never thought of herself as the type of woman someone would want to tie themselves to for the rest of their life. But there she stood. Six months postpartum, feeling more beautiful than she ever had.

Harmon's family had welcomed her with open arms. They had been at the house the day they'd brought Novak home. They treated her as if she had always been part of their family, and they had accepted Novak in a way she never could have dreamed. They were his grandparents in every sense of the word that mattered. She dreaded the day when he would be old enough that she had to explain to him why he had blue eyes and blond hair while his dad had dark hair and eyes. She only hoped he never thought he was anything but the best part of her life. They both were. Watching Harmon dote on him from the day he was born was a blessing she would never get over.

"Ready, rascal?" Jerry asked at the doors that would lead her down the aisle to her soon-to-be husband.

When CJ had lunged for Jerry, his scalpel had sliced him from shoulder to elbow. The scar still looked terrible, but it had healed well. She looped her arm through his, and they walked down the aisle.

As the wedding march played out and Skylar smelled the fragrant lilies in her bouquet, she tried to focus on what she had on this gorgeous day and not what she was missing. No matter the love she was showered with, she couldn't help feeling that part of her was still broken. Her mother was gone, her sister in prison after a plea deal, but she was surrounded by friends and Harmon's family.

CJ had been taken to prison. His wife was being tried as an accessory, and his parents had written him off in the public eye. His attorney had tried for a plea bargain, but once he was arrested and his mother was no longer there to protect him, people stampeded forward to bring to light all the harm he'd done to those around him. Once the new evidence had been brought against him for various other crimes, the judge had refused to consider a plea bargain.

Releasing a long, slow breath, Skylar looked up from the petals running down the aisle just in time to catch Harmon swallowing back tears. The emotions this man drew from her amazed her every day. After everything they'd been through, the fact that they had still made it to this point told her all she needed to know.

Novak's baby babble rose over everything from his seat in the front row on Harmon's mother's lap. The happy tears Skylar had been trying to hold back spilled over before she was even halfway down the aisle. Zelda and Lara stood at the front, also blinking back tears. They were the sisters she wished she'd always had. But they'd arrived in her life when she needed them most. And they, too, had stayed through it all. Verity sat next to Harmon's mom with her daughters, who had been Skylar's flower girls, and her son, who had been their ring bearer.

Porter and one of Harmon's friends from college stood by his side. When Skylar truly focused on him, her chest ached at the love she saw reflected there.

Jerry kissed her temple. "You have always deserved the world. Make sure he never forgets that, sis."

His whispered words sat heavily in her heart. He was the big brother she often needed. She squeezed his arm in thanks as he turned to take his seat in the front row with the rest of their close circle. She didn't trust herself not to melt into a sobbing mess.

Harmon took her hands in his as if he sensed her need for comfort and grounding, and he gently rubbed the tops of her hands. "You look stunning, Skylar," he whispered.

With those simple words, she could relax and fall into an easy place as she married the man of her dreams, with the son she was lucky to have in the front row.

About the Author

E. Lynn has loved reading since her mother read books to her as a child. Something about being able to get lost in a book took hold of her imagination. It was not until the pandemic, spending long days and weeks at home, did she begin writing. She found a release in letting out the ideas that clogged her mind. As one story swam to the surface others would find their way into the pool of possibilities. With many more novel ideas on the horizon, E. Lynn hopes to pull people in with her own stories of love, loss, and suspense.

She has lived in Vermont her entire life but has enjoyed traveling with her husband. The first of hopefully many trips will be taking place soon, and although she knows she will miss her kids desperately, she is getting more and more excited as the days pass. They hope to do much more traveling when their children are older. So, until the day she can wake up and walk out to the beach each morning she will live vicariously through her characters.

ACKNOWLEDGEMENTS

Thank you for choosing my novel to read. This was one I wrote because I felt Harmon needed a story of his own. It is so often talked of the emotional impact of child loss on a woman, but how does it impact the father? So, I wanted to give Harmon a chance to tell his side of the story no matter how wrong he had been.

I then would like to thank my sister again for her critical eyes and willingness to help me in this journey. I can say that it is getting easier to people who know me to read my writing. Even though my stories seem to range in their content, I hope you will be ready for all the stories to come and will continue to be in my corner.

I would also like to thank everyone from Red Adept Editing for their assistance. The editors and proofreaders helped me to create something that I hope will pull you readers in. Their criticisms have helped me to grow as a writer and have given me so much to think about when I work on my future stories. I hope to work with you all for a while to come.

I hope you will continue on this publishing journey with me.

ALSO BY

The Depth Series
The Depth of Their Scars
The Depth of Their Regrets
Coming Soon:
The Depth of Their History

Roadrunner Motel
Sequel coming soon

Holiday and Seasonal Rom-coms
Spring in My Step
Coming Soon:
Bazaar Holiday

If I Had Been There

Coming Soon a fantasy trilogy.